SLOW DANCING
ON PRICE'S PIER

Slow Dancing on Price's Pier

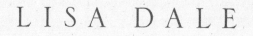

Lisa Dale

BERKLEY BOOKS, NEW YORK

THE BERKLEY PUBLISHING GROUP
Published by the Penguin Group
Penguin Group (USA) Inc.
375 Hudson Street, New York, New York 10014, USA
Penguin Group (Canada), 90 Eglinton Avenue East, Suite 700, Toronto, Ontario M4P 2Y3, Canada
(a division of Pearson Penguin Canada Inc.)
Penguin Books Ltd., 80 Strand, London WC2R 0RL, England
Penguin Group Ireland, 25 St. Stephen's Green, Dublin 2, Ireland (a division of Penguin Books Ltd.)
Penguin Group (Australia), 250 Camberwell Road, Camberwell, Victoria 3124, Australia
(a division of Pearson Australia Group Pty. Ltd.)
Penguin Books India Pvt. Ltd., 11 Community Centre, Panchsheel Park, New Delhi—110 017, India
Penguin Group (NZ), 67 Apollo Drive, Rosedale, North Shore 0632, New Zealand
(a division of Pearson New Zealand Ltd.)
Penguin Books (South Africa) (Pty.) Ltd., 24 Sturdee Avenue, Rosebank, Johannesburg 2196,
South Africa

Penguin Books Ltd., Registered Offices: 80 Strand, London WC2R 0RL, England

This book is an original publication of The Berkley Publishing Group.

Copyright © 2011 by Lisa Dale.
"Readers Guide" copyright © by Penguin Group (USA) Inc.
Cover design by Rita Frangie.
Cover photograph by David Fischer / Photographer's Choice RF / Getty.
Text design by Laura K. Corless.

PRINTING HISTORY
Berkley trade paperback edition / April 2011

Library of Congress Cataloging-in-Publication Data

Dale, Lisa.
  Slow dancing on Price's Pier / Lisa Dale. — Berkley trade paperback ed.
    p. cm.
  ISBN 978-0-425-23995-7
  1. Triangles (Interpersonal relations)—Fiction.   2. Newport (R.I.)—Fiction.   I. Title.
  PS3604.A3538S57 2011
  813'.6—dc22

                                              2010036371

PRINTED IN THE UNITED STATES OF AMERICA

10   9   8   7   6   5   4   3   2   1

To Matt, because I kinda like you a little bit

From "The Coffee Diaries"
by Thea Celik

The Newport Examiner

What I love about coffee is this: the dramatic change a coffee cherry goes through before it becomes a coffee "bean."

If you've ever dumped out a bag of fresh-roasted coffee beans, you've probably stolen a sniff of that gorgeous, earthy aroma. You must have marveled at that glossy, dark sheen.

But that smell and those oils simply did not exist in the coffee cherry when it was little more than a hard green fruit growing on a mountainside.

It's fire that forces the transformation from seed to bean. Roasting alters the seed's makeup—an intense molecular restructuring.

In that way, I think coffee cherries aren't much different from people. Heat and pressure change us. When we walk through fire—and we all do at some point—we come out the other side to find ourselves altered. If we're lucky, we become richer, more complex, more alluring people because of our trials. But sometimes, we just get burned.

ONE

By the first day of summer, everyone on Price's Pier had caught wind of Thea's impending divorce from her husband—though not everyone had the facts straight. The more conservative among the gossipers speculated that Thea wanted another baby but Jonathan did not. Or that Jonathan wanted to play a bigger part in the coffee shop, and that Thea had shut him out. Some made accusations that took on a tabloid smuttiness within the rumor mill: there was talk of sexual perversion, secret photographs, and dirty money changing hands. One or both parties were often accused of cheating.

Most of the time, Thea could tell what her regular customers believed simply by the way they looked at her when they came in for their morning coffee. Suspiciously slanted glances and cold *I'll have the usuals* meant that the story they'd heard placed the blame on Thea. But shyly raised eyebrows, pitying smiles, and somber nods meant that Thea was the one who held their sympathies in the game of picking sides.

Thea treated all of her customers—regardless of their

allegiances—exactly the same. She talked with them about coffee, the weather, or her latest column when it suited them to chat. Or she let them simply lapse into brooding quiet as she poured their drinks. Eventually the rumors would die down. The strange and sudden silence that had descended on her life like dust after an explosion would begin to feel normal. But until then, her plan was to simply yield to the surreal feeling of time suspended. She brewed big carafes of coffee; she picked her daughter up from soccer practice; in the evenings she swept beneath the tables and turned off the lights. It was business as usual. She pressed on.

"A toast!"

Jonathan watched as his brother pushed out his chair and stood at the pub table, nearly sending tequila sloshing onto his poker chips. Six of them—a group of men that Jonathan had never met until he'd moved in with his brother a week ago—sat together at a private booth in a Providence bar. The lights were dim except for a single green lamp that hung over the center of the sturdy round table. In the corner, a man in a flannel shirt stuck out his chin and closed his eyes, reaching for high notes in a Led Zeppelin sing-along. The waitresses were gruff until they got tipped and the beer was skunked—but since the bar was nearly empty, it was a great place for long hands of poker on a Tuesday night.

"No toast," Jonathan said. "No toast. Let's just knock 'em back."

"No—I insist." Garret bowed his head, something princely in the gesture. He smiled his wide, genuine smile that had wrapped so many women and congressmen around his little finger. His California blond hair gleamed gold in the light. "It's not every day a guy gets to throw his brother a divorce party."

"But . . . a toast?" Jonathan said lamely.

"C'mon! We're celebrating here. You're a free man." Garret laughed and clasped him on the shoulder. "The single life's the only life. Right, guys?"

Garret's friends—unmarried corporate types with their work shirts opened at the collars and their sleeves rolled—gave a *hear, hear.*

Jonathan shifted uncomfortably in his seat.

"Don't look at me like that," Garret said, laughing in his good-humored way. "I'm not gonna stand up here and bad-mouth . . . anyone. That would be low. Even for me!"

Some of the men chuckled, and Jonathan could feel them looking at him, watching to see what he would do.

He hadn't wanted a divorce party, but once Garret got an idea into his head, there was no sense in arguing. Garret was in the business of persuasion—a lawyer turned lobbyist. Of course, if he had really known how much the divorce party bothered Jonathan, there was no way he would have insisted. After ten years of little more than Christmas and birthday cards, Jonathan hardly knew his brother anymore. If he could reconnect with Garret, at least some good might come of his impending divorce. He lifted his glass a little higher and motioned for the toast to go on.

Garret cleared his throat. "Sometimes a man has to take the long way to find out a woman isn't who he thought she was. You know what they say. It's hard for a man to lose a woman. Sometimes, it's damn near impossible. Believe me, I've tried."

"Jeez, Garret." One of his friends cut in. "Whose divorce party is this anyway?"

Garret turned his eyes a bit guiltily toward his brother, and for a split second Jonathan saw what the other men did not. The nervousness. The frustration. The too-wild, too-bright glare in his brother's eye. Garret's bravado was usually unpracticed and care-free, but tonight something in his words rang false.

"I'm really screwing this up here, aren't I? The point is"—
Garret lifted his drink to the height of his shoulder, his voice
faltering—"the point is, you made the right decision. This isn't the
end of a marriage; it's a new beginning. This is the first day of the
rest of your life. And nobody deserves happiness more than you."

For a moment, he and Garret locked eyes. Solid. Loyal. Like
they used to be. And it occurred to Jonathan that only the two
of them—him and his brother—knew what this toast was really
about. Garret wouldn't have told any of these men about his past.
His pride was too big, his ego too fragile. Tonight was supposed
to mark the end of an era in Jonathan's life with Thea—but it was
closure for Garret too.

Jonathan nodded at his brother solemnly. "Cheers," he said.

They lifted their glasses and threw their heads back.

The way Thea told the story to her daughter was this: *Your father
is going to stay with Uncle Garret in Providence for a little while.
No, it's not that he doesn't like us. He would just rather stay there
than here right now.*

The way Thea told the story to her mother was this: *Jonathan
and I are taking a break. Because we are. No, I don't need you
to move in with me—and I'm not going to live with you either.
Well, partly because Irina and I don't speak Turkish. Don't worry.
Everything's going to be fine.*

The way Thea told the story to Jonathan's father Ken was this:
*These things happen. Yes, I'm sorry too. I understand that this is
going to change things for all of us. Thank you. That's very kind.
I'll always love you guys too.*

The way Thea told the story to herself was this: *He says it meant
nothing, and I don't think he's lying: I don't think there's anything
between them. I feel like she's just an illusion. Like there's two*

of us in the room—me and Jonathan—and we're fighting over a third person who doesn't even matter and isn't even there.

The way Thea told the story to her friend Dani was this: *I can't say I'm completely surprised. And what's strange about it is that I don't feel devastated. I should, but I don't. Is that wrong?*

The first time Thea met the Sorensen boys was in the salt-crusted gloom beneath Price's Pier, where the shifting softness of beach sand rose up and met the dark, hard underside of the planks along the pier. Occasionally Thea would encounter a couple making out or some high schoolers smoking cigarettes or getting high. But mostly, no one knew how to get beneath the pier, and those who did were put off by the smell of dead fish and the decaying bodies of crabs.

She'd heard about the Sorensens before she saw them—the new neighbors who lived in the old Pinker place on the richest side of town. One of her girlfriends had made up a system for grading guys on their hotness: The Sorensen brothers were "totally rated R."

In the safe anonymity of the hallways between classes, Thea watched for them. There was Jonathan, the tall, smart, older one—the one who always wore shoes instead of sneakers and who was in honors math. And there was the one in her grade, Garret, the one who played soccer. The one who allegedly left a hickey on Annie Reed's thigh. She listened to her girlfriends' gossip about the new kids with giddy speculation, but she had no information to contribute. Just a funny knot in the pit of her stomach, eagerness and fear at the same time.

Yet, when Thea finally met them—the legendary Sorensen brothers squatting low in the shadows beneath the old pier, their spines hunched and their heads bent in concentration—they didn't seem so adult and mysterious at all. Instead they seemed like little boys. In school they were royalty, practically men. But in the smelly shadows of the pier they were no different from any of the other boys. They were playing with little green army men—practically baby toys—with utter seriousness and concentration. Their words were furtive and rushed.

The crash of the tide climbing up the beach filled the cavern between the damp, smelly sand and the high pier, and it took a few minutes before she understood what it was they were doing. She saw a cigarette lighter winking gemstone blue in slatted sunlight. And the pile of army men, a lumped green heap, weapons and body parts melted down.

These Sorensen brothers were not the experienced and sexy vagabonds her girlfriends had so badly wanted them to be. They were just *boys*—boys playing with fire as kids were known to do. She wanted to see their toys melting, to watch their soldiers' bodies wilt and puddle like wax. So she simply stepped out of her hiding place and said, in the clearest and loudest voice she could, "Hello!"

She must have startled them. Because Jonathan jumped. The lighter went tumbling. And Garret spent the afternoon in the ER with a second-degree burn. Officially, Thea had scarred him before she'd even known his name.

The coffee shop was bustling, the summer throngs having arrived in Newport for the season. All along Ocean Drive, tall mansion windows had been thrown open to the cool easterly breeze coming in over the harbor. On Thames Street, where seventeenth-century homes huddled together, the sun baked the cobblestones and tempted tourists to wrap their sweaters around their waists. On Price's Pier, among the restaurants, boutiques, and bars that clustered in friendly bunches at the water's edge, some of the newcomers to the area were finding their way down the maze of narrow, shadowy alleyways that led to the Dancing Goat.

Thea stood at the counter, relishing a moment of temporary quiet in between morning rushes. At the moment, her only two customers were Hollis Cooper and Dean Gray. They sat together at a small chessboard in the corner, one that had been worn down by years of weekly matches at the coffee shop. They'd never claimed to like each other: as far as Thea could tell, one man had never said to the other, "How is your wife?" or "What are your kids up to these days?" And yet neither of them had ever missed a match. It was always the loser who got the bill. "I don't know why I keep coming here," Hollis would often grumble. "Coffee used to be a quarter a cup when I was a kid. Not these five dollar an ounce mocha-latte-cchio-split things."

Or Dean would complain, "Don't know why I bother with such bitter coffee if I have to doctor it up with so much sugar and cream."

But Thea didn't mind their complaints, and when they showed up to play their weekly game of chess with each other, Hollis with the old wooden chess case tucked under his arm, she was glad to see them. People like Hollis and Dean were the reason Thea had fallen in love with the shop.

The Dancing Goat had never been meant for the tourist trade. Thea's parents had established the business back in the seventies—but not to cater to the blueblood families that still maintained their traditions of summering in Newport. Instead, the shop was intended to be a locals' place: no designer decor, no menus printed on recycled paper, no waiters to suck up and smile. Thea's parents had one main goal—to make good coffee at a good price. No frills, no fuss. And over time, as word began to spread, Newport's summer visitors began to think of the simple little coffee shop as a novelty—their hidden gem—and each man who visited told his friends about it as if he were the first to have discovered it and wandered inside.

Thea loved the shop—had loved it since she stood at her mother's elbow and learned to measure scoops of coffee beans. The clunky old cash register of her parents' generation held an honored space in her office, though it was no longer used. The smell of coffee would never come out of the curtains no matter how many times Thea washed them. Thea had inherited the coffee shop from her parents when they'd moved back to their home overseas—just like she'd inherited her house from them. But she'd never questioned her love for the place. The doors of the Dancing Goat were open to everyone—enemy, stranger, or friend.

"So here's what I'm thinking."

Thea looked up from the rosette she was doodling in latte foam to find her daughter squinting at her with sly eyes. At ten years old, Irina's interest in making conversation never waned. She'd made a niche for herself talking up espresso drinks, many that she'd never even had. With her slightly too-big teeth and perpetually too-short jeans, her specialty was convincing middle-aged men to buy "one for the road."

"This better be good," Thea said.

Irina crossed her skinny arms, one hip leaning against the counter in a parody of a woman twice her age. Her brown hair fell to her shoulders, straight and ashy as Jonathan's would have been if he'd ever worn it long. "Here's my idea. We call up Grandma Sue and tell her she doesn't need to watch me today. And I stay home by myself while you go to the roasters. Okay?"

"I don't think so," Thea said. She took a quick sip of her latte. "Grandma Sue's going to be here in a minute."

"But why can't I stay by myself?"

"Your grandma Sue wants to see you. Don't you want to see her?"

Irina's "Yes" was begrudging.

I want to see her too, Thea thought.

For her entire adult life, Sue had been a second mother to her. In the emergency room on the first day that Thea had met the Sorensens, Sue had put her arm around Thea's shoulders, walked her to the snack machine for a candy bar, and told her that it wasn't her fault—Jonathan and Garret shouldn't have been playing with a lighter in the first place. When Thea was fifteen Sue took her aside to explain how to use a tampon so she could go in the ocean with "the boys." And even when Jonathan had announced that he and Thea were getting married, Sue had never voiced her initial disapproval, though she had every reason to worry that they'd married too hastily and too young.

But now that she and Jonathan were separating, her relationship with Sue was in real jeopardy. The Sorensens were the closest family she had since her own parents had moved back to their home country shortly after her high school graduation. If and when Thea signed on the dotted line to divorce her husband, would she divorce his family too? Could a woman get visitation rights to see her in-laws?

Irina screeched when Sue pushed through the coffee shop door, and she ran to give her grandmother an awkward tomboy's hug. Sue was dressed beautifully—as always: a blue boatneck sweater, freshly pressed capris, and pearls at her ears and throat. Her thinning blond hair was pulled back in a ponytail.

Thea met her in the center of the room. This was normally the point when Sue leaned in, kissed her on the cheek. Instead, she just nodded and held tight to Irina's hand. "Hello."

"Sue! How are you? Can I get you something to drink? Iced tea?"

"No, I'm fine thanks. Just fine. How's things?"

"Not terrible," Thea said. "Thanks."

Sue nodded. A moment passed. "Well . . ."

"Are you okay with keeping her for dinner?"

"Oh, that's no problem. Not a problem at all."

Thea smiled. She wasn't sure what else to say. Years of Sunday shopping trips and drinking white wine spritzers into the wee hours of the morning with this woman—and she couldn't think of a thing to say.

"Well, we've got a lot to do this afternoon," Sue said brightly.

"Oh, all right. Call if you need anything."

Sue gave Irina's hand a shake. "Ready?"

"Yeppers!" Irina bounced on her light-up sneakers.

Sue nodded once, and her blue eyes were as somber as a cold morning mist. After they left, Thea was no longer in the coffee shop. She was remembering. She was sixteen years old, sitting at the edge of Sue's flowered bedspread, her eyes red and puffy from crying. Her parents had been talking about moving back to Turkey. It was just talk, but it was enough to scare her. She'd gone running across town to the Sorensens' house in the Bellevue neighborhood, seeking refuge in the most perfect place she knew. Garret and Jonathan weren't home, but that didn't matter. Thea was always welcome.

Sue had listened patiently to Thea's plight—her fear that her parents would take her with them and her fear that they would not. As Thea spilled her guts, Sue sat patiently brushing Thea's long hair. *You know*, she'd said. *I always wanted a daughter. And if God had seen fit to give me one, I would have wanted her to be just like you.*

The moment was such a meaningful part of their past, a precursor of things to follow. But the divorce would likely rewrite what that moment had portended. Thea picked up a rag to wipe down the counter. She loved the Sorensens—all of them. Love did not bloom one day and die the next. It couldn't be neatly severed or cut cleanly out of the heart. (At least, not for most people—though Garret might have been the exception.)

She would do what she could to remain a part of the Sorensen family—regardless of what had happened or what might yet happen with Jonathan. She just had to give herself over, to trust in their kindness—and to hope that Garret would not succeed in poisoning his family against her once and for all.

The morning after the divorce party, Garret woke hungover and wretched. He'd kicked his covers to the foot of the bed in the middle of the night, so they were in a great black heap on his warm toes while the rest of him pebbled in goose bumps. He pulled on his boxers and dragged himself to the bathroom, his face bearing a sandy blond stubble, his fair hair going this way and that.

After a certain point, he couldn't remember much of last night. Drinks, laughs, cigars—the memories were smeared and blurry as a dream. There was the toast, of course. He'd botched it. And a ninety-dollar bottle of champagne that Jonathan wouldn't let him buy. But after that, just blur.

He hoped he hadn't done anything too outlandish. He'd wanted the divorce party not to feel like a divorce party at all—no games of "pin the blame on the ex" or faux voodoo dolls. Instead, he'd hoped that it would become the bachelor party he'd never gotten to throw, that his toast would become the best man speech he'd never gotten to make, that he could finally show support for his brother without any awkwardness or rage.

Instead, what was meant to be a coming-out party had felt like a pity party, and just who was being pitied it was hard to say.

Garret bent down and washed his face in mint cleanser and

ice-cold water. He rinsed the sleep from his eyes. For a moment he leaned his weight on his forearms and watched the water go sluicing down the drain.

It's her, he thought. *Always her*.

His brother's decision to separate from Thea had put her front and center in Garret's mind. For years Garret had practiced the delicate art of not thinking about her. Of avoiding any thought that might jog a memory or trigger a flash of feelings long gone. But when he got his brother back a week ago, he got his memories of Thea back too. As it turned out, the mental wall he'd constructed to block her from his consciousness had been no stronger than a tower of cards.

He pulled on an undershirt and walked down the hallway, his body feeling heavy and clumsy. Jonathan was already in the kitchen, drinking a cup of coffee and reading in the bright, mid-morning light. Jonathan was dark where Garret was fair, lanky where Garret was stocky. He peered up at Garret over the top edge of a novel—dragons and craggy mountains on the front cover. His dark eyes were alert and friendly.

"Morning." Garret went to the counter to pour himself a cup of black coffee.

"How you feeling?"

"Like a million bucks that just got washed down a sewer."

Jonathan laughed. "It was a good night."

"I'll have to take your word on that," Garret said, joking. He leaned against the counter and blew the steam of his coffee into the sunlight. Beyond the floor-to-ceiling windows was the steel-and-glass heart of Providence, with its tall buildings and busy thoroughfares.

He loved his kitchen in the morning. He'd had it redesigned last year to include brand-new matching stainless steel appliances, a backsplash of imported blue glass tiles made by Venetian artisans, and Brazilian cherry cabinets. Garret thought they should fire up the built-in grill one of these days (since he'd yet to use it). But his brother had little interest in much of anything. Mostly Jonathan worked late at the office—where he was an accountant and book-keeper for investment firms—and then he came home to watch sitcoms or read science fiction novels until he passed out.

Garret walked barefoot to the table and sat down. "Hey. You doing all right?"

"Not bad." Jonathan nodded and put down the novel. "It's just so different here."

"How do you mean?"

Jonathan looked around, and Garret knew he was no longer seeing the cabinetry or recessed lighting but instead was imagining his own house, *Thea's* house—the inside of which Garret hadn't seen since he was a kid. "It's just really quiet here in the mornings," Jonathan said. "I'm not used to it."

Garret nodded. "You miss your daughter."

"She usually sings show tunes in the hallway until I get out of bed."

Garret set down his coffee cup. "It's only been a week. And you just talked to her yesterday."

"I know. But it's different on the phone."

"So why not go see her?"

"Honestly? Because I'm just not ready to see Thea in person yet."

"Why? It's not like you meant for this to happen. I mean, look at you. You're not the type of guy who sleeps around."

Jonathan gave him a mean, sidelong glare.

"Well, yes, you did pull a one-nighter." Garret ran a hand through his hair, searching for words. "But I'm sure that whatever went down, Thea must have driven you to it."

"Careful," Jonathan said.

Garret rubbed his face with his hand, trying to clear his head.

He felt the tug of memories between them; they were both think-ing of her in their different ways.

"Ask me if she told Mom and Dad what I did," Jonathan said.

"Did she?"

"No. They don't know a thing about it. She could have ratted me out, made things really messy. But she didn't."

"At least not yet," Garret said. "She's just waiting for the right time."

Jonathan stood and dumped the remains of his coffee in the sink. "I understand what you're trying to do," he said. "But Thea's not the bad guy here."

"Why don't you write her an e-mail?" Garret suggested. "Or I'll do it for you, if you want."

"Yeah?"

"Sure," Garret said lightly, but he was already doubting him-self. To write Thea an e-mail was to acknowledge her. Since Jon-athan had married her he hadn't opened that door—not even a crack. He wasn't sure he had the strength to do it, even now. But his brother needed his help, and Garret was so grateful for the opportunity to prove himself that he would have jumped before a bullet if Jonathan was in its way. "Sure, I'll e-mail her for you. As long as you'll promise never to let me do that many shots again."

"Which reminds me. I wanted to thank you. For the party. It was just what I needed."

"No it wasn't," Garret said gently. "But you're a good man to say that. And you're welcome any time."

On Thursday morning, after Thea had dropped a very tired Irina off at the babysitter's but before Thea fired up the espresso machine at the Dancing Goat, she stood alone at the edge of Price's Pier, watching the sunrise. She blew on her convenience-store coffee, sending threads of steam rippling against the heavy morning air. The brew was salty and bitter—cheap robusta that never failed to make her jittery, broken up by flecks of coffee grinds. But she relished it—stubbornly—if only for the fact that it was a cup of coffee that she herself did not make.

If her mother were here, she would insist on squinting into the wreckage of coffee beans in the bottom of her cup to discern Thea's future. Her mother always saw the same shapes; she saw them so often that Thea suspected they were the only symbols she knew. The fish meant *luck and good fortune*. The bird meant *someone will come to you with good news*. The heart meant—what else?— *you will have love*.

But what would her mother say now? she wondered. She drained the last of her coffee and waited a moment—as she'd been taught—for what few grinds there were to dry a little and stick to the sides. But when she looked into the bottom of the cup only a thin line of brown spots greeted her, scalloped as the wrack line at low tide.

What will I do with myself? she thought.

She'd gotten married when she was practically still a schoolgirl. The structure of her life had been blocked out into three massive cornerstones: (1) she was the owner of a coffee shop, (2) she was a mother, and (3) she was a wife. Each role was precarious at times, her strengths always shifting. But remove one support entirely, and the whole trivet of her life would come tumbling down.

From far away she heard the sound of a cart rattling over the boards of the old pier, probably Khalid staking out territory for his hot dog stand. And in the distance, Xavier and the other lobstermen were shouting loudly, laughing occasionally, and punctuating their Spanish with English swears. Even this early in the morning, when the city's rich vacationers weren't even dreaming of waking up, Price's Pier was busy, striving, hurried . . .

Perhaps that was the message she was supposed to take from the coffee grinds—that she should get to work—just keep doing what she'd been doing her whole life, and that would get her through.

When the coffee shop was up and running, and the summer hires had arrived to tackle the morning rush, Thea ducked into her office to catch up on paperwork. Her heart dropped out of her chest when she saw Garret's e-mail address in her in-box. She thought for a moment that he was e-mailing her to tell her off—to rant and say all the things to her that he hadn't said all those years ago. Instead, his message was simple, curt.

> *Jonathan wants to see Irina tomorrow. He plans to pick her up from school and keep her for the weekend. Please let her know she should expect her father then.*
>
> *G*

She leaned back in her chair, considering the computer screen with the feeling that she was sitting before a chess board and pre-paring to make her next move. Was this how it was going to be, then? Jonathan wanted to pick up his daughter, and Garret was to broker the deal?

She looked for long moments at his signature line, which was not a signature line at all—not even a name. She had the feeling that if his message had been delivered over a phone line rather than a computer screen, she would have heard him trying not to gag. Did he sign every e-mail that way? So impersonally? Or just e-mails to her?

Dear G,

Irina's school has ended for the year. I'm sure she'll be very excited about staying at your place for the weekend. But is it suitable for a ten-year-old girl? She gets hungry at the most unpredictable times (beer and pretzels will not suffice). She needs a night-light to fall asleep. And she's probably going to break something—though it's hard to predict what.

From,
Thea

To her surprise, the reply was nearly instantaneous:

Thea,

Men too get hungry at unpredictable times (there will be plenty of kid food on hand). I can leave the hall light on for her at night. And there's nothing here she can break that I can't afford to replace ten times over.

Garret Maxwell Sorensen
Sorensen Consulting, President
Providence, RI
Sent from my mobile phone

Thea sat back against the wooden slats of her chair; there was no reason to keep Irina from going to Garret's for the weekend. Irina wanted to see her father, and Jonathan no doubt was longing to see Irina too. But Thea worried. She didn't know Garret anymore. Was he still so angry at her? So bitter?

She hated that Garret hated her. She meant to live her life as a good person. She told the truth—even when it made her look bad. She deferred to other people's wishes graciously. Some days, she felt her heart was full to bursting with love—for her family, for her customers at the coffee shop, for the coffee shop itself. She was not perfect, but she tried. She suspected that most people generally thought she was nice, even when she couldn't connect with them on a personal level.

But Garret hated her—despised her so deeply he'd split his family in two over her. It pained her, some days, the ache coming on when she least expected it, like an old injury that flares up days before the rain. To everyone she met she was a good person—to him she was a monster. From his absence at birthday parties and holidays, Thea could feel his indignant fury, an unrelenting, stubborn rage. And now she felt that sending her daughter off to Garret's house was like putting her in a rowboat and shoving her out into a stormy sea.

She covered her face with her hands and leaned on the desk before her. She'd been working on her newspaper column the night before, and her scribbled notes were strewn across the surface of the desk—along with Irina's crayon drawings of horses and bears. Irina was a smart kid, bold and strong. Thea was a hundred times more nervous about sending her daughter away than Irina ever would be about going. Thea just had to trust that Jonathan would defend her—if Garret started filling her daughter's head with his hate. She wouldn't let Garret drive yet another wedge between the members of her family.

Dear Garret,

All right. I'll have her packed up and ready to go on Friday afternoon. Jonathan can pick her up outside the coffee shop, if he prefers. I'll send her out if he texts me when he gets there.

I'll also send her with a quarter pound of Guatemalan Hue-huetenango, since he's probably running out.

Thea

Again, the reply came lightning fast. Thea thought: *So he's the plugged-in type.* Life at the speed of light. Her heart gave a little cry to think of him compulsively watching his phone.

Don't need coffee. Just the kid. I'll pick her up, not J. Will text you to send her out.

Garret Maxwell Sorensen
Sorensen Consulting, President
Providence, RI
Sent from my mobile phone

The kid, she thought. *My kid.*
She would be sending Jonathan his coffee anyway.

From "The Coffee Diaries"
by Thea Celik

The Newport Examiner

Coffee is the official and unofficial drink of friendship in many cultures.

In Ethiopia, the coffee ceremony is a fundamental rite of friendship. To be invited to a coffee ceremony is a sign of honor and respect. Guests drink three cups with their hosts and by the third cup, it's said they are friends.

Coffee plays such a big part in that country that it has infiltrated the language. "I don't have someone to have coffee with" means "I don't have close friends." Mothers warn their children, "Don't let your name be mentioned at coffee time."

Sometimes the age of coffee corporations and flavor crystals can make it feel like coffee has lost its connotations of friendship. But the connection between coffee and friendship persists.

Look around and you'll see old men drinking coffee and talking shop at the countertops of sleepy diners. Women smiling and pausing for coffee between errands, chatting with a friend in the line.

Coffee has been bringing people together for centuries. And as the coffee business grows, so too do our conversations over coffee, whether they are meaningless and silly or the most important moments in our lives.

TWO

The first few months after Jonathan had moved from New Jersey to Newport had been filled with one wonder after another. And Thea herself was one of them. She knew every back alley, every unofficial path leading to the beach, every person in town. She became indispensable—their secret weapon in neighborhood water gun fights and games of manhunt. She showed them sand dollars, touristy key chains with dirty jokes, anarchist graffiti on the underside of the pier, a grave with a pirate flag, and so, so much more.

She was the perfect combination of him and Garret. She was as smart as—if not smarter than—Jonathan, and he saw himself in her and admired what he saw. She could talk for hours about Newport history—about the 300-year-old architecture, about the Vanderbilts and Morgans who built their American castles at the water's edge, about how to tell a tourist from a local just by sight. She was an honors student and a first chair trumpet player. She liked to argue, and she was good at it too. Occasionally, Thea was able to sneak into the Dancing Goat and steal a little cupful of espresso. Then the three of them would hide in the alleyway behind Crook's Pub, where they would pass the cup around like a joint to sip bitter coffee that none of them were allowed to have.

Jonathan was in awe of her, half in love the first day they met. He wanted to think they were kindred spirits, that they shared their way of looking at the world. But for all that she was like Jonathan, she was like Garret too—distracted, restless, always wanting more.

Sometimes she took them to the warehouse that hosted the fish and lobster market at the farthest edge of Price's Pier, where brownish green "chickens" scuttled over one another in enormous, shallow blue tanks. Jonathan hated trips to the lobster market. The first time Thea had brought him there he'd had to fight back tears. Living lobsters were nothing like the crustaceans they ate for dinner—their shells so plastic and red they could have been toys.

But Thea was fascinated by the lobsters, grotesque and awful as they were: the culls that had only one claw to wave about uselessly, the pistols that scuttled armless over the bottom of the tank, the sleepers that were too listless to move, the soft shells that rattled around in their own peeling bodies.

While Jonathan dragged his feet, Garret and Thea bent by the hips over the open tanks and competed to spot King—the biggest lobster in the bunch, the lobstrosity. Jonathan had tried to tell Thea and Garret that there was no King, that every week someone came and bought the biggest lobster ("to eat it!"), and that King was a different animal each time they saw him. But Thea and Garret didn't care. They goaded each other mercilessly: *I dare you to put your hand in. I dare you to touch his claw.*

Jonathan and his brother had always been quick to fight, but that first summer with Thea, things between them settled down. Garret was the one who was most likely to steer them into trouble.

Jonathan was the one most likely to bail them out. And somewhere between was Thea, who commanded the whole enterprise of their friendship even when none of them knew it. The balance was perfect. At least, it had been for a while.

For the first time in longer than she could remember, Thea faced down a Friday night that included neither her husband nor her little girl. She had no idea what to do with herself, but the world had given her plenty of options:

From her mother: *You know what you should do? Tell your husband to come over so you can cook him dinner. That's all you need. One dinner, he gets a little tired, a little homesick, and now he might as well just spend the night. Call him. Tell him you're cooking right now.*

From Irina: *I know! You can go to a bar. Wouldn't that be cool, Mom? You never go to bars. Kristi's mom does it all the time. You could go with her!*

From her friend Dani: *You know what you should do? You should go shopping. Seriously. Buy new underwear. That always helps me.*

For most of her life, Thea had been good at taking advice. She'd taken her mother's advice that she marry one of the Sorensen boys—though not the one everybody expected. She'd taken Jonathan's advice that she buy a minivan instead of a Subaru Impreza. She'd taken Irina's advice that LOL was better than ha-ha.

But none of the advice she'd received about what to do with her first Friday night alone seemed right. She'd cleaned the house, she'd caught up on bills, she'd called a few friends—but all were busy cooking dinner for their children or going out with their husbands (if they picked up the phone at all).

Loneliness squeezed her heart, and so before Thea gave in to sitting on the couch, eating Oreos, and watching reruns of decade-old sitcoms, she left. She headed back to the coffee shop, walking the five blocks from her house to the pier with her hair pulled up in a baseball cap and her work sneakers on. At seven p.m., the pier was in full swing—music playing through the open windows of bars, pedestrians crowding shoulder to shoulder in the thorough-fares. But because the Dancing Goat was tucked away at the end of a narrow alleyway, it was often a somewhat more peaceful refuge away from the panic and frenzy of the main pier. The head barista, Jules, was surprised—if not a little dismayed—to see Thea when she came through the door.

"Thea!" Jules put his cell phone in his pocket but not so quickly that Thea hadn't been able to see that he was texting when he should have been working. A few customers were sitting together at the tables, talking easily and sipping their drinks. The apprentice baristas—Rochelle and Claudine—gave her a quick wave before going back to their conversation with the couple at table eight.

"Hi, guys!"

"I wasn't expecting to see you!" Jules said.

Thea walked behind the counter, feeling better already. "I fig-ured you'd need some help with the refrigerator project."

"We just finished," Jules said.

Thea opened the display fridge and peered in. It was sparkling clean. "Oh." She stood up, put her hands on her hips, and scanned the shop to see what needed to be done. "Slow night?"

"Eh. Pretty slow," Jules said. "For a Friday. But it's a little early yet."

Thea heard a faint buzzing and saw Jules's eyes go wide with surprise. His hand jerked toward his pants pocket to stifle the sound, and inwardly, Thea smiled.

Jules was twenty-one years old, a junior in college whom she'd hired every summer since he was sixteen. He was an art major—long-haired and frail-boned—and he frequently came to work with paint splotches on his jeans and under his nails. Though he worked hard, he partied hard too. His phone book was a who's who of the Newport club scene. Sometimes, it boggled Thea's mind that he was just one year younger than she was when she'd had Irina. At twenty-two—while he was partying and literally painting the town—she'd been learning to breast-feed.

"Listen," she said. "I'm not doing anything tonight. If you want me to take over for you, I'm happy to do it."

Jules eyed her suspiciously. "Really?"

"It's no big deal," Thea said, and she walked to the tall white locker that held their aprons. "Go out. Have a good time."

Jules took a step toward her, put a hand on her shoulder. "I don't mind staying," he said. "I mean, if you want to, like, go out. You know? Go get into some trouble?"

"*Please,*" she said, laughing. "Women with ten-year-old daughters don't cause trouble."

Jules stepped back, crossed his thin arms over his black T-shirt. "How old are you? Thirty? Thirty-one?"

"Thirty-two," Thea said.

Jules's smile tipped up at one corner, and he gave her an exaggerated once-over. "You could definitely cause trouble, Thea. Believe me."

She chuckled and turned away. "Get out of here. I'm ordering you. I'm the boss."

"All right, but . . ."

"Nope. Out." She finished putting on her apron as he took his off, and she watched him out of the corner of her eye as he dug his car keys out of his pocket.

"So, I'll see you later?" he said.

"Yup! Later!" She picked up a rag and began to wipe down the counter. Then he was walking out the door, and another customer was walking in, smiling, and a few minutes later the first rush of a Friday night was pushing through the door, and the world was beginning to slip back into place.

By three a.m., Garret had had enough. He'd already gone to the gym, gone for a walk, and gone for a beer, and now there was nowhere left to go but crazy. Irina had hit her head on his bookshelf just when Jonathan had been about to put her to bed, and now she simply would not stop crying. She'd told Jonathan that she didn't want to stay over—that she wanted her and her father to go sleep *in their house*. And for a while, it had seemed his explanation held. But once she'd hit her head and the tears had started, there was no end.

Jonathan came into the living room where Garret was pretending to watch a late night horror movie—though he'd hardly been able to focus on it over Irina's bloodcurdling screams. She was still weeping in Garret's bedroom, but she was beginning to sound tired now, the sobs less forceful, the tears probably dried.

Jonathan dropped down on the sofa beside him. He was wearing dark navy pajamas, a matching top and bottom that had doubtlessly been purchased by Thea. His skin was pale and dull, and his brown eyes were glassed-over. "I don't know what else to do."

"Thea's going to think we tortured her."

"Irina's always had a flair for drama." Jonathan rubbed his face. "I think she's just . . . uncomfortable. It's her first night in a strange place."

"She wants it to feel normal, but it just isn't."

"And I can't help," Jonathan said.

Garret shrugged and decided to take a different approach. "Don't worry so much. She's a kid. She'll fall asleep. She just has to get tired enough."

"I don't think so," Jonathan said. "She's stubborn. You of all people can appreciate that."

Garret reached for his bottled water, took a long pull.

He'd thought of Irina over the years, thought of her often. For every one time he saw her, he'd dropped three birthday cards for her in the mail. He hadn't meant to neglect his niece, but Irina was Thea's daughter—and Garret had sworn to himself that where Thea went he would not go. Holidays had been notoriously uncomfortable—and lonely. Knowing that his family was at his parents' house on Christmas, opening presents and eating candied walnuts, nearly killed him every year.

Now, Thea and Jonathan's daughter was whimpering and talking to herself unintelligibly in Garret's bedroom. Her parents' separation was hitting her hard. Garret had last seen her two years ago, and she was getting to look like Thea more and more every day. She had Jonathan's face—his narrow, high cheekbones, his pointed chin—but she had Thea's hazel, almond eyes. Garret had been looking forward to Irina's visit; he missed her. She was, after all, his brother's daughter. He wanted to be a part of her life.

In the other room, Irina's crying regained momentum, part sob and part protest. But Garret knew that no matter how hard she cried or pretended to cry, she wouldn't be able to bring her parents back together. Wearily, Jonathan got to his feet. "I'm really sorry about this."

Garret shrugged. "Eh. What're you gonna do?"

Jonathan put his hand on his hips, his chest sinking visibly as he sighed. "Maybe I should take her home."

"Really? Now?"

"Maybe this wasn't such a good idea. Maybe I just should have kept her for the day."

Garret sank deeper into his leather couch and focused on the

TV. "Let's give it five more minutes," he said. "Then Uncle Garret
and Irina will have a little talk."

The first year Garret spent in Newport, Thea had not been a girl
to him. Girls were smiley and lively. They wore little skirts that
showed off the long backsides of their legs, and they smelled like
candy or flowers. Girls liked to shout at him when he was walking
down the hallway or they strutted next to him when the school
day ended and the mass of his classmates pushed their way outside.
Girls pulled him behind the bleachers at lunchtime to kiss him and
put his hands on their breasts. When he didn't pay attention to
them, girls cried.

And so by these standards, Thea was not a girl. She wore unre-
markable jeans, too-white sneakers, and her glasses were purple
plastic. The only thing about Thea that intrigued Garret was her
hair—her beautiful, dark hair that fell so effortlessly into inky,
rolling waves. When they wrestled or fought, as they often did
when Garret wanted to play video games and Thea wanted to go
outside, Garret would sometimes get a fistful of that beautiful hair
and tug—not to hurt but just to feel the strength of it and the
sound of her voice as she squealed.

At some point during the summer before his freshman year,
Garret had found himself beginning to use Thea as the butt of his
jokes—especially when he wanted to embarrass his older brother.
He'd discovered Jonathan had a fear of anything remotely sexual,
and Garret wasn't afraid to use his big brother's discomfort with
the same practicality that he might use a lever or a wedge.

"You want to make out with Thea, don't you?"

"Eww. Shut up."

"You pervert. You want to put your tongue right down Thea's
throat."

"I said, shut up!"

There was no faster way to get on Jonathan's nerves than to accuse him of wanting to mess around with Thea, who—in all ways but one—was just one of the guys. If Jonathan wouldn't leave Garret alone while he was watching television, Garret would threaten to tell their parents that Jonathan and Thea were having sex. If Jonathan wouldn't agree to go to the movies instead of to mini golf, Garret would say, "That's because you want to do Thea behind the waterfall." Sometimes Jonathan would fight him, viciously. Black eyes and bruised ribs and mangled egos would end with them both being grounded for days.

But Garret's taunting had an unexpected consequence as well.

His mother pulled him aside one day, leaving Garret to watch as Jonathan and Thea went tripping out the door, as fast as their legs would carry them toward their bicycles. Garret twisted out of his mother's grip.

"You've got to be careful with her, Garret."

"With who?"

"You know who," his mother said, her voice dark with warning. "And you know exactly what I mean."

Garret's skin had prickled. How had his mother known?

That evening as the three of them sat on the big rocks along the water's edge, Garret had been relentless, unmerciful in his teasing. Jonathan deserved to be embarrassed—for ratting him out. For being a coward. For making it look like Thea was the one who was uncomfortable when, as far as Garret could tell, she didn't care.

With the waves crashing against the jagged rocks and a buoy bobbing in the rough surf, Garret pulled out all the stops: he thought of every nasty thing he'd ever heard of people doing. He used every dirty word in his vocabulary. Jonathan pelted him in the head with a stone and broke the skin above his eyebrow, but still, Garret couldn't stop being angry. Wildly, powerfully angry.

The taunts just kept coming, each worse than the one before. He hardly noticed Thea at all—not until she stood up from the rock where she sat, marched up to him, and said, "That's enough."

She stood before him, the last summer she was an inch taller, in her boxy gray T-shirt, her wind-mussed ponytail, her dorky white tennis shoes. He'd seen her walk up to the meanest teacher in school and insist he'd graded her test unfairly. He'd seen her split open her knee on the pavement and refuse to cry. But that night, her eyes had gone red, filled up with tears, and her lips pulled into a frown.

"Thea . . ."

She turned away and ran as quickly as she could toward the road, where their bikes were kicked over on their sides in the dust. He saw her hair, caught in a long black ponytail, wagging at him as she ran away.

"Nice job, dilhole," Jonathan said. And he punched him hard in the chest, almost knocking the wind out of him.

Garret rubbed the spot absentmindedly, his own eyes beginning to water. Shame and guilt warred. "It's not my fault you're a couple of prudes. I was just joking around . . ."

"Real funny," Jonathan said. "Don't follow us. We don't want to see you."

And Garret realized that Thea was at the top of the hill, a silhouette in the fading light, waiting, but not for him.

Thea stumbled through the darkness of the kitchen to the door, and when she opened it, Garret was there. Behind him, the street was quiet and still, holding its breath. The streetlight cast his shadow in blurry orange on the ground. Irina was settled against his chest, her arms around his neck, her back folded gently forward.

"Garret."

He held a finger up to his lips. "Shhh."

He turned sideways as he slid through the doorway, past her, and Thea saw her daughter's face—splotchy from crying but peaceful too, as if sleep had been hard-won. An hour ago, Garret had texted Thea to tell her he was bringing Irina home. He didn't say why.

"Where's her bedroom?" Garret mouthed.

Instead of answering, Thea led him through the house with its very tiny square rooms, low ceilings, and narrow doorways. Nestled in the heart of Newport, not far from Price's Pier, the downstairs level of the house had been built before the Revolutionary War, and Thea had done what she could to keep its colonial feel: folk art, antiques, original flooring, few embellishments. She wondered: Did her house look like what Garret expected? Had he expected anything at all?

She was too conscious of him as he trailed her on the stairs in the dark—to have him following, so close, gave her a strange sense of vulnerability and made her want to turn around and walk backward. His hair was glossy, neat, and as blond as when he was a kid, and his skin was so perfect that she wondered if he'd started tanning. He was taller than she remembered. Bigger across the shoulders. All traces of the heart-on-his-sleeve boy she'd fallen so desperately in love with had been usurped by this harder, more unreadable man.

She, on the other hand, hadn't seen the inside of a gym in years. What did she look like to him? Childbirth had changed her body, had taken her young woman's angles and swollen them into more sloping, softened curves. Her skin was older too, she knew. In bad light, there were traces of lines around her mouth and eyes. She'd found her first gray hair this past spring—a shock of white like a lightning bolt against a black sky—and now it seemed they were coming on like armies. She hated that he made her so very conscious of herself, and it wasn't until they got to the top of the stairs that she realized she'd been holding her breath.

She bent to turn on the night-light in Irina's little room. In the soft pink glow, she watched Garret pull back the light quilt on the bed and then bend over carefully to settle Irina down. His hand cradled the back of her head, and though she groaned a little and her eyes fluttered open long enough to see where she was, she didn't seem interested in waking. She turned her back to them in the semidarkness and curled deeper into the bed.

Thea pulled the door closed behind them, leaving it open half an inch. She didn't speak until they were in the kitchen, standing beside the simple wooden table in the center of the small room. And even then, a whisper was the most she dared. "What happened?" she asked. "Is she sick?"

He shook his head. "She's been crying for hours."

"Why?"

Garret shifted uncomfortably. "She wanted her and Jonathan to come here. But that's obviously not an option. Anyway, she finally fell asleep on the ride home. And by that point, I figured she'd rather wake up here than in my condo."

"Why didn't Jonathan bring her?"

"He doesn't want to see you," Garret said.

Thea stood quietly a moment, not sure what was to come next. Everything had been said—the facts exchanged—and now there was nothing more.

But Garret made no move to leave. He just stood, looking at her. His eyes were the exact steel blue of the harbor on a fall day.

Thea felt some shadow of her old feeling for him rising up. Longing. Regret. A wish deeper and bigger than she could name. *Don't hate me anymore,* she thought. The Sorensen family believed that Garret had been avoiding her since her marriage to Jonathan. What they hadn't realized was that she had been avoiding him too.

"Was she good otherwise?" Thea asked.

"Fine. I didn't know she plays soccer."

Thea nodded, again at a loss. She wanted him to stay. To talk. To tell her everything that had happened since she saw him last. *Let me make you a cup of coffee,* she thought. And yet, the vast bulk of missing years was wedged between them, and there was nothing to say.

"She seems to trust you," Thea said.

His lips curled into a sneer. "She didn't get it from her mother."

She took a step back—and just like that, he'd smacked her in the face with the past, the blunt force of it knocking her composure down. "Garret, we should talk—"

He held up his hand: stop. Then he pushed open the screen door and went outside. She followed him to the doorway, watching him for a moment as he shoved his hands into his pockets and walked with his shoulders back and straight. Her heart cried out—traitor that it was. She hadn't seen him in so long.

"Garret!"

She pushed open the door, one foot inside her house, the other on the sidewalk. The street was narrow, old, more alleyway than thoroughfare. He stopped and turned to look at her, the streetlamp just above his head, orange light falling down.

All at once, shyness overtook her. With one word she felt as if she'd thrown herself at him. She pulled herself up straighter and tried to be cool.

"Thanks for doing this," she said.

"This was for Jonathan," he said.

And then he turned, whistling, and walked away.

Coffee has been controversial since its discovery, and the debate continues even now.

Some studies proclaim coffee to be a miracle drug—its antioxidant properties are touted as the cure for cancer and age. Other studies decry coffee as the instigator of various diseases, since caffeine can trigger stress responses in the body and interfere with overall health.

Caffeine wakes us up on rainy mornings or keeps us going when we lag, but it shouldn't be forgotten that caffeine is a drug. One hundred cups of coffee will kill an average man.

In nature, caffeine has a practical purpose: It's a pesticide, a natural bug deterrent. Caffeine emitted from the roots of a coffee tree will keep other plants (including other coffee seedlings) from growing nearby.

But there's a downside to having a built-in toxicity. Caffeine becomes more concentrated with time, so if a coffee tree lives long enough, the caffeine that protects it from being harmed can also kill it in the end.

THREE

Jonathan hadn't gone looking for trouble. He'd never liked to make waves. But one night, when he was on a business trip meeting with a potential new client for the firm, there she was, at a hotel bar in Boston. She was not some femme fatale in a backless dress, not a wallflower either, but she was there, cliché as any stranger seems on first glance, so that later Jonathan felt that she might have been waiting—if not for him, then for someone like him. He—and she—could have been anyone.

She was a graduate student passing through town to visit a friend. Her hair was highlighted blond and her laugh was easy. They'd struck up a conversation about Boston, and soon they were talking about baseball and then cooking and then politics, and then they were ordering another round of beers.

He hadn't made the decision to sleep with her lightly. Instead, he'd felt what had happened was a thing that he had let happen—as opposed to a thing he had done. He simply had to accept, to receive her, and not say no. In the musty elevator she'd pressed against him, her hips circling, and his body had responded with quick desperation. He was still vital. Alive, after all.

In a hotel room that could have been any hotel room, she'd left him with bruises and bites. Jonathan was sure Thea would see the dark shadows her mouth had made on his chest—she would notice them at night when he took off his shirt. Or when he toweled off after a shower. Or when he climbed into their bed. He couldn't separate his fear of the moment from his anticipation of it. Thea would see. She would yell and scream, and he would know they had a chance.

But days passed. Then a week. Then the bruises faded. And Thea, if she saw, had never said a word.

Dear Thea. Just a quick e-mail here. You looked terrible when I came to babysit Irina. You've lost weight. Here's what I'm thinking: it's a good thing for you and Jonathan to be spending some time apart. Absence makes the heart grow fonder. Might get the spark going again. Hopefully we'll all look back on all this one day, and it won't be any more consequential than a bad dream. Just keep loving him—as I know you do—and I'm sure he'll come around. Sue.

Dear Sue,

Thanks so, so much for your kind words. I needed them. I miss you (and Ken too). Can I see you? Can we get lunch? I'd really love to talk.

Thea

Thea. I would love to have lunch with you. But you understand, I'm in sort of an uncomfortable situation. I worry what Jonathan would say. Sue.

Because Sue and her husband Ken had held a standing reservation for the corner table at the Dancing Goat on Thursday nights, and because they'd stopped coming when Jonathan moved out, and because Thea couldn't stand the empty spot in the coffee shop where she wanted them to be, and because the babysitter was fine with keeping Irina for an extra hour, Thea was thrilled to comply when her baristas asked if they could hang around a while after the shop had closed.

She and Jules worked prepping drinks while the other baristas pushed the tables together and changed the music to something poppy and fun. She'd always felt that she could tell a lot about people by how they liked their coffee—and her baristas were no exception.

For Claudine, the French ex-pat whose talkative African lover had left her after learning he was eligible for dual citizenship, she brewed a good strong cup of yerba maté, made from a South American shrub.

For Rochelle, a pretty blond freshman who was majoring in biomedical engineering but who had yet to master perfect cappuccino foam, Thea made a raspberry-vanilla latte with mountains of whipped cream.

For Lettie, a hobbyist piano player with arthritic hands who had been working at the Dancing Goat since before Thea was born, she set out a pot of ginger-peach white tea.

Jules had made himself a slushy iced coffee with a drizzle of caramel before he sat down. And for her friend Dani, who was not a barista but who could probably run the place because her regular police beat brought her to the shop three times a day, Thea made a cup of coffee. Splenda and skim.

"So what do you think about my new marketing idea?" Claudine asked, smiling mischievously at Thea. Her eyebrow ring caught the light and gleamed. "We can call it Naughty Lattes."

Jules laughed. "Robusty Brews."

"Sexpresso Station," Rochelle said, her voice dripping with phone-sex cliché. "Gives new meaning to *hot* coffee."

"I think I'm gonna have to stop walking this patrol," Dani said, leaning back in her seat and adjusting the high waist of her uniform. "But maybe . . . Café au Lays?"

Thea heard Lettie groan at her side.

"Don't worry," Thea said. "Nobody's wearing a bikini to sell drinks. We're not that desperate."

"Really?" Jules's grin was wide. "But a bunch of coffee shops out West are doing it. And I figured we'd put Lettie out at the front of the alley to wave people in."

"Not if you want them to keep their food down, you won't," Lettie said, chuckling and pulling her lavender cardigan closed.

The conversation wore on, but no one seemed to be in a hurry to leave. Thea was glad for their company. Lettie had been with her so long she was practically family; Jules had charmed her when he'd showed up on his first day with a glossary of coffee terms; Dani had been Thea's friend since she'd wrestled a guy to the ground for trying to leave without paying; Claudine, in her thrift-store tank tops and thinning bandannas, offered provocative insight that Thea found fascinating; and Rochelle—she was still new, but like all of the baristas that Thea hired, she meant well.

Thea supposed she should have known that filling her shop with such good-hearted people would mean they might be up to something, asking to stay late at work. And it wasn't long before she understood the real reason they had decided to get together. Gradually the conversation came around to Thea, and the hints were clear: *You seem to be working so much.* And *What are your plans for when Irina's away with her dad?* They were worried, all of them, about her.

"All right, let's have it," Thea said. "Come on. Tell me. What do you want to know?"

For a moment, the little group went quiet.

It was Claudine who broke the stalemate. "Well then, for starters, how did you find out about the affair?" she asked, her accent making the word *affair* sound much more romantic than it was.

"Did you barge in on them?" Jules asked. "Catch them in the act?"

"No. Oh—no. I didn't walk in on them," Thea said. But already, her brain was building alternate histories, layering them up like scenes of a filmstrip. She hadn't "walked in." But she could have—maybe. She saw herself naively opening the door to her bedroom, white sheets, naked legs splayed, Jonathan's head lifting in surprise, his mouth shiny, the scramble and fumbling as he said, *Thea! What are you—*

"I did not walk in on anyone." She pushed the images from her head. Her husband—sleeping with another woman. She was more repulsed than hurt.

"Then how did you find out?" Lettie asked softly.

"He told me."

"Just like that. He told you." Dani paused, her coffee in the air.

"Is that so hard to believe? He felt guilty. He's a good man."

"But he told you because you had a suspicion, no?" Claudine asked.

"No idea at all," Thea said. "I don't think he'd planned it. It happened so fast."

"Maybe it's not serious," Rochelle said gently. A bit of whipped cream had dotted her chin, and Jules motioned for her to wipe it off.

"Ridiculous." Claudine pursed her lips. "Of course it was serious. It's not worth a man's time to confess a one-night stand."

"Maybe not to you," Jules said, and Claudine elbowed him.

"Do *you* think it's serious?" Lettie asked, her hand, cold and papery, pressed for a moment on Thea's arm. "Because my first husband always said it wasn't serious. But every Thursday night when I'd go off to orchestra, he'd have a different girl. And a whole

bunch of little 'not seriouses' end up as one steaming heap of serious in my book."

Thea shook her head. "He says it didn't mean anything. And I
believe him."

"Why?"

Thea looked down at her hands. "It's hard to explain. But I
trust him. Even now. If that makes any sense."

"Thea." Lettie's voice was gentle. "Were you unhappy?"

Thea felt them looking at her, waiting.

She picked up her own drink, decaf coffee with a splash of
milk and mint. She bought time by taking a sip. She and Jonathan
had done everything right as husband and wife. There was a lot to
love about the lifestyle they'd built together—a good house, a good
income, a beautiful daughter. When Thea got an occasional case
of the blues or the what-ifs, she'd written it off as commonplace.
What woman didn't doubt her job or her marriage from time to
time? "No, I wasn't unhappy. I don't think I was, anyway."

Rochelle was looking at her, studying. Her cute round face
was full of compassion—but a kind of intelligent scrutiny as well.
"There's more, isn't there? There's more to this than your husband's affair."

"Is there someone else?" Claudine asked.

Thea shook her head, appalled. "I've never been unfaithful."

Claudine's lips curled into a grin. "That doesn't quite answer
the question," she said.

It hadn't taken much convincing to talk Jonathan into playing
hooky from work—he always was easy to persuade—and so on
the last Tuesday of the month, they bought tickets for the ferry
and decided to spend the day on Block Island, away from the crush
of the crowds. Now Garret floated with his brother in a shallow

saltwater cove, the tide barely moving their kayaks along the surface of the water. The air tasted of salt and sunshine, and Garret watched as the color began to come back into his brother's face.

"Not bad, eh?" Garret took a big breath, felt his nostrils flare with the effort. Low green reeds edged the glassy water around them. "Worth bailing on work?"

Jonathan laughed. "And then some."

"Come on!" Garret began to paddle, leading them deeper into the verdant, snaking rivulets of the salt pond as the nose of the kayak cut a path through the water. The sun beat down hot on the back of Garret's neck. Schools of fish darted beneath them, and birds twisted in the air overhead. Garret's arms began to burn, and when Jonathan caught up with him, they were both breathing hard. They spent a few minutes drifting to catch their breath.

"Do you do this a lot?" Jonathan asked.

"Enough," Garret said. "I try to get out here a few times a month during the summer. At least that."

Jonathan adjusted the brim of his baseball cap. "We've got to get Irina out here with us next time. She'd love it."

"Yeah. She's quite an athlete."

"She gets it from her mother," Jonathan said, smiling. "That and her stubborn streak."

As long as that's all she got, Garret thought. And from the way Jonathan turned his head, he wondered if his brother had heard.

"Can I ask you a question?"

Garret trailed his hand in the cool water, the pressure of the current pushing against his palm. "Shoot."

"I know you were mad at Thea for marrying me—"

"Water under the bridge," Garret said, laughing.

Jonathan frowned. "The question is, why weren't you mad at *me* for marrying *her*? Why didn't you stop talking to me too?"

Garret laughed again. "I did stop talking to you."

"But only for a little while," Jonathan said.

Garret dug into his lunch bag for a bottle of water. He hadn't brought his brother out here for a heart-to-heart. And yet, he should have seen it coming. He and Jonathan had almost always been on speaking terms, but there was no denying that their relationship had cooled—maybe even frozen—in the years since Jonathan and Thea married. Only the potential for divorce had made an opening for Garret to truly seek out a friendship with his brother again.

"That's all in the past," Garret said. "Let's just forget it. Upward and onward. We've got a lot of life ahead of us now—to make up for lost time."

"I guess you're right. I'm just trying to understand."

Garret screwed down the cap of his water bottle overly tight. He knew exactly what Jonathan was getting at—but the subject was off-limits. Over the years Garret had come to terms with his brother's marriage to Thea. Where Jonathan was concerned, Garret had done what he could to forgive and forget. Jonathan was his brother, after all.

But he would never in his life offer that concession to Thea. Just because she was a good person to Jonathan didn't change the fact that she had *not* been good to him. She'd been cruel and unforgiving. Hateful. As kind as she appeared to others, Garret knew there was a hardness in her, a maliciousness, that only he had ever seen.

Unfortunately, running into her again—in her quiet kitchen, her dark hair mussed and voluminous, her T-shirt falling off one shoulder, her feet bare and small below the hemline of cartoony pants—had made it difficult to cling to his hate.

She didn't look like the demon he'd conjured of her in his dreams. Instead, she was far more terrifying for how beautiful she appeared. He'd wanted to take her face in his hands, to look at her and have her look back, wordless, as if that might make her understand what he couldn't find words to say.

Now, floating among the reeds and salty inlets in bright, revealing sunlight, he knew that instant of tenderness he'd felt for her was only a mirage. He couldn't let his anger at her go. He wouldn't. He and his brother might finally reconnect in a way that was more than just lip service—if only because the woman who had broken both their hearts had united them, finally, as their mutual enemy.

Jonathan leaned back against his seat, his paddle resting on the kayak parallel to the waterline. "Thanks for taking me out here today. I think I needed a change of scenery."

Garret back-paddled a few strokes. "All good. I'm glad we can do this."

Jonathan turned his head, his dark eyes shaded by his baseball cap. "So am I."

Her sophomore year, Thea's girlfriends had started throwing around the word *love*—not in relation to shoes or movies or food but in relation to men. Sometimes Thea judged her friends to be silly in their love—as if they were trying to feel it by acting like they felt it. As if a person could *think* her way into love.

But then she would find herself in the girls' room between classes, listening to a friend crying in the bathroom stall, and her own heart would crack because she herself knew that pain, knew what it was like—that love was not a spike driven into the heart, but rather, one pulled out of it: a hollow wound.

Garret was one of her best friends. Jonathan too. And so she'd taken care to treat them both exactly the same—never favoring one over the other, never teasing one more than the other, never spending too much time alone with one brother if the other wasn't there. It wasn't until Garret had pulled away from them that the truth became clear.

Her feelings astounded her: she couldn't make sense of them.

No single word could pin them down. Back in eighth grade the three of them had discovered that if they took twenty breaths very, very fast they could make themselves lightheaded, dizzy, so that the world spun on its side. They would compete to see who could take the most breaths, who could stand the sweet and terrible dizziness the longest. Now, when Thea saw Garret coming down the hallway, he made her feel just that way—as if her head might lift off her shoulders. He spent less and less time with her. She wanted to believe that it was soccer that was keeping him away. But it wasn't.

Garret had splintered off from their little group and struck out on his own. He started hanging out with a new crowd, going to parties, forcing her or Jonathan to be his alibi. She and Jonathan could do nothing but speculate. Without Garret between them, some of the energy had gone out of their shrunken tribe.

Sometimes she saw him in the hallways, leaning near a locker. And when she went to say hello to him, she realized he was not alone, and that he was not leaning against a locker at all but was leaning on another person, a girl. She wondered, with bitter envy, if he was having sex. She figured it was a given.

She also saw him on the soccer fields, since she and Jonathan had not stopped going to his games simply because he'd stopped hanging around with them quite so incessantly. He'd changed in the last year. His face was different, though she couldn't put her finger on precisely what feature—his nose? his jaw?—had changed. His body grew lean and hard from days of practicing, cuts of new muscle just beneath the surface of his skin. When he ran into the end zone, he left her breathless with his confidence. His teammates crowded around him, all wanting to be the first to congratulate him for a big win, and from the bleachers, Thea clapped and called his name. Sometimes he would wave in her direction. But there were many people in the stands—and Jonathan at her side—so she was never perfectly sure that he was waving at her.

Her friends, many of whom seemed to have a crush on him as well, commiserated with her in the line for the cafeteria. And Thea hated them for it. The way they loved him was different from the way she loved him. They had not seen him step in and take the blame (and the grounding) when Jonathan had accidentally scratched his father's Mercedes. They had not seen him the day he grabbed her by both arms and pulled her up from the side of the breakwater before she fell in. They had not seen him working on his algebra homework, Jonathan patiently helping. They did not know he got so frustrated sometimes that tears came into his eyes.

"Why don't you go out with Garret?" her friends would ask her, agreeing that if anyone among their little circle had a chance, it was her.

Thea's reply was always the same, though it killed her to say it. "He doesn't like me that way."

And it was true. He didn't. Not then.

Dear Sue:

I didn't mean to put you in an awkward position by asking you to lunch. But Jonathan is very understanding. Even before he and I married, you and I were friends—and I don't think he will have forgotten that. I hate not seeing you. How about this? What if you ask him what he thinks? If he's against the idea of our meeting, then I won't ask again.

Thea

Thea: Well, you were right, dear. You know him better than I do. Let's meet one day next week. I'm looking forward to it. Sue.

* * *

"Thea?"

She knew his voice immediately, though it was the middle of the day on Wednesday and there was no sound on earth she'd expected less than the chill of her name when he said it. Around her, the coffee shop was busy with the lunch rush, locals stopping in to pick up fresh fruit and simple sandwiches on whole grain bread. Jules had just spilled an entire pitcher of scalded milk down the front of the counter, and Rochelle was about to break into tears before an angry customer who'd been given regular vanilla syrup instead of sugar-free. Hell was breaking loose, the calm of morning cracking open and chaos bursting through.

But Thea stepped away from it, the phone to her ear. Stepped away, behind the black curtain and into the quiet of the storage closet, as time slowed down. For an instant, pandemonium gave way to the jolt of memory, and she was in the dark of her bedroom, when he held her and they whispered together for hours.

"Yes. It's me," she said.

"It's Garret."

She closed the black curtain behind her, the closet going dark. "I know."

"We need to talk."

"All right."

"About Irina. Jonathan wants to set up a regular visitation schedule. He wants to see her again."

"I want him to see her too. We just have to figure out the best way."

"I'll come pick her up for the day on Saturday mornings. Let's say ten. And I'll bring her home in the evening around eight."

"That sounds okay." Thea leaned her shoulder against the cluttered shelving. "What else?"

"Nothing else. What else would there be?"

"I don't know." Thea took a breath. "I just don't see why Jonathan can't talk to me about this directly."

"Well, what did you do to him?"

"Sorry?"

"Jonathan acts like it's his fault. But I know better. What did you do?"

"Nothing," she said, hating how defensive she sounded. "I didn't do anything."

"My brother isn't the type to cheat, and you know it. You must have done something wrong."

Thea was quiet. Garret had always known just how to strike her deepest nerve. For weeks she'd suspected herself of being more guilty than Jonathan—even though it was he who broke his vows. She loved him—she always had. And if he hadn't left, she would have stayed with him forever. But did that make her blameless? She had her doubts.

"So what did you do?" he pushed. "Steal money?"

"Garret . . ."

"Did you apply the wifely thumbscrews? Crowd him? Not let him breathe?"

"None of those things," she said, trembling now.

"Did you cheat on him?"

"No!"

"You're lying."

"I'm not," she said, anger rising like fire within her. "I never cheated. And it's only between me and Jonathan if I did."

"Then what did you do, Thea? Because when Jonathan married you he was the happiest person I knew. And now he's a shadow of that guy."

"Are you talking about him? Or yourself?"

"Please," he said. "Don't give yourself so much credit. Life's moved on."

"Has it?" she asked, surprising herself. She had no intention of having this conversation with him today. But here it was, astonishing as a ghost manifesting before her eyes. She took a step deeper into the closet, not wanting to be heard. "If that were true, Garret— that you've moved on—then why haven't you said two words to me since we were eighteen? If what we were doesn't matter anymore, then why can't you even write your name on the bottom of your e-mails to me?"

He laughed, as if they weren't on the brink of a meltdown. It was a practiced, perfect laugh. When he spoke his voice was cool. "As far as I'm concerned, you don't exist. I don't want to hear about you. I don't want to see you. And I sure as hell don't want to be talking to you. I'm only doing this because Jonathan asked me to. I'm not interested in a trip down memory lane."

Thea held her breath, fuming. Fury choked her. She couldn't stand this new side of Garret—the side of him that had become so callous, so willfully obtuse. Didn't he know how much she'd thought of him over the years? How much she wished things were different?

"Why can't you forgive me?" she asked.

"What would be the point?"

She let her forehead rest against the shelving. All those days she'd thought herself in love with him. All those nights her conscience had gnawed like rats on her heart. All the years she'd wished she could go back to do things differently.

"There's always a point," she said.

From "The Coffee Diaries"
by Thea Celik

The Newport Examiner

Every story has a beginning, and coffee does too. Ethiopian folklore holds that coffee was discovered one day when a goatherd lost his goats.

When he finally found them, they were playing and frolicking—and they were also nibbling the cherries of a nearby tree. Intrigued, the goatherd tried one, and he was immediately energized—and hooked.

At any moment that you're drinking a cup of coffee, you're still connected to those first people who discovered the coffee bean. Sure, it may be hard to relate a sugary and icy mocha mint blend with the mashed-up seeds and lard that the ancients used as the first energy bars.

And maybe it's difficult to see why an espresso—brewed with intense heat and steam—has anything to do with cultures that make "coffee" not from the beans of the tree but from the gently boiled leaves.

But all in all, coffee connects us to our roots—a reminder of our nomadic and unindustrialized origins, and a reminder that no matter how distant we get from our beginnings, we're never very far away at all.

FOUR

In the dream it goes differently. She's eighteen—beautiful. She's wearing the same clothes she wore that day: an aqua T-shirt that shows a little of her belly. Denim shorts that are frayed to white at the bottom edge. Garret pushes open the door to the falling-down barn, knowing what he'll find on the inside: old tires, a coil of rope the width of his leg, rust-crusted shovels, flattened beer cans, remnants of charcoal and ash.

But instead, as he leads Thea inside the barn inside the dream, he doesn't find the detritus of a falling-down silo, but instead, he walks into paradise: pinkish sunlight, pillows and candles, grapes and wine.

She's not nervous and neither is he. This isn't their first time anymore—not in the dream. They've been doing this forever; he knows every inch of her body, every inch of flesh that's round or sharp, dry or wet. He's in no rush as he leads her to the plush and silken bed, the promise of her soft, slim fingers in his, the slight sheen of her lips where she's licked them. Desire is restless but tender, greedy but patient—the want of old lovers, not new. The kind of passion Garret's never known with anyone, least of all Thea, except in dreams.

On a peninsula jutting westerly into the waters of the Narragansett, the Pennant Inn appeared to Thea to be overwhelmingly regal, as if the perfect green lawn sloping away from the building was created to display the architecture like a velvet pillow displays a crown. At a table in the restaurant, Thea and Sue sat before a long line of curved bow windows that offered near panoramic views of the shoreline and foaming white breakers. Though they'd never explicitly talked about it, it was always understood that Sue paid.

The busboy refilled their glasses of cucumber water, the ice sparking in the sunlight, the sound of classical music covering a long lull in the conversation. Nervous, Thea picked up her glass. Lately, she'd been working extremely long hours at the coffee shop, and she'd looked forward to her lunch date with Sue. They'd already covered the unusually cool weather, the traffic on the bridge, and the drop in numbers of tourists. But the truth was that neither one of them had come for chitchat.

Thea shored up her courage. "Have you spoken to Jonathan?"

"I talked to him. And he seems fine. But he always seems fine." When she spoke again, her voice was gentle. "What happened— if you don't mind my asking. I thought everything was going so smoothly . . ."

"So did I." Thea squeezed Sue's hand; her friend's compassion showed clear on her face. "He clammed up in the last year. Like he was going through the motions but nothing else. I wish he would have talked to me. Warned me that something was wrong."

"Sweetheart. It sounds like he did."

Thea was quiet. As far as she knew, no one had told Sue about

Jonathan's infidelity. And Thea wasn't about to. What she wanted from Sue was guidance. Understanding. Wisdom. All the things she had come to depend on from her good friend. "Please. Tell me what I should do."

Sue drew her hand back and picked up her white wine, her fingers almost as thin as the crystal stem. "Did you know Ken cheated on me once?"

"He did?"

Sue nodded, her usually gentle smile marred for a moment by nerves. "I don't know if I should call it cheating really. It was more of an emotional affair. And they may have fooled around a little bit . . ."

"How did you find out?"

"He felt so terrible about it he confessed everything. He bought me a new car that I left sitting in the garage for six months. I thought my life was ending, and if it wasn't for the boys holding us together, we might have come apart."

"But you didn't."

"No, we didn't." Sue looked out the window, where the sun was spraying the water with gold. "We toughed it out. And now that I can look back on it, all I see is a moment that made us stronger—that brought us together. We got through that. I think we could get through anything."

Thea sat back in her seat, moved by the thought that Sue's perfect-looking marriage wasn't always so perfect, and she wondered again how much Sue really knew. Sue's resilience in the face of pain was meant to be encouraging, but instead, Thea had the sense that her own marriage to Jonathan was nothing like the relationship that Ken and Sue shared. And when Thea found out that Jonathan had cheated, she hadn't felt angry so much as resigned, as if the inevitable had finally arrived.

Since her friends had asked her whether or not she'd been happy, she'd been thinking about the circumstances of her marriage. She'd assumed that because she wasn't unhappy she must have been happy. And yet now she was beginning to see that there was a third state—one she'd never considered before—and it felt an awful lot like happiness but wasn't quite it.

The waiter brought their salads, loaded with nuts and fruit, but Thea didn't pick up her fork. "And what about us? I mean, you and me."

"We've been through worse than this. You know that."

"So you're saying this won't be a big deal. That we can stay friends."

"Of course we'll stay friends! But if it starts to get too messy . . . Oh never mind. I can't imagine this getting messy—you and Jonathan are both such well-meaning people. As long as Jonathan is okay with it, I see no reason we can't keep having our harmless little lunches from time to time."

Thea picked up her fork. It wasn't quite the declaration she'd hoped for—not a pledge of undying loyalty—but she felt comforted nonetheless.

"So tell me," Sue said, stabbing at her salad. "What are your plans for the week?"

On days when school was closed and the snow went whipping down the narrow streets, Jonathan, Garret, and Thea bundled up in hats, sweaters, mittens, and scarves, and then headed outside. The snow piled here and there, blanketing cars and frosting windows, and the whole city was thrown into a familiar and intimate silence—one it had once known so well, four hundred years ago.

Much as Jonathan loved days off from school, Garret was always especially reckless in the snow—so much that it made Jonathan nervous for them both. And when Thea wasn't around, Garret's foolishness knew no restraints. He was so much more likely to do dumb things if she wasn't there to stop him—like jump off the roof of the bakery into a snowdrift or decide to go sledding down the middle of the street. Jonathan tried to keep his little brother from being irresponsible, but Garret always ended the argument with the word that never failed to sock Jonathan in the gut: *coward.*

Unfortunately, Garret's antics were just the first half of Jonathan's torment; the other half he owed to his parents. After Garret had been grounded or sent to his room, Jonathan could never shake the sense that his parents secretly admired Garret for his outrageousness and daring. Family friends would ask, "What's Garret grounded for this time?" and always Sue and Ken would answer with an amused twinkle in their eyes: "Oh you know. Boys will be boys." Though Jonathan worked hard at his studies, never forgetting his homework, always getting A's, Garret never failed to outshine him with little more than a good drive down the soccer field or a zinger of a joke that cracked up his class—even if it landed him in detention.

Maybe if Jonathan hadn't been so pissed off on the day of the snowstorm during his junior year. Maybe if Thea hadn't been sick, and had been there to distract Garret from his need for adrenaline, and Jonathan from his need to compete. Maybe if it hadn't snowed, and they weren't bored, and the rungs leading to the tops of the telephone poles hadn't been quite so appealing . . .

Maybe then Jonathan wouldn't have said, "Yes, but let's make it a race."

On the steely, cold rungs of the telephone pole, Jonathan's boots squeaked, but the treads held firm. His muscles worked until he perspired beneath his snow pants. He wanted to beat his brother so bad it made little black stars creep in at the edges of his eyes. As the ground disappeared beneath him, falling away inch by inch, the frozen white sky growing closer—he heard Thea's voice. She'd come out after all; she'd found them. She was calling up to them, her voice cracking the air, calling *get down*, and he looked to see that he was ahead of Garret—*ahead!*—higher and higher than his brother, and he thought, with the thrill knights must have felt climbing towers for maidens, *I'll win this one for her, for her, because she's watching*—

Right before he lost his footing and fell.

At the hospital, tucked into a hard white bed, his parents stared down at him in disappointment and shook their heads. "You should have known better," they said.

And Jonathan could only close his eyes and pretend he was sleeping, because they were right: he should have known better. He *always* was supposed to know better—better than Garret anyway.

"Irina!" Thea called to her daughter, who was out on the floor, talking to Hollis and Dean as they set up their chessboard. She'd just come from practice. Her hair was pulled into a ponytail that hung down thin and straight, and her entire left side was a grass stain. She was telling them about it like a fisherman might brag about his catch of the day. "Irina!"

Irina glanced over at her, then looked back at the chess players, going on with her story as if Thea hadn't just called her name. Hollis, who was placing black pawns one by one on their squares, rolled his eyes—just enough so that Thea would see.

Thea finished making a café breve of espresso and cream, and she set it on the counter for Claudine. "Will you take this to table six?"

Claudine smirked. Her big bracelets clacked together as she picked up the drink. "*Mon Dieu.* She's a talker, that one."

Thea didn't bother to answer. She hurried over to her customers' table to save them from her domineering kid, wiping her hands on her apron as she went. "Sorry about this," she said, smiling sweetly. "She's always been a chatterbox."

"It's fine," Hollis said.

"Let's just get to playing," Dean said.

Thea tugged her daughter by the arm away from the old men. Later she would bring over a few little butter cookies, on the house, to thank them for their patience. But for now, she glared at Irina—embarrassed that she would so publicly and purposefully misbehave. "Irina, I was calling you."

"I know," Irina said.

"Your uncle Garret is going to be here any minute," Thea said. "Now come with me."

Irina didn't simply *follow* Thea back across the room, she *stomped*. Once behind the counter, Thea bent until she was at her daughter's level, where they were both hidden from prying eyes by the tall, refrigerated pastry case. She had to hold her daughter's shoulders to make her stand still.

"Mr. Cooper and Mr. Gray don't want to talk right now. They're here to play chess and complain about coffee. Not to talk to little girls."

Irina was petulant. "How do you know?"

"I just do," she said.

"You don't know anything!"

Thea frowned. Her daughter was never so surly. Thea could only guess that she was upset about having to go visit her father—not because she didn't want to see him, but because she was reacting to the disconnect and pressure of having to make such a production about going to see the man she once saw every day. The only thing Thea could do was assure her: this would begin to feel more comfortable with time.

"You're going to have a nice day today," she said.

"I know."

Thea let Irina go. "Do you have everything you need to go with Uncle Garret? Do you have your backpack?"

"Yeeeees."

"Did you put all your toys in it that you want to bring?"

"Yeeeeees."

"All right. So there's nothing to worry about. Stay back here until your uncle gets here, okay? No more going out on to the floor today."

Irina pouted.

"Understand?"

"Yeeeeees, Ma," she said, and then she found a chair in the corner where she could kick her legs out and sulk. Thea picked up a clipboard and went back to work, counting the number of gallons of milk so that she would know how many more to order.

A moment later, Claudine was standing beside her. "She's taking it hard," she said under her breath.

"She doesn't like being away from home."

"Of course not. She gets it from her mom."

Thea glanced at Claudine, not sure what to say. Claudine had never been catty, exactly, but she didn't mince words. "I like my house," Thea said. "It's . . . where I live."

Claudine draped an angular arm around her for a moment. "It's a very nice house."

"Thanks," Thea said, and rather than reading into Claudine's odd comment, she put it out of her mind.

Ten minutes later, Claudine had gone out back for her break and Thea was wrapping a blueberry scone in wax paper when Garret came in, his cell phone pressed to his ear and his mouth seeming to go at a million miles an hour. She swallowed her nervousness. He was wearing khaki shorts, a nice black polo that stretched snugly across his shoulders, and flip-flops. He pushed his dark sunglasses up to rest on the top of his blond hair, then snapped the phone closed.

"Where's Irina?" he asked.

Hello to you too, Thea thought.

"Present," Irina called out. She pushed herself off of her chair, slumped forward with cartoonish glumness. Her footfalls were heavy against the tile.

"Ready, kid?" Garret asked hopefully. But Irina didn't so much as smile.

Thea crouched down and spoke softly. To her dismay, she saw tears swimming in her daughter's hazel eyes. "Listen to me, sweetheart. You're not staying there overnight again. You're just going to go hang out with Daddy for the day. Doesn't that sound like fun?"

Her lower lip trembled. "Why can't you come with us?"

Thea took Irina's hand and led her around to the side of the counter where Garret stood waiting. "I bet you and Daddy are doing something really fun today."

Irina tugged her hand hard. "But you should come too. I want to see Daddy and you. At the same time."

"Irina . . ."

"Why can't you come with me?"

Thea faltered, and amazingly enough, she found herself looking to Garret for help. She didn't expect him to be good with kids—though at one time she'd believed he wanted to be a father—but even a complete numskull would know how to help with this if he knew how to take a hint. "Garret? Why don't you tell Irina what you're doing today?"

He answered without hesitation. "Playing mini golf," he said, and he flashed his big, charming smile. "Have you ever played mini golf?"

Irina nodded.

"Do you like it?"

She nodded again.

"I bet you're not very good at it though," he said. "Your mom never was."

"I'm good at it!" Irina said, and she let go of Thea's hand. "I'm awesome at it. I'm the best in my school!"

Thea glanced at Garret, thankful—and trying not to remember the night he kept hiding her golf ball under windmills and fiberglass stones. "Irina, why don't you go use the bathroom before you get in the car?"

"But I don't have to go."

"Try," Thea said.

Irina dragged herself in the direction of the small unisex bathroom. Thea's heart ached for her daughter. What kind of family didn't see each other? And what kind of parents could communicate the duties of parenthood only through a messenger like Garret? If Jonathan didn't get in touch with her, personally, soon, she would get in touch with him.

She glanced at Garret, the blue of his eyes so sharp and disarming. She crossed her arms. "So, are you really going mini golfing?"

"We are now." He flipped open his phone, stared at the screen. "Excuse me," he said.

"Oh. I just remembered. I have something for Sue—" Thea hurried over to the locker and retrieved a silver pen from her bag. When she returned to the front of the counter, Garret wasn't on the phone. He was watching, waiting for her.

"What's this?" he asked, taking the pen and turning it in his hand.

"Sue left it when we had lunch the other day. If you could give it to her when you see her, that would be great."

He scoffed. "You had lunch with my mother."

"We always do."

He shook his head. "Not anymore, you don't."

"Jonathan knows about it," she said. "He's fine with it."

"Jonathan doesn't know what's good for him right now."

"And you do?"

"Thea—you're not a part of this family. Jonathan left you. You're not attached to us anymore."

Thea felt her eyes burn. "It's not that easy."

"What's not easy about it?" he asked. "Jonathan needs his mother right now. His family. You owe it to him to steer clear."

She stared at him, and for the first time, it occurred to her that she had no idea who he was anymore. Though she hadn't seen him in ages, she'd assumed that the deep fundamentals of his being would still be recognizable. She thought she might still know him and understand him if only because of how close she'd been to him years ago. But now she saw that maybe she'd been wrong—that he'd changed so much that he was no longer the same person in any way. When she looked at him now—the strong bones of his face, the familiar shape of his hands and fingernails, the unaltered blue of his eyes—she was no longer looking at the boy she'd once loved.

"Are you really such a monster?" she asked.

He was quiet for a moment. She thought his voice would be mean, cruel, when he spoke again. But it was not. "Are you?"

Irina came back from the bathroom, dragging her feet, and Thea put on a cheerful smile. "Did you go?"

She nodded.

Thea bent down and tucked a strand of her daughter's pale brown hair behind her ear where it had fallen out of her ponytail. "You're going to have a great time."

"How do you know?"

"I asked the coffee grounds in my cup this morning."

"Really!" Her eyes brightened. "What did they say?"

"They said you're going to get a hole in one."

"Told you so," she said, glancing at Garret.

He laughed—a real, unpracticed, and not at all sarcastic laugh. His face seemed ten years younger. It tugged at Thea's heart.

Irina kissed her on the cheek. "Love you!"

"Love you too, sweetheart."

When she stood, she saw that Garret was watching her. Staring. The anger had melted from his expression, replaced by something quieter, more forlorn than mad. She wondered what he saw, what he was thinking. She wanted to go to him, to wrap her arms around him and hold him—to clasp all that anger and sorrow that she saw in him and heal it, somehow.

But all she could think to say was, "You'll bring her back this evening?"

"At eight," he said. He looked down at Irina, who was now holding his hand. "Ready, kid?"

Irina smiled, enchanted by her uncle. Like mother, like daughter. There was no hope for either of them. "Have fun," Thea said. She watched them walk out the door—her daughter and the man who might have been her husband, if life had taken a slightly different turn all those years ago.

Thea was on the Harvest Dance decorating team during the fall of their junior year, but much as she loved school dances, she didn't think she would attend. She'd had to play her cards close to her chest: *Of course I'm going,* she told her friends. *I don't need to have a date to go.*

But the truth was, she'd been hoping that Garret would ask her. And when she'd heard he'd asked Carin Woodhouse instead, she knew she wouldn't be able to stand watching the two of them slow dancing under the basketball hoops, which had been decorated with a garland of paper pumpkins that she had made.

The night of the dance, Thea bailed without telling her girlfriends. She and Jonathan rented a handful of prom slasher movies, and they curled up under blankets on opposite ends of Sue's couch. Thea had spent the afternoon making chocolate-covered espresso beans with her mother—the caffeine and chocolate combo was her mother's prescription for Thea's bad mood—and she and Jonathan sat crunching beans between their teeth and laughing at campy murder scenes until at last Garret came home.

He was wearing nice clothes—grown-up clothes—and unlike other boys his age, he wore them well. To Thea, he looked like a prince—or some dignitary from a different time, come to visit their century. He took off his jacket and hung it behind the door.

"Hey!" Garret leaned on the arm of the couch, glancing at the Farrah Fawcett haircuts and polyester gym shorts on the TV screen. "Is this *Carrie*?"

"Yeah," Jonathan said coolly.

"Why didn't you guys tell me you were watching movies tonight?"

Jonathan glanced at Thea. Her heart went fluttery in her chest, and she found herself going quiet—as she so often did when Garret was around these days.

"It was a last-minute thing," Jonathan said. "Sit down if you want to sit down."

Garret did. He plopped on an overstuffed armchair and began to take off his shoes. Thea was rapt by the muscles moving under his shirt, the way his gold hair flopped forward as he leaned down. When he looked up, his eyes found hers immediately, as if he knew she'd been watching.

"I thought you were going," Garret said to her. "Everyone was asking me where you went. Are you sick or something?"

She shrugged. "I'm okay."

Jonathan threw a handful of popcorn at him and told him to shut up and watch TV. Now that Garret was with them, the atmosphere had changed. Jonathan clammed up around his brother these days—he was a totally different person. It wasn't long before he excused himself and went to bed.

Later, when the movie had ended, and Thea was getting her

jacket on to go home, she knew the subject of the dance was about to come up again. Garret had never been one to give up easily; she would have been disappointed if he was.

"You did such an amazing job on the gym," he said. The light from a black-and-white movie flickered in the otherwise dark room, and the house was so quiet Thea worried he might hear the beat of her heart—too fast for explanation. "All those little white lights. And the hay bales and cornstalks. It must have taken you forever."

"It did," she said. "Thanks."

"That's why I don't understand why you didn't go," he said, his eyes narrowing suspiciously. "I get why Jonathan didn't. He just doesn't 'do' dances. But you . . . You didn't really want to sit around and watch TV all night, did you?"

She focused on the buttons of her windbreaker as she snapped them closed. *Oh please let him not know,* she thought. *Oh please let me not do something stupid.*

"Is it because you didn't have a date?" he asked.

Kill me, she thought. "No. It's because I wanted to stay here. Keep Jonathan company. I didn't want him to be alone."

Garret nodded, but she could tell he didn't quite believe her. "Well. It would have been more fun if you were there."

She felt her face flushing and she could barely speak. "Did you have a good time?"

"It was okay," he said.

She wondered what that meant—if he wasn't in love with Carin Woodhouse after all. She picked up her backpack and pulled it onto her shoulders. "Are you going out with her?"

"No." He looked down at her face as if he was looking for something. She hoped that whatever it was, he found it. "Maybe next time I'll skip the dance to stay in with you and Jonathan."

She smiled, warmth blooming within. "You'll always be welcome," she said.

From "The Coffee Diaries"
by Thea Celik

The Newport Examiner

Much as people love coffee today, rulers of the past had every reason to fear coffeehouses. Coffee causes trouble. It gets people riled up. It incites.

One theory holds that coffee changed the way people interacted socially on a grand scale. Prior to coffeehouses, much public socializing was done in pubs, where beer made conversation apathetic and sloppy. When coffee arrived in public venues, it sparked alertness and intellectual debate.

Coffeehouses became places of radical thinking and political uprising—and those in power feared them. England's Charles II attempted (unsuccessfully) to ban the existence of coffeehouses. Frederick the Great mandated that his people forgo coffee for beer. Some regimes and leaders went as far as punishing coffee drinkers, with repeat offenders paying the ultimate price: death.

In this country, coffee maintained its revolutionary reputation. Coffee became the symbolic drink of the patriotic due to the British tax on tea. Coffeehouses, which sometimes fused with pubs in colonial America, were places of uprising and revolt.

Though perhaps the scale has diminished a bit, the dramas of our lives continue to play out in coffeehouses today.

FIVE

Every year on the Fourth of July, the Sorensens took Ken and Sue's sailboat out into the Narragansett to watch the fireworks. And every year, Thea had looked forward to it—to packing a picnic basket with grapes, crackers, hard white cheese, juice boxes, and wine. She loved the moment just before the fireworks went off, when the water that cradled the boat's hull turned black as coffee under the night sky.

But this year, Thea had not been invited along.

Now, the fireworks having ended an hour ago, she stood waiting at the marina, her forearms resting on a cool metal railing as she watched the boats and dinghies coming in one by one. They were late to get back, but Thea wasn't angry. Though she hadn't been with her family tonight, she had nothing but good wishes for them.

When at last she heard the familiar sound of her daughter's laughter, faintly echoing across the water, her skin began to prickle. The sailboat came to the dock with excruciating slowness—inch by leisurely inch. Irina was bouncing on her tiptoes and waving toward the shore, a green glow stick making wild arcs in the darkness, and Thea waved back. Garret and Jonathan were busy getting ready to secure the boat, and Sue was packing things into a big canvas tote while Ken stood at the wheel.

"Mom! Mom!" Irina leapt onto the dock, barely waiting for the boat to stop. Her flip-flops pounded the wooden boards as she ran and hugged Thea tight round the waist. "Did you watch them? Did you see that one that looked like an American flag?"

Thea pushed her daughter's wind-ruffled hair back from her face. "I saw it! It was awesome!"

"Dad says the blue ones are the most expensive." She glanced over her shoulder, to where her father and Garret were securing the boat. "You know, Dad's right there. You can go say hi . . ."

Thea hesitated. She wanted to be a good example to her daughter. To show that she was not so petty that she refused to talk to him. But she didn't want to make him uncomfortable either. "He's tying up the boat right now, hon. Let's just give it a minute, okay?"

Sue and Ken came up the dock, their arms full of bags. Sue wore a white visor and capris; Ken's seersucker shirt was half-open across his burly chest, and his face was mottled where his sunglasses had left the faintest tan lines.

They both kissed her on the cheek, and Thea smiled, glad for their kindness. She hadn't been able to go with them, but they weren't acting strange now that she was there.

Yet she couldn't shake the feeling that she was being watched. She found herself wondering if her khaki shorts were too short for a woman over thirty. When she glanced toward the boat, she saw that Garret had stopped working and was staring at them—but especially at her. There was something disconcertingly feral about him—the way he stood half-bent over a coil of rope, his head lifted, his eyes focused—like some wild animal catching the scent of danger in the air.

"Did Irina tell you what we did today?" Sue asked.

Thea reined in her focus. "No. What?"

"Tell her, Rina!"

Irina took Thea's hand. "I caught a huge fish."

"Really?"

"Yes. Grampa Ken helped me."

"That's wonderful!"

"Dad took my picture with it, and then we let it go!"

"That's great," Thea said, her voice slightly tight. She could envision the scene perfectly. It was so very normal—for the family to be rallied around Irina, cheering her accomplishments. The only thing that wasn't normal was that Thea hadn't been there.

"Well, we're about to head off to the Merrys' house. Thanks for coming here to get her," Ken said.

"You're welcome," Thea said cheerfully.

Sue shuffled the bags in her arms to reach out and squeeze Thea's hand. "See you soon," she said so softly it was almost a whisper.

Thea's heart cracked. She hadn't realized how badly she'd needed to be reassured. "Hope so," she said.

A moment later they were gone, and Irina was tugging on her arm so hard it pulled all the way to her shoulder joint. Then she let go and ran ahead. "Come on, Mom! Let's go tell Dad bye!"

Thea resisted only a moment. She wanted to see Jonathan. She missed him. There was something open and unresolved between them. She took a deep breath and began to walk slowly forward, to the white boat that was rocking gently in the coal-dark water. With each step, her courage built. Something deep within her cried out in gratitude, already rejoicing in the decision she'd made.

As the months of their junior year passed, Thea did her best to keep her feelings about Garret to herself—to hide the ebullient joy that bubbled up within her when she heard him shout to her in the hall-way, to secret away the intense desire of something she couldn't quite name. Garret had been her hero from day one; he was bold, friendly, and he loved to make people happy. When his mother was having a bad day, he cheered her up, teasing her until she laughed and shooed him away. When a favorite teacher was taking flack from an unruly student, Garret wasn't afraid to step in and put his own reputation on the line.

Much as Garret enjoyed helping those around him, it was the way he'd helped Thea that truly touched her. On their junior class trip just before summer break, he waited in line with her, stifling hot and unspeakably thirsty, for a roller coaster that no one else in her group would ride. When she forgot her lunch money, he bought her a sandwich, whether she wanted it or not. As the daughter of working-class parents—the girl who didn't have a future in Ivy League colleges or sorority halls—only Garret's public support saved her from complete outcast status.

Once, when they were at a party together, some kids playing volleyball on the beach, others surfing small waves along the shore, and others grilling burgers and shish kebab, someone had thought it would be funny to tell Garret that Thea "liked" him. She sat with her plastic plate on her lap, her face turning red as ketchup while everyone laughed, and she couldn't even find the poise to lie and say "That's not true."

Garret had saved her then. He'd gone to sit by her, to turn the whole thing into a joke. "As if I'd be that lucky," he'd said, and he put his arm around her, her skin and his separated only by sticky, gritty sand.

He spared her the mortification of having her secret displayed like the banners flown by planes above the beach—and yet some part of her felt that he'd failed her. Someone had told him she loved him, but he hadn't cared enough to ask if it was true.

*   *   *

As the sailboat approached the docks, Garret had spotted Thea before anyone else had—just a blotch of white against the landscape—and since that moment he hadn't stopped watching her, if only from the corner of his eye.

He'd seen more of Thea in the last few weeks than he'd ever thought possible, especially since he'd never wanted to see her again. She brought out the worst in him—everything that was cynical, begrudging, and snide. He knew that in some twisted way, his discomfort wasn't a fear of seeing her, but a *hope* of seeing her—she, the woman who'd torn him from his family and broken his heart.

He watched Irina charging down the narrow dock toward her father, her footsteps clomping along the wood and resounding against the night. Thea, in shorts that showed more of her skin than he could stand to see, was following.

Oh no, you don't, he thought.

He jumped from the boat, landing on one foot and immediately moving into a jog. His brother and Irina didn't notice him, but Thea did. At the other end of the long and narrow dock, her walk slowed. Her eyes widened. She pulled herself up straight, as if she knew she was about to cross a line.

"What's going on?" He stood before her, blocking her way.

She peered around his shoulder. "I'm trying to collect my daughter."

"She'll be done in a minute," he said.

Thea crossed her arms, looked up at him. Her hazel eyes glinted green and gold in the light above them. "So you're protecting him from me now? You're his bodyguard against his intimidating soon-to-be ex-wife?"

"When he wants to see you, he'll let you know."

She put her hand on her hip—frustration making her toes curl in her sandals—and he thought of how many times she'd given him that pissed-off look when they were kids. "I don't want to chew him out—certainly not in front of my daughter. And I don't want to ruin anyone's day. I just . . ."

"What?"

"I just . . ." The frustration in her face slowly abated, leaving something sorrowful and yearning in its wake. "I just wanted to say hi."

Garret felt the clouds gathering in around his heart. He hated to see any softness in her. He liked her better when she was mean and hard and angry. Like him. At least then he knew how to relate to her—and how to feel.

"Please don't do this," she said.

"Do what?"

"Try to cast me out of your family. I won't go down without a fight."

Garret pulled himself up straighter. "If standing between you and my family is what it's going to take to keep this family together, then that's what I'm going to do."

"I see," she said, her eyes narrowing. "It's me or you, is it? You're afraid if Sue and Ken still want to see me after the divorce, you'll be forced back into your self-imposed exile again."

"You honestly think they'll pick you over their own son?"

Thea looked at him a long moment. "I wouldn't ask them to—"

"What's going on here?" Jonathan stood at Garret's side, Irina's hand in his. Her wide eyes were filled with a kind of mystified attention.

"Hi, Jonathan." Thea offered a friendly smile. "Was Irina good for you today?"

"An angel," he said. He kissed the back of his daughter's hand.

"You all set, hon?" Thea asked.

Irina nodded.

"Okay then. C'mon, Irina. Bye, guys," Thea said, as cheerfully as if she departed from them all the time. As if nothing extraordinary had passed. Irina followed behind her, making big loops with her glow stick and skipping along the boards.

Garret watched them go. What had he hoped would happen? And why did every encounter with her leave him so furious—and yet ready for more?

"What the hell was that?" Jonathan asked.

"Nothing," Garret said.

In the following days, Irina began to have trouble sleeping. Firecrackers popped and boomed in the streets and in the sky overhead, leftovers from the holiday, and the lingering daylight hours meant the sidewalks beneath Irina's bedroom windows were busy with pedestrians. Irina flailed and screamed at bedtime, begged to watch one more TV show, demanded one more glass of milk, or refused to brush her teeth. The babysitters threatened to revolt.

One slow night at the coffee shop, Thea left Lettie in charge of the open mike and headed home early in an effort to spend as much time with her daughter as possible. Surprisingly, Irina was on her best behavior once the babysitter left. When it was time for bed, she got herself into her pajamas, brushed her teeth, and then asked Thea for a story so sweetly that there was no way she could have said no.

Thea sat on the edge of her daughter's bed, speaking quietly, hushing her when she tried to ask questions or interject. The story she told was an old one she'd learned from her mother, about a Turkish princess who was "as beautiful as a fourteenth of the moon." To test the character of a suitor, the princess dressed up as a peasant, and she wasn't surprised when the prince rejected her and sailed away.

"She has to teach him a lesson," Irina said, her sheet drawn up to her nose so only her eyes showed.

"That's right," Thea said. They both knew how the story ended. One day, the princess sailed to the prince's island in a ship made of diamonds, and when she waved to him from beneath the shimmering sails, he fell desperately in love with her. Luckily, the princess was as generous as she was beautiful, and once she'd taught him a lesson, she forgave him. Their wedding was celebrated for forty days and forty nights, and they lived in great happiness for a long time.

Thea had started to say the traditional closing for a Turkish story when Irina interrupted. "But what happened after?"

"There is no after. That's the end of the story."

"But you said they get married. Do they stay married?"

"Of course they do," Thea said.

Irina's eyes narrowed suspiciously. "That's only in stories."

"Now, that's not true. Look at Grampa Ken and Grandma Sue. They've been married longer than you've been alive."

Irina sat up, throwing the covers off so fast that the air stirred the hair around her face. "So then why did you have to make him go away? Why can't Daddy live here with us anymore?"

"I didn't make him go away . . ."

"Yes, you did!"

"Irina." She touched her daughter's arm. "I didn't kick him out."

"Well, can he move back in?"

Thea shook her head.

Irina's eyes began to fill with tears. "This is all your fault!" She dove into her pillow, burying her face.

"It's no one's fault."

She pulled the covers up over her head. "I don't want to talk to you right now. Go away."

Thea stood up from the bed. She knew that Irina was angry—and that she had a right to her anger. Anger was a stage in dealing with what was happening, and Thea would be wrong to take that away.

But she couldn't allow Irina to be disrespectful either. She stood in the middle of the room, a hand pressed to her forehead, uncertain about what to do.

"It's no one's fault," she repeated gently. "Not your father's or mine. And not yours either."

Irina kicked her foot against the wall but said nothing.

"I promise you, it's all going to be okay."

Thea waited for a long moment, and when Irina didn't answer, she walked to the doorway and turned out the light. In the dark, she could hear Irina's uneven breathing. She couldn't bear to end the day on such a sad note.

Quickly, she walked across the tiny room, stepping over splayed books and a teddy bear that Irina had pulled the stuffing out of, and she bent down to rub what she thought was her daughter's back through her blankets. "I love you," she said. "Nothing will ever change that."

Irina's voice was muffled and small. "I love you too," she said.

After seeing Thea on the Fourth of July, seeing her and realizing that he *could* see her and speak with her, and it really wasn't that hard at all, Jonathan made arrangements to meet with her in private to talk. He walked the planks of Price's Pier, then waited for Thea to join him outside a jewelry shop, the window full of sparkling purple and mother-of-pearl. To meet with her at the Dancing Goat was too risky: she knew too many people there. He did too. All day long, customers came in and out of the café, expecting and finding friendly conversations that lasted a moment but could cheer a person up for a full day. And Jonathan didn't want to ruin that, to monopolize his wife who was soon to be not his wife at all.

He sat down on the edge of a large cement flower bed and watched the tourists pass. The sun had gone behind the clouds, but the afternoon was hot. Until he'd seen Thea standing under the stars on the Fourth of July, Garret blocking her path, he hadn't known just how absurd it was that he'd been avoiding her. He'd reasoned with himself that his need to stay away from her had to do with fear of facing his own failure. Seeing her would make him unable to stand himself.

But then on the Fourth, when Thea was there looking fresh and sun-kissed on the pier, he realized that he wasn't afraid of taking responsibility for what had happened at all. In fact, he forgave himself for what he'd done. If something was holding him back from speaking with her, it wasn't self-blame. It was something else.

Of course, forcing himself to meet with Thea had a practical purpose, as well as an emotional one. He didn't want to lean on Garret anymore. His brother had done enough—more than could have been expected, given the circumstances.

Now, Thea was coming toward him, smiling hesitantly. Her warm-toned skin was made even darker by a summer tan. Her shirt was one of many in her closet that was the exact shade of coffee—best to hide the spills. And her hair was a loose knot on the top of her head, a few tendrils spiraling down.

"Jonathan."

He stood to meet her but did not embrace her or even extend his hand. "Want to walk?"

She nodded and fell into stride beside him. The pier was a circus today, almost literally. A man on a unicycle juggled flaming torches, and the smell of gasoline mixed with scents of popcorn, hot dogs, and salty sea air. Jonathan had seen the man's act a few times now—the plate spinning, the broom balancing, the one-liners that were as old as time. Thea waved at the performer, and he winked. Something curled in Jonathan's belly.

He steered them away from the pier's busiest thoroughfare,

away from the coffee shop, to where they were less likely to meet people they knew. When the crowd eased, Thea finally spoke.

"It's good to see you," she said. Her voice was friendly.

"Same here," he said, though the words stuck.

"You've been having Garret do your dirty work."

"Did he do something mean?"

"No," Thea said. "I'm just glad you're talking to me again."

He looked down at his loafers moving along the weathered boards. "I figured you wouldn't want to see me. That it would be easier for both of us if he handled things."

"Why wouldn't I want to see you?"

When he looked at her, the bewilderment on her face was real— a complete lack of comprehension that completely cut him down. He balled his hand into a fist.

"I just thought . . . never mind," he mumbled.

"Of course I want to see you," she assured him.

"I figured you wouldn't."

"Why not?"

"Oh, I don't know. Maybe because I slept with someone else."

The moment he said the words, he regretted them. Thea's face lost all its friendliness. He'd expected her shock—because he'd never been an outspoken man—but he hadn't expected how good seeing that shock would make him feel.

"I don't want you to be unhappy," Thea said. "And I'm not mad at you, for what it's worth."

"Not mad at me? Not mad? You should be *furious*."

"I'm just trying to tell you that I forgive you. That I understand."

"What do you understand?" He stopped walking. They stood near an old industrial building that had been converted into condos, long wooden stairways leading down to the level of the street. "What *exactly* do you understand?"

Thea looked up at him, her brown eyes dark like oubliettes. "That maybe there was something you needed that I couldn't give you."

"But that's just it," Jonathan said. "You *could*. If you wanted to."

The breeze picked up. It blew a strand of Thea's hair across her face. And Jonathan saw that the gray in the sky was from clouds that had not yet formed into storms. He hadn't realized how angry he was. How deeply, powerfully, resentfully angry. Until this moment—Thea looking up at him, the slight shadow of disbelief in her eyes—he'd thought the entirety of their failed marriage fell on his shoulders, and his alone. But now, a kind of fury he hadn't known himself capable of was raising the temperature of the blood inside him—and it didn't feel bad.

"I tried to tell you," he said. "A thousand times. A million. But you wouldn't hear it."

"Jonathan . . ."

"Where did you *go*, Thea? After we got married. Where did you disappear to?"

"I don't understand—"

"You left me alone. *For years*. And I'm sick of it. I was there, Thea. For you, for Irina. For our family. I was there. But where were you? Tell me. Where?"

Thea held her ground. "Are you saying it's my fault that you slept with someone else? Like I locked you naked in some room with her and made you do what you did?"

"No," Jonathan said, his head getting clearer by the moment. "But what I'm saying is that I don't need you to assure me that you're not mad at me. That you *understand*. That you forgive me. Because from where I stand, you should be asking me to forgive *you*."

Thea made a small noise, the sound she made sometimes if he accidentally stepped on her foot or caught her hair on his ring. And Jonathan felt fantastic. He took a few breaths, then started to walk away from her. It amazed him—how good he felt. When was the last time he'd had a fight with Thea? He couldn't remember. They should have fought more often. The thought made him mad all over again.

He turned to her over his shoulder. "I'm glad we had this talk," he said cruelly.

She hurried a few steps to catch up with him. He saw there were tears in her eyes. "What about Irina? Do you want her to have parents who can't stand to be in the same room as each other?"

"The kind of father I am isn't your business anymore," he said. He stopped walking. "I love Irina, and I'll be the best father I can be to her. I'll see her all the time. But as for you . . ." He thought of their first Christmas together, of their fifth anniversary when he gave her a diamond-crusted wedding band, of the way she slipped her hand in his pocket when she got cold. "You'll be hearing from my lawyer," he said.

Then, with the wind nudging him forward, he walked away.

July wore on. The City by the Sea steamed and sweltered, and the speed of pedestrians walking down the streets grew slower and slower with each rising degree. The tenor of the crowds changed like the tides: one weekend it seemed everyone who had come to Newport was under thirty—drinking fruity cocktails and making out in the streets—and the next weekend Thea found herself surrounded by rich Wall Street retirees. For relief, they signed up for cruises and boat rides, or they left the congestion of Newport for the cooler vistas of Aquidneck Island's nature reserves and parks.

On an especially hot Saturday evening, Dani had invited Thea and a few of the baristas to her house in Middletown—her way of saying "thank you" to the baristas who normally had her regular order ready even before she walked through the coffee shop door. Her home, occupied by herself and her two teenage children, was a small but comfortable bungalow on a hillside near a Christmas tree farm.

On Dani's deck, Thea leaned back in her chair and sighed with pleasure. It had been a long week. She was glad for the chance to get away. The air was oppressively hot, and the citronella torches did little to ward off the mosquitoes, but the sky was turning a gorgeous orange pink. She would slip an extra twenty in Jules's paycheck at the end of the week to thank him for manning the shop tonight.

Dani slid into the chair beside her, biting a corn chip in half. "Glad you could make it," she said to Thea.

"Irina's been staying later and later at Jonathan's, so I've got a few extra hours to myself these days." Thea closed her eyes as a hot, gentle breeze made her hair stick to her skin. She thought of her daughter, of Jonathan's words yesterday afternoon. *Where were you?* She hoped Irina was having a good time.

"That's probably a good thing."

"Irina does seem to be getting more comfortable being away."

"I mean it's a good thing for you both," Dani said.

Thea's best friend was no stranger to divorce. Thea had met her years ago—more years than she cared to count—not long after she married Jonathan. In that time, Dani's children had gone from elementary schoolers to teens who gave their hard-nosed mom a run for her money. With dark hair cut severely short, Dani fought hard for her family even when her ex-husband stopped paying child support. She'd gone back to school, went to the police academy, and ultimately earned a position with the city. But it hadn't been easy. Thea admired her determination and grit.

On the other side of the table, Claudine, Rochelle, and Lettie had been having a conversation of their own, and when their laugher crested in a wave that rolled out over the green countryside, Dani butted in.

"Hey now. What's going on over there?" she asked.

Claudine, cross-legged in her chair, filled them in. "Lettie won't say her new man is her boyfriend."

"Women my age don't have boyfriends," Lettie said. Despite the heat, she'd draped a light, lacy scarf around her shoulders. "He's just a friend."

"Yeah. And I'm Joan of Arc," Claudine said.

Lettie pulled herself up straight with all the bearing of a duchess. "And should we call that young thing you've been hanging around with your *boyfriend*?"

"What *young thing*?" Rochelle asked, her ponytail bobbing. "You didn't tell us about a *young thing*."

Claudine laughed. "He's not that young. He's nineteen."

Thea sat up a little, and the backs of her legs stuck to her chair. "You're dating a nineteen–year-old? He's—what—seven years younger than you?"

"I wouldn't say I'm dating him. More like—" Claudine pulled a cigarette from her purse. "What do you call it? *Tutoring*."

Thea laughed. "That's not a *boyfriend*. That's a boy *toy*."

Claudine coaxed a flame from her lighter, then puffed on her cigarette until it was a deep orange blister against the dusk. "What about you?"

"Me?" Thea asked.

"Don't you have a backup plan? You know—a man to fall on."

"You mean, 'fall back on,'" Rochelle said.

"Oh, no," Thea said. "No man."

Claudine's breath was gray with smoke. "Was Jonathan the only man you've ever slept with?"

"Well, I . . ."

"You don't have to answer that." Rochelle smacked Claudine's arm. "And *you* shouldn't *smoke*."

Thea reached for a sip of lemonade, not really afraid of telling the truth but not sure of how to explain it either.

"So, let me understand." Claudine slouched in her chair, something catlike in her long fingers and curling spine. "You married your high school sweetheart. You took over your parents' café, where you'd been working since you'd learned to talk. *And* you inherited your house from your parents—all before you were twenty years old."

"Not all of us want to be globetrotters," Lettie said. "I've known Thea since she was a baby. And she's had a very exciting life. More exciting than she wanted, I'd bet."

"Thank you, Lettie," Thea said, and she hoped her friend, who had been a part of her life for longer than she could remember, who had seen how her relationship with Garret had changed all their lives, would leave it at that.

"Claudine's right." Dani canted her head, thoughtful. "Look. I know a thing or two about getting divorced. You've got a whole new life that you've got to get used to now."

Thea put down her lemonade; the glass was dripping wet with condensation. "What do you mean, a whole new life? I like my life."

"You're divorced now," Dani said. "Life's going to change. And you might as well be ready."

"It is like this." Claudine uncrossed her legs and sat up, leaning her arms on the table. She tied her dark blond hair in a spiky bun as she spoke. "People have to collect experiences—like I do. I try to collect *all* experiences, good and bad. This is a great time for you to become a bigger person, *n'est pas*? Branch out. Try new things."

"Like what?" Thea asked.

Lettie's voice was soft but hopeful. "Whatever you like or don't like," she said.

Thea got up, unsticking her sundress from her skin, and went to the railing of the patio. A hundred pint-sized fir trees were lined up like little soldiers, the evening shadows sinking into the gulfs between rows. The air was heavy, and haze softened the distant hills so they were nearly indistinguishable from the sky.

Dani's words echoed in some deep place within her: *You're divorced now. Life's going to change.* Already, she could feel the primary purposes of her life—her reasons for living—being relegated to the sidelines. She'd felt so comfortable in her role as wife, as mother. But perhaps Jonathan was right. Perhaps she'd been operating on autopilot for a few years too long.

"Irina's been going to see her father every weekend," she said, her back to the group. "And I'm glad he wants to be with her so much. But it feels so strange . . ."

"Why?" Rochelle asked gently.

"Irina gives me these in-depth reports. What Jonathan ate for breakfast. How the bathroom at her uncle's house has water jets in the walls. It makes me feel so . . . left out."

"Understandable," Dani said.

"But there's more." Thea turned around to face them; it felt good to be talking. She hadn't realized how much she'd bottled up. "Some days she'll come home and say, 'We all went kayaking down the river in Providence,' or 'We all played Yahtzee and I won.' And I realize, she's talking about *all of them*—my family. Everyone getting together, but not me."

"They can't very well invite you." Claudine put out her cigarette on the bottom of her flip-flop. "You're split up. It would be weird."

"Hush," Rochelle said. She turned to Thea, her doe-brown eyes full of compassion. "Have you tried talking to them about how you feel?"

"They *must* know," Thea said.

"You gotta speak up for yourself." Dani's voice had gotten louder. "Are you still not talking to your husband?"

"I saw him yesterday. It . . . didn't go well."

"Hmm," Lettie said.

"So, *no*. I guess we're still not talking."

"But you must see him when he comes to get Irina," Dani said.

Thea shook her head. "Garret picked her up again this morning. Which means Jonathan's back to giving me the cold shoulder. I think it's meant as punishment. The silent treatment, with the added bonus of making me deal with Garret—who is not exactly my biggest fan."

"The brother? Is he a jerk to you?" Rochelle asked.

"No more than could be expected."

"Still acting like a child," Lettie said, shaking her head. "And after all this time."

Thea laughed a little to herself. "He once said marrying me was the worst decision Jonathan ever made."

"Good Lord," Dani said. "The man's a beast."

"No," Thea said. "Just hurt. The point here is that the whole situation feels terrible. To know that the family—my family—is going on these outings without me. It makes me feel so alone. There's a gap in my life—a pit—that used to be filled up by them. But that's not the worst of it."

"What's the worst?" Dani asked.

Thea scrutinized a spot in the center of the table. A breeze rolled over the hillside, but did nothing to cool her down. "The worst is knowing that as hard as this has been for me for the last few weeks, this is how Garret must have felt *for years*."

"He thinks you stole his family from him," Lettie said.

"Yes." She looked over her shoulder, where the orange of the sunset was fading to blue. "And maybe I did."

From "The Coffee Diaries"
by Thea Celik

The Newport Examiner

At one point in history, coffee held as firm a place in apothecary shops and doctors' offices as it did in coffeehouses.

In fact, coffee was thought to be so important a medicine that at one point a group of physicians in England were said to have petitioned the Crown to make coffee a controlled substance.

Today, proponents of coffee's healing properties proclaim that Americans get more of their daily antioxidants from coffee than they do from vegetables. Coffee has been used in skincare products, has been said to fight cancer, and allegedly wards off the signs of aging.

Regardless of whether or not you believe coffee can heal, many of us agree that coffee feels good—that there's something invigorating about the brew, even if it's not technically medicinal.

Is it any wonder that when we want to help a friend feel better, we offer her a cup of coffee? Sometimes, it's the best we can do.

Six

Thea's mother had never been a gentle woman. When Thea was sick, her mother's voice was like sandpaper on glass. When Thea was upset by something that had happened at school, Thea's mother rarely showed sympathy with kind words and soft smiles.

And yet, a person who thought Thea's mother was gruff would be wrong. Her tenderness came in different ways. On days when Thea was not feeling well, she would go to her daughter with bowls of broth, with strong black tea, with bread that steamed from the oven. When her parents fought, Thea knew she and her father would eat like royalty for at least a week—her mother cooking the richest foods, buying the best cuts of meat, preparing desserts and candies to make her mouth water.

She would not accept refusals. *Take this. Eat. Drink.* Only as an adult did Thea come to understand the deep satisfaction that came from offering another human being the fleeting pleasure of good food.

* * *

Newport on a weekend evening during summer vacation had no patience for adolescents who could not yet drive, and so Garret, Thea, and Jonathan had been forced to improvise. The evenings buzzed with an energy Garret hadn't quite been able to put his finger on—something adult and off-limits, something to do with sex and alcohol and jokes that went over his head. On those nights, all he and his best friends could do was watch from the sidelines as Newport swung into high gear, the parties revving up around them but without them.

When they were bored, they sat on the grass in the park and spied on the various groups of people who rented out the fire hall for music and dancing. Different communities showed up on different Saturdays—sometimes Asians, sometimes Latinos, sometimes people speaking a language that Garret couldn't identify. The lights in the hall blazed through wide-open doors—a bright, warm glow against a cooling blue evening—and from across the street, Garret could glimpse the occasional girl in a bright skirt and listen to the cheerful beat of a salsa band. If the mood struck her, Thea would take off her shoes to dance and spin in the grass.

"Why don't your parents hang out with the other Turkish people?" Garret had asked her once.

"Because we don't know any in Newport," she'd said.

For Garret, going over to Thea's house was always an experience. Her parents were friendly enough, but their mannerisms threw him off. Her father was loud, and he always wanted to talk about the exchange rate—which Garret knew nothing about. Thea's mother was doting to the point that it made Garret uncomfortable, but he'd learned early on never to tell her *no*.

At other people's houses Garret got to eat pizza and hot dogs, but at the Celiks, he had to choke down lukewarm, vegetable-laden meals: white beans and tomatoes in olive oil, raw meatballs, wheat salad with onion and mint, and fifty kinds of eggplant. Only the dessert made up for the strange dinners; he, Jonathan, and Thea would wait eagerly for colorful little squares of Turkish delight or baklava.

Occasionally Garret could see the Celiks' culture in Thea's behavior, like when she insisted that he put a knife or scissor on the table instead of passing it directly to her, or when she wore a little blue bead at her wrist to keep away the evil eye. But mostly, Thea was as different from her parents as water from stone. She didn't have her parents' accent and couldn't speak their language. When she got in trouble, her parents accused her of "being too American." Garret couldn't help but feel she fit in better at his house than she did her own.

"Do you wish there were more Turkish people in Newport?" Jonathan had asked her one night while they sat waiting for the Saturday revelers to begin filling the fire hall.

Garret had held his breath.

"Nah," she said. And she punched Jonathan so hard he had to rub his shoulder. "Why would I? I have friends like you."

Dear Jonathan,

Just a quick e-mail to let you know I got the divorce papers in the mail. The terms are fair—of course I'll sign them—and I guess we'll have this whole thing behind us in about three months. But I hate to think of the words "joint custody." Sounds like we're transporting a prisoner.

I don't know how Irina's been acting with you, but with me, she hasn't seemed like herself lately. If we're going to have "joint custody," we have to be joint parents. We have to parent together—whether we're married or not.

*The last time I saw you, you said some things. I need you
to know that I'm not afraid to hear them—whatever it is you
need to say. I know I wasn't the best wife. And I'm sorry for
that. Lately, I've had a sense of myself like I'm just a mirage.*

*Still, I'll do whatever it takes to be a good parent. I know
you will too.*

I hope to hear from you.

Thea

There was a long line on Saturday morning at the coffee shop
when Garret arrived to pick up Irina—at least three families, and
tourists probably, given their shopping bags and amped-up chatter.
The small room was warm despite the buzz of the air conditioner,
and he listened, sweating, as the people in line before him hemmed
and hawed over the menu, running their choices past each other,
changing their minds.

From behind the counter Thea caught his eye, and he did what
he could not to shift his weight, not to glance away, not to give any
indication that she affected him. Her hair had been pulled back at
the top, and the rest fell gently around her shoulders in waves. She
wore no makeup, but she was beautiful nonetheless—dark eyes
offset by darker lashes, the glow of her skin from heat and work.
She went about her tasks—a young woman with a pierced eyebrow working beside her—with studied focus. But he knew she
was aware of him. She *always* was. He knew because he felt it
too—that magnetism that was something more than attraction. A
compulsion. A pull.

He closed his eyes for just a moment. When he was a kid, running down the alley to the coffee shop's door had been like falling
down the rabbit hole, an escape into some enchanted kingdom.

And now, all these years later, he still had that slightly heady feeling of possibility and desire and allure creeping up on him—though it was no longer the illicit thrill of sneaking sips of coffee that compelled him. It was something far more intriguing and disallowed.

"Garret."

He opened his eyes. The line had moved forward without him. And Thea stood beside him in a coffee brown tank top that showed off the dark freckles and smooth skin of her shoulders. He had to look away.

"What were you doing with your eyes closed?" she asked.

"Falling asleep," he said. "Is this a marketing ploy? The heat and the lines? You're trying to get your customers good and droopy so they'll order more caffeine?"

Thea chuckled, and he was glad to see it. "What can I get you?"

"Nothing. Where's Irina?"

The slight pull of a smile tugged her lips. "Come on."

She walked away, and he hesitated to follow her. She motioned for him to stand slightly behind the counter, and despite his better sense, he did. "Let me guess. Double espresso?"

"Yeah. But *ristretto*." He liked his espresso to be brewed stronger than the standard "long shots" that had more water but less flavor. "What gave it away?"

"Just going on what I know about you," she said. "I'd guess you'd want the efficiency of espresso. If you could, you'd take your espresso the Italian way—standing at a counter, one quick shot and then—done." She glanced at him, a quick sweep from head to toe that made him pull himself up straight. "I'd also guess that you watch your dairy and fat intake, if I were a betting woman. So espresso seemed to fit the bill. And short shots make sense too."

He laughed—he couldn't help it. He meant to hate her, but for now—for this one second—it didn't seem to hurt anything to relax. "You're good. You're damn good."

"And don't forget it," she said. She smiled; her face lit with playful and mischievous light. But no sooner had he seen that glint of good nature than she'd caught herself smiling and turned away.

He watched her grind the beans—the smell of them filling the air—press them gently with a silver tamp, and then set the espresso machine to brew. When she was younger, she'd timed her shots with a stopwatch—twenty-eight seconds—but now she no longer needed it. She tapped the leftover espresso out of the portafilter so it emerged as round and flat as a hockey puck. The dull *thud* of the handle banging against the knock box was a sound Garret had heard for years in his dreams.

He flipped open his wallet to get a few dollar bills as she walked past him.

"Don't even think about it," she said. "Come with me."

With no choice—she was holding his espresso hostage—he followed her. The hallway had been painted white, and Irina had drawn all over it—horses, clowns, birds, a few bright, smiling suns, and the ocean. This was no furtive and prohibited drawing that would get her grounded; Thea had left a bucket full of crayons for her at the end of the hall. He felt as if he were a voyeur being allowed to peer for a moment into Thea's life.

Thea pushed through a thick fire door, and then he found himself standing with her in the sunshine, in the littered back alley behind the brick of the shop. A stray orange cat sat halfway in a splotch of sunlight, blinking up at them sleepily. Seagulls waddled aimlessly where the pier ended and the pavement began, plucking at bits of garbage and food.

"Why do I get the feeling that Irina's not back here waiting for me?"

She handed him the espresso; the demitasse was hot against his fingertips. He noticed how short her nails were. How her cuticles were split and chapped. She worked hard. Too hard, he guessed.

How often was she at the coffee shop? Did she ever take a break? The tired circles under her eyes confirmed his theory—she worked to avoid her life. Not that he could blame her. Most days he did the same.

"How's the espresso?" she asked.

He took a sip. The espresso was rich, pleasantly bright with hints of citrus, but chocolaty too—low notes of something dark, heavenly, and forbidden. He wanted to close his eyes, to give himself over to the taste and weight of it on his tongue. It was a damn good espresso, but then he knew it would be. *She'd* made it. It burned a little going down.

"It's all right," he said.

"I need to talk to you."

"I'm a busy man. I've got things to do, places to be."

"Stop." She grabbed his arm; her hand was strong. "Just shut up and listen for a second. You can do that."

He watched as she gathered her composure. He felt her fingers loosen, and even after she'd dropped her arm he still felt the imprint of her palm.

"I owe you an apology," she said.

He crossed his arms, careful not to spill espresso.

"Anytime something's gone wrong, I've always had my family to depend on. Well, I've always had *your* family to depend on. Since I met you, they've been my entire life."

He pressed his lips together. Wherever this was going, he planned to resist. She'd get no sympathy from him.

"But now," she went on, "I feel like I'm losing them. If they're not already gone."

He took a sip of his espresso to cover his reaction. "What do you want me to do here, Thea?"

"Nothing. Nothing at all."

"I'm afraid I'm not following you."

She looked down at the ground or maybe at nothing; he couldn't tell. And when she spoke again she seemed to be struggling to find the right words. "I know you didn't want Jonathan to marry me." She raised her eyes to him, and he was struck by their color—the deep, rich hues of espresso ringed faintly with gold. Why hadn't he noticed the similarity before? "I just wanted to tell you that I'm starting to understand how you felt. All those years you couldn't see your family because you didn't want to see me. I get it now. And I'm sorry for it. If I'd known what this was like . . ."

He waited, aware that he was scowling but unable to stop.

"If I'd known what this was like, I would have done things differently," she said.

"Like what?"

Her face was shy. "Like, I would have worked harder to make things right with you."

He threw back the last of his espresso as if it was vodka. "Impossible."

"Why impossible?"

"I wouldn't have let you."

"At least I should have tried. I owed that to you. But instead, I just . . . it was easier, you know? Easier not to see you. Easier to let you stay away."

He looked into his empty cup, the golden crema disintegrating like broken lace. He knew what she meant—but he couldn't let her get to him, not again. He didn't know her anymore. Was she really trying to make peace? Or was she just trying to convince him to call off his campaign to keep her away from his family?

"All right," he said carefully. "So maybe now we're even. I thought I'd go the rest of my life living an arm's length away from my family. But instead it's your turn. There's nothing I can do to change that."

"I'm not asking you to do anything," she said. Her voice was quiet, as if the words were hard to form. "I'm just saying I'm sorry. For everything you had to go through. Because of me."

The sunlight in the alleyway had shifted a fraction of an inch, and the cat who had been sitting in the sun got up and moved with the light. Garret took in a deep breath. He'd imagined this moment a thousand times. And in his imagination, when Thea had come to him—groveling, as he saw fit—he showed her no mercy. He rejected her apology. He insulted her, so she knew what she really was to him. There was nothing she could say to make him forgive.

But in real life, he was a different man than he was in his fantasies. Something within him that had been festering and gnarled for a long time began to loosen. Instead of anger and resentment, tenderness welled up. It scared him.

"Look," he said. "This conversation is going nowhere . . ."

Thea stepped toward him, her eyes searching, questioning. And, before he could force himself to move away, she was pressed against him, clasping him to her after so much time had passed, her two hands wrapped around his waist, her cheek pressed against his chest. Her hair smelled of vanilla, espresso, and spice.

For a moment he held himself upright, away from her, so she could feel that he was not about to hug her back. He let her rub her face against his chest; he let her widen her hands on his back as if she wanted to feel every inch of him at once. And then—though he tried to think of anything, *anything* that would make him remember why he hated this woman—there was nothing but the warmth of her body, her gentleness, melting the ice of his anger, filling him with a longing he couldn't withstand, and he wrapped his arms around her, gathering her closer, folding her into a deeper embrace. He felt her inhale against him, the slight lift of her ribs and breasts. She was so warm. There was nothing false in the soft sound she made when she sighed against him.

He didn't owe her forgiveness, he knew that. But it shocked

him to discover that, for his own sake, he *wanted* this—as if some part of him had already forgiven her long ago, though it had lain dormant, waiting for this moment, to be realized.

He let himself hold her until he could no longer stand it, then he pushed her away. He didn't know what to make of this—the sudden urge to accept the past, and by accepting it, let it go. Now more than ever he needed to make it clear that his allegiances were to his brother. He needed to keep Thea out of his life—out of all their lives—if he wanted to feel some semblance of normalcy with his family. But he wanted *this* too, this feeling of completeness that had come upon him so unexpectedly, and yet as if he'd been inching toward it—toward her—for a long time. He had no reason to forgive her for hurting him except that she'd asked for his forgiveness. And yet that had been enough.

"Tell me one thing," he said.

She nodded, and he knew she would tell the truth.

"You did love me once, right? I didn't imagine it?"

Irina pushed through the fire door with a bang. "Mom! Uncle Garret!"

"Hey, kid!" Quickly he changed modes, already hating himself for the question his ego couldn't help asking. What did it matter if she'd loved him once? She didn't love him now. She didn't *know* him now. What was the sense in asking such a stupid thing?

"Uncle Garret, come see what I did! We made a diorama in class about our parents' *professional establishments*, and Mom helped me make a volcano with coffee trees and everything!"

"That sounds great!" he said.

"Come on!" She grabbed his hand and pulled.

For a fleeting second, he caught Thea's eye, her smiling apology as her daughter tugged and tugged on his hand. Thea's words were soft and rushed just before Irina pulled him inside.

"Of course you didn't imagine it," she said.

*   *   *

In the evening after what she was coming to think of as her *encounter* with Garret, Thea was restless. A huge weight had been lifted from her shoulders, and she needed something to do with her excess energy. She stayed at the coffee shop though her shift had ended, on the pretense that she needed to taste test the new biscotti samples that had come in. Claudine and Lettie were happy to help, and at some point, Dani had wandered in, her uniform giving her an imposing look that was not at all in keeping with her warm smile.

At a table in the corner, eight new types of colorful biscotti were laid on a white plate before them—samples from a company hoping to get her business. Thea took little bites of rock-hard biscotti one by one: mint and chocolate, strawberries and vanilla, espresso and cranberry, kahlua and cream. Some were traditional—straightforward biscuits that packed no surprises but that got the job done. Others had been frosted with pink, green, and white icing, little chocolate shavings or flecks of fruit perched along the top like birds on a line.

Lettie wiped some crumbs away from her lip. "Mmm. This almond biscotti gets my vote. Delicious."

"No way." Dani held up a stick of biscotti that was bubble-gum pink and turned it like a scientist examining an ancient relic. "Really? The plain ones? Lettie—you're so booooring. Live on the edge. Try the frosted strawberry."

"No, thank you. I like the plain. They remind me of when I used to be a little girl."

"I didn't know they had biscotti in the Bronze Age," Claudine said, grinning.

Lettie chuckled. "We had *manners* back then too." She dipped the tip of her biscotti in her coffee, watching it turn a darker brown.

"What do almond ones remind you of?" Thea asked, curious.

"Oh, well." Lettie hesitated, and Thea knew she didn't want to bore anyone. Thea offered her full attention, hoping she would go on. "We lived in Austria until I was five—my father was in the army, you know. And when I walked home from school, I'd stop sometimes at a little bakery opened up by a young Italian couple. I never had much money for treats, and sometimes I'd go in, look at all the pastries, and walk right back out empty-handed."

"Oh, Lettie," Thea said, imagining Lettie as a child. Her white gray hair was probably long and blond, her gentle smile more youthful but promising wisdom to come.

"One day the young woman who owned the bakery—she was so beautiful, I thought she was the most beautiful woman I'd ever seen—asked to see a test I'd taken in school. For every test I brought to her with top marks, she would give me a treat."

"An almond biscotto," Dani said.

"The end pieces that she couldn't sell. But I loved them. The taste still makes me think of her to this day."

Dani snapped off the top of her bright pink biscotto and talked with her mouth full. "You know what this makes me think of?"

"What?" Thea asked.

"Easter. My mom always made these hideous homemade lollipops of eggs and bunnies. She said it was white chocolate with strawberry, but it was like biting into a brick of pink candle wax. Kinda like this."

"*Blech.*" Claudine frowned and shook her head. "So why do you keep eating the biscotti if it's disgusting?"

Dani shrugged and bit off another piece. "Dunno. I guess 'cause it's familiar? Makes me think of being a kid? Don't get me wrong—this is gross. Thea, *please* don't buy them. Because if you do I'll come in and order them all the time and there will be no excuse for it."

"It's amazing how much food is attached to memory," Thea said.

"Certain foods bring you right back to the past," Dani said. She put her biscotto down. "I really need to stop eating."

"Okay—I won't get the strawberry," Thea said, pulling the plate of nuclear pink biscotti away from her friend.

"Or the anise," Lettie said. "You always hated the anise. But it brings back memories, I'm sure. I remember when you and Jonathan and Garret would come bursting through the door of the coffee shop like a motorcycle gang, dropping your coats and book bags on the tables, getting your fingerprints all over the front of your mother's pastry fridge. Of course, that was before you and Garret were joined at the hip . . ."

Claudine perked up a little, her fine eyebrows arched high. "You dated Jonathan's brother?"

"It was a long time ago."

"Garret—the man who came in this afternoon?" Claudine pressed, her voice bright with excitement.

"We weren't together long," Thea said. "We were just kids."

Dani put down her coffee. "Less than a year."

"Right," Thea said. She stood and began to gather the empty plates. "So, which biscotti did we decide on? Just the almond? Lettie, you think this brand is better than the one we already have?"

"Hold on a sec," Claudine said. "Garret—the gorgeous guy you dragged outside to be alone with this afternoon?"

"To *talk*," Thea said. She piled the plates into the crook of her arm, balancing them there. "I had to talk to him privately for a moment."

"I'm sure you did," Claudine said.

Thea laughed and carried the plates behind the counter, where she loaded them one by one carefully into the industrial dishwasher. She'd stayed at the Dancing Goat later than usual this evening because she'd wanted to *not* think about Garret or Jonathan or even Irina—just for a few minutes. And yet even the most innocuous moments were filled with emotional land mines.

She'd been planning for days to apologize to him—if only for the sake of her self-respect. She'd prepared for him to be angry with her. To yell and get in her face. Instead, he'd seemed to become *less* angry—as if what had happened to them standing beside the Dumpsters behind the shop was something they'd both been waiting for, a conversation they'd both needed to have. The moment she'd stood in the circle of his arms she felt as if she was cradled by a patch of warm, welcoming sunlight. There were a thousand nights of her life that she'd dreamed of reaching out to him—to know she was forgiven. But now that she was being slowly but surely pushed out of Jonathan's family, his forgiveness had come too late.

On the counter, one last bit of biscotti was left in the wrapper. She picked it up between two fingers. She had no idea what it was, but she popped it into her mouth. *Anise*. The flavor that she hated held so many memories for her. It had been Garret's favorite. She wondered if it still was. She wondered what he would think if he knew just how long it had taken her to forget him and how much she still remembered.

From "The Coffee Diaries"
by Thea Celik

The Newport Examiner

Coffee trees thrive only in equatorial regions, with the best arabicas grown slowly at high altitudes, and so the cost of importing coffee has been known to be prohibitive—especially during times of war or financial hardship.

And yet, because the desire for coffee doesn't abate even when the supply of coffee dwindles, many countries have been forced over the years to rely on replacements.

During World War II, the most widely used coffee substitute was chicory—that stalky bluish wildflower that grows beside highways and in waste places on a hot summer day.

The root of the chicory plant can be roasted to resemble the color of coffee, and it can be ground to look like coffee beans. But chicory is not coffee. To mitigate chicory's rough palate, Italians began serving their chicory-laced "espresso" with lemon peel on the side.

The fact is, there's nothing in the world like a good cup of smooth, dark coffee—but as with so many things, sometimes it takes a substitute to make you appreciate the real thing.

SEVEN

Though technically Garret hadn't been old enough to drink at his cousin's wedding, no one noticed what he slipped into his glass. His parents pranced about and mingled on the parquet dance floor, and he hung around with his brother and Thea at the table that had been marked for the three of them with a place card that looked like a violin. In true Sorensen family fashion, the wedding was lavish. The mansion where they celebrated dripped with gold-leaf swags and scrollwork. A series of crystal chandeliers hung from a high ceiling. Pilasters capped in acanthus leaves flanked elegant French doors. Garret didn't mind the overzealous decor—as long as no one noticed that his Coke was spiked with rum.

Jonathan, whose soda remained uncorrupted on the tablecloth, sat beside him watching the dancers laugh and wiggle on the dance floor. "Hey. Have you seen Thea?"

"Bathroom."

"She should have been back by now."

"She's mingling," Garret said. "Leave it alone."

He took a long swig of rum and Coke that burned his throat, and he tried to look unconcerned. But the truth was that he too had noticed that Thea was gone, and he'd been keeping an eye out for her for quite some time. She hadn't been acting like herself today. In her deep red dress and dark eye makeup, Garret had expected her to outshine the bride. Instead, she seemed listless, disinterested. She loved dancing—but she wouldn't get up even for her favorite songs.

"I'm going to get another drink," Garret said, pushing back his chair. "Want something?"

"I'm fine," Jonathan said.

"You okay here sitting by yourself?"

"I like people watching," he said.

Garret made his way among the revelers, on the lookout for flailing elbows and knees as he cut across the dance floor. When he got across the loud room to the bar, he kept on walking. He walked until he got to the lobby, with its sparkling marble floors and light-studded ficus trees. But Thea wasn't there. He stood for a while outside of the ladies' lounge, watching a parade of cousins flutter in and out, but it did no good. He checked the coatroom to see if her coat was there; it was. He pushed open heavy, random doors and walked down echoing, random halls, but she was nowhere to be found.

Fifteen minutes later he was beginning to get nervous. He didn't want to ask his parents or Jonathan if they'd seen her because he didn't want to alarm them. He thought of his cousin Eric, who'd been making passes at her all night, and his stomach did an unexpected little turn. Had she ducked away into some hidden room with him? No. Not her. Thea didn't date. Though he'd always wondered why she'd yet to hook up with anyone, he didn't ever question her. He liked her being unattached.

When he finally found her—at the lowest point of a stairwell, where the underside of the stairs sloped sharply to meet the floor and made a kind of cave—she was alone, a shock of red against the dull planes of the cinder blocks. In this forgotten corner of the house, the finery had been stripped away so only the unadorned bones of the old structure showed. The damp air smelled of dust and Pine-Sol.

Thea jumped when she saw him, turning away.

"Garret!"

"What are you doing here?"

She didn't turn to face him, nor did she explain. Her back was a study in layers, the fall of her dark hair, the rich red sheen of a sheer wrap, the thin straps of her dress across her shoulder blades, and then, finally, the smooth expanse of her skin and muscle beneath.

"Thea . . ."

He didn't know what to do, how to help. He laid his arm along her shoulders, and to his surprise she turned into him, the backs of her hands pressed into his chest where she covered her face. He looped both arms around her; she fit so well against him. He resisted the urge to press his cheek against her hair. "Tell me what's wrong so I can fix it," he said.

She brushed the tears from her cheeks and brought herself to stand up straighter. Her eyes darted away. "I don't want to say."

"There's no way I'm leaving until you tell me what's going on."

She sniffed, drew her shawl closer around her shoulders. "I wasn't going to tell you until I knew for certain. I mean, there's no sense in getting everyone upset until I'm sure."

"Sure of what, Thea?"

She looked up at him from beneath her dark and clotted mascara. "That I'm leaving."

"Leaving. Where?"

"My parents are talking about closing the coffee shop and moving back to Turkey."

It took a moment before the news sank in. "Are they serious?"

"They started looking into it weeks ago," she said.

He saw that the tears were rising up again, and he handed her the handkerchief in his pocket. He was stunned—completely at a loss for what to say. Thea—*leaving*. In all of his visions of the future—his intention of being a soccer star, of living the good life, of making his family proud—Thea had been there, right beside him. The idea of a future without her challenged the certainty he felt about all of his plans.

She dabbed the inside corners of her eyes. "Seeing everyone here at the wedding. Your cousin. Your aunts and uncles. Your parents . . . you. How can I leave this, Garret?"

"You don't have to," he said, taken aback by the swell of his own determination. "You're not going anywhere."

She shook her head. "If my parents go, I've got to go too."

"Would they make you?" he asked.

"I don't think they'd make me do anything," she said. "I want to graduate high school with you and the rest of our class next year. I don't want to go. But they're my family. And as much as I'm afraid of leaving, I'm afraid of *not* leaving too."

Garret sighed, feeling suddenly uncomfortable in his borrowed tux and tails. A feeling of possessiveness gripped him. Thea *belonged* with him. He simply couldn't believe that she would just up and leave him, and she would never see him again.

He stepped toward her. He'd touched her a moment ago, and now he wanted to touch her again. She didn't resist when he took her in his arms. She melted against him, her own arms going around him tight. Life without Thea—he simply couldn't imagine it. He felt the press of her from his sternum to his waist; he thought he'd never touched a woman so intimately before—and not just any woman. *Her*.

He gathered her closer, as tight as their bodies would allow.

As far as he was concerned, she wasn't going anywhere. He would find a way.

At Garret's apartment, Jonathan watched as Irina and his brother played video game baseball, Irina swinging the bright white controller with two hands. "Your back foot should come up, Uncle Garret. Like this. It comes up. Look. Watch me."

Jonathan sat back in his chair in Garret's kitchen area, his favorite Le Guin novel open next to his laptop. He'd just checked his e-mail: Thea had sent him a note to say she'd received the papers from his lawyer. And in a matter of time she would no longer be his wife. He was struck by a strange feeling—not the notion that she had been uprooted from his life but that *he* had. She'd been his anchor: now he was supposed to set sail. But to where?

"Hey."

Jonathan didn't notice that Garret had stopped playing the game until his brother sat down next to him. "What's up?"

"I've got good news."

"What?"

"I talked Irina into sleeping over. And I texted Thea to tell her not to wait up."

"That's easily the best news I've had all day. How do you do it?"

"Do what?"

"You've always had a way with people. I've never been able to figure it out."

Garret dusted his fingernails on his shirt, blew them off, and grinned.

"How did you really do it?"

"Okay, you got me. I promised to take her with me to the gym tomorrow morning if she stayed."

Jonathan laughed a little and looked back to the computer screen, where Thea's e-mail stared back at him with unapologetic candor. *I don't know how Irina's been acting with you* and *I know I wasn't the best wife.* Since he'd unloaded all his hurt and anger on her, the feeling of freedom that had come over him had worn off, and he was beginning to doubt himself again. It bothered him that Irina was so hesitant to stay with him. He knew as well as Thea did that they would have to work together if they wanted to be good parents. But could they do that? Or would they become like so many other ex-couples, who spent more time fighting about their kids than raising them?

"What's bugging you?" Garret asked.

Jonathan glanced up to see if Irina was listening, but she'd gone into the bathroom, he guessed. "Has Irina seemed like she's been acting up to you?"

"She seems fine to me."

Jonathan rubbed his eyes, thinking. Irina acted like a tough little soldier when she was with him, but he didn't doubt that Thea was telling the truth about her deteriorating behavior. Now that the separation was going to be permanent, things were going to change—for good. And he worried that Irina would have a tough time with the transition. "Thea got the papers from the lawyer," he told his brother.

"And?"

He leaned his forehead on his hand. He'd told Garret of his meeting with Thea. He hadn't needed to go into detail for Garret to understand that it hadn't ended well.

"I don't know what I expected," Jonathan said. "Part of me wishes . . . I don't know. Wishes that she would have been angrier."

Garret was quiet.

"I want to separate from her, but I don't want to let her go."

"I'm afraid it doesn't work that way," Garret said.

Jonathan looked up at him. "*You* should have married her."

"Please. I've never exactly had a reputation for being the smarter brother. But I knew enough not to get married. Especially to her." He clasped Jonathan on the back. "You're going to love the bachelor's life. Trust me. But you've got to embrace it. Start living it, instead of just watching from the side."

"So is that your way of saying it's time for me to move out?"

"You can live here until you're a hundred and four." From the living room, Irina called Garret's name, challenging him to another round. Garret grumbled as he got to his feet, but Jonathan could tell he was happy. He wondered how his brother—the most social person he knew—could have lived alone for so long. "Duty calls."

Jonathan stopped him. "You know, I was worried at first about moving in with you. It's been a long time since we've really spent any time together. But instead it feels like we picked up right where we left off."

Garret clasped his brother's hand, halfway between a handshake and a hug. "I'm right there with you," he said.

The unofficial party for Jonathan's senior class graduation was held at the same beach house where it was held every year, and Garret had no doubts at all about crashing it. Nor was he surprised when it hadn't been difficult to talk Thea into crashing it with him. She sat beside him on a thick tree trunk of driftwood that was twisted and smooth. A small fire surrounded by lichen-speckled stones made her hair shine gold and red. At their backs, a huge clapboard house was lit up against the pitch of night, and newly liberated seniors made their way to and fro between the keg on the deck and the water's edge. Already the party was getting sloppy— couples disappearing together, the sound of someone retching in the darkness, laughter bubbling and boiling over into the night.

"Come on," Garret said. "Let's get out of here."

He took Thea's hand and led her away from the fire, away from the crowd. He had a slightly dizzy and tipsy feeling, but not because he'd taken a single drink all night. Lately, Thea made him feel that way. He liked the smell of her perfume and the way she felt when he hugged her, which he did whenever he got the chance. She wasn't rail-thin like so many of her friends; he'd been with skinny girls—all their sharp angles and planes. He liked them well enough. But in recent weeks he'd discovered that Thea was more comfortable, touchable somehow.

They walked to the edge of the water, which was unusually calm. Something about the blackness of it, the darkness, brought out its liquid nature, so that the ocean seemed more like itself at night than it did during the day. He led her down along the beach, not giving up the warmth of her fingers. Why hadn't he ever held her hand before? And what kept her from pulling away now?

"I have good news," he said. "I've been waiting all day to tell you."

"What is it?"

He gave her hand a squeeze. "My parents said you can move in with us, if you need to, so that you don't have to leave the country. You can graduate with us, here."

In the moonlight, he saw tears come into her eyes, silvery as the surf that washed up on the sand. "Really?"

"Why are you crying? Aren't you happy?"

"Of course I'm happy. I'm happy your parents would be so kind to me. I'm happy that you are. I don't know what to say."

He stood to face her, his heart racing in his chest and all of his awareness concentrated on the feel of her hand in his. "Say you'll move in with us and that you won't go."

Slowly, the hope and pleasure ebbed from her eyes. "I don't know. I think it would be better if I go."

"But why?" he demanded, frustrated. "Why wouldn't you move in with us? I thought it's what you would want."

She pulled her hand away from his. "I just can't."

"Thea . . ." He balled his fingers into fists, too angry to know what to do. Yell at her? Shake her? Beg? She couldn't leave. She couldn't. "I'm telling you . . . asking you . . . not to go."

"Why?"

"Because I'm not ready to lose you," he said.

"But what do you mean, *lose* me?"

"Thea—" He ran a hand through his hair, frustration making every muscle in his body go tight. And because he didn't know any other way to show her, to make her believe, he kissed her.

He'd meant—after years of strict friendship—to go slowly, to coax and tease the way he'd learned to when a girl wasn't certain about being kissed. But his head swam, his heart raced, and Thea's arms came around him, her fingers pressing hard into his skin, so that all thoughts of being slow and gentle vanished like a match burning down to his fingers. His hand found the back of her neck, cradling her head, and when her mouth opened beneath his, he felt whole worlds of desire open as if the earth had dropped away beneath his feet. Thea—his Thea—had been holding out on him. There was something inside of her that he wanted, *needed* more of, a light in her like a lantern in the darkness, and he chased it—deepening the kiss, reaching into the shadows of her mouth, seeking more.

He was startled by the punch of cool air when she pulled away.

"I don't want to be just another one of your girlfriends," she said, her voice a whisper.

"Thea." He threaded his hands into her hair, marveling at the just-kissed sheen of her lips, the openness that she gave so freely to him. "You're not," he said. "You could *never* be." And much to his surprise, the words were true.

*   *   *

In the darkness of his kitchen, where he stood drinking a glass of water in the middle of the long night, Garret knew there were a million reasons he should not be thinking of Thea. And there were a million thoughts of her that he should not have been having.

And yet his mind replayed their conversation in the alley a hundred different ways. He saw the sunlight gleam on her hair. The kindness in her eyes. He thought of her calloused hands, her tired skin. He thought of the little knot of bone at the edge of her wrist when she'd handed him his espresso. He thought of the feel of her against him—he'd thought of it so much that when he'd dozed off earlier, it was to thoughts of being with her, holding her— and then the thoughts that had lulled him to sleep were the exact same thoughts that woke him up with sheer misery and loneliness, because he realized he'd been dreaming.

He refilled his glass of water, drank it down. *Where is she tonight?* he wondered—and then he chastised himself for the thought.

So he'd forgiven her, or she'd forgiven him—or both. Really, it meant nothing. Forgiveness didn't change the way he would proceed in the future, and it certainly didn't entitle him to wonder what she was doing so late at night while he paced the floors.

And yet, despite the strength of his longing, he couldn't deny that forgiveness had made him feel lighter, better, more human than he'd felt in years. In fact, it wasn't worry that was keeping him awake—it was something else entirely. He actually felt fantastic. Liberated. And he wanted to take the feeling—the freedom and joy and shock of it—and do something with it. Put it to good use. He wanted to share the feeling with the woman who'd given it to him.

And this, he realized, was exactly the reason he had to keep his feeling to himself. Why he had to stay away.

From "The Coffee Diaries"
by Thea Celik

The Newport Examiner

In theory, there's no wrong way to make a classic cup of coffee.

In Turkey, coffee is ground powder-fine in a mill and then brought to a frothy boil three times in an *ibrik*.

In Italy, it's pushed at high pressure and heat through the tamped grinds in an espresso machine.

In Vietnam it's brewed with a hatlike, individual-cup filter, and it's dripped directly onto a few spoonfuls of condensed milk.

In Paris it's ground coarsely and brewed in a French press.

In America, a cup of coffee will be brewed by an automatic drip coffeemaker, everywhere from greasy-spoon diners to five-star restaurants.

Despite the many ways that countries around the world have evolved in their preparation of coffee, one thing remains the same: It all comes down to the coffee bean.

EIGHT

The hallways of Jonathan's high school had always been filled with rumors. Whispers flew from locker to locker like moths picking their way among flowers, and they spread beyond the classrooms as well, spilling over into crowded cars, shops, beaches, and homes. So when Jonathan caught wind of rumors that Garret and Thea were dating, he paid no more attention to them than to a whisper of music coming through the windows of a passing car.

Mostly, the gossip was easy to ignore. To Jonathan it had seemed that high school kids were too shallow to understand how he and Garret could be friends with the same girl, and he was glad to have graduation over and done. Everyone had been certain that a friendship of two brothers and one woman could not last—that one brother, the better brother, would "take home the prize."

But Jonathan knew and took refuge in the truth—that even though Garret was so much more popular and accomplished and praised than Jonathan had ever been, they were equals in Thea's eyes. She did not favor one of them over the other. Her parents had decided not to move away until after Thea graduated, and as far as Jonathan was concerned, that meant they could go on as friends forever, proving the world wrong. They had no secrets among them.

Or so he'd thought.

On the day that changed the course of his life forever, he was supposed to have been at the library tutoring a summer school student, but he'd returned home earlier than planned. His parents' house was quiet—the large, first-floor rooms filled only with sunlight and breeze—and so he assumed no one was home. He climbed the stairs two at a time to the top of the turret, where he often spent long hours reading or playing at writing books, and he ditched his backpack on an old couch. It wasn't until he'd settled into a window seat with a notepad that he realized he wasn't alone after all.

There, at the edge of the property, Thea and Garret sat together sunning themselves on one of the large flat rocks. The ocean water came in around them, frothing playfully at their feet. Thea was leaning on her elbows, her long hair falling to brush the beach towel beneath her, her legs crossed at the ankles. Garret was at her side.

All at once, Jonathan felt time slow to an indescribable crawl— the second hand on his watch unable to click forward, the tops of the trees gentling in their sway. He'd just begun to think to himself, *I'll go down and see them*, when—even before he could finish the thought—his brother's hand lifted—lifted so that somehow Jonathan knew what was about to happen, that the certainty of his place in both of their lives was about to crumble—and he saw his brother reaching to touch Thea's hair, to put his hand around the back of her neck, and to draw her in with all the lazy entitlement of a man who had repeated the gesture many, many times.

The sun ducked behind a cloud. And Jonathan stood there a moment, numb behind the window. Thea had chosen. He wondered how long it would take them to tell him—if they were going to tell him at all.

A few days a week, Thea snuck away from the coffee shop—leaving it in Jules's hands—and she took her iced coffee and newspaper to the marina not far from Price's Pier. She didn't like to stay overly long away from work, just long enough that she could clear her head.

Carefully, she climbed aboard the *White Whale*, a small pristine yacht that belonged to one of her customers whose family also was close friends with Sue and Ken. Ron Madden and his wife were rarely on the bathtub-white boat during the day, and some time ago they had offered it to her as a refuge for occasional lunch breaks. Ron was one of her favorite customers. She'd watched his son turn into a teenager, summer by summer, growing out of his sneakers and growing into his overlarge feet and hands. She and Jonathan had gone out to dinner with the Maddens a number of times, and always, they'd met as a foursome. Thea wondered: what now—since four had turned to three?

She tried to put the thoughts from her mind as she sat on the deck of the Maddens' yacht, not caring that her skin was warming in the brutal, late July summer sun. On the pier, people were packed in shoulder to shoulder—raised voices, hyper children, the smell of coconut suntan oil, dollar bills flashing—but here on the yacht, she enjoyed the emptiness of the space surrounding her like a pocket of air. She sipped her iced coffee and sketched out her notes for her upcoming article in the local paper. She kicked off her sandals and put her feet up on the side of the boat. She closed her eyes.

"Thea?"

When she opened her eyes, she saw Sue standing on the dock,

sounding unsure about interrupting. Thea pulled her feet off the railing and sat up straighter. "Sue? What's wrong? Is everything okay?"

"Fine," Sue said, stepping carefully into the boat. "Don't panic. Everyone's fine."

Thea let out a deep sigh of relief. "How did you find me?"

"Jules told me you'd be here." She looked down at Thea, shading her eyes with her hand. Her sunglasses were big and black—old Hollywood. Her blond hair was curled in gently at her chin, bleached nearly white by the bright and relentless sun. In light blue cotton, she always seemed to Thea to be so wonderfully put together, as if she'd never in her life broken a sweat.

"I know you don't have much time," she said, "so we have to talk."

"Oh?"

"Jonathan said he had his lawyer draw up divorce papers."

Thea nodded. "Yes. I have them."

"Did you sign them yet?"

Thea hesitated, glad her own sunglasses were there to hide her reaction. "No."

"Oh thank goodness," Sue said. She walked toward Thea, hugged her briefly and lightly. When she pulled away, the thin line of her mouth had softened into something that neared a smile. "I knew you wouldn't do anything rash."

Thea leaned back in her chair. Sue didn't want her to sign the divorce papers. That much was clear. But Thea could not go on living as husband and wife with a man she did not love and who did not love her. If she was guilty of something, it was letting things go on for so long.

"I haven't signed them yet," she said. "But I'm going to."

"But . . ." Sue flattened a hand against her rib cage. "Why?"

"Because Jonathan's right," she said.

Sue shook her head. "How can you say that? Thea . . . this is just a bump in the road. You can't give up so easily. If every couple threw in the towel at the slightest bit of discomfort, no one would be married at all!"

"I know that. But Jonathan's right. People who save their marriages are people who have something to save. But Jonathan and I, the way we got married wasn't exactly well thought out. We rushed. You know that. We can't restore our marriage to what it was, if it wasn't much to begin with."

Sue's perfect posture faltered. "Maybe that's true. That you rushed into marriage. I always thought you got married way too young. But that's exactly why you shouldn't make the same mistake again, and you shouldn't rush into anything permanent until you're sure."

"I'm sure," Thea said.

"And what about Irina?" Sue asked. "You're not even going to try to keep it together. Not even for your daughter?"

Thea had to look away. Irina was a sore subject. Her tantrums were getting bigger by the day. "Plenty of couples raise their kids together, even if they're not married."

"Name me one."

The wind blew, cooling the sweat on Thea's skin. In the sky, the clouds were bilious and white—the innocent-looking harbingers of a storm. "I can't," Thea said.

Sue nodded, her expression softening. "You know I love you like a daughter. I always will. But I feel no small responsibility for this family. And so I just want to be sure that we exhaust all avenues before . . . before it's too late."

"I understand that," Thea said.

"All I'm asking is that you not make this final until you're sure."

Though the day was hot, goose bumps rose on Thea's skin. "So what do you think I should do?"

"Don't do anything final until you talk to Jonathan. In person. None of this e-mailing or Twittering or whatever it is you young folks do. You have to meet him, and you have to talk."

"But he won't see me," Thea said. "We tried talking . . . It didn't work."

"Oh really?" Sue pulled up straight. Though she was a tiny woman, she sometimes summoned a kind of bigness and gravity that made her seem three feet taller than she was. "I'll take care of Jonathan," she said.

Garret had learned enough about persuasion to know that where logic and emotion competed, emotion usually won. It was not logic that convinced the public to pass a law increasing the penalty for sex offenders; it was emotion—the feeling stirred by images of the victimized and abused. It was not logic that compelled senators to vote for a complex restructuring of the financial sector; it was emotion—the anger of the people at big business, the restless urge that something be done.

And so Garret knew well enough that he could not fight his own emotions with logic—though he had mastered every rhetorical argument technique in the book. Emotions could not be talked or reasoned into submission—especially not when they were as deep-seated as those he'd felt for Thea ages ago. For unwanted emotions to stop, they had to be cut off at the source.

On Thursday evening, he and Jonathan sat at a pub on Newport's quieter side, away from the edge of the harbor and away from the crowds. The Black Horse Tavern was a tiny, dark pub—Garret had seen walk-in closets on Ocean Drive that were bigger than the old watering hole. A limited selection of liquors lined the shelf behind the bar, and there was room only for a few tables and six seats at the bar. But Garret liked the place. Heavy timber beams in the ceiling still bore the marks of axes hundreds of years old. Tiny, four-paned windows let only the barest amount of light reach the dark-stained pine of the walls. It made for a nice stop on the way home from his parents'. He took a long swig of beer, preparing to make his gambit, easing in.

"So I've been thinking," he said.

Jonathan waited, then laughed. "About . . . ?"

"You still haven't got word on the divorce papers?"

"Nah." Jonathan took a sip of beer. "Maybe she's having a lawyer look them over. That's what I'd do."

Garret turned his beer in a circle, where it left a puddle on the wood of the bar. He couldn't claim to know Thea very well anymore, but he did know that she was trusting to a fault—to the point of not hiring a lawyer. Garret wondered why Jonathan didn't see the same thing. "Are you anxious?"

"About getting it finalized?"

Garret nodded.

"Oh yes. Anxious isn't the word. I feel like I can't move on until it's official. Like there's things I'm not allowed to do or think about doing until it's all over."

"Like what?"

"Like—" Jonathan cut himself off, shook his head.

"You mean like other women," Garret offered.

"That's part of it," Jonathan said. "It's about getting on with my life. Whatever that means."

Garret signaled the bartender for another beer. If Jonathan was thinking of dating again, he could probably handle the scenario that Garret was about to propose. "Do you think it's time to start picking up Irina by yourself?"

"Why?" Jonathan asked, turning toward him. "Is something wrong? Has Thea been giving you a hard time?"

"She couldn't give me a hard time if she tried. No—nothing

like that. I just wanted you to know that whenever you're ready to take over, let me know. I'm not going to stand in your way."

"I didn't think you would!" Jonathan laughed. "If it's getting to be too much for you . . ."

"Not at all."

"Are you sure? Because . . ."

"No really. It's fine. I don't mind," Garret said, but already he could feel control slipping away from him, his plans failing. He couldn't bear to see Thea anymore. She was making him feel tangled up and anxious, more each day. And yet he'd sworn to be there for his brother—Thea or not.

"I owe you," Jonathan said. "It's not for much longer. I think I'll feel better about the whole thing once it's official. Once the papers go through."

"It's no big." Garret shifted on his barstool, and the bartender brought them another couple of beers. In the dim light from the stained glass lamp over their heads, the ale shone a crisp, deep amber. "This isn't any kind of talk for two bachelors at a pub," Garret said. "We need to be talking about sports. Or women."

"I don't really do sports."

"Women it is," Garret said, lifting his glass to clink his brother's. "So tell me. Not that I'm rushing you into anything. But when you *are* ready to start playing the field again, exactly what kind of woman are we looking for?"

"I'm not sure."

"Come on, Jon. What type are you into? Curvy blonds? Petite brunettes?"

"I don't know," Jonathan said. "Maybe . . ." He looked around the small bar. Old men sitting alone, minding their own business. A few women in the corner, their heads bent low. "Maybe someone like her? Maybe?"

Garret glanced over toward a woman in the corner, and his

throat went a little tight. "All right," he said. "That's a start. Now we're getting somewhere."

"So what do we do?"

"We go up to her. Buy her a drink. See if she's wearing a ring."

"It's that easy?" A light danced in Jonathan's eyes, just the faintest dim flicker. But it was a light nonetheless.

"Come on," Garret said, not giving his brother a choice. He readied his most charming smile as he walked across the room, ignoring the sinking feeling in his chest, toward the woman who looked, for all the world, just like Thea.

When Thea was young, long before Garret and Jonathan had moved to Newport, she'd had her first kiss. She'd known something was up when the boy, whose name she no longer remembered, had asked her to walk home with him. His backpack was stuffed with books, his sneakers were gray and worn, and his hair was a dazzling, otherworldly red. When he tugged her into an alleyway between two buildings, the smell of mold and damp assailed her nose—but she didn't hold back.

Five seconds, she'd said. *We have to kiss for at least five seconds. Like on TV.* The boy's tongue had been alien and strange bumping up against hers. His mouth had seemed like a cave—the space behind his teeth was wet, dark, vacant. His kiss did not draw her in, did not make her go misty-eyed and smile against his lips like the heroines in movies. And when his watch beeped and five seconds was over, she picked her backpack up off the pavement and walked herself home. She'd found the precise taste of disappointment inside his mouth.

But years later, she knew: what had passed in the alley had been nothing but a choreographed meeting of lips—and not a kiss at all. When Garret kissed her, his mouth was not some dank and fearful cave: it was a darkness to fall into, a darkness that swallowed her up, left her with so much pleasure it was close to pain.

She could not get enough of him. They made plans to meet between classes, to sneak into a quiet stairwell to steal a fast and risky kiss where no one could see. She couldn't stop herself from thinking of him, from anticipating the next time they would meet—and kiss again—so that at every moment it felt as if he was with her, a secret companion who kept her company even when she was alone. The thought of him and what they'd come to share gave her the feeling that no woman on earth had ever fallen in love before her—that she was the first, the last, the only one.

And yet, all her extremes of brightness came with extreme dark. Garret had insisted that she not tell anyone about them— *What,* he asked her, *is there to tell?* He made no promises to her. He did not say he loved her. On some days he seemed to forget her. He flirted outrageously with other girls, touching them, smiling at them, while Thea bottled up her pain as she passed him in the hallway without so much as a wave. Or he turned down her offer to help with his homework in order to play foosball with his friends. She was sure that each and every instance that he ignored her was a sign that he no longer cared for her at all—that his glance over her shoulder signaled the end. On some days, she knew he did not love her, did not even like her, and was on the brink of casting her aside.

Only his kiss could save her from herself, her doubting. One kiss, rushed in secret in the parking lot or gym, could lift her whole day out of the mire of despair, could make her feel as if she were shining under her skin. His mouth could not lie. His lips didn't speak of mere passing infatuation—what he wanted from her was serious, intense, a thing that he starved for and that no other girl could give. And she wanted to give—everything that she was. Body and soul. She was not a prude, and if he were another man she would have already let his frustrated kisses play themselves out on every part of her body—that, and more.

But she loved him. She knew him. She'd seen the tides of his interest in other girls swell and then fade, and she was not about to join their ranks.

And so in the hallway, when his hands strayed too far, when his hips against hers made her want to fall against the wall behind her, she forced herself to do the thing she wanted least in the world—she pushed him away.

For a long time, Thea had avoided giving the drinks at the Dancing Goat overly cutesy names. She served three types of coffee every day—the dark house blend, a mild blend that she changed up every week, and decaf. Coffees that were flavored with hazelnut or raspberry were not given silly monikers that appealed to happy tourists; they were simply called hazelnut coffee or raspberry. But in recent weeks Irina had been getting on her case about changing the names of her drinks, saying that zanier names would draw attention to the drinks they wanted to move, and Thea was beginning to wonder if her precocious daughter had a point.

Now, on the first scorching day of August, she sat with Dani, Lettie, and Irina at a table in the coffee shop while Claudine and Jules manned the counter. Thea had conceded that she would add three "drinks specials" to the menu that would have unique names—on a trial basis. If Thea's lobstermen customers got tongue-tied and embarrassed while trying to order coffee, then the experiment would be considered failed.

"It's gonna work, Ma," Irina said. "Trust me."

"What's the first drink?" Dani asked.

Thea handed them each an espresso cup filled with a decaf sample of her latest concoction. "It's a vanilla latte with a hint of cinnamon.

I wasn't going to put this out until the fall, but since we're going public with new drinks now . . ."

"Oh, wow," Dani said, her voice trailing off as she looked up from her cup. "This is delicious."

Lettie closed her eyes. "Very good."

"Now we have to think of a nàme," Irina said.

Thea took her own sip—the drink really was good, comforting smooth vanilla, a little kick of cinnamon, and rich espresso as the foundation that held the other flavors up—but she wasn't too keen on playing the name game. If Irina wanted a cute name for a drink, she would have to invent it.

"It's like a hug from the inside out," Dani said, cupping her hand around the tiny drink.

"No, it's more like a snuggle," Thea said. "Because it lasts longer than a hug."

"It's a huggle!" Irina said. "It's a vanilla-cinnamon huggle."

"How 'bout just vanilla huggle," Lettie said, delighted. "And the cinnamon is a surprise."

"Vanilla huggle." Thea rolled her eyes, but wrote the name down. "Why do I get the feeling that none of my locals are going to be ordering the vanilla huggle?"

"They will, Mom!"

"What about the men?" Thea asked.

"The men can have it too," Irina said. "Let's do the next one!"

Thea pushed another set of coffees toward them, careful not to mix up regular with decaf. She didn't want her daughter to be up all night. "This is coffee flavored with banana and walnut extract. Like, banana nut bread meets coffee."

"I like it," Dani said.

Lettie wrapped her hands around her cup, her thick knuckles pressed against the heat. "But what do we call it?"

Irina gave the drink her fullest concentration, her eyes closed to focus on the flavor before she swallowed. "Something about banana . . . nutty banana. Split. Like a banana goes crazy and splits up from a nut."

Dani laughed. "I'm not sure that quite rolls off the tongue . . ."

"How about the No-Fault Split?"

Thea felt the blood draining away from her face. She hadn't been talking to her daughter about the intricacies of divorce—the logistics of it all. But she should have known Irina would hear. She heard everything.

"That's not a very cheery name," Thea said. "I wouldn't order it."

"No—it's a good name. It's funny."

"I don't like it," Thea said. She could feel Dani and Lettie watching her.

Irina threw her hands up. "Well, I don't know what you call it then!" she shouted. She pushed her palms against the table edge, toppling cups and splashing coffee on the floor. Thea jumped, avoiding the flood, but a few ounces of coffee spilled on Irina, soaking her legs. Luckily it hadn't been too hot.

"Oh dear!" Lettie got to her feet. "I'll get some towels."

Thea leveled a serious gaze at her daughter. "Okay, we're done with this for the night. If that's how you're going to act, then we'll have to finish this up when you can behave."

"I *am* behaving," Irina said. But her face was already turning red, and her eyes were already filling with tears. She was about to blow. "It was an accident."

Thea took a deep breath. "Go to the bathroom and clean yourself off, and then we're heading home."

"But we still have one more drink!"

"Irina . . ." she said, her voice full of warning.

"Fine." Irina stomped toward the bathroom to get what coffee stains she could out of her pants.

When she was gone, Thea stood still for a moment to close her eyes and regain her composure. Lettie returned with paper towels and a garbage bag; she and Dani set to work cleaning up.

"You don't have to do that," Thea told them.

"Nonsense," Lettie said.

Dani wadded big fistfuls of paper towels in her hands, soaking a puddle of coffee that had landed on the floor. "She okay?"

"I don't know," Thea said. "It's not like her to be so angry. I don't know what to do to make her stop hurting. I feel like a terrible mother."

"Stop that," Dani said, standing. "You're a great mother, and you know it. Irina's just going through a difficult time. You all are."

Thea held open the garbage bag for Dani. "Sue thinks Jonathan and I are being reckless. That we shouldn't do this so fast."

Lettie's voice was gentle as she blotted the coffee rings that had formed under their cups. "Of course she has to say that. She's concerned about her family. And rightly so. But only you can know what's right for you in the end."

"I'm not so sure that's true," Thea said. "Maybe I should try harder. Tough it out. For the sake of the family—for Irina, but for Sue and Ken too."

Dani shook her head. "You can't stay married to Jonathan because you're afraid of losing his family."

"I don't want to be the cause of anyone's pain," she said, and strangely enough, she didn't find herself thinking of Jonathan and Irina, but of Garret—of all the years he'd stayed away from his family because of what she'd done. "I've been there before. I don't want to do it again."

Dani took the garbage bag away from Thea. "Here's what it looks like from where I stand—and keep in mind that I've been through this before. You're in a good position to stay friends with Jonathan right now. But not if you keep drawing things out until they get messy."

Thea nodded. "You're right. You know that? You're right. I think Irina will feel a lot better once we get into a routine."

"Let us know what we can do to help," Lettie said.

Thea glanced toward the hallway, where Irina was walking as slowly as she possibly could, foot over foot, to rejoin them in the shop. "I may take you up on that."

Dear Thea,

It's come to my attention that before we turn in the divorce papers and make it official, we should probably meet—just to make sure we both have a clear vision of the road ahead. Hopefully this e-mail will find you before you drop the papers in the mail.

Garret said he'd be willing to watch Irina tomorrow evening, if you can get off work and you want to meet. A year ago I wouldn't have let him—since he doesn't have much experience with kids. But now that I'm getting to know him again, I promise Irina will be in good hands. Frankly, she'd probably rather hang out with her uncle Garret than her dear old mom or dad.

So, are you amenable? Can we meet?

Jonathan

From "The Coffee Diaries"
by Thea Celik

The Newport Examiner

Serious coffee drinkers know the importance of decaf coffee when it comes to round-the-clock consumption. But how does coffee get decaffeinated, since caffeine is so vital to the life and protection of the coffee seed?

Don't think that a label indicating that a bean is "naturally decaffeinated" means that the bean was engineered to grow without caffeine.

In the early days, the process of decaffeinating coffee was horrifying: coffee beans were steamed in brine, then given a dose of benzene—but the method was deemed unsafe. Not surprising, given that benzene was an ingredient in early napalm.

New methods include steaming the beans and then washing them with ethyl acetate or methylene chloride. When the ethyl acetate is derived from plant sources, the beans are said to be naturally decaffeinated.

Health food stores have begun to stock coffee that has been decaffeinated by soaking green coffee beans in a mix of water and coffee itself.

Whatever the method of decaffeination, most decaf coffees still contain some small amounts of caffeine. There's just no way to get rid of it completely. Nature insists.

NINE

To be with Thea during their senior year was not what Garret expected—it was pushing a boulder up a hill. It was swimming upstream.

For brief moments between classes, when he could be with her, touch her, he felt as if he was seizing for himself something illicit and dangerous. The notion that a friend, his friend, could have been hiding within herself the ability to give him so much unthinkable pleasure was more than he could understand. How could he not have seen it before? Thea, going breathless under his hands, gave him the same incredible adrenaline rush that he felt on the soccer field. He wanted more than quick, fumbling gropings between classes—he wanted to see how far he could take her, if he was good enough to make her lose herself to him. But how much longer could he stand to be held at arm's length?

At night, he went to her house, climbed the drainpipe as quiet as a mouse, and his whole body became a bundle of nerves even before he'd reached her window. Mostly, he wanted to make out.

And it was what she wanted too. They'd spent their whole lives talking. He knew her soul-deep. No amount of conversation could knit their souls more tightly together than they already were.

He campaigned hard for permission for every new kiss, for the first time she let him taste the skin above the button of her jeans, the first time she let him slide off the strap of her bra. Always, she resisted—as if he was asking something she didn't want to give even as he knew by the tremble in her voice that she wanted to give it. She left him confused and—when the pain of frustration built nearly to bursting—angry.

Who was this girl who seemed to be such an innocent in the dark? Thea—his Thea—was not timid. He'd seen her volunteer to light firecrackers on the beach while other girls cowered and squealed safely in the shadows. He'd seen her climb the steep face of the cliff wall at the edge of the ocean—no rope, no hesitation, no fear. When Garret had broken his arm playing Frisbee, so severely that the bone showed, she barely flinched, but instead calmed him down and held his good arm as she walked him to the nearest open store to call Sue and Ken.

But on the floor in her bedroom, she seemed half terrified of his hands—at least, there was no other way to read her reticence. When Thea wanted something, she went for it. And yet she did not give herself, no matter how he pleaded and coaxed and demanded, with words and without. Her hesitation could mean only one thing—she was unsure of him. She didn't trust him. He guessed she was a virgin and—with a kind of desire that was almost too embarrassing to own—he wanted her virginity.

But she would not give in.

As he lay in the darkness of her room, the hard floor under his shoulder blades, Thea buttoning herself up at his side, he began to wonder if he'd made a mistake. Perhaps they were meant only to be friends after all. He vowed to himself that he wouldn't get any closer to her—that he would keep his options open with other girls if he needed to—because if her hesitation was real, and she really didn't trust him, then he didn't know how he would be able to stand it when she finally, completely turned him down. Thea had the power to wound him more deeply than any other person on the earth; he needed to be careful not to put too much of his heart in her hands.

Thea leaned against the warm grill of Jonathan's black sedan, her toes getting dusty from the gravel parking lot, and Jonathan leaned beside her, popping green grapes into his mouth and occasionally sipping iced tea from a blue plastic cup. Far below the hill where they stood, the water of the bay was an opaque, shocking blue punctuated here and there by swells of land and polite, tree-covered islands. All that was left of the sun was a sliver of pinkish gold over the far edge of the horizon, and from Thea's vantage point, she had the strange sense that she was closer to the sky than the sun was.

The high ridge had always been Thea's favorite when she and Jonathan needed to talk. They'd agreed early on that discussions and arguments should always happen in neutral places—in restaurants instead of their kitchen, in sleepy parks instead of in their bedroom. From the beginning, they'd approached their marriage as a thing to be accomplished—almost a job. When he'd asked to meet her here—in the place where they'd hashed out whether or not to send Irina to private school, whether or not Thea should work or be a stay-at-home mom—she knew that he hadn't thrown over his thoughtful and logical nature simply because of the looming specter of a divorce. And she knew that this time, he wanted to talk without fighting. To approach their divorce like he'd approached their marriage, with reason and convenience leading the way.

"More iced tea?"

Thea looked into her cup—the yellow gold of green tea that

had been infused with hibiscus and mint. Her standby for hot summer days. "No, thanks."

He poured a bit more for himself. So far, they had tiptoed around each other, chatting about inconsequential facts, gingerly testing the conversation as if poking a wound to see if it would reopen and bleed. They hadn't talked about anything overly significant—Irina's summer schedule, Sue and Ken's volunteer work with the Newport Historical Society, Jonathan's overbearing boss—no mention of their reason for meeting today.

"So what did she do?" Thea asked, smiling.

"Who?"

"Sue. Did she threaten to cut off your inheritance? Will everything to Garret instead?"

Jonathan laughed. "Not exactly."

"So how did she get you to come out here?"

Jonathan rolled a fat green grape between two fingers. "She asked me to," he said.

Thea nodded. In some distant and invisible place, children were playing, squealing, their happy cries carrying upward into the sky. Of course Thea knew that Sue would never threaten. But she wanted to tease Jonathan a little, to let him know she wasn't mad.

"Sue wants us to reconsider," Thea said.

"I know." Jonathan crossed his arms, the dark hairs rising slightly in the breeze. "She told me to ask if I could move back in with you. Temporarily. Just to see."

"Do you like living with Garret?"

Jonathan looked out over the water, hundreds of feet below, his expression thoughtful. "I miss Irina. And I miss you."

Thea smiled gently.

"But, yes. I do like living with him. It's hard work—to be alone. But I feel like I need to stick it out. To see . . ."

"I know what you mean," she said. She squeezed her plastic

cup, and when she let go, it snapped back into shape. The sudden urge to tell Jonathan what she was feeling—what she was going through—was inescapable. In some small way, she wanted his permission to move on.

Their marriage had never been especially passionate. They'd married young and waited until after their wedding to have sex. Thea hadn't expected much. Her love life with Jonathan hadn't been like jumping headfirst into a bottomless pool but instead like creeping inch by inch into deeper waters, until she was just deep enough to feel like she was submerged without getting in over her head. At some point, the pressure to work toward a healthy sex life vanished entirely, and Thea was almost glad when it did. She felt that her job as Jonathan's wife was to offer him comfort and refuge—he felt the same way toward her—and they set about making their lives easy for one another. Somewhere along the line, good intentions had eroded into complacence like stone becoming sand.

Thea couldn't help it; she put down her cup and embraced him, hugging him tight, and she felt his arms come around her back, those same arms that had held her so many times when she was upset—a good friend's arms.

"Oh Jonathan." She buried her face in his shoulder. "How could we have messed things up so bad?"

It was a moment before he replied. "Maybe we didn't." He let her go, pulled away to look into her eyes. "Maybe we did everything right. Maybe we were meant to get married, have Irina. And now maybe we're meant for this too."

"There are so many stories of people who get divorced and they mean for it to go well, but then it all goes wrong." She squeezed his hand. "I don't want that to be us. If you have something to say, if you're upset about something, if you think something isn't fair, then come tell me. Talk to me. Jonathan . . . of every couple I know, I think that you and I have the best shot at staying friends."

He nodded. "I feel that way too."

She let go of him, leaned her backside against the hood of the car once again. The sun was gone now; it had vanished while they weren't watching.

"So I guess this is it," she said.

He nodded.

To her amazement, she felt a slight clearing within her—the parting of curtains or clouds. At once, she could see the path of her life before her, and Jonathan had a place in it by her side, as if he'd finally slipped into the role he was meant for at last. They would be okay—the two of them. They were fine before. Now they would be *better*.

"When did you know?" she asked, braver by the moment.

"After Boston," he said, his eyes holding hers, confident in the truth. "I made up this long, convoluted story about why I couldn't call you that night at the hotel. I must have rehearsed it a hundred times in the train on the way home. And when I got back, I told it to you while you were getting ready for bed. But when the story was over, it was like you hadn't heard a word."

Tears came to her eyes; she hated to think that Jonathan had suffered because of her. "I'm sorry," she said.

He bumped his shoulder against hers. "Don't be. Okay?"

She nodded. "I knew it too. Even before Boston."

He gestured for her to go on.

"When me, you, and Irina went to the carnival that came through last year, Irina and I were running around like lunatics, playing games, standing in line for the rides, eating everything in sight . . . it was like you weren't there with us. Like you were just . . . somewhere else."

"I'm sorry," he said.

"Don't be. Okay?" She nudged his shoulder. "Like you said. I disappeared sometimes too."

They sat together in silence while a black and gray tern moved smoothly against the backdrop of the sky. The voices of the children in the distance trailed off. They could hear the faint hiss of traffic far below them, but otherwise, the evening was silent and pristine.

"I hope you find someone who makes you happy," Thea said.

He took her hand again, held it. "I hope you do too. And I mean that. In every way."

"Does this mean you can start picking up Irina again on the weekends, instead of sending Garret?"

He laughed. "I think he might volunteer anyway. He's taken a real liking to Irina."

"Well, that's one thing going for him," she said, and she smiled to let him know she was teasing. Mostly. She still wasn't certain that Garret had backed down from his vow to exile her from his family. She thought: *How ironic.* She had more hope of being friends with her ex-husband than with him.

She glanced at Jonathan, those familiar features that gave her so much comfort, even now. If she had to go through a divorce, there was no man she trusted to be sensible more than Jonathan. "So," she said. "How are we going to break the news to Sue?"

He grinned. "I'll take care of my mother," he said.

Garret sat on the aluminum bleachers at the soccer field, his butt getting sore. The steeply pitched gables and dormers of Newport broke up the softness of twilight, black angles silhouetted against a yielding sky. Out on the grass, Irina's sprint was beginning to slow to a jog as she dribbled the soccer ball from one end of the field to the other, narrating an intense, winner-take-all competition that only she could see.

Garret flipped open his phone, wondering if he'd missed a text from Jonathan. He hadn't. The only text he'd received so far was from a buddy he used to go to school with years ago:

Hey Gare. It's on tonight. My yacht. Moored at Price's Pier. Can u get here by 9?

At this rate, he wasn't sure he would make it to the party. Jonathan had yet to give him the signal that he and Thea were done talking. Anxious, with a strange knot in his gut, he shut his phone.

"Garret!" He looked up to see Irina jogging toward him. She wore loose green shorts and a white tee. Her hair was pulled back tight.

He stood, feeling the creak of his old knees, and he laughed a little to himself and shook his head. Once he'd been as serious as she was about soccer—if not more. He'd meant to devote his entire life to the sport, to play pro or at the very least become a gym teacher—anything to stay close to the game he loved. When he was her age, he was as certain of his future in soccer as he was of the necessity of breathing. But life had gone a different way.

"I was just gonna call you," he said to Irina. "Sun's going down. We have to head in soon." He tucked his phone into his pocket, still anxious to hear from Jonathan.

"No, Garret! Come kick a few balls at me. Please! I want to practice tending goal!"

"We really have to get going . . ."

"No, we don't," she said. "Mom and Dad are going to be a while yet."

"How do you know?"

"They always stay out late when they go out on dates."

"I don't think they're on a date, Rina."

She shrugged. "They're doing something together. It's probably a date."

Garret, a professional conversationalist, an expert at small talk and evasion, had no idea what to say.

Irina braced the ball against her hip with her elbow. "Garret?"

"Mmm."

"You know my parents are getting divorced?"

"I'd heard that. Yes."

"And did you know that kids who come from broken families are more likely to do drugs?"

"Who told you that?"

"My teacher." Her face was fraught with tension. In fact, if he didn't know better, he thought she might be about to cry. "I don't want to be a junkie."

"That's ridiculous. Of course you won't."

"It's not ridiculous." She wiped at her face. She was crying now; there was no getting around the sniffling. Garret marveled that the tears had come on so quickly. He could only imagine what it was like to be a ten-year-old girl, going through such a hard time with her parents and suffering from emotional whiplash. "I saw on the television that kids whose parents get divorced do drugs. And my teacher—"

"Your teacher doesn't know that your uncle Garret would never let you do any drugs," he said. He squeezed her closer and was oddly surprised when she let him. She was such a tomboy—so tough. He wasn't sure how to comfort her without making her feel pitied. "Being a junkie is out of the question."

"What about being a teen mother?"

Garret tried to keep his face placid. "You don't have to be a teen mother as long as you, um—" He fumbled. Sex talks were advanced parenting, but he was still in babysitting 101. "There's ways of protecting yourself against becoming a teen mother."

"Like what?"

"Like keeping your eye on the ball. Like deciding you want to be a teen soccer star instead."

"Well, I already know that." She grinned, and he thought he was out of the woods until she spoke again. "Why did they break up? They told you, didn't they? They never tell me anything."

Garret sighed and led her to sit down on the bleachers. "It's not really my place to talk about it, Irina. You need to talk about it with your mom and dad."

"But they won't talk to me."

Garret rubbed at his face. He wasn't sure what to say. To his own ears, his voice sounded wooden—an adult trying to act like an adult for the benefit of a kid. He didn't want to talk down to Irina; she didn't deserve that. But he also didn't know how he could help or even explain.

"I think it's my mom's fault," Irina went on. "I think she told him to leave."

Garret leaned back so his elbows were on the seat behind him. In the far corners of the field, lightning bugs were beginning to sparkle greenish gold. He thought of Thea—of how a few weeks ago he would have sworn to anyone that Jonathan's infidelity was her fault, that she *must* have done something wrong. And yet the idea that everything was her fault . . . it no longer sat so comfortably. Before, he'd wanted his brother's breakup to be black and white—Thea was a terrible person, and it had simply taken Jonathan too long to find out. But now he knew that he could not make her into an enemy, no matter how much he wanted to.

"You know that both of your parents love you. That won't change."

"Everyone keeps saying that."

"Because it's true. You've got a family that would do anything for you, Irina. And you can include me in that too."

She stood with a sigh that was far too worldly for a girl so young. She bumped the soccer ball with her knee, then pinned it with her foot to the ground. "You really mean that?"

"Would I lie?"

"Ha!" Her face lit up, and she kicked the ball to him. "Then I've got you. Legally you have to come kick a few balls for me. You said you would do *anything* . . ."

He laughed. "Great. Just what the family needs. Another attorney."

She ran toward the goal, and when he stepped away from the bleachers to follow, she let out a happy *woo-hoo!* So much of Irina's life had gone by, and Garret was only now getting to know her. For a while—especially over the last few years—he'd begun to doubt that he'd ever truly liked kids. Other people's children were needy and snotty and loud. They were conversation pieces for small talk but little else. He'd started to think it was a good thing that he'd escaped being saddled with parenthood.

But Irina wasn't just someone else's kid, interchangeable with a hundred other kids. She was a person, her own person—and what's more, he *liked* her. She was pushy and funny and so, so vulnerable sometimes that he knew if she tried to sell him the Golden Gate Bridge he would get out his wallet without batting an eye.

"Come on!" Irina shouted. She stood at the end of the soccer field, haloed by the net behind her. Garret kicked a ball in her direction, just inches to her left. He cheered when she caught it.

"Oh, Uncle Garret," she said. "You're gonna have to do better than that."

That night, after she'd heard all about Irina's evening with Garret, Thea made herself a cup of decaf tea—plum with a bit of valerian root to soothe tired nerves—and climbed into the attic for an old box of photographs she'd been meaning to organize for some time. Tonight, they'd called to her. She sat on the floor of the spare room, surround by a hundred pictures of herself from the past, each picture a judge with a hundred things to say:

Remember the day you had Irina, when Jonathan took this picture of you and your just-born daughter, and for a moment you were so sure that you'd done the right thing, as if Irina's perfect little face was a sign that you'd made the right decisions after all . . .

Remember this day, here you are on ice skates, holding Irina's two hands and pulling her around; remember the way Jonathan sat on the side, watching, and you thought of how after years of marriage he still seemed so distant . . .

Remember your wedding day, the dress, the veil, the robotic feeling of going through the motions for reasons you couldn't at the time understand—and remember your faith in friendship, that marrying a friend was better, safer, than marrying a man who could, if he wanted to, turn your heart to ash . . .

She sat, looking into her empty hands.

And remember the days that have no pictures. The moments that changed everything but that no one would dare document with something as offensive as a photograph. The day in the barn, Garret's weight. The night that was filled with lights, red and blue glaring, decisions you can't take back . . .

She couldn't let herself think that she'd made the wrong choice in marrying Jonathan. They'd done their best. They'd tried, like two dedicated workers, to build a life together as if laying out bricks and mortar would be enough. No—she would never for a moment regret the years spent with him.

But when she looked at the pictures of herself spread out around her, the woman she saw was the same woman in every picture—from high school graduation until today she had not, in even the smallest sense, changed a bit. Maybe Claudine and the other baristas were right—maybe she hadn't taken enough risks or tried enough new things.

What, she wondered, would she do with herself now that she had such an unsought opportunity—a second chance she didn't quite know she'd needed until now?

In a seat on Jamie Rigby's small yacht, Garret opened another beer and tipped his head back to drink it. The hazy lights of Newport wharves in the distance obscured most of the constellations, but a few stars poked through, crisp against the dark sky. The boat bobbed gently on the swells, hip-hop playing from built-in speakers, Jamie and his friends flirting recklessly with a couple of undergraduate girls.

Garret leaned the back of his head against the side of the boat, pensive. He didn't like this feeling—the indescribable sensation of being empty but not being able to put his finger on why. He never felt this way, so self-pitying and lonely. So what on earth was making him feel that way now?

"Hey. What's up?" Jamie gave him a quick punch on the arm and sprawled in a chair beside him. He wore orange Bermuda shorts and a hemp necklace, as if Newport was some New England Malibu.

Garret looked around at the partiers, some familiar, others not. Those he'd been closest to five years ago were nearly all absent, replaced by a different crowd. "Is it just me, or is everyone getting younger?"

Jamie laughed and held up his beer for a toast. "The fountain of youth, bro."

"Really. Where is everybody? Where's Stubs? Where's Rocco? Where are those guys?"

Jamie shook his head. "It's over for them."

"What do you mean?"

"Married. All of them. They're probably off at a dinner party or something equally lame. Maybe they're playing Scrabble. Stubs's wife is pregnant with their second kid."

"*Jeez,*" Garret said, not surprised to hear that they all had married but surprised at the pang of jealousy that ripped through him head to toe.

"Tell me about it. Now if you want to have a good time, you've got to pick your friends up in town and bring them back here. Which is my preferred method."

"Which is why your friends are hot single women."

"Nothing wrong with that."

Garret leaned his head back again, feeling old and out of place. Most of the men he worked with had been married for such a long time it seemed their anniversaries could be measured in geological periods. Once, Garret had every intention of getting married and having children. He'd thought those desires had been burned out of him long ago; he understood now that they'd been forgotten but not gone.

"Hey. Perk up," Jamie said. "Life's good, man. You're not married yet. Go work the crowd. Seriously. They're mostly from out of town."

"Maybe," he said.

"No maybe about it. Or are you doing the celibate thing again, like when we were in school?"

Garret flinched inwardly. "Definitely not."

"So . . . ?"

Garret watched a cute redhead push away one of Jamie's younger brothers—she was hot. He had to give Jamie that. "We'll see," Garret said. But inwardly he still wished he was back on the terra firma of the soccer field with Irina, kicking the ball around while the sun went down.

From "The Coffee Diaries"
by Thea Celik

The Newport Examiner

On the surface, preference seems straightforward: there's bad coffee and good coffee. There's the kind you like and the kind you don't. We come to rely on our favorite coffees each morning to nudge us awake, to brighten our passage into the day.

But coffee is sly—often giving one impression while being something entirely different.

Many of us were taught that espresso—that strong, muscular, and most efficient of all coffee drinks—has the most concentrated dose of caffeine.

But that's just not true. A cup of regular coffee has more caffeine than a shot of espresso.

And while many think that dark roasts, with the strong flavors of earth and burned wood, are more potent than light roasts, the fact is that lighter coffees are more caffeinated than dark roasts. So don't be fooled: just because the cup in your hand tastes strong and vibrant doesn't mean it's the powerful mood changer you want it to be.

TEN

On Monday at the art museum, Thea stood in an airy white room, shifting her weight from one foot to another, tipping her head to the side to see if maybe it would help her "get" the tangle of iron and plastic lettuce leaves hanging from the ceiling. It didn't.

So, she thought, *I'm not into art.*

On Tuesday, she swapped out her usual turkey wrap and water for Indian food; her lunch was so spicy that she ended up trashing it in one of the public garages on the pier and eating a pistachio ice-cream cone instead.

On Wednesday, she took Irina to a poetry reading, because once when Thea was younger she had an idea that she loved writing poems, and she wondered if some part of her still did. One soft-spoken poet after another, Irina's boredom became fury—somehow she kicked over her own chair while she was sitting on it. And as far as Thea was concerned, it was the most exciting thing that had happened all night.

On Thursday morning she left it to Jules to open the shop and instead decided to go jogging, because it seemed to her that people who were on a journey to find themselves also got fit. She jogged until she couldn't breathe and until she grew so bored listening to the sound of her own thoughts that she decided to jog herself into the local pastry shop for espresso and a cheese Danish.

And on Friday of the second week in August, she gave up.

"I just don't know that there's anything to this whole finding yourself thing," she told Dani over the phone. "I try new things, and I don't like them. So why not just stick with the old things that I already know I like?"

"Maybe you're just not trying the right new things," Dani said.

Dear Thea,

I can't say I'm thrilled to hear that you and Jonathan have decided to quit, but since you seem friendly toward each other, I have high hopes. It's been my wish all along that the rift between you and Garret would mend. Odd that divorce might be what brings this family back together again.

So—that said—Ken and I are married fifty years next month. Can you believe it? Fifty years with him and each one better than the last. We'd like to have a big party at the Marriott, and we're wondering if you might consider catering. Of course, we don't want to invite you as "help," darling. But the Dancing Goat makes the best coffee in town, and those little almond tartlets and vanilla biscotti and mousse-stuffed cupcakes that you order—just divine. If you don't want to do it—because you'd rather attend as a guest, which will certainly be more fun than working—then don't think twice about turning the offer down.

Oh, and until I know that there won't be any problems, I'd prefer if you let me tell Garret that you're coming—if you're coming. Jonathan agrees this is a good idea as well.

We're so close to having peace, I think. I'm crossing my fingers.

Yours,
Sue

Thea sat in the near darkness in her office; it was too early for bright light. She tapped the tip of her pen on her desk. In theory, she was supposed to be thinking about her next column—what would she write? But instead, she found herself thinking of her parents. The heavy wooden desk where she sat had been her father's; she had many, many memories of him sitting here, layers of memories, one on top of the other, blurred slightly at the edges. She remembered him writing checks, marking sales for the day in pencil in a spiral-bound ledger, typing on a loud calculator that printed equations in faint blue ink.

She'd seen her parents last fall, when she and Irina had gone to Turkey for a visit, and she was eager to see them again. Within her extended family, her parents were considered too modern, too American. The fact that they hadn't forced Thea to return with them to Turkey had nearly made them outcasts. She supposed she could have been bitter that her parents had left, but she knew they'd never felt entirely comfortable here—while she could never feel entirely comfortable someplace else. They'd made their own sacrifice for her, the sacrifice of understanding, of respecting her choice to stay, even though it went against their nature. For that, she'd always thank them.

It was six thirty in the morning in Newport. It was midday in Turkey. She decided her column could wait, and so she picked up the phone and dialed.

"*Merhaba?*" Her father's voice was sleepy.

"*Babacığım*, it's me."

"Thea!" She could hear the smile in his voice.

"I've missed you," she said. "Is Mama there?"

"No, *fıstığım*. She's out harassing the nice girls who work at the market."

The last time she'd been to Turkey she'd seen her mother in action, working for the best prices. Thea was lucky to have inherited some tenacity from her; it helped when she was negotiating the price of beans from local roasters.

"So," her father said. "How are things with the . . . what is the word from the airplane . . . ?"

"Airplane . . . ?"

He murmured under his breath for a moment. "Turbulence."

"You mean with Jonathan?" In Newport, thousands of miles away from him, she leaned her elbow against the desk that used to be his. "It's more than turbulence. It's put your head between your knees and hold on tight."

"Your mother said . . ."

"I'm sure she didn't want to worry you," Thea said. "We've decided to separate."

Her father was silent a moment. She tried to picture him—did he have a mustache now? Was he wearing the same sweatpants and sweater ensemble that was so often his leisure wear here in the States? Did he sit down, she wondered, when she told him the news?

"You feel happy about this?" he asked.

"Yes."

"If I divorced your mother every time I thought of it, I would have divorced her a million times by now. But I didn't."

She paused for a moment. Her father had always been unfailingly supportive. She didn't quite know where he stood, though, on the divorce. "Jonathan's a great man," she said. "We're going to be model divorcees. Believe me."

"And what does his family think of this? What about Sue and Ken?"

"I think it's going to be okay," she said. "But it will take some getting used to."

"And what about Garret?"

"Garret?"

Her father laughed. "I'm sure he's got strong opinions."

"He always has strong opinions."

"Have you seen him lately?"

Thea swallowed. She hadn't expected his line of questioning to veer quite this way. "Yes. He's been picking up Irina on the weekends."

"And . . ."

"And *nothing*." She heard a slight pinch in her voice, and she didn't like it. But her father's questions were making her uncomfortable. He should be asking about her and Jonathan—not her and Garret. "Garret doesn't factor into any of this at all—except that I think he wants to keep me away from his family now that I'm separating from Jonathan."

"And who can blame him?" her father said. "You broke the man's heart."

"I broke *his* heart? I think you're remembering things backward."

"Thea. You've always been a strong woman. You and Garret were in love in the way that only kids can fall in love, and you survived it. You went on, got married, had a baby. You can withstand a lot of unhappiness—without even knowing whether it's unhappiness or not—because you're optimistic and you're tough. But Garret . . . what did he do after you? Nothing: that's what he did."

"I hardly think going to law school and becoming a lobbyist is nothing."

"You misunderstand." Her father's voice was strained. "You're not going to be married to Jonathan anymore."

"So?"

"You believe Garret isn't thinking about that?"

Thea was quiet, stopped in her tracks. Was Garret thinking about her again—thinking about her as more than his brother's ex? She'd only seen him a couple of times. Each time, their meetings were charged and intense—something between them crackling and snapping like fire. Maybe it was his anger. Her regret. Some combination of the two—she couldn't tell. But she didn't think it was . . . *interest*. She'd been with him in high school for less than a year. One tiny little year—a moment so small it should have been inconsequential and forgotten.

It should have been.

Either way, it was trouble. Garret had sworn himself to keeping her away from his family. Even if some small part of him was still curious about her—even attracted to her in some vestigial sense— it didn't matter, and she shouldn't even be thinking about it.

The rest of her life would be a life without Garret—she'd made peace with that the moment she said, "I do."

"Garret's not going to be an issue," she said. "Sue, Ken, and Jonathan aren't going to shun me—I trust them."

"I know you do, sweetheart," her father said, his voice suddenly filled with melancholy. "They're good people. I'm so glad you have them."

Thea wished she could give him a hug. But all those miles of ocean . . . it was hard to bridge the gap. "Maybe you and Mom will come visit again soon. Or maybe Irina and I will go there."

"I would like that very much," he said.

* * *

The campus of Brown University, where Jonathan had gone to college, was friendly enough—its collegiate brick buildings with white-trimmed windows, its large green courtyard dotted with austere trees, its elegiac columns and dignified white pediments. And yet, for all its charms, Jonathan felt that going just a few dozen miles away to school was like being sent to the moon.

During fall break, he found Thea walking home from school on a chilly autumn afternoon, when the sidewalks were covered with leaves and the sun was deceptively bright. He knew her by her walk, her jeans cut close to her body, her corduroy jacket showing beneath the arms of her backpack. He beeped the horn lightly, not wanting to scare her as he pulled over to the side of the road. He expected she would be pleased to see him—that she might run to his car to give him a hug. Instead, he saw the flash of recognition in her eyes when she turned, and then she climbed into the car as if her body was too heavy to drag around.

"What happened?" he asked.

She adjusted her backpack on her lap. "What do you mean what happened?"

"Were you crying?"

"No," she said.

"Thea . . ."

"It's no big deal," she said.

He took a deep breath and put the car in drive. He wanted to be there for her, more than he'd ever wanted to be there for anyone. His heart cried out for her secrets, her burdens. He would carry them, and her, as long as she needed him. But how to tell her that? And even if he offered to listen, what made him think she would *let* him?

They drove along the familiar streets of Newport, four-square colonial mansions, cottages from long-forgotten farms, carriage houses converted into family homes. It took a moment before Jonathan plucked up the courage to say what was on his mind.

"I know about you and Garret," he said.

She stared out the window, where the trees were passing in a green and red blur. "Are you mad?"

"No," he said. But he wanted to tell her, *yes, I am.* "Did my brother do something stupid?"

She shook her head.

"Did you break up?"

Oddly enough, she laughed—a sound completely out of place given her tears. "I saw him on the soccer field with Krissy Spelling. They were just joking around, but he was pretending to, like, dance with her, you know? Like in the old days. Picking her up and twirling her around while she was laughing . . ."

"And he doesn't do that sort of thing with you."

"No. Not anymore." She wiped her face—the only sign that she was still crying. "He won't let me tell anyone about us. Jonathan—" She took one of his hands from the steering wheel, held it in hers. Her skin was damp. "I'm so glad you know. It's been killing me to keep it a secret. There's no one I can talk to . . ."

Jonathan's chest grew tight. He pulled his hand away to turn the wheel. "Have you . . . um . . . did you—you know—"

"Sleep with him? No. Not yet."

"Good." Relief washed over him as he pulled up in front of her house and stopped the car. "Don't."

She looked at him. Her eyes had turned more green than brown, the effect of tears.

"Hear me out," he said. He put his arm around the back of her seat. "The two of you have been just friends for so long. And I think there's a reason for that. I think you make sense as friends.

Garret's always wanted to have everything. And I think once he gets everything from you, he'll go on to want whatever the next thing is that catches his attention."

"I know what Garret is," she said.

"I'm not blaming him. I don't think he'll try to hurt you on purpose. It's just his nature." Jonathan leaned toward her, overwhelmed by concern for her. "Just promise me that you'll, I don't know, go slow. Okay?"

She held still, quiet but listening.

"If you guys can hold out until the end of your senior year, like the week of graduation, then maybe you'll have a chance."

"The week of graduation?"

"Yeah," Jonathan said. But he didn't think they would make it until graduation—Garret's longest relationship had lasted a mere five weeks. Probably this whole thing would blow over soon, especially since Garret was already flirting with other girls. If Thea could hold off on sleeping with him, she might save herself worlds of regret and pain. "I just don't want to see you—*you know*—just to lose him. You deserve better than that."

"I guess it couldn't hurt to make a timeline . . ."

He nodded and took her hand. "I hope Garret sees how lucky he is to have you."

She leaned toward him—an awkward hug and a kiss on the cheek. "Thank you for your help. And for the ride home. It's good to see you."

He smiled, felt a little better. He liked being useful to her in a way his brother could not. "What are friends for?"

On a Saturday in late August, just after the sun had gone down, Thea stood in front of her open closet—a million voices ringing in her head and none of them her own.

From Dani: *Of course you have something to wear to the bar. Here, this black camisole. Is this silk? Yes, I know it's supposed to go under another shirt, but isn't that the point? To show some skin?*

From her mother: *Don't change your clothes. That husband of yours never cared what you looked like, and you shouldn't either. You should stay home and read a book. Or I'm sure there's something you can find to clean.*

From Irina: *It's not about the clothes, Ma. It's about the makeup. I know—I read it in a magazine when we were in line to pay for groceries. If you put on enough makeup, you won't look old!*

From Garret: *What you're supposed to wear? You shouldn't ask me that question. Really—don't.*

Thea had forgotten how loud the night could be—the music, the crowds yelling over the music, the way everything seemed so inflated and larger-than-life. Dani had changed out of her ubiquitous uniform to wear curvy dark jeans and a neon orange satin shirt. There was no question that she was turning heads. She talked as loud as she laughed, and people came from across the bar just to stand near her to see what had everyone so lively and entertained.

Thea wasn't feeling too bad herself—she'd pulled on a red tank top that made her look curvy but not trashy. She'd also managed to put on makeup beyond her usual mascara and blush, and she'd been happy with the extra effort: Her eyes looked smoky and even a little sultry. Her dark curls fell softly around her shoulders. Her lips were full and red.

At the bar, she drank cheap Coronas and danced—she was thrilled to discover she still knew how. At some point during the night, she got the feeling that Dani was sending men over her way, telling them to flirt with her, to buy her a drink and show her a good time. The bar became hazy, kaleidoscopic, all color and smiles and laughter, and Thea gave in to it. She could still flirt. She could still drink. Maybe this was what she was meant for—more people, more laughing, more parties. She yelled to Dani over the music: "This is better than staying home."

One of the men she'd been talking to—a tall guy who looked like something of a cowboy—stuck around. She could barely hear a word he was saying, but somehow, she found there was a lot to laugh about. When the band dropped into a slow song, the last of the night, he put his arms around her waist, and she could feel his breath in her ear.

As the bar emptied out, he took her hand and brought her tripping over the planks of the pier and into the dark. They stood by the railing, the water far below, the stars far overhead, and distant lights of yachts and dinghies watching them from the black of the bay.

She wasn't at all surprised when he kissed her. She felt his hands on her back, crushing her against him. She felt his lips, thin though they were, and the press of his tongue in her mouth. She had the sense that she wasn't actually kissing him but was instead looking down at herself kissing him, watching with detachment as the scene played out.

She felt the cowboy's hands sliding down into her jeans pockets, and she pulled away. This man wanted her to go home with him—she could feel it, emotionally and physically too. Some part of her was tempted, just to see if she could, until it occurred to her that she didn't know his name.

"You're the most fun I've had in a while," she said.

"Why do I have a feeling there's a 'but' coming?"

She took his hand from her waist, held it in hers. "I just don't want to move too fast."

"Did you have a good time?"

"Yes. Lots of fun."

He took out his wallet, pulled out his business card. "Then call me if you ever want a good time again."

She laughed, and he kissed her again. She felt the barest spark of heat—a tiny flame, but a promising one. Maybe her future wasn't entirely sexless after all.

"Thanks," she said. And she slipped the card in her pocket before he took her hand and led her back in the direction of the closing bar.

The winter of her senior year, Thea developed the senses of a cat. She swore that she recognized the sound of Garret's particular brand of sneakers on the sidewalk under her window—a sound distinct from the foot traffic of other pedestrians. She thought she could hear the tap of his finger on her window even before his skin touched the glass.

Some nights, he didn't even say hello. He simply came in, kissed her, reached for buttons and hems. He slid under the covers of her bed, whispering, asking, pushing her to the edge of what she could stand. The press of his fingers was strong and greedy. His mouth was hot. When the creaking of the bed threatened to give them away, they moved to the floor. She'd insisted that they keep their underwear on, a frail and absurd barrier—and she couldn't take it, fabric so thin it drove them both crazy, how easily it could be pushed aside, inches this way or that, and all the agony of the moment, built to excessive and terrible pressure, would be eased. Sometimes her whole body trembled uncontrollably so her skin jumped beneath Garret's hands, and the word that would have ended the torment perched on the tip of her tongue even while Garret dared her to speak it.

And yet she stopped him. She had to. It hurt to hold herself away. "Garret."

His breathing was rough, his focus not quite meeting hers for some moments. When he raised his head from her chest, his eyes were glassy, unfocused too.

"I need you to know something." She pushed his hair back from his forehead. Why couldn't this man in her bedroom be the same man she saw in the halls of the school each day? "I can't sleep with you yet. I think we should wait until graduation."

His sigh was a puff of air on her face, and he dropped his head back down. "Why?"

She looked to the ceiling. There was no way to explain.

"Don't you like this?" he asked, his hands moving over her.

She felt the tug between them. "Yes."

"So why wait? Thea, it's going to be . . . perfect. I promise."

She propped herself up, the hard floor hurting her elbows. "Why can't we tell anyone we're seeing each other?"

He sat up, ran a hand through his hair. "Is that what this is about?"

"Jonathan knows."

"He does? Did you tell him?"

"No." She reached for her nightshirt, pulled it on. "I just don't understand why we can't tell. Are you . . . are you ashamed of me?"

"No," he said.

"This isn't serious to you?"

"I've never been more serious about anything in my life." The look in his eyes was fierce, and she wanted to believe him.

"Then what is it?"

He stood up, crossed the room. She felt the space between them widen like rising waters. He grabbed his jeans from where they were crumpled in a ball, and he tugged them over his hips. When he sat down on the bed, she joined him, and the mattress sagged.

"I don't know how to explain," he whispered.

"Try."

He looked away. "I like keeping you to myself. I like this being . . . secret. Just you and me."

"Really?" Thea sniffed. "Because I thought maybe it was that you just like people thinking you're still single, so that way you can keep on flirting with whoever you want to flirt with and keep getting all the attention you need."

His lips pressed together. "I do like attention, I guess."

"And girls do like to give it to you."

"Can I help it if I'm magnetic?"

She shook her head, but inwardly, she was laughing.

"So what do you want to do?" he asked. "You want to tell everyone? Let everyone in? Be . . . what we are in front of everyone?"

"What are you so afraid of?"

"What if we break up?" he asked.

She pulled away, looked at him with new comprehension. She thought, *So that's what this is about.* He was afraid they wouldn't make it. And that having the entire school in on the heartbreak would make a bad situation unbearable. He didn't do well with public failure—the thing that drove him to be exceptionally brave on the soccer field was, ironically enough, a deep and secret fear. Thea wanted to reassure him.

"There's nothing in the world that would make me want to break up with you. Ever," she said.

"Really?"

"There's a lot of things you have to worry about," she said. "Losing me isn't one of them."

He looked into her eyes, kissed her hard. She felt the press of a kiss that branded them both, one to the other, a promise so ongoing and endless that it could never be completed or entirely kept. When he pulled away, the look in his eyes was desperate.

"We'll tell everyone tomorrow. It will be all over the school in seconds." He kissed her again, softly. "I don't know if I can wait until graduation."

She didn't speak. She ran her hand along the ridge of his jeans. *Me neither*, is what she didn't say.

In the pre-morning dark, Thea fumbled with her key chain at the door of the coffee shop, but her fingers felt clumsy and numb, and she couldn't seem to find the right key. She was glad when she saw Jules appear in the alleyway, his ripped jeans slung low on his hips and a yellow plaid shirt untucked and hanging from narrow shoulders.

"Thea? What are you doing here? You're not opening today," he said. He stood beside her, his pale face still puffy from sleep, and he noticed that she was juggling her keys to find the right one. "Here, let me do that."

"Thanks."

He opened the door, and she followed him inside, glad to be out of the dewy chill of morning. She turned on the lights and headed behind the counter to put her purse away and get her apron.

"Coffee?" Jules asked.

"Shot in the dark."

"Wow. Espresso and coffee together?" He laughed and set the espresso machine to backflush in order to clean it out. "Rough night?"

"Does it count as night if you never go to sleep?"

"I've often wondered the same thing myself," he said.

For the next twenty minutes, they worked in silence, booting up the register, brewing coffee, and getting ready for the morning rush. The fresh pastries were delivered, and Thea began setting them out for display in the glass-front fridge. When their coffee was finally ready, they stopped a moment to drink. Through the pressure between her temples, she could feel Jules looking at her, puzzling her out.

"Do you feel okay?" he asked.

"I just have a bit of a headache."

"Oh my God, Thea . . . Are you *hungover*?"

She glanced at him out of the corner of her eye; a shooting pain made its way from one eye to the other. "Fine. Yes. Maybe a little. Okay?"

He laughed and held up his hand for a high five. She gave it begrudgingly. "That's awesome. Good for you, getting out there. What'd you do?"

She took a tentative sip of her coffee. The java and espresso combo was bitter and thick—exactly what she needed. She wished she could get it pumped directly into her veins. "I went out with Dani. Then we stayed up for a while talking. At some point, it made no sense to go to sleep."

He leaned hard on one hip, indignant. "You shouldn't be here. Go sleep in. I'm on the schedule for this morning."

"I don't mind working," she said.

"What's wrong?"

She shrugged. "Nothing."

"Did you get crazy? Are you *overthinking*?"

"Probably," she said.

She breathed in the fragrant steam from her coffee. Last night—or perhaps it was early this morning—she'd kissed a man who wasn't her husband. She supposed she'd needed to do it, and looking back, she realized that she'd had high hopes for the kiss. She'd wanted to know she was still sexy and appealing, and that she could still feel that spark of electricity and promise of new romance. And yet, what she'd learned from the experiment was slightly disappointing. Her future of kissing men was a future

SLOW DANCING ON PRICE'S PIER

filled with *common* kisses—not unpleasant—but not the kind that made her wild for more.

The truth was, she'd only been in love once in her life. One great, juvenile, operatic, and misplaced passion. The shape of that first falling in love had been coming back to haunt her in recent weeks, and yet it was nothing but a cruel, empty shell of what it had once been. No amount of kissing strangers could bring those feelings back.

Jules leaned on the counter, his arms crossed. "Well, I'm proud of you. You needed to go out. And you're supposed to try new things."

"Even if it gets me in trouble?"

"Especially if it does," he said.

She smiled and felt some of the pressure of her hangover abate. She'd behaved badly. She knew that. She was not some twenty-something who should be dancing on tables and making out with strange men. If she made a self-discovery, it was not that she'd discovered who she was—but rather, who she wasn't. Still—it was a start.

"If you're going to be staying out all night, then we've got to get something straight," Jules said sternly.

"What?"

"You're the boss. And when you stay out all night, you're not allowed to come in at six a.m. the next day."

"But—"

"Nope." With one tug, he pulled the string of her apron. She grabbed for it when it fell. "If you don't go home and go to bed right now, you're going to have to find yourself another token male barista. Seriously, Thea. This is me putting my foot down."

"You're not a token—"

"Out. Now."

Thea barely had time to get her purse before Jules shooed her out of the coffee shop. Outside, the sun was rising, and the mist was fading from between the narrow buildings of the pier. She took a breath, and the cool, clean air filled her lungs and cleared her head. She felt different, a little bit more certain—though she wasn't precisely sure what she felt certain about. The mire of tiredness gave way to bright waves of energy and triumph. Newport was waking up. Dawn was becoming day. All the hours were before her and full of possibility. She thought, *I couldn't possibly go to bed.*

And yet, when she got home, her pillows beckoned. And she fell into a slumber that was dreamless, restorative, and deep.

From "The Coffee Diaries"
by Thea Celik

The Newport Examiner

In the early days of coffee cultivation, many Arab countries prohibited the export of even the smallest number of green coffee seeds. However, enterprising explorers found ways to spread coffee across the globe, and their stories have taken on a larger-than-life mythology.

Coffee is said to have made its way to India courtesy of a seventeenth-century Sufi named Baba Budan, who taped a few green coffee seeds to his belly to smuggle them out of Yemen.

Gabriel-Mathieu de Clieu, an eighteenth-century Frenchman, claimed in his memoirs to have brought a single, fragile coffee tree to Martinique, but in order to get it across the ocean, he had to protect the plant during violent storms, pirate attacks, sabotage from envious fellow sailors—and when the ship's water rations wore down to nothing, de Clieu is said to have risked his life by sharing his last cup of water with the tree to keep it alive.

My favorite bit of coffee mythology comes from Brazil. When a Brazilian lieutenant seduced the wife of a prominent French official, the woman gave her lover a parting gift that changed history. Tucked inside of an innocuous bundle of flowers was a cutting of a coffee tree—a small green shoot that gave rise to a coffee empire.

ELEVEN

A hundred times—a thousand maybe—Thea had told her daughter, *It's going to be okay.* When Irina had been learning to ride her bike and she'd scraped her knee so that there was hardly any unscratched skin to speak of, Thea had told her, *It's going to be okay.* When Irina was six and she'd come tearfully into Thea's bedroom to confess that she'd broken the living room lamp, Thea made room for her under the covers and said *It's going to be okay.* And last week, when Irina had purposely snapped her toothbrush in two because Thea wouldn't drive her over to Providence at almost nine o'clock on a weekday night to see her father, Thea summoned all her patience and assured her daughter, *It's going to be okay.*

Irina needed to know they would get through this. All of them. And yet to assure another person *It's okay* was also to acknowledge that something was wrong.

"I don't know what to do," she told Dani over the telephone. "Tell me what to do. How do I handle this?"

"Hey." Dani's voice was soft. "You're freaking out."

Thea forced a deep breath. "I know. I'm sorry. I'm just worried about her."

"I know you are. But honey? You've got to believe me on this one. I've been there, done that."

"Believe what?"

"One way or another," she said. "It's going to be okay."

Garret didn't have enough information to do any kind of formal comparison to determine if other men were more talented in bed than he was, but the anecdotal evidence—offered in breathless and bewildered gratitude moments after orgasm—all pointed to his being more dexterous than the average guy.

In college, he'd thrown himself into discovering ways to please women with the same passion that he'd once brought to the soccer fields. He'd pored over the hints and tips in dirty magazines that his friends passed furtively from one dorm room to another. He soaked up lessons like a sponge: "What Women Want," "Five Secret Fantasies of Real Women," "How to Kiss a Woman (but Not on the Mouth)."

But eventually, snippets in men's magazines began to seem predictable and inadequate. *Of course* he knew about the G-spot. *Of course* he could pay attention to the back of a woman's knee. And so he sought education elsewhere. It didn't take him long to give up on watching porn for pointers; silly scenes of nurses and delivery men were choreographed for the visuals, not necessarily for the pleasure of the parties involved. When skin flicks failed, he turned to books, their covers plastered with pictures of half-naked couples, the gentle contours of candlelight and shadow obscuring strategic body parts. Unlike movies, the books made a promise that he wanted so badly to believe: all he had to do was follow the instructions to a T.

In crowded common rooms of the boys' dorm, where his friends played Ping-Pong and dropped coins in the vending machine, he made no secret of his studies. And the guys mocked him ruthlessly—not because they weren't impressed but because Garret was the only one of them who never got laid. He read, studied, and learned—he even counseled others on what he knew when they needed advice—but he didn't put theory to practice. Not until years down the line.

Now—an adult out on a promising date—he stood in the quiet marble lobby of his building with Gemma, a gorgeous blond he'd met on Jamie's yacht. They'd returned from a nice dinner together at a gourmet steak house in Providence, and she was looking at him expectantly, waiting for an invitation to join him in the elevator.

"Thanks for dinner," she said. Her lips were red and shiny, set in her tanned face. Her hair, touched with perfect highlights, smelled of flowers. "Are you up for dessert?"

He looked into her eyes—past her dark makeup to the shock of blue that may or may not have been contacts. His entire life, he'd prided himself on making his dates happy. And this woman—he could make her *very* happy.

But when he tried to imagine walking her through the rooms of his condo, where Jonathan was probably reading a science fiction novel on the couch, and Irina was sleeping soundly in the room they were all coming to think of as *hers*, he simply didn't like the idea of bringing her inside.

Oddly enough, he'd found himself enjoying the company of his brother and his niece more than he ever could have anticipated. Sure there were inconveniences—Jonathan left the toothpaste cap open and tended to be a bit of a slob, and Irina had the television in a stranglehold of endless cartoons. But generally, he enjoyed the friendly, quiet hours they spent together, and he knew it would upset the balance if he were to bring this woman home.

"You have no idea," he said in his deepest, sexiest voice, "how much I want to take you upstairs right now."

Her smile flickered.

"But the trouble is my niece is with me for the weekend. And she's too young to explain why her uncle has house guests."

"You're so thoughtful." She ran her fingers along his tie. "But we'll be quick. In and out before you know it."

"I see you're going to make this difficult for me."

She sidled closer, twining her arms around his neck. "I'll sneak out before morning."

And I bet it's not the first time, he thought. For a moment he had the odd sense that he was on the wrong side of a seduction, and he didn't like it. He wondered if the women he'd seduced over the course of his life had also felt like this—the slight discomfort that was not dangerous and exciting, but more of a pain in the ass.

"Rain check?" he asked.

She dropped her arms from his shoulders. "This might be a one-time offer."

He nodded, relieved. He held the glass door of the building for her as she walked outside, her green dress making a perfect hourglass of her curves, and he shook his head at himself.

The doorman appeared by his side, watching his date walk away. "Rough night?"

"No," Garret said. "Not at all."

Thea didn't realize that she was staring off into space until Irina looked up from her summer reading and stuck out her tongue.

"Sorry!" Thea said, and they both laughed.

At a table in the corner of the coffee shop, Irina looked like a miniature version of the writers and college students who regularly brought their work into the coffee shop. With a mug at her side and her foot tucked under one knee, she took on their posture—their veiled gaze and air of studious boredom—perfectly. Some days, she was ten going on thirty. Other days, she was still a baby in Thea's mind.

Thea looked up when she heard the brass bell over the door ring, and she saw Jonathan walking into the Dancing Goat right on time. He was still dressed for work: gray pleated slacks, an oxford shirt with a tired collar, and a light purple vest. His briefcase hung from his fist.

"Dad!" Irina scooted off her chair. She threw her arms around her father's waist, her face pressed into his belly. "What are you doing here?"

"Visiting the love of my life," he said, and he kissed her forehead.

Thea came around the counter to say hello. It felt ridiculous not to greet him with her usual kiss on the cheek—such a platonic gesture, even when they were married—and so she leaned toward him and gave him a quick peck. Irina's eyes lit up with an optimism that made Thea's heart break.

"What are you having?" Thea asked. "Iced tea?"

Jonathan glanced at the chalkboard above the counter, deciding what to drink. "No iced tea. I'm feeling adventurous. Give me . . . let's see . . . a vanilla huggle."

Irina's face lit up, her head snapping toward Thea. "I *told* you men would like it. Didn't I say?"

"Yes, you were right," she said happily, and she headed behind the counter to make Jonathan's latte. Her daughter had not only been correct that the lobstermen felt no discomfort about the vanilla huggle, but the men in particular ordered it twice as often as the women. They also ordered it twice as often as when it was simply called a vanilla-cinnamon latte. Thea was convinced of her daughter's genius for marketing. Irina had a future in the Dancing Goat—if she wanted it someday.

Thea made their drinks, left instructions for Claudine to give a shout if she needed help, then she, Jonathan, and Irina headed back into her office for privacy. Thea pulled the chair around from behind her father's desk, Irina sat on a stool shaped like a red dog, and Jonathan got comfortable on the small love seat that had been pushed against the wall for the last ten years.

For a while, they talked easily—like they used to. Thea felt as if her life had gone back to normal. Irina seemed to have made it her goal for the evening to make her father laugh, and Jonathan was a willing audience. They were very different—father and daughter. Irina didn't let Jonathan coddle and spoil her half as much as he would have liked. But Thea could tell that one day, they would be more than just relatives: they would be friends.

First, though, they had to get through the next hour.

She could tell from Irina's constant chatter that her daughter was nervous, as if talking about soccer and mean teachers would keep more adult discussions at bay. But Jonathan had come for a serious conversation. He and Thea had been planning it for days via texts and e-mails. There was no sense in prolonging the inevitable.

"Irina," Thea began, "we need to have a discussion. You know how your father's been staying with Uncle Garret . . ." She hesitated, trying to find the right words. "Your father and I . . . we've decided . . ."

"We've decided we can no longer live together," Jonathan said. "And so we're going to permanently separate."

"That means divorce," Irina said slowly.

"Right. That is what it means." Thea could feel Irina looking at her hard, watching for cues about what to say and how to react. Thea kept her voice as light as possible. "Basically, things are going to be the same as they are now. You'll stay with me for part of the week and your father for the other part."

"At Garret's?"

"Not forever," Jonathan said. "Just for a little while."

"I *knew* this would happen." Irina sighed and looked down at her lap. "I don't like it. I don't want you to live apart. I want everything to be like it was before."

"I know. And I'm sorry," Thea said, surprised by Irina's lack of theatrics. "There's no other way."

"Is it just for now?" Irina asked.

"No, honey. It's permanent," Jonathan replied.

"Don't you love each other anymore?"

Thea caught Jonathan's eye, saw nervousness flash across his face. "Yes," she said quickly. "Of course we still love each other. We'll always love each other."

"Then why can't you be together?"

"Because we love each other like friends do," she said. "Not like husband and wife."

Irina glanced at Jonathan, something sly and conspiratorial in her eye. "This is her fault, isn't it?"

"*What?*" His face showed blank shock. "No—no, it's not her fault. Irina, listen to me. It's not anyone's fault. It just happened."

Thea resisted the urge to take Jonathan's hand. She wanted to draw them both toward her, to embrace them and protect them. "Any questions you want to ask, you can. That's why we're all here together. Even if it takes all night."

"All right," Irina said.

For an hour that seemed like ages, they talked, Irina asking questions that had no good answers. The minute hand made its slow crawl around the clock over the filing cabinet. Thea's coffee grew cold, and Irina's eyes began to droop with fatigue.

She and Jonathan had married for the wrong reasons, and now their relationship had not been broken so much as they had finally accepted what it truly was. Thea could see that now—the truth of it. But how could she explain that to her daughter—if she should explain it at all?

Eventually, the conversation grew tortuous and repetitive: Irina asked the same questions over and over, and with each iteration Thea and Jonathan struggled to find new answers, better answers, ones that satisfied. They might have gone on that way forever if Irina hadn't finally yawned and said she was getting tired. She slid off her low chair and settled down on the rug that looked like a map of a town. Her feet rested beside a herd of cows grazing on a hillside; her head was propped on her arms, not far from a bank.

Jonathan moved her hair to kiss her check. "I'll see you this weekend," he said. "We're going to have fun, okay?"

Irina was mute, eyes closed. For a moment, Jonathan stood beside her, hesitating as if he might apologize. Thea saw the sadness in his eyes, the hesitation that said he too wondered if they were doing the right thing.

She put her hand on his shoulder. "Come on," she said softly. "I'll walk you out."

Outside, they stood together under the light above the door of the Dancing Goat. The wind blew down the alleyway, smelling of fried food and salt from the sea. Thea rubbed her arms against the slight chill of the air.

"How do you think it went?" Jonathan asked.

"It's too soon to tell. She's been so angry lately. I don't know if we made it better or worse."

"Will she be okay?"

"I hope so," Thea said. "We'll do our best to help her be okay."

He looked at her for a long time, his expression soft in the yellow light. His face gave her comfort: his heavy eyebrows, his strong nose, the little brown birthmark barely visible on his cheek. "For what it's worth, I don't think she could have a better mother."

"Her dad's not too bad either, I have to say."

Jonathan gave her a quick kiss on the cheek. "Call me if you need anything."

"I will."

She watched him walk down the alley, his familiar ambling gait, the slight slope of one shoulder where his briefcase dragged his arm down. Whether or not Irina was satisfied by their groping attempts at explanations, she wasn't sure.

But what she did know was that she would fight for the happiness of her family—despite the new and surprising form that happiness had taken—and she was thankful to know she wouldn't be fighting alone.

Garret had bought a new suit for the occasion of his parents' anniversary party—the pretty saleswoman had told him that the deep navy color brought out the blue in his eyes, which in turn had brought out the green in his wallet. And while Garret hadn't bought the suit because of Thea—since he wasn't certain whether or not she was going to have the audacity to show up—she was on his mind. If he absolutely had to see her, he wanted to be in top shape. The fewer cracks in his armor, the more time he could spend on offense instead of defense.

The party was in full swing when he arrived, a lifetime's worth of his parents' friends gathered, drinking, laughing, and even dancing. The ballroom had been sparingly decorated—just a few hearts here and there hanging from the ceiling on strings, tables covered in red cloth, tall tapering candles in gold holders, and a lively band playing oldies. He scanned the room and saw Irina holding court in the corner with a group of children. His brother was talking without animation to a distant cousin.

"Garret!" His mother pushed her way through the crowd, smiling her gracious smile. She wore a gold dress with black beading that on any other woman might have looked too young. But Sue, so slim and youthful, pulled it off beautifully, and he told her so as he hugged her.

"I have to warn you," she said. She pulled the sleeve of his jacket to bring his ear a bit closer. "Thea's here. Oh, don't look around for her like a cornered cat. I just didn't want you to be caught by surprise."

He pulled himself up straight. "You invited her."

"She's very generous. She's helping me out."

Garret shook his head and laughed to himself. His mother was a genius—through and through. Because Thea had been asked to cater, she *had* to show up at the party—she would never turn down a request for help. And Sue, in the meantime, got to make a public show of support for her ex-daughter-in-law despite a divorce that would be unpopular among her conservative Newport friends.

"Oh! There she is now," Sue said, brightening instantly. She stood on her tiptoes and waved Thea over, and to Garret's disgust, he felt his nerves leap—excitement, annoyance, frustration . . . He wished he or she hadn't come. Life had been so much simpler when he'd hated her and never saw her.

Sue spoke to him through tight lips, her worry not putting so much as a dent in her smile. "Are you going to make a big scene at your father's anniversary party? Or are you going to smile and be friends?"

Garret sighed. "It's gonna cost ya."

"You'll be fine, darling. Just treat her the same way you'd treat some political person you don't like."

"You want me to pull some strings and get her fired?"

"I want you to be charming," she said.

He rolled his eyes and tried not to notice Thea crossing the room to meet them. And yet he couldn't help it: she compelled him to look. She was dressed not as a guest but as staff. She wore trim black pants that made her legs look curvy and strong, a maroon dress shirt, and a black, buttoned vest that hugged her from ribs to hips. Though she was all business walking toward him, he didn't miss the apprehension in her fake smile.

"Hello," she said. She glanced at Garret only for the briefest of moments before her eyes landed back on Sue.

"How's everything going?" Sue asked her. "Are we working you too hard?"

"Oh, no!" Thea said, and Garret wondered if his mother could hear that slight tinny pinch in her voice. "We're all set!"

Sue knocked Garret on the shoulder. "Aren't you going to say hello to Thea?"

He looked at Thea, her serious oval face. Something in his chest went taut. "Hello to Thea."

"Oh, good Lord. Garret—I think sometimes you're still a thirteen-year-old boy inside that head of yours. I've got to go say hello to the Whartons. So you two play nice. Got it?"

Thea laughed. "That's what you always used to say."

"And who would have thought I'd still have to say it now?"

Garret watched as his mother joined a group of friends on the other side of the room. And then he was with Thea—just her— the two of them standing still together, so the bustle and sweep of the crowd around them was like a river parting around an island. She smelled like vanilla and coffee, and she was wearing makeup. The effect of it—her eyes darkened to black, her lips shiny and pinkish brown—stopped him. Thea, the innocent he'd once known so well, had been replaced by this dazzling and worldly woman.

He did what he could: he steeled himself against her before he spoke. "So what is it that you're not telling my mother is wrong?"

"What makes you think something's wrong?"

"I can just tell." He leaned toward her, lowering his voice. "It's me, isn't it? Years of pent-up lust that you just can't get under control."

She laughed—a tight, nervous hiccup. Her eyes darted around the room, and he knew she was searching for a polite way to excuse herself. "Fine. If you must know, my head barista stood me up."

"What's she doing?"

"*He* just called and told me he's hungover, sleeping on somebody's floor, and can't get a ride here."

He glanced over at the coffee carafes and espresso machine that had been set up on a cloth-covered table in the corner. A young woman was frantically making drinks while partygoers waited in line. This was barely controlled chaos, and if he knew anything about Thea, it was probably driving her nuts. She prided herself on two things: coffee and customer service. And from the looks of the way that the barista was rushing through her cappuccinos, it seemed neither was being handled adequately.

He unbuttoned his suit jacket and put his hands in his pockets. "So I guess you'll need some help?"

She looked up at him, suspicious.

He smiled—the smile he always used when he wanted something. But usually he was angling to *receive* a favor, not the other way around. He cleared his throat. "You know . . . if you asked me to help you, I *might* be willing."

"You want me to ask you for help?"

"I'll make you a deal. You don't even have to say *please*."

"Thanks." She crossed her arms, glaring. "But I'll figure it out on my own."

He shrugged. It was stupid to have offered. *Of course* she would turn him down. "Suit yourself," he said.

Then—though it took everything in him not to tell her to stop acting stupid—he waved to his brother standing on the other side of the room and made himself walk away.

Garret had never liked English class—the poetry especially. *Shall I compare thee to a summer's day? How do I love thee? Let me count the* . . . He didn't care. Falling in love had not been part of the blueprint he was drawing of his future. He would graduate high school, get accepted to Notre Dame for soccer, then maybe—once he'd had plenty of time to date and rake in his social capital as a national soccer hero—he might think about falling in love and settling down.

But in his senior year, lying on a single beach towel with Thea, their feet sloping toward the whispering surf and the stars clear and unusually bright above their heads, he was beginning to see that love had taken the plans he'd so carefully laid out and burned them to the ground.

He'd thought, growing up in the shadow of his parents' relaxed companionship, that he would have more say in the logistics of falling in love, like picking the first player for his team in gym class. He'd believed he'd have some authority over *when, where,* and *why.* Based on what he saw between Ken and Sue, lasting love meant easy love—love that took afternoon naps, love that exchanged sections of the newspaper over breakfast, love that ran errands to the car wash and the bank.

But what he had with Thea was nothing like what his parents had—the way he felt about her was wild and greedy and intense. This was love that had him by the balls, love that led him like a dog through the hours of his own life. This was love that tormented him, moment by moment, with the threat of crushing his heart into sand.

He adjusted his legs beneath hers, denim sliding along denim. The surf whispered, and the moonlight caught the froth of the waves.

Regardless of what love was or wasn't, Thea had altered his plans. He no longer saw himself as a bachelor. Thea had dedicated herself to taking over the Dancing Goat after high school, and he worried about how they would be able to stay together during his semesters. He had to believe they would find a way.

He closed his eyes, airplanes gliding silently along the black sky, the cooling earth pushing the breeze out to the sea. The moment was perfect. He half thought of waking Thea up to say, "You don't want to miss this." But then it occurred to him, she was *this*—everything that was beautiful about the moment. All the promise and peace and completeness of it. He guessed that's what the poets were trying to say.

At the makeshift espresso bar, Thea did her best not to appear hysterical. Most of the guests knew her—or at least they knew Sue and Ken—and so they'd been exceptionally patient, some of them waiting a half hour for a latte or a shot. If Jules were here to help her as the third person on her little staff, she would have had the situation completely under control. But with each moment, the line was more fidgety and impatient. She was furious—and it was hard to tell if her anger was because Jules hadn't shown up, or if it was because he'd left her to embarrass herself in front of Garret—not to mention everyone else in town.

"Miss! Miss! What's an Americano?"

"It's a—"

"Excuse me," a man with a red bow tie cut in, "but I ordered a café breve ten minutes ago, and—"

"It's not done yet," Thea said.

"Terrible caterers at this hotel," a woman said.

Thea cut the flow of espresso when it turned from dark brown to the color of weak tea. She hated this. Failure at the Sorensens' party was more than just a personal disappointment; it was a reflection on her business. It could hurt her reputation among the Sorensens' Newport friends. She needed this to go well—or at least to be passable.

She plucked up her courage, tugged down the hem of her vest. She never broke down while she was working. Never. Rude customers had never made her duck into the back room to cry. Persnickety coffee snobs couldn't hold a candle to what she knew about her craft, and not even undecided customers who stood hemming and hawing while the lines grew long behind them could get under her skin. No, she never broke down.

But today, with the party going so badly and Jonathan across the room oblivious to her distress, and Garret glancing over from time to time as if he was enjoying her struggle—*enjoying* it, the bastard—

She lost her grip on a cup, and hot coffee dripped down the front of her.

"Rochelle." She put down the half-empty mug. "I'm taking a two-minute break. I'd tell you to hold down the fort, but it's probably too late."

"Do . . . do you have to?" Rochelle asked, panic showing in her childlike eyes.

"Yes," Thea said.

She walked out of the party, past Jonathan who had said only three polite words to her earlier and now didn't seem to notice her go. She wound her way down a maze of paisley-carpeted hallways until she eventually found a ladies' room. She leaned her hands on the granite sink, catching her breath. The brutal lighting and large mirror sugarcoated nothing: Her face was flushed, and not from makeup. Her hair was coming out in springy little curls around her face. She pressed a soft paper towel against the spot on her shirt and did her best to blot the stain.

"Come on," she told herself. "Get it together. You're fine."

And by the time she was making her way down the hall toward the party, she thought she was fine—really—until she got back to the espresso station, where Garret had taken off his suit jacket and rolled up the pale gray sleeves of his shirt and was pouring cold milk into a silver pitcher with such concentration that he didn't even notice when she stood by his side.

"What are you doing?" she asked.

He glanced at her over the hiss of the steam wand. A lock of blond hair fell across his forehead. "Making a dollop of foam for an espresso macchiato."

"You can make espresso?"

"I spent some time in Vienna. Long story."

She touched her forehead. Vienna? It sounded like such a crucial part of his life. How had she missed that?

He shot her a grin that would have felled a lesser woman. "You going to just stand there? Or you going to deliver that caramel latte to Mr. Richardson?"

She didn't need to be told twice. She picked up the latte, smiling as pleasantly as she could, and brought it to Ken's friend.

Over the course of the next twenty minutes, she found that everything was sliding slowly but steadily into place, the deluge becoming a more manageable trickle. Garret, to her amazement and consternation, awed her with how cheerfully and efficiently he'd taken on the jobs that needed to be done. At first, she bristled each time he handed her another drink for delivery—hating that he'd bailed her out, hating that the ship was sinking and needed bailing. But as the fast-flying minutes grew slower and less frantic, she realized that she liked the way he worked, the way he picked up on her system quickly, the way he joked with impatient people and put them at ease, the way he needed to be told something only once, if at all. Silently, the three of them tackled one drink after another, until at last the line dwindled down to nothing, and Thea felt as if the very air around them had gone slack with relief.

"Can I have a break?" Rochelle asked.

"Absolutely," Thea said, and she hadn't completely formed the word before Rochelle was walking away.

She stood with her hands on her hips, watching Garret tidy up a tray of abused sugar packets, and she felt the slight disorienting shift of going from insane busyness to having little to do. Though her body wanted to keep pressing frantically forward, she forced herself to breathe out, to consciously relax. She had one last thing to deal with before the madness was over.

"Garret." She tucked a stray curl behind her ear. "I don't know how to thank you."

He straightened up, abandoning the sugar. His perfect hair was mussed and his face was slightly sweaty. His pristine and expensive gray shirt was speckled with flecks of brown. "Don't worry about it."

"I've got it handled from here."

He wiped his hands with a cloth towel. "Are you going to fire the barista?"

For a moment, she thought he was talking about himself. But then she realized: "Jules? Nah. I have a feeling it was just a miscommunication."

Garret shook his head. "You're too easy on your employees."

"I've been running this business since I was nineteen," she said. "I think I do okay."

He frowned a little, and she could tell he hadn't meant to make her mad. Seeing him working—doing the menial job of taking orders and preparing drinks in front of the crème de la crème of Newport—something inside her opened to him. She wondered: Was this a peace offering? Or was he just trying to save the party from being an embarrassment to his parents?

"Last order," Garret said, and he handed her a mug of steaming coffee. It was warm against her cupped hands. Her body ached with tension, her head pounded. She pulled her shoulders back, scanning the crowd. "All right," she said, calling on her last reserves of energy. "Who does this go to?"

"No one," he said. "It's for you."

For a moment, she said nothing. When she looked up at him, his understated smile, his kind eyes, what she saw nearly undid her.

She took a sip of coffee, feeling strength return. "Thanks, Garret," she said.

From "The Coffee Diaries"
by Thea Celik

The Newport Examiner

When roasting coffee beans, it's critical to be able to control the heat levels, so that between the "first crack"—when the bean makes a popping sound—and the "second crack," when the bean is finished roasting, the temperature is raised slowly and carefully.

Timing is critical because there's more to good roasting than applying the correct external heat. After first crack, coffee beans stop *absorbing* heat from the outside and start *giving off* heat from the inside. For a brief period, they are no longer "being roasted"—instead, heat flows from within each bean into the environment, intensifying temperatures around them.

For that reason, roasting is an extremely delicate process—one that requires attention, precision, and care. Success, or sometimes failure, is in the smallest of details.

TWELVE

The city of Newport could tell by the color of the Narragansett that tourist season was officially gone. The friendly summer blue of the harbor had deepened, becoming a stark and uncompromising cobalt. The sidewalks and piers emptied out, boutiques along Newport's busy thoroughfares closed their doors earlier and earlier, and Thea too felt the shift in energy at the Dancing Goat that signaled the slow decline toward winter.

Claudine and Jules had cut back their hours to go back to school, and after a teary going-away party, Rochelle had left for the season altogether. The glossy veneer of summer tourism had worn down to a dull film, and on Price's Pier the rough-and-tumble, workaday roots set down by generations of New Englanders began to show through once again. Strangers were replaced by men and women who had known Thea since she'd been too small to see over the countertop of her own shop. Bins of notebooks and pencils went on sale, and all over the city parents laid out their children's new clothes for the first week of school.

Like Newport, Thea too could feel herself changing with the season—or at least, she felt herself itching for some kind of change. She tried kickboxing with Dani, and though she'd wound up falling flat on her butt and knew that she would never be quite the jock that Dani was, the experience had been worth a shot. Claudine had pressured her into going with her to see a French movie—since Thea had accidentally confessed that she'd never actually seen a foreign film—and though she ultimately decided she would rather watch her movies than read them, she couldn't shake the persistent need to try new things.

Deep edginess gripped her, a restlessness that should have been settled after the divorce went through. Newport itself seemed to fuel her uncertainty. New England seasons were fickle— sometimes shy and bashful, sometimes cruel. She'd seen a hurricane come up the coast, making the waves boil up over embankments and battering boats into smithereens. She'd seen snow descend silent and gentle as starlight to blanket the beaches, deceptive in its aggression and the damage it did. In the summers, she'd watched the thunderstorms that popped up out over the water, lightning touching down in the distance, long dark smears of rainfall against the sky, nearing the shore.

She'd survived all those things throughout her life in Newport. And as the weather cooled and she needed to wrap a light sweater around her shoulders in the evening, she began to feel glad, even relieved, that the season was ending—because it seemed to her that the entire summer had been a kind of storm. And somehow she'd survived that too.

Garret hesitated near the enormous old anchor that had been propped up as a monument on Price's Pier, not far from the dark little alley that led to the Dancing Goat. Along the edge of the pier, tall-masted sailboats with gleaming wooden decks bobbed in the water. Crude lobster boats, pulling at their tethers, were strewn with thick chains and tarpaulins. The afternoon might have been perfect for a short stroll and a long nap, but Garret was too racked by nerves to enjoy it.

"So?" His buddy Jamie stood at his side, squinting into the sunlight. He wore a blue and white shirt covered in hibiscus flowers—he'd not yet been persuaded that summer was gone. "So, are we going for coffee or just standing around lapsing into caffeine withdrawal?"

Garret checked his watch as if he had anywhere else to be. "Yeah. All right. If you want to."

"I'm pretty sure you're the one who brought it up. Come on. Unless you changed your mind . . ."

Garret started across the redbrick wharf toward the Dancing Goat, forcing Jamie to follow. "It's fine."

"I know your ex sister-in-law works there. If that's going to be a problem . . ."

"It's *fine*," Garret said, and he walked a little faster to make a point.

For as long as Garret cared to remember, the main problem of his otherwise impressive life had been the fact that he hadn't wanted to see or even hear about Thea. The mention of her name at his parents' dinner table had made him cringe, made him want to throw down his fork and say, "No more." News of Jonathan's life coming to him from a distance—in conversation with a cousin, in matter-of-fact e-mails—plagued him with reminders that his relationship with Jonathan had been damaged by a woman he'd once loved. Since the day Jonathan had married her, Garret had spent much of his time trying to solve the problem of how to connect with his brother while refusing to see her.

And yet now, the problem had turned on its head. His difficulty was no longer that he didn't want to see Thea. The difficulty was that he *did* want to—with far more curiosity than was acceptable. He felt more unsettled now that he'd made peace with her than when all he'd known was anger. Since Jonathan had started picking up Irina, Garret no longer had a reason to see or even call her. He had the sense that something was off that he couldn't quite pinpoint, as if a cold draft was seeping into his life, and no matter how he searched he could not find its source.

He wondered about her. Was she still the woman he once knew?

His heart pounded alarmingly hard as they walked down the alley toward the coffee shop door. He knew he shouldn't go inside. He should wait out here. Pretend he had to make a phone call. Give Jamie his order.

And yet, he saw his hand reach for the door handle. Saw himself moving through the jamb into the small room, with its board and batten walls and glass pastry display that came up to his chest. He was eager, ready. He wanted to see Thea, wanted her to know that he'd come expressly for the purpose of seeing her. He was prepared to say, "I just happened to be in town," and he trusted her to know exactly what the words would mean.

Unfortunately, she was nowhere to be found. The boy making coffee was young, skinny, with long dark hair and paint under his nails. A question was burning on the edge of Garret's tongue, and he almost heard himself voice it: *Is Thea here?*

But of course, he kept quiet. It shouldn't matter if she was here. He had nothing to say to her—no message to deliver from Jonathan, no excuse for saying hello. What right did he have, after so many years of hatred, to take the liberties of friendship? He ordered a cup of coffee. In a way, he was glad she wasn't here. Otherwise, his whim—which had seemed like such a good idea moments ago—would have embarrassed him.

He felt Jamie clasp him on the back while the barista made change. "Hey, man. Look at that. You lucked out."

"Looks like," he said. His coffee burned his hand.

As Thea neared her high school graduation, the days grew longer and longer—not because of the seasons but because she could hardly wait to put the matter of her virginity to rest. It had taken on monumental importance in her mind, constantly occupying her thoughts while she watched her geometry teacher sketch triangles on the blackboard or listened to her history teacher drone on about FDR. She loved to torment herself with the question (*what would it be like?*) and the promise (*it would be soon*). Sex would hurt for a moment—she expected that—but Garret was experienced, and she trusted him to be gentle. She imagined that afterward, he would hold her close and tell her he loved her, that they might drift off to sleep in each other's arms.

In the hallways of her school—papered with red and black streamers for one senior class function after another—she walked past rows of lockers with the feeling that she was being watched. She and Garret were public now, and while no one was completely surprised, there was some general consternation that the boy who had been chosen prom king had fallen for *her*. But she held her head high, ignoring jokes and barbs alike, because Garret loved her—he'd chosen her—and soon she would give herself entirely to him.

Of everyone who'd learned of her relationship with Garret, only Jonathan had truly worried her. Her parents were thrilled, doting on Garret as if he'd proposed. Sue had actually gone a little teary-eyed when she'd learned that Thea and her son were officially a couple. And Ken had clasped Thea's shoulders and said how pleased he was, since Thea was the only girl in Rhode Island who could keep Garret in line.

But Jonathan had changed. He no longer loaded up his car with duffel bags full of dirty laundry and made weekend trips to Newport—though she'd called and called and asked him where he'd been. The early days of running amok through the crowded beachgoers at King Park or making faces at the eerie funerary statues of Island Cemetery were becoming a distant memory. Jonathan grew especially cold toward Garret; at one point, just days after Garret had learned he'd gotten an athletic scholarship that would guarantee he could attend Notre Dame, the brothers had a shouting match over a sink full of spaghetti-crusted dishes, and for the first time since Thea had met them, she worried they would come to blows. From where Thea stood, the brighter Garret shined, the duller Jonathan became.

"I'm warning you," Jonathan told her one night at a burger joint after his spring semester had ended. "Things are going to go wrong. I've been picking up the pieces after my brother for my whole life. And Thea, I don't want to have to pick you up too."

She'd laughed at the time, leaned her shoulder against his, and told him to stop acting more motherly than his mother. But in her heart, she worried. She felt almost as if Jonathan was preparing her for the day that Garret would push her away—and the day that Jonathan would be ready and waiting with open arms.

Thea stood in front of the espresso machine with the barista she'd hired to replace Rochelle, a boy who had written down his name as Frank Radfern, but who insisted that everyone call him Tenke. Thea had taken an immediate liking to him—his jagged dark hair slicked severely to the side like a raven's wing, the three stars tattooed on his neck, and his enormous dark-rimmed glasses and skinny jeans. Tenke might not have had a future in corporate America, but as a small-business owner Thea knew that the best employees sometimes came in the most irregular packages.

"And now for the fun part," she said. She pulled two separate shots of espresso into mismatched demitasses, so shimmery gold crema floated evenly on the surface of each cup. "I want you to know what a good cappuccino tastes like. So that means you get to drink."

"Do I have to, like, pay for stuff while I'm working?" he asked.

"You don't," she said. "But no making free drinks for your friends."

She talked him through the process of making microfoam first, showing him that perfect steamed milk for a latte had no visible bubbles and a consistency that was more creamy than foamy. For fun, she topped off his latte with a bit of artistry—a rosette of brown and white swirls, which she etched with a coffee stirrer.

"Do I have to do that too?" Tenke asked.

"Not on your first day."

She heard Jules chuckle a few feet away. "Show-off."

She winked at him.

"Are you going to tell him about the monks now?" he asked.

"None of your business," she said.

While Tenke sipped his latte, she made him a cappuccino so he could see how different the frothing techniques were when done properly. Cappuccino foam, she told him, should be airy, with bubbles of even size, so it could sit on top of a shot of espresso rather than sink down into it. "What we don't want," she said, "is dish-sponge foam, like the kind that suds up when you're washing your hands. Macrofoam should be dry but not overly stiff. Don't worry, you don't have to be able to master it all today."

"What's this about monks?" Tenke asked, dipping the tip of his finger into the foam of his cappuccino.

"Coffee lore," Thea said. She glanced up as Lettie came through the door and stopped for a moment to chat with a few of their regular customers.

"I'll tell him about the Capuchins," Jules said, taking the cloth for the steam wand from Thea's hands.

"Why?"

"Because I owe you one."

"For the anniversary debacle? You owe me ten," Thea said.

"Right," Jules said. He turned abruptly to Tenke, giving Thea his shoulder. "So one day there was this monk who wanted to wear a brown hood—the Italians called it a *cappa*—but the other monks wouldn't let him . . ."

Thea rolled her eyes. Jules had always been such a social creature, the hub around which her younger baristas perpetually spun. But he was damn good at making espresso, and she trusted him to train her new hires right.

At the other end of the counter, away from the training session, she helped Lettie with the bags she'd picked up at the sandwich shop on her way over to the Dancing Goat. Lettie regularly got away with wearing something other than the typical coffee brown that Thea usually insisted upon. In a grasshopper green shirt and elastic-waist jeans, she was the only person who had been working at the coffee shop longer than the dress code had existed. Thea figured that made her the exception.

"Can we take lunch now?" Lettie asked, digging around in the paper bags for her sandwich.

"Sure you can."

"No, I mean, can you and I take lunch now? In your office?" Lettie asked.

"Of course," Thea said casually, though the hair at the nape of her neck stood on end.

Together, they carried their food into Thea's small office. Lettie had to clean off a chair that had been covered with Irina's toys in order to sit down at the desk. Thea unwrapped her eggplant sandwich, the smell of fresh basil rising up and making her stomach rumble.

"How have you been doing?" Lettie asked.

Thea had started to take a bite, but stopped. "Fine."

"Well you *seem* fine, I have to say. But how are you really?"

"I'm . . . *fine*," Thea said. "Should I not be?"

Lettie rested her wrist on the cracked black-leather arm of her chair. "I just thought someone should tell you. He didn't notice me because I was working in back, but Garret came in the other day. To see you."

Thea blinked. "Did he ask for me?"

"Well, not that I heard."

"He didn't say he was here to see me?"

"He didn't have to say it, dear—"

"Then he must have just wanted a drink," Thea said, and she took a big bite of her sandwich.

Lettie made the face that she always made when she was disappointed that Thea didn't get something right away. "I mean—given your history and all . . ."

Thea shook her head and covered her mouth when she spoke. "*Ancient* history. I don't think you should read anything into it."

"If you say so," Lettie said. "Forgive me for saying this, but I remember how it was. You two kids were about as in love as Romeo and Juliet. I may be seventy-seven, but I know that if my husband—rest his soul—walked in the door right now after twenty-three years, I wouldn't assume it was because he was thirsty for a *drink*."

Thea swallowed too big a bite. It hurt going down. She hoped she was doing a good job of making it seem as if Lettie's news hadn't affected her. But the fact was she'd been thinking of Garret ever since his parents' anniversary party, and some part of her was beginning to feel curious about him, about the *new* him, whoever he might be. Given his unusual, voluntary cameo at the coffee shop, she wondered if he was thinking the same thing.

"I appreciate your telling me this," Thea said. "You've always looked out for me. But you might be happy to know that Garret and I had a long talk, to get everything out once and for all, and it looks like we're going to be—I don't know—maybe even friends. In fact, he bailed me out at Sue and Ken's party the other day when I needed help."

"He did? That was nice of him. I'm so sorry I couldn't go . . ."

"You were missed," Thea said, and she breathed a sigh of relief to think that they might be done talking about Garret. "Sue and Ken had a great time."

Lettie dabbed at her mouth with a napkin. When she spoke again, her eyes were wells of tenderness and care. "Darling, I know you don't need advice on how to live your life. But it's seemed to me that you've always been very good at being happy. That whatever life throws at you, you just make do with it."

"I would think that's a good thing," Thea said.

"And it is! Oh don't get me wrong, it is! But you didn't used to be that way."

Thea leaned back in her seat. "Do you mean that you think I'm doing something wrong?"

Lettie gave a small frown. "On the contrary. I think you're starting to do things right. And I'm happy for you. I really am."

"Thank you," Thea said, though she still felt a bit unsure about what Lettie was getting at. "I think I've got everything under control, actually. The divorce went through, but Jonathan and I are getting along. Things with his family are good. Irina's a little touch-and-go lately, but otherwise, everything's okay."

"I'm glad," Lettie said. "But the thing is . . . contentment is for when you get old and lazy. Happiness takes work. You have to risk something to get it. I'm just saying that, well, if you find something that makes you happy—wildly, blissfully, amazingly happy—you'll go and get it and not hold back."

Thea looked up, guilt-stricken. It occurred to her: perhaps it was no coincidence that Lettie's pep talk was coming on the heels of a conversation about Garret. She was sure there was a connection. Was Lettie rooting for her and Garret? The idea was so preposterous it would have made Thea laugh aloud—if she wasn't so horrified. "I hope you're not saying I should chase after Garret. I don't even know him anymore."

"Rubbish," Lettie said. "But anyway, I'm not only talking about Garret. I'm just saying that whatever it is that makes you happy, you should go after it. Your heart *knows*. You just have to listen. That's all."

Jules knocked on the open door and stuck his head in the room. "Thea? You told me to tell you when the milk delivery guy is here? Well, he is."

Thea stood up from her chair, glad for the excuse to interrupt the conversation. Had Garret come to the Dancing Goat looking for her? She couldn't bring herself to believe it. And yet, some part of her wanted to.

"Excuse me," she told Lettie. "I have to go argue about an overcharge."

"Of course." Lettie picked a bit of wilted lettuce from her sandwich. "Just think about what I said."

So how are you doing? was the question people asked Jonathan again and again. And they didn't mean *So what are you up to these days?* or *How is your morning going?* Each *So how are you doing?* had its own cautious and unsaid meaning.

From his mother: *Are you happy, my love? Is there anything I can do to make you happy?*

From his coworkers: *I know what happened to you, poor bastard. You brought it on yourself, but still, I hope you're hanging in.*

From Garret: *So what comes next, now that the divorce is final? When do you want to start dating? When do you get back on your feet?*

From Thea: *I'm not sorry this happened. And I want you to be okay.*

Mostly, Jonathan's answers were the same, no matter who asked the question. And in fact, he was getting on rather well. His divorce had not been the radical life change that it might have been if he and Thea were different people. He still had his daughter. He had his brother again. And his ex-wife didn't feel like an ex at all, but instead, like a long-lost and newly rediscovered friend.

He read more books, started training for a marathon, and saw his daughter on the weekends. He fought against loneliness with everything in him.

How are you doing? he asked himself.

The answer: *All in all, okay.*

On the aluminum bleachers at the soccer field, Thea sat watching her daughter run from one end zone to another in the first scrimmage of the year. The other team was winning by one goal, and Irina seemed to have taken the error personally, her face crumpling in intense concentration and her little legs pumping as fast as they would carry her downfield. She'd tried a couple shots on goal, and Thea had gripped the cold edge of the bleacher in anticipation, her jaw clenched and her gaze riveted. But Irina just couldn't seem to score.

Thea sat quietly, clutching her cup of hot chocolate and espresso.

Where Irina's love of soccer had come from was completely baffling. It seemed to have arrived so abruptly, independent of Thea or Jonathan's interests. A spontaneous generation. Jonathan had never once watched a soccer tournament; neither had Thea. No one had breathed a whisper that Irina should take an interest in the game.

Yet even before Irina had been old enough to sign up for soccer, she'd been obsessed with it—begging her parents to record the New England Revolution's game so she didn't miss a moment, begging to stay up past her bedtime to watch the end of a half. Thea and Jonathan could only sit with her, far more engrossed by their daughter's astonishing and unexplainable enthusiasm than they could ever be in the score.

Thea wasn't surprised when she saw Jonathan making his way toward the bleachers; though he didn't follow professional soccer, he'd always loved watching his daughter play. But she *was* surprised to see that the man walking beside him wasn't a fellow soccer dad but was Garret, holding a hot dog on a paper plate in one hand and his cell phone in the other.

She waved toward them as if she hadn't been taken aback, and she tried to reason with herself to stay calm. It wasn't surprising that Garret would come to see his niece tear up the turf. In fact, Thea was glad that Irina and Garret had something in common— even if, during Irina's younger years, Thea sometimes had the sense that the universe had conjured a passion for soccer in Irina because Thea had once stolen that same passion from Garret. Irina would be thrilled to see her uncle and father—and even more committed to winning the game.

And yet, the question that Thea could not overlook, the question that she could not grip firmly enough to cast aside—was whether or not Garret came not only to see Irina, but her too.

"Hey guys!" she smiled up at them and scooted down to make room. Jonathan slid in beside her, Garret beside him.

"How we doing?" Jonathan asked, scouring the field to find his daughter.

Thea pointed. "Not so great. Coach just benched her, put in a substitute."

"Bull," she heard Garret say.

"Was she due to sit out?" Jonathan asked.

Thea shook her head. "I don't think so. But she was getting a little too . . . intense."

"Shame," Jonathan said.

Garret leaned forward so Thea could see him. He wore a Red Sox baseball cap over his blond hair, but beneath the brim was the sparkling blue of his eyes. "Want me to talk to the coach?"

Thea laughed, and then she saw he was serious.

"What? She wants to play, she should be allowed to play. I'll have her back out there in fifteen seconds flat."

"I'm sure you will," Thea said, and she meant it. Garret had a silver tongue, a way of persuading people. He would probably talk about the team's record, about how all the parents—even those whose kids weren't exactly athletes—would rather leave here celebrating a win than see their kid play for an extra five minutes and lose. In Thea's mind, there was no doubt that Garret could persuade the coach to put Irina back in. But Irina had to learn to fight her own battles.

Jonathan glanced at his brother. "Hey, remember that time you talked Mr. Fairfax into giving you and Thea permission to cut last period so we could go to Adventureland?"

Garret laughed. "And there was that bumper boat operator who thought Thea was cute, so we could just keep jumping the lines?"

Thea couldn't help but smile a little. "True. We had your powers of persuasion to thank for that day."

"That and your denim shorts," Garret said.

She heard Jonathan snicker beside her, and though she felt a little jolted to remember the shorts in question, which Garret had unbuttoned too many times to count, she too couldn't help but laugh.

"She's talking to the coach," Jonathan said, nodding toward the field. Irina had risen from the bench and made her way over to the adults on the sideline. She stood directly in front of the head coach in her red nylon shorts and shin guards. If she were tall enough, she would have stared him down, eye to eye. "Ten to one says he puts her back in."

They watched quietly for a moment, all of them rooting for her. Thea couldn't hear a thing over the shouts of the spectators around them, so she was scrutinizing body language: Irina's head was held high, her ponytail bobbing violently as she talked, so that Thea knew she was lecturing. The coach's bemused smile, his crossed arms, the tilt of his head said, *I'm listening.*

A moment later, they were cheering and clapping together as Irina jogged back onto the field, back into the game. Jonathan put his arm around Thea and squeezed. Garret punched a fist into the air.

So this is how it's going to be, Thea thought. The three of them. Together. Just like in the old days. On the fading grass, Irina made a charge for the ball, running out in front of the crowd with fiery resolve. Maybe they had come full circle, at last.

In the fourth quarter, when Irina tumbled into another player, Garret knew she was hurt. He couldn't tell exactly what had happened. She and another girl had gone rolling onto the ground together like a pinwheel of arms and legs. She got up—of course— fast to her feet, and she'd even managed to run three more steps, never losing sight of the ball, the goaltender, the one point that would secure them a win. But her pain reflexes were delayed— Garret knew from personal experience how fast adrenaline kicked in—and after three steps, she crumpled, rolling to the ground, grabbing her ankle, her face contorted with pain.

He didn't wait. He jumped from the bleachers, running onto the field. He didn't care if he was breaking some kind of unwritten friends-and-family policy. Jonathan had left an hour ago, realizing he'd forgotten his laptop at work. Thea had gone in search of a restroom, and Irina needed help. He beat the coaches to her, sprinting past them while they jogged, and when he got there, she was lying on her side, not crying but dazed.

"What hurts?" he said. "Your foot?"

"My foot?" She lifted her head to look down at it; it was swelling. "My foot and my head."

He ran a hand lightly over the spot just above her ear; a hard knot was already swelling. They would need to get her checked out. The coaches huddled around her, stooped with their hands on their thighs, asking questions. Panic flashed in Irina's eyes—fear that seemed to be fed more by the coaches' worrying than by pain.

"What happened?" Thea was beside him, breathless. He saw her focus sharpening, the intense concentration in her eyes. She wasn't overreacting; he could see her mapping out the situation, drawing up plans.

"I think she sprained her ankle. The coach is getting ice."

Thea nodded. "It's not broken?"

"I don't think so," Garret said. He took Thea's arm and stood with her, taking a few steps away from Irina for a moment and leaving her in the care of another player's mom. A cold wind sliced through the fabric of his jacket. "There's something else. I think she got kicked in the head. We should take her to the doctor, ASAP. Get her checked for a concussion."

"We walked here. I don't have a car."

"Not a problem," he said.

The walls of the high school locker room were imprinted on Garret's mind. A lattice of red steel lockers. Water bottles and crumpled jeans. Fountains too low to drink from. The bright, high energy of the gym after victory. The solemn and gloomy trudging to the showers after defeat.

He remembered what it was like to play hurt. A shin bruise the size of a saucer and the color of eggplant. A twisted knee or ankle, pain that nearly crippled him walking from one hallway to another, but that somehow vanished the moment the starting whistle blew. In the weight room he trained his muscles to be strong and agile, and on the field he trained for pain. When he went pro, the presence of pain would become more normal than the lack of it. But he welcomed it—all because of the game.

He remembered too icing his elbow in the locker room or bandaging an ankle, while around him his teammates ribbed each other and gossiped as much as, or more than, the cheerleading squad. On good days—like Fridays, when the amped-up expectations of the weekend were setting in—it never failed that talk in the locker room was talk that veered in the direction of women and then of sex. Garret loved it. He'd discovered somewhere along the line that he was a great storyteller—good at capturing the attention and the imagination of a crowd. He'd never been self-conscious about bragging—or embellishing when it came to things he hadn't quite done. And over time he'd acquired a reputation for scoring bigger, higher, and faster than any of his teammates—and not just on the soccer field.

The trend didn't stop when he started dating Thea.

You banging her yet? his friends wanted to know.

Garret had tossed his soccer uniform into his duffel bag, buying time. He knew it was inevitable—that it would come to this, as it always did. If Thea were any other woman he might have given them details—insinuations about skill or assets, kinks or trysts. But she wasn't any other woman. He wanted to clam up and say *butt out*. The trouble was, if the guy who had spent years going into detail about his sex life suddenly wouldn't tell them a thing, he would give away too much.

So he did the only thing he could do. The thing they expected him to do. He gave them a few details. He let them read between the lines.

And though he didn't know it at the time, the kind of pain he was in training for had nothing to do with wrists or knees— nothing to do with soccer. He would learn soon enough that he couldn't ice down heartbreak. And he couldn't heal injuries that weren't his own.

Thea leaned against the refrigerator door, cool air and soft light falling on her bare feet. The window over the kitchen sink was beginning to go dark, and she had no idea how long she'd been standing there with the notion of getting something to drink. From the kitchen, she could hear the television set playing softly in the next room, where Irina was settled into the couch, a sprained and bandaged ankle propped up on the armrest and a bowl of three-color ice cream on her lap.

"Need something?"

Garret was behind her, and she wondered when he'd come back from the bathroom and how long he'd been standing there. Discomposed, she reached into the fridge to grab herself a bottle of water, then thought better of it and reached for white wine. "I'm guessing you're a beer drinker," she said. "But all I can offer is chardonnay."

"Anything's fine."

She took two glasses down from the cabinet, poured, and handed him a glass. In her favorite pair of worn-out jeans and her fleece pullover, with the day's stress no doubt showing on her face, she was sure she looked terrible.

They'd spent the entire evening together in the emergency room—talking to doctors, talking to each other about Irina, talking to Jonathan on the phone—and yet in spite of all they'd been through in the course of a few hours, being alone with him in her kitchen was making her feel edgy and self-conscious. Everything familiar about him standing in her kitchen was butting up against everything unfamiliar, and it made her feel a little like she'd gotten mixed up in layers of time.

"It looks like I have to thank you again," she said.

"Don't think I'm not going to call in a favor," he said, smiling. "It's part of my job description."

She handed him a glass of wine. Something in the motion, the transferring of weight from her fingertips to his, felt too intimate to bear. "Do you always do that?"

"Do what?"

"That smooth, joking around, small talk thing? Do you do it all the time or only when you're uncomfortable?"

He laughed heartily; she thought that it, too, was fake. "I live to entertain."

She couldn't help looking at him a moment, his face that had always been so handsome. His soft blond hair and slightly over-sized lips. She nearly laughed to think of how many times she had kissed him, promised her future to him. And yet, all of that seemed a dream now.

"Did you come to the coffee shop last week?" she asked. To her surprise, she thought she saw some color touch his cheeks. She'd embarrassed him.

"Who told you that?"

"My baristas are my front line. Nothing gets by them." She watched him carefully, not hiding the fact that she was watching. Garret seemed uneven to her—sometimes his words sounded so false and overly cheerful, and other times she felt as if he wore his heart on his sleeve. She found herself watching for those moments of honesty, for the real Garret, like sun shining between clouds. "Why didn't you mention that you'd stopped in?"

He rubbed the back of his neck. "Ever since you gave me that double shot of espresso, I can't go back to the old stuff. I stopped in for another round."

"So I ruined you for other baristas."

"Don't be so modest," he said.

She laughed, and then they both were laughing, more than the joke deserved.

"You like running the coffee shop?" he asked.

"Sure."

"Jonathan said you're there all the time."

"I like to work."

"Do you?" he asked. "Because I could never tell if running the coffee shop was something you really loved doing, or whether you just sort of fell into it."

"Why does everyone keep saying that?"

He looked at her for a long moment over the rim of his wine-glass. Thea held herself perfectly still. She supposed she knew what was coming.

"Why did you marry him?"

She turned away on the pretense of loading a few dishes into the dishwasher. "It wasn't revenge, if that's what you're thinking."

"Telling me why you *didn't* marry him doesn't answer the question."

She rolled her eyes. Talking with Garret had always been inter-esting when they were kids; now that he was trained in the art, it was nothing shy of thrilling. She liked that he pushed her, that she didn't know what he was going to say next. "I love him," she said. "He asked me to marry him, and I couldn't think of a better way to spend my life."

"You mean a *safer* way."

She said nothing.

"Everyone knew you weren't right for each other," he said. She bristled at the confident tone of his voice. "You had no chemistry."

"What was I supposed to do?" she asked, angry now. "Wait around for you?"

His pretty smile fell clear off his face, and she felt instantly gratified.

"You're a lot different now than I thought you'd be," she said. She finished loading a few of Irina's plastic cups into the dishwasher. She wished there were more. She dried her hands and picked up her wine.

"How so?"

"I figured you would have gotten married. Started a family. You'd always talked about it."

"Momentary insanity." He flashed his blockbuster smile. "We were kids. Neither one of us knew what we wanted."

Yes we did, she thought.

"You, on the other hand, are living exactly the life I thought you'd live. Settled down. Married. In your parents' house. Running the shop. Having a kid . . . Thea, your life could have been a paint by numbers from those days to this."

"You're wrong," she said.

"How do you figure?"

She held his eye. "I've been trying new things. Taking risks. Meeting people."

"Oh really."

"And anyway, I'm not settled down. I'm divorced."

"Right. From my brother," he said.

For a moment, the seconds stretched long between them. The window to the street had darkened, so only the faintest glow from the streetlight came in. The clock above the table ticked loudly. The blue of Garret's eyes was flecked with nickel and a question Thea didn't quite know how to read.

For years she had been telling herself that there was nothing left of him inside her—that he'd become irrelevant to her present life. But she saw now that she was wrong, that there was still some part of him that was important to her. Some part of what had passed between them had shaped her, continued to shape her, even while she was married to Jonathan, and even now.

"I should go," he said.

She put down her wine. He did the same. "You were great today. I don't know what I would have done without you."

He crossed the room, silent, and she summoned up all her cordiality, her good feelings toward him. She wanted to treat him like she would treat any old friend.

"Thanks again for everything," she said. "Get home safe."

He frowned at her from where he stood near the door. "You should know something."

She waited.

"We may have found some sort of . . . I don't know . . . balance, or whatever you want to call it. But what you did to me . . . I don't think we can be friends."

"Suit yourself," she said as lightly as she could. And she opened the door.

Beneath the last of the light fading in the sky, Garret walked to his car. And then he walked past it, the sidewalk leading him on. Her street had changed little in the last fifteen years, owners wishing to preserve the historic character of the city—shutters and sash windows, steep gables and wrought-iron lamps. It was as if the neighborhood was a time capsule, a place that had been preserved until his return.

He'd learned something today—a thing that made him want to leap for joy and cry into his hands all at the same time. He still knew her. All this time, and he still knew her. She hadn't changed so much that he could no longer recognize that which was fundamentally *her*.

At the hospital today, he'd seen that she was still generous, still caring. Everyone near her was drawn in by her, children especially. In the waiting room she'd temporarily adopted a scrawny five-year-old with a stick-on tattoo, but she didn't skimp on paying attention to her own child. Her calm and assurance when the doctors shined a bright light into Irina's eyes made her daughter—and even him—feel like she had everything under control.

It dazzled him that so much of her was still in place. Little things had changed, like the way she did her hair or the way she took her coffee or what she liked on her pizza—but he knew her, still. And somehow, the thought made him feel like he could still mean something to her, which in turn made him feel gratified and hopeful and happy—and just plain terrible too.

For years he'd built Thea into something she wasn't. He'd determined that everything good he saw in her must have been the result of self-delusion, and everything bad about her was fact. He'd begun to wonder if he'd imagined her.

But tonight he knew he had not. Though friendship was probably impossible between them, she was real flesh and blood. Real enough, he knew, to be missed.

From "The Coffee Diaries"
by Thea Celik

The Newport Examiner

If you've ever given a little kid a sip of coffee, you probably had a chuckle at the child's reaction to the brew.

Coffee, some people say, is an acquired taste. Most of us aren't born loving that bitter tang coffee leaves in our mouths. Other common foods that don't immediately please our palates are beer, olives, and wine.

It's still something of a mystery to scientists that the sip of coffee that made your nose curl in agony as a child can make you salivate in agony as an adult. Repeated exposure to unwelcome tastes is thought to encourage appreciation, changing flavors that must be acquired into flavors that are enjoyed.

But there's a danger in purposely trying to acquire an acquired taste. If you don't like coffee, it is entirely possible to make yourself believe that you like it—to the point that you actually do start thinking you like it, even if you don't.

The trick is knowing yourself well enough to grasp the subtle difference between embracing an acquired taste and conforming to expectations—whether society's or your own.

THIRTEEN

Thea was sitting at her desk paying bills when her computer made the noise that meant she had a new e-mail.

Dear Thea,

I'm writing to you about your daughter Irina. I'm concerned about her behavior. Would you be willing to come in and speak with me one day next week?

Lori Caisse

A knot formed in Thea's stomach. Lori Caisse was Irina's homeroom teacher. Not good.

Dear Lori,

Of course. Just name the time and place.

Thea
P.S. I hope everything's okay.

In the lunchroom and the library, speculation was only natural: Thea had expected her friends to ask: *Are you sleeping with Garret?* And though it wasn't their business, she'd never been one to withhold facts. She'd told them: No.

But every few days, they asked again. And again. *How long,* they said, *can you hold out?* She became so used to answering their endless questions that she very nearly became comfortable doing it. Until one day in the morning before school as they lounged outside near the flagpole, she affirmed for the hundredth time that she was not sleeping with Garret, but she didn't get the usual response.

"Really? That's not what he says."

The blow had landed like a punch in the gut. She could picture the scene perfectly—Garret talking to his buddies. Making her the same as all the other girls he dated. Kissing and telling. The thought made her sick.

"Well, we're not," Thea had said.

All day she carried the shame of revelation with her. All those hundreds of invisible eyes that were turned on her in friendly speculation now seemed to be turned on her in malice, and as she walked down the hall, her books clutched to her chest, she saw herself as they saw her: She was telling them that she was not sleeping with Garret and he was telling them she was. She didn't know how she would make it to the end of the day.

And yet, she did make it. At first she didn't say anything to

Garret about what she'd heard. He came to her in her bedroom at midnight, kissed her, panted against her neck, until all their bittersweet and tenacious want had finally burned itself out without having been satiated. He lay with her, his breath light as clouds, his body hot beneath her hand, his eyes closed in exhaustion.

She asked him, "Did you tell the soccer team that we're sleeping together?"

He was quiet a moment before he answered. "Yes."

"Why did you?"

He propped himself up on one hand. "To get them off my back."

"But you bragged to them. You brought everyone in. This was supposed to be ours . . ."

"You don't understand what it's like," he said.

He kissed her forehead. She turned away slightly, the floor hard beneath her head, and in the darkness she could just make out the shape of boxes and blankets beneath her bed. She didn't know what to make of this—of everything surrounding sex. Girls much younger than her had been doing it for years, with hardly a thought, it seemed. For them, there was no gravity, no deep-seated fear, no desperation. They liked sex the way they liked a good meal or a trip to the amusement park—things to anticipate joyfully and easily, and afterward, things that could be let go.

But with Garret, Thea did not have that uncomplicated, breezy feeling. She worried about what Jonathan had said—that Garret was only after one thing. And that once he got it, he would go.

"I wish you hadn't told them one way or the other," she said. "But I guess there's worse things."

She felt his hand along her spine, his fingers tracing the ridges where her hair trailed down. She tried to hold herself away from his touch—so much want collecting within her like rainwater, near to overflowing.

She leaned down, kissed the contours of his mouth that she was getting to know so well. "Next month we graduate," she said. She kissed his cheekbones, the ridge of his eyebrows, the bump of his chin. "Can you wait that long?"

When he looked at her his eyes were steely and clear. "No," he said. "But I will."

Thea stood at the kitchen counter, folding slices of Swiss onto turkey sandwiches for her and Sue. Irina's swollen ankle had apparently translated into a great excuse for Sue to shower her granddaughter with presents: a remote-controlled car, a bag full of new books and DVDs, and the promise of a trip to the Providence Children's Museum once Irina was "back on her foot."

Sue came into the kitchen and sat down at the table. The day was unusually hot for September, and she was fanning herself with a women's magazine.

"Do you like avocado for your side salad?" Thea asked.

"I can stand it if it's in something," she said, a slight lilt to her voice. "But otherwise, no thanks."

Thea finished preparing their plates, then took one into the living room, where Irina was lounging in her pajamas. She set the plate down on her daughter's lap.

"No, Maaaaa," Irina whined. "I don't like avocado."

"Try it anyway."

"I have tried it; I don't like it."

"Try it again," she said, laughing to herself. She hadn't liked avocados as a girl either, but she loved them now.

When she got back to the kitchen Sue was already nibbling at her salad, and Thea joined her, glad for adult company. Irina was driving her crazy these days; her appointment with her daughter's teacher could not come soon enough.

"She seems to be doing well," Sue said.

"Pretty well."

"And how's Mom?"

"I'm okay," Thea said.

Sue sprinkled a bit of Italian dressing on the dark leaves of her salad. "Garret told me he went to the hospital with you."

"He was great with Irina the other day. I'm glad he was there to help."

"Help you or Irina?"

"Both," Thea said.

Sue worked a bit of salad onto her fork. "That son of mine gives me more gray hairs than I know what to do with. I've been trying to set him up with Kate Cooper for three weeks now. They'd be perfect together. Did you know she's a rock climber? Yes, along with being the VP at the hedge fund, she also climbs rocks—with no ropes. She's perfect for him. But of course, you know Garret. He won't even meet her."

Thea wiped her hands on her napkin. She could picture Garret turning on the charm for a woman as a favor to his mother, but she couldn't imagine him dating unless he really wanted to. He didn't like be told what to do.

"Maybe he likes being single," Thea suggested.

"He doesn't," Sue said. "He's never liked being single. He just likes to pretend. You must know that, Thea. Even as a kid, he was so serious about his relationship with you. And kids who are that serious when they're that young don't usually grow up to be dedicated bachelors."

Thea took a bite of her sandwich. She didn't know why, but Sue's voice seemed different. Tense. Thea couldn't remember the last time Sue had mentioned her and Garret in the same sentence. To Sue, it was as if Thea's brief relationship with Garret had never happened. Once Thea and Garret had split, Sue had never looked back. Until—Thea watched her friend pull a piece of turkey out of her sandwich and pop it in her mouth—now.

"Maybe there's something I can do to help," Thea said. "Something that might speed the process along . . ."

"That's sweet. But once Garret digs his heels in, there's nothing anyone can do. And anyway, whether he wants to meet her or not, he'll have to meet her at the Gilded Age Society Ball next week. You are coming, right?"

Thea glanced down at her fork. "I wasn't sure if you'd wanted me to go this year . . ."

"Of course I do! You're family. And family must be there!"

Thea smiled. Every year the Gilded Age Society held a major fete in one of the enormous mansions the society supported. The old homes were as glamorous and jaw-dropping as any European palaces—the fact that they were called "cottages" only added to their outrageousness. They were white elephants: treasured for their rareness and beauty but astoundingly expensive to keep up. The annual ball was meant to help offset costs. Sue and Ken always paid. "I'm glad you want me to go. I love going."

"Will you . . . will you be bringing a date?"

Thea took a bite of her sandwich to stall. A date? She'd never needed a date before—to anything. Either Jonathan or Garret had always been on hand. "You guys are going to be there, right?"

"Yes. And the boys."

"Then I don't need a date," Thea said. "Unless you think I do."

Sue touched her arm. "Thea. I know you and Jonathan are newly divorced. But if you want to date, you have my blessing. You and Jonathan both deserve to fall in love—for keeps this time."

"Thank you," Thea said, lacking a better answer. "But I don't imagine I'll be doing the dinner and roses thing any time soon."

From the other room they heard Irina ringing the little porcelain bell that Thea had given her a few days ago—a bell that Thea was beginning to hear clanging in her dreams. She pressed her hand against her forehead and stood. "Why I ever thought that was a good idea . . ."

"Stop." Sue rose and pushed aside her chair. "I'll go."

"But . . ."

"A grandmother doesn't turn down the opportunity to spoil her only granddaughter."

Thea stopped her before she could leave the room. "Sue . . . thank you. For everything, I mean."

"What are friends for?" she said.

Jonathan walked down the hallway of the elementary school, holding Irina's small hand. The corridor was dark, the school mostly empty. As their footfalls echoed down the long, straight hall, copies of paintings of presidents stared solemnly from the shadows. Even as an adult, Jonathan felt intimidated enough by the menacing portraits to be on his best behavior. He could only imagine how well they worked on the kids.

Irina stopped him when they reached her teacher's room. "This is it."

"All right. You wait here," Jonathan said, seating Irina in a wooden chair outside the door.

She snarled at him like a tiger.

"I mean it. Don't get out of this chair until I get back. I shouldn't be very long." He waited until she nodded, then he walked into the classroom. It was empty except for Irina's teacher, who was sitting behind a big desk at the front of the room. Behind her the whiteboard was marred with the blue smudges of half-erased lessons.

"Hi, I'm Jonathan Sorensen," he said, not certain she would remember him.

She looked up, then put her hand to her heart and laughed.

"Oh, you startled me. Sorry!" Her smile was pretty, just a little too wide for her face. Her hair was pulled back into a neat brown ponytail. Jonathan had met Lori Caisse before, at back-to-school night last month. Then, as now, she left him with the impression that she'd just wandered out of a storybook. "Nice to see you again. Have a seat."

Jonathan looked around for a grown-up-sized chair. "You mean here?"

She came around the front of the desk, a textbook in her hands, then slid effortlessly into one of the tiny chairs. "I spend so much time around kids, I forget everything isn't adult size."

"My daughter's waiting in the hall."

"This shouldn't take long. You can close the door."

He did as she asked, then eased his lanky frame behind one of the small desks alongside her. Strangely enough, he felt nervous— as if he was the one in trouble, and not his kid.

"First off, Irina's a wonderful student," Lori said. "She's bright, funny, and really a team player. But I have to show you what she did." She opened the textbook; the cover showed a picture of a globe surrounded by a rainbow. When she picked the book up, pages went cascading out and onto the desk.

"Oh no." Jonathan leaned down to pick up one of the pages that had fallen to the floor. "She tore them out. All of them?"

"No. She missed the last one," Lori said, and then she looked away, busying herself with the pages, as if she wanted to give him a moment of privacy to collect his thoughts.

"We'll take care of this," Jonathan said. "How much do you think it will cost her to replace the book? We'll take it out of her allowance."

"I'm not really sure, to tell you the truth. I think you could decide what's fair . . ." Lori lowered her eyes. "May I ask if Irina is having any trouble at home?"

Jonathan adjusted his tie, which had suddenly become too tight. "Thea and I are newly divorced. She couldn't be here tonight because she got held up at the coffee shop that she owns. But we're still very committed to parenting as a team."

Lori nodded. "Irina will benefit from that. She's lucky."

"I feel like she's acting out little by little, more and more, doing these slightly destructive things." Jonathan shifted against the hard wood of the seat. He felt as if he was failing his daughter—as if he'd already failed her. "So what can we do? What specific step would you recommend we take to stop the cycle?"

"Just keep communicating with her," Lori said. "Stay involved in her schoolwork too. You can go online and see what her homework is. Check up and be sure she's studied. Kids don't like it, but it makes them know you care."

"I guess it's a little harder to pinpoint who has what job now that Thea and I don't live together. I'll talk to her. We'll work something out."

"The other thing you can do is enroll her in counseling here at school. Mrs. Leightner is trained to work with students from broken homes. Her group meets after school on Wednesdays for an hour. I can make the arrangements, if you like."

"Thank you," Jonathan said. "I'll let Thea know. I'm sure she'll be glad."

"There are always a few families that split in the course of a year. But I've met you and Thea both, and it seems like Irina really does have a fighting chance." She smiled, the brightness returning to her face again. Something about it pulled Jonathan in. He thought she must break a dozen fourth-grade hearts a year.

"Do you have children?" he blurted, embarrassed by the question the moment he asked it.

"Yes. I have eighty this year. Ninety the year before that. But none of my own."

He stood with some awkwardness, bumping his thighs on the bottom of the desk and nearly lifting it off the ground. He was about to thank her again and duck out when a Philip K. Dick novel on her desk caught his eye.

"You like Dick—I mean—oh Lord."

She suppressed a smile, standing. "I'm into dystopic fiction."

"Funny, I never would have pegged you for the type. I'm writing a science fiction novel. I just started. It's . . . I'm sure it's terrible. But I'm amusing myself."

"You could come to our reading group!" she said, her face entirely without reservation. "We meet on the second Thursday of the month. We're reading Isaac Asimov next!"

"Well, thanks." He tried to look nonchalant, but something in him thrilled at the invitation. "Great tip. Maybe I'll come by."

She was next to the door now, pushing it open. "Don't feel weird about showing up. We're a bunch of SF geeks. An easygoing crowd."

"That's great. I—" He paused. In the hallway, Irina was no longer in her chair—she was on it. The chair had been laid on its back, so her legs jutted into the air, perpendicular to the floor.

"I'm still in my chair," she said.

Jonathan shook his head. Before he could think of joining a reading club, his obligation was to get Irina back on track. "Thanks again," he told Lori.

"Don't hesitate to be in touch," she said, and he could hear that her voice had shifted slightly, back into a more professional caliber.

He held out his hand for his wayward daughter and wasn't surprised when she didn't immediately right herself. "Come on, sweetheart," he said.

Once the baristas at the Dancing Goat heard about the Gilded Age Ball, they insisted Thea go shopping. She protested: she already had a dress—a tried-and-true black cocktail dress that seemed to get just a little smaller every year.

"But you're trying new things," Dani said. "You have to get something new."

"Maybe you'll land a rich new husband," Claudine said.

"The old dress is fine," Thea said.

"I hate that old dress." Dani smacked her lightly on the arm. "The old dress is one you picked out for Jonathan. The one you wore publically when you dressed up in the role of Jonathan's wife."

"True," Claudine said. "I cannot get on the wagon with dress shopping, because I would never wear one, but for you? You get to pick out a dress for yourself that is only for yourself. Not for a date. Not for a man. For no one but you."

Thea thought of her old dress hanging in the closet, where it stayed 364 days a year. Now that she was thinking about it, she'd bought it because it was on sale. It hadn't been her first choice, but it had been acceptable. It had made her feel pretty enough.

But compared to the pinks, teals, and purples that flirted with her from the gleaming window of Athena's Closet, her old cocktail dress was fit for a woman that Thea hadn't been in quite some time—and she wondered, When was the last time she'd done something impulsive? She used to be impulsive. She wanted to be impulsive still.

She looked at her friends, who were anticipating her pronouncement with the eagerness of kids waiting for the school bell to ring. "Okay," she said. "You talked me into it. But we don't have much time."

All along Bellevue Avenue, the traffic dragged inch by inch along the pavement, brake lights blinking red against the dusk, buses dressed as trolleys stopping and putting their hazard lights on, drivers waving for other cars to go around. On Ochre Point, Garret parked across the road from the big Italian Renaissance arches of the Breakers, and he could hear the tour guides giving their normal spiels through the open windows of a trolley.

"Yes, I recommend you take a tour of the Breakers. But no, not tonight."

Tourists leaned out of the trolley, snapping pictures as Garret walked past them. Probably, he could give a tour of this part of Newport by heart. He, Jonathan, and Thea had spent hours here, riding their bicycles down the road, sneaking onto the cottage properties to wonder at the oversized mansions and ditching their bikes to climb on the rocks at the water's edge.

The Breakers was the most excessive residence in a long line of excessive palatial summer homes. The tall front gate was gnarled iron scrollwork and soldierly limestone, so that it almost seemed to snarl as any guard dog might. From where Garret stood, not far from the porte cochere entrance, the mansion itself was simply too much for the eye to take in—its high red terra-cotta roofs trumpeting Mediterranean flair, its many thickset chimneys, rounded arches, balconies, quoins, and gardens. One had to step back a bit to be able to handle so much in one glance.

The interior was no different. Garret walked into the mansion and followed the sound of voices to the indoor Italian piazza, two stories from floor to ceiling, so that he never failed to suffer the strange vertigo of feeling like he was outside when he was actually in. High Corinthian pilasters drew his gaze up to the second-story loggia, and a dramatic, red-carpeted staircase descended to the first floor like a waterfall.

Garret glanced casually around the room to see who was in attendance that he knew. He always looked forward to evenings of small talk, of mingling, of meeting new people and making connections. He liked the challenge of it, the thrill of not knowing who he might meet next. Careers were made or broken over glasses of champagne, and he loved that about Newport life—the crude and wild undercurrents beneath all the gentility.

But before he could work the room, he needed to pay his respects to his family. To better scan the crowd without having to walk through it, he climbed the circling stairs that led to the second-level balcony. Fresh, warm air blew in from the sea, and beneath him the throng of revelers was thick and lively. He looked around until he saw his mother standing with a tall brunette who was just his type. As he waded back through the crowd to greet them, he prepared his most charming smile.

"Mom," he kissed her on the cheek. She was wearing an apricot spangled dress, square cut and modest, but stunning on her. "You look beautiful."

"Thank you, darling."

Garret shook his father's hand and gave him a quick nod. With his full head of silver white hair and his navy suit, Ken looked as much at home in the Vanderbilt mansion as he did baiting lines and drinking beer on the bay.

His mother tapped his arm. "Have you met Kate Cooper, of Cooper-Simon Holdings?"

"Kate Cooper . . ." He held out his hand. She wore a gray satin dress that was so thin it would have shown every bump and curve, if she had any. She was athletic and wiry, with a strong face that could almost be described as handsome. "So nice to meet you."

"I've heard a lot about you," Kate said. "You've got quite a reputation."

"For what?" he asked, laughing. "What's my mother been telling you?"

"Only that you're a good man to know around here. That you can get things done. Actually, I wanted to ask you a question. You see, my company . . ."

He didn't hear the rest of her story. Not a word. And he was only vaguely aware when his mother picked up the slack where he'd dropped it.

Thea had come into his line of vision, and if he hadn't been so wrapped up in his own reaction to her appearance, he might have laughed at himself. He'd caught a movement out of the corner of his eye and even before he'd turned his head, he knew it was her—could feel that it was her—somehow. He'd been looking for her, though the search had never been a conscious one.

She was wearing a burgundy dress that had no tolerance for understatement: swags around her midsection showed off a trim waist and flared hips, and a halter top made her breasts alluringly plump. Her hair fell down around her shoulders, and his reaction to it was the same as when they'd been kids.

"Thea! Look at you. You're gorgeous!" Sue exclaimed.

Thea kissed Sue and Ken. Garret was next in line, and when she didn't move to kiss him, he did it for her, leaning down, dusting her cheek with his lips as quickly as he allowed himself, then moving away.

"Where's Jonathan?" she asked.

"He'll probably show later," Sue said. "He never liked these kinds of things."

Thea shook her head, smiling. "Tell me about it."

"So who's watching Irina?" Garret asked.

"My friend Dani," Thea said.

They talked for a few minutes of nothing consequential: food, history, the incredible building, and the days of an economy before income tax. Kate was new to Newport, and she'd heard very few of the stories about the Breakers—the ghosts of servants, the luxury of pipes that ran both water from the town and water from the sea. It wasn't long before Ken and Sue excused themselves: they had to mingle. Garret, Kate, and Thea were left alone.

Garret stood listening to the women debate whether or not the Hawaiians or the Ethiopians made the best coffee. He tried to pick up the thread of the conversation, but something was off. He gazed out over the crowd, forcing his shoulders and face to relax. But the restlessness that gripped him did not let up—he felt as if he was waiting for something to happen. He couldn't quite understand it: he usually felt so comfortable in crowds.

Thea laughed, the sound seizing him physically as if she'd wrapped her hands around his wrists and tugged. And then he knew what he wanted: he wanted Thea alone. The urge to have a private moment with her was intensely distracting, almost painful. He didn't even care what people might say or what they might not say. He knew only that he wanted her undivided attention, to claim a few stolen minutes of her life for himself, minutes he once thought he would never get again.

When the band in the corner struck up an old Frank Sinatra tune, he held out his hand. "Care for a dance?" he asked. Not his smoothest move, but he'd lost his appetite for patience the moment she'd arrived.

Thea glanced nervously at Kate. "It's a little early in the night yet."

"Oh, don't worry about me," Kate said, her hard face giving away nothing. "I've had my eye on an old friend I haven't seen in a while. If you'll excuse me . . ." She glanced at Garret. "Have fun this evening."

He nodded, and when she disappeared, he fixed his eyes on Thea. Her dark hair fell around her face in gentle curls. "Are you going to come up with an excuse to turn me down?"

"No," she said. She gave him her hand.

He led her to the center of the great hall, beneath the high corniced ceiling. Her fingers in his were small and light, and he could feel her calluses on his palm. She stood close to him, her spine schoolteacher straight, and when he put his hand on her lower back, heat rushed through him like fire. Her dress was backless. Her warm skin was naked under his hand.

"You look . . ." he searched for the word. How could he tell her? He thought of the mansion, so big that he'd felt he couldn't quite grasp it unless he stepped back. "Breathtaking."

She narrowed her eyes, but he didn't miss the playful spark behind the cynical stare. "Are you hitting on me?"

"If I say yes?"

"Your mother will disown you."

"Maybe it would be worth it," he said.

She laughed and looked away from him, past his shoulder. When he flirted with women, it was usually an automatic response. He liked making women smile, liked seeing their color change beneath the luster of a little compliment. Thea was no exception. He told himself: flirting with her was far more ordinary than *not* flirting with her, and so he wasn't going to stop.

"That was terrible what you just did to that woman back there," Thea said. "Ditching her like that. Your mother wanted you to dance with her, not me."

He grinned. "You forget which son you're talking to."

Her face changed, the light in her eyes fading into something less carefree and much, much more aware. "It wasn't more than a couple of days ago that you were telling me you could never like me again. Now you ask me to dance?"

"A couple of days ago you weren't wearing that dress," he said. And just to see what she would do, he didn't stop himself from looking down at her, the slope of her shoulders and the swell of her breasts.

He saw her throat work as she swallowed. "How can you be so hot and cold?"

"It's easy," he said. "I'm faking."

He felt her muscles stiffen under her skin, under the tips of his fingers where they pressed her spine. He couldn't help it, he moved his thumb. A little forward. A little back. "I fake everything," he said. "It's part of the job description. I'm an expert faker."

"Some things are real," she said, and he heard the hitch of her breath in the noisy room with all the clarity of a pin dropping in an empty cathedral. "So which is it?"

"What do you mean?"

"Which is real? The hot? Or cold?"

He adjusted his whole hand on her back, spreading his fingers as wide as they would go, the texture and warmth of her skin coming alive when he brushed over it. "Which do you think?"

For a fraction of a second, her gaze fell to his mouth. Then her grip on his hand loosened, and she stepped away.

"Thea . . ."

He followed her through the crowd, hanging back just enough so that she wouldn't notice he was behind her. She walked out of the back of the house, down the long green lawn toward the water. The crescent moon was bright and high, and the waves were breaking against the dark rocks at the edge of the harbor, sprays of silver white arching then splattering like rain. He stopped to watch her and consider if he should follow her. She stood alone against the moonlit ocean, the roaring breakers, the endlessly clear sky.

When they were kids, he'd felt they were on the brink of an adventure—the people they could become. As an adult, he'd assumed all that potential was behind him. And yet now, the shape of her silhouette against the ocean made it clear that there was more promise in his future than he ever could have expected in the past.

He walked up to her slowly; he didn't want to startle her. But when she turned her head, she seemed to expect him.

"Don't do that," she said. Her eyes were sparkling with moonlight.

"I'm sorry. It didn't mean anything. I flirt with everyone."

Her cheek twitched. "Exactly."

He shoved his hands in his pockets, needing to do something with them. When he'd gone out on his last date, and he'd sent Gemma home without taking her upstairs, he'd told himself it was because he hadn't wanted to make Jonathan uncomfortable and that he didn't want to have to explain a strange woman to Irina in the morning. But he knew now that he was lying to himself. The reason—the real reason—he hadn't taken that woman to bed wasn't just his family. It was the woman standing in front of him right now.

He looked at her; he wanted to hold eye contact, but she wouldn't let him. He studied the slope of her nose, the gentle curve of her jaw, her high forehead. Did she know how beautiful she was—even more beautiful now than when she was eighteen? As if she heard what he was thinking, she turned away.

"Why are you still here?" she asked.

The waves crashed on the rocks along the shore, a persistent roar. Strains of frivolous music floated from the old mansion's bright windows through the salt-heavy air. He supposed he'd known, all along, that if he ever saw her again—this woman who had broken him so unforgivably—he wouldn't be able to pretend. Desire had been incubating inside of him like warm coals, heat that needed very little tinder to flare back to life. When he spoke, words fell with shocking easiness from his tongue.

"I still want you," he said.

He watched the emotions dance across her features, but he couldn't read them. Her lipstick had worn off, and he wanted to kiss her with a need that verged on pain. For a moment, he thought she might let him. Her eyes were clouded, her lips parting on a breath. But then her expression turned hard—and a wall went up in his face.

"We're not doing this again," she said. And she was marching away in her heels, walking over the lawn with difficulty, back toward the lights and sounds of the party. This time, he knew not to follow again.

From "The Coffee Diaries"
by Thea Celik

The Newport Examiner

That anyone ever drinks a truly good cup of coffee is nothing shy of miraculous. There are simply too many variables that can go wrong.

The soil might be too heavy with minerals, such as salt, or too depleted. The cherries can mature too quickly in full sunlight, instead of being slowly shade grown. The farmers might inadvertently pick green cherries along with the ripe, red ones—tainting the lot.

The beans might ferment or grow slightly moldy if not washed and dried properly. If left to sit too long, they will take on the flavor of the bags they're stored in.

When the roaster gets the beans, he might over or under roast them (each type of bean is best served by a unique type of roasting). Then, once roasted, the beans might sit on the shelf too long before being brewed. Or the delicate process of infusing water with the essence of the beans might be mishandled.

And even if nothing in the whole process goes wrong, brewed coffee will go stale in less than three hours, so that the time for drinking the perfect cup is incredibly brief.

When you do find that perfect cup, savor it. There's a miracle in the making of the drink in your hand.

Fourteen

In an alternate time and place, the day before graduation goes differently. Thea does not meet Garret in the old barn. She doesn't despair over the concrete floor veined with thick cracks and crumbling by the door. The smell of cobwebs and dirt doesn't dissuade her. The old rusted shovels, dusty ropes, and the light—the ominous and accusing light that slices the boards of the old barn in neat vertical lines—doesn't make her second-guess. She doesn't smile nervously when Garret takes her hand; she doesn't put all her faith in an idea of perfection.

When Garret lays her down on the bundle of blankets and pillows that he's stolen from his mother's house, she doesn't feel a lump in the back of her throat, doesn't give in to the feeling that what should be a beginning is instead an end. She doesn't notice that he's rushing. That he's greedy, loutish, and obtuse. She doesn't feel tears come into her eyes when she tries to tell him to slow down, even—halfheartedly—to wait, but he can't seem to hear her. She has no choice but to pretend she's not there. She doesn't feel the pain—no sharp, stinging stretch, no blunt bruising and unwithstandable invasion. She doesn't feel that she's just given her most vulnerable moment to a stranger. She doesn't notice that there are tears running into her hair.

And when it's over, Garret doesn't pull on his clothes, doesn't bullshit his way through niceties, doesn't take off running and leave her in the old, ghostly barn. No—in the alternate timeline, he holds her. Says sorry. They talk about what went wrong, and then they try again, they figure it out, and Garret doesn't stop calling her. Thea doesn't spend the next weeks of her life making excuses because she's stopped eating, because she can't bring herself to face the sun through the blinds in the morning. The story moves backward, through all the what-ifs, possibilities collapsing on themselves, a house of mirrors teeming with choices—but only one way out.

The apartment was nice—two bedrooms, a small balcony where Jonathan and Irina could eat their dinners and watch the sailboats on the harbor, wood floors, high ceilings, and plenty of sunlight. After days of looking, Jonathan was beginning to suspect that they'd finally found the right place.

"Well?" Garret said, opening the refrigerator door to peer in. "Is this the one?"

"Maybe," Jonathan said, and he couldn't keep the excitement out of his voice. Overall, he liked living with Garret—their evenings spent talking about old memories and making new ones. Garret was good for him—he thought—and vice versa. Garret pushed him to jump feetfirst back into life-after-divorce, and Jonathan felt he and Irina brought a kind of happy disorder to Garret's once perfect and overly neat life.

But much as he loved living with his brother, there were plenty of reasons that he needed to get his own place too—Irina being the most pressing of them, since he wanted to get a place in Newport that would make it easier for her to stay with him on school nights. And of course, there was also his desire to get back on his own two feet.

"Listen." Garret shut the refrigerator door and crossed the room to stand before his brother. The Realtor had honored their request to be left alone to talk, and Jonathan could tell that his brother had something on his mind. "Are you sure you're ready to move out? That it's not too soon?"

"I've more than overstayed my welcome."

"Screw that," Garret said. "You can stay as long as you want. What I'm trying to tell you is that . . . that you don't have to go if you don't want to."

"I think I'm ready. I feel okay about being on my own."

Garret motioned for him to sit on the couch that was still in the apartment. "I'm not going to lie to you. Living alone is hard. I don't know if you're ready for it."

"I'll have Irina—and not just for the weekends either. I'll have her for a few days a week now that I'll be able to take her to school."

"Yeah, but it's different. Trust me."

He looked at his brother—Garret's soap opera–star face, his salon-cut hair. Jonathan was only just beginning to know Garret again and understand what made him tick, but one of the fundamental traits of Garret's personality seemed to be a die-hard commitment to living alone. And yet now Garret was saying—almost asking him, it seemed—not to move out just yet.

In a way, Jonathan was glad to see a crack in his brother's armor. It meant he was human—subject to loneliness—after all.

"You don't like living alone?" Jonathan asked.

"Oh—I have no problem with it," Garret said, puffing up a bit. "But you're not used to it like I am. It's going to be a jolt."

"What else?" Jonathan asked.

Garret stood, sighing heavily. "Look. Here it is. Once you move out, that's it—you move out."

"So . . . ?"

A muscle in Garret's jaw tightened. "I don't want things to go back to the way they were."

Jonathan resisted the urge to smile—the wrong reaction. But he was touched by what his brother was saying: Garret liked living with Jonathan after all. "That won't happen again," Jonathan said. "I'm divorced from Thea now, so we're fine."

"You sure?"

Jonathan stood. "Hey, of course I'm sure."

"Can you promise?"

Jonathan felt a slight shiver go up his spine. "What could happen that would put our friendship in jeopardy again? I mean, what could be worse than what we've already gone through?"

"Nothing, I guess."

Jonathan reached out, clasped his brother by the wrist. After months of needing Garret's reassurance, it felt good for once that the tables were turned. "We're fine. From here forward. We're brothers. Nothing can come between us again—not money, not a woman, not even geography."

Garret smiled, but it was not the beaming-with-confidence smile that Jonathan would have liked. He let go of his brother's arm. "Let's get the Realtor and write him a check."

If cell phones had been common when Thea was eighteen, she would have been checking hers constantly the day of graduation, the day after the barn. She would have felt the heaviness of the phone pulling down her pocket, the gentle bump of it against her thigh, but instead, since the possibilities promised by a phone were absent, there was only the weight of her own grief and hope and no tangible thing to make into the altar of all that emptiness inside.

"What happened?" her friends asked. And she could only give them the vaguest of answers. The possibilities were staggering and dangerous, layering up like snow on ice on snow. She thought of Jonathan's warning: Garret had only wanted her for one thing. Garret was a sportsman—she'd known going into it that he measured his life in goals and girlfriends. She'd become one more, and it was nothing less than she'd expected.

But there had been an additional element, one that she hadn't seen coming, and that had been her utter failure on the concrete floor of the barn. She'd done something wrong—something mortifyingly wrong. She'd expected the pain, but not the way Garret had been so careless of it, almost as if he'd meant to use it against her—or to use her in spite of it. How he could be so cruel, so purposely ungentle, she couldn't understand. And then, as if her humiliation hadn't been complete enough, he'd left her there, alone, so that she could hear the scrapes and squeaks of birds that were nesting in the rafters, and she pulled her clothes on, mindless of blood, and made her way out into the early dusk.

She'd tried to talk to him the morning of their graduation—to play it normal. But he was cold and disinterested, so that when she said, "I guess we're finally free, huh?" his reply barely sounded like words at all.

And she tried again later, after anger had swelled up and replaced all her sadness. She'd cornered him outside the locker room, hating herself for her own neediness, and told him, flat out: "You hurt me."

If he knew what she was talking about, he didn't let it show. "It's supposed to hurt," he said.

"Not like this," she'd replied.

*   *   *

Garret had known his mother was up to no good when she'd invited him over to her house on a Friday evening in late September. She greeted him in the marble foyer wearing a pink track suit and diamond earrings. She placed a small kiss on his cheek then led him into the living room, where Tara—the girl who helped Sue with housework—was arranging biscotti on a small silver tray. Beyond the gauzy curtains, the trees were bright red and gold against the blue slate of the ocean.

"Have a seat," Sue said.

"Why do I have the feeling I'm in trouble?"

"Because you are in trouble," Sue said. She poured herself a cup of tea, and the smell of lemon and chamomile pervaded the room. "What did you think of Kate?"

"So that's what this is about? You're mad because I didn't get down on one knee and propose in the middle of the piazza?"

"That's textbook rhetoric, dear," she said calmly. "Exaggeration. What I expected was for you to have a conversation with her. What I didn't expect was to see you dancing with Thea the next time I turned around."

Garret rolled his eyes and bit off the end of a biscotto. "You told me to make nice with her."

"Make nice," she said. "You looked like you wanted to make *something* with her, but it wasn't *nice.*"

His biscotto turned to dust in his mouth, and his face grew warm.

"You don't have to say anything," she said. "And I won't bring this up again. But Garret—for once in your life—listen to what I'm telling you. Thea's always made you go a little crazy."

"That's not tru—"

"Hear me out. You get reckless around her. Careless. You and your brother are finally settling into friendship. Don't ruin it. Not now."

Garret shook his head, looked down at his lap. His task was clear before him: he needed to convince his mother that she was worrying for nothing. But the truth was that Thea had been on his mind 24/7 since the moment she'd left him standing on the lawn at the Breakers. Thoughts of her—memories—popped back into his mind at the most uncomfortable moments. And even when he wasn't thinking a specific thing about her, he felt as if she vaguely permeated every moment of his days and nights, much like the smell of lemon tea that now filled the room.

He had to make it stop—the torture of how much he thought of her in her absence. There had to be a logical way to make the longing end. But in the meantime, he had to convince Sue that she was overreacting.

"You do realize that was the first Gilded Age Society Ball she went to without Jonathan," he said.

"Of course."

"I wanted her to feel comfortable. Especially with me."

"Well, that's very admirable of you, but—"

"And did you or did you not see me talking with Kate later in the evening?"

"Well, you—"

"Did you or did you not?"

Sue sighed. "Yes, counselor. I did."

"No further questions," he said.

"I'm trying to look out for everyone's best interests here." She got up from her armchair to sit with him on the couch. Her eyes were soft, pleading, and she put a hand on his arm. "Just promise me you won't go off the deep end with Thea again. Promise that you'll do whatever you need to keep both feet on the ground."

He held his breath a moment, then let it go. His mother had

seen through him—she always saw through him. He could fool senators and judges, but not his mom. Some part of him almost felt relieved that she knew the truth, even if he felt compelled to deny it. Her reaction made one thing clear enough: Thea did get under his skin, more than any woman he'd ever met. He couldn't think straight when it came to her. Sue was right—he needed to stay grounded going forward.

"You're overreacting," he said. He put his hand over his heart. "But if it makes you feel better, I'll swear. I won't do anything crazy."

"I think we have to discuss the meaning of 'crazy' in this context."

He kissed her cheek. "And you wonder where I get it from."

Thea knew she had a serious problem—Claudine had pointed out that she'd mistakenly made a decaf espresso instead of a regular, Jules had mentioned that she was wearing her shirt inside out, and even Tenke had pulled her aside to ask if she realized that she'd replaced the stack of coffee filters with a pile of napkins.

She'd laughed and made jokes about going senile—which Lettie told her she knew nothing about—and she tried to stay on track. But the fact was, she was uncontrollably distracted. The memory of just three simple words that Garret had spoken—*I want you*—raced through her blood and made her feverish as a virus. Her body went hot and cold, heat spreading through her at the most innocent moments. Her head swam and her imagination took her rational brain hostage, replacing reality with fantasies of seeing him again—at the shop, at the beach, in her bed.

One evening while Thea was closing up alone, Dani wandered in wearing her blue uniform, her face set in determination. Dani locked the door of the café, swept under all the chairs, and when

Thea started to say "Thanks so much for your help," Dani told her to sit down.

"Spill," she said. "What's going on?"

Thea rolled her head to one side, fighting the muscles that had been tightening bit by bit over the last few days. "You're not going to like it," she warned.

"I might not like what you have to say, but I'm willing to hear it."

Thea nodded. "Something happened with me and, okay, with Garret."

"You slept with him?"

"God no," she said. "Something trickier than that."

"Go on . . ."

"He was flirting with me. Hard-core flirting. Like, I want to take you home and have my way with you flirting."

Dani laughed. "And that surprises you? Thea—he talks to every woman like that. It's just how he is."

"I don't think it's the same."

Dani sat back in her seat. "So what are you telling me here? That you want him too?"

"Well—"

"Because that absolutely can't happen." She smacked her hand on the table. "If you want a rebound lay, you're going to have to pick someone else. I know I've been encouraging you to try new things, but I don't think anyone was talking about your ex's brother."

Thea got up, not because she needed to stand, but because she felt too close to the conversation. Dani always had a way of cutting right to the bottom line when she had a problem to solve—and whether she hit the bull's-eye or not, she stood by her convictions.

Thea paced, caught in the sting of pent-up frustration. Dani was right to suspect what Thea hadn't allowed herself to suspect—that she was looking for a rebound, that it was only natural. After years of a lackluster love life, she was overdue for some toe-curling, sheet-twisting sex. But even before Garret had told her he wanted her, she'd been feeling uneasy—leading her to suspect that her sex life was part of the problem, but not all.

"It's not entirely about that," Thea said. "It feels like something else."

"Like you need closure."

She nodded.

Dani leaned an elbow on the table. "Oh I see. It makes sense. You've got closure from Jonathan. It's probably in a drawer in your filing cabinet with the Rhode Island notary seal on it. But with Garret, things are still a little open-ended. You've got to find a way to close things off."

"How?"

"Get it all out in the open. And then, you just . . . let it go."

"Let it go . . ." Thea thought of a balloon lifting toward the sky. A wave pulling out to sea. Lovers coated in sand. She swallowed hard. "You think so?"

"Talk to him," Dani said. "You've got to march straight up to your problems and face them head-on. As soon as you can."

"You're right," Thea said.

The week following his graduation, the local paper did a story to highlight where some of the more successful students of the senior class were headed during the coming year. Garret's picture had been on the front page. A soccer ball was suspended in space just before contact, his body was lifted off the ground, and his lips were open and drawn back into a roar that rang out even from the silence of a photograph. Garret's parents had cut out the clipping and hung it on the refrigerator, and his mother had planned to have it laminated for future family albums. That way, when Garret was signing autographs and getting sponsorship deals, his family would have proof that he came from the same place as the rest of them.

That was the vision that Garret's family had of him—their boy who stood on the brink of a dazzling future. But in the weeks after graduation he carried a vision of himself that was much different than what the paper showed.

Once, when he was young and his family still lived in New Jersey, he'd gone to summer camp with Jonathan. The camp was in the northwestern part of the state, so that the hiking trails and lean-tos of the Boy Scout–owned property were surrounded by green hills and crystal lakes. Garret had thrived at summer camp—playing pranks, sneaking to the girls' cabin at midnight, kicking ass at scavenger hunts and other games.

But one day, while everyone gathered at rows of picnic tables to eat their desserts, the winds changed. Garret was struck suddenly by a hot, gnarled pain low in his stomach. He fled to the boy's room. His guts turned themselves inside out in every way possible, leaving him gasping for air and wiping tears from his cheeks. Later, they would tell him it was food poisoning. He splashed water on his face and did his best to put himself back together. He didn't want to look weak, and he thought no one would notice. But when he got out of the bathroom, his cabin supervisor was waiting for him in the hall.

What he didn't know was that while he was getting sick, one of the camp counselors had quieted the group of a hundred middle-school campers for announcements. And everything that had happened in the bathroom—the puking, the shitting, the stomach turning inside out—had echoed through the high rafters of the mess hall. He had to walk through the crowded cafeteria to the infirmary, his eyes on the floor and his face burning, as the other campers, all seated and looking up at him, laughed and laughed. He'd vowed to himself never to be in a position that could cause him so much embarrassment again.

And yet, what had happened in the barn with Thea could not even begin to compare to his childhood humiliation. The way Thea looked at him with her big, trusting eyes said that she was prepared to put not only her virginity in his hands but everything else too. And he knew that when he slept with her, it would be more than just the sweaty and greedy sex that he'd so often begged her for on the floor of her bedroom. It would be the equivalent of getting married.

He'd told himself, as he sat bouncing his legs beneath his chair in Spanish class, watching the clock tick closer to his rendezvous in the barn, that he was just having a little performance anxiety—and that the edginess was a good thing: nervousness electrified him before an especially big soccer game and made him run faster, play harder than he might have played if he simply didn't care. He and Thea had made plans months ago for the specific time and day that they were going to do it. He would not let himself be so cowardly as to back out.

He'd had to accept failure instead. What happened between him and Thea in the barn had seemed to be an event entirely separate from the stream of hot encounters that happened on her bedroom floor. He felt removed from her—as if he was carrying out an act. He let his body dictate the terms, and afterward, he was horrified to see that Thea had been crying. He was a boy walking through the mess hall—having just committed the most humiliating act of his life—all over again. But this time, there was more at stake.

In the days that followed, Thea had made a couple of awkward attempts to speak to him—not to say *I miss you* or *I love you*, but to say, in not so many words, *You were a horrible disappointment.* Eventually, she stopped speaking to him altogether.

The days grew longer and hotter. The nights were suffocating and damp. And there, on his parents' refrigerator, was a picture of him snapped at the height of his power, a good-looking, promising young winner about to kick a game-changing goal. He really wanted to be the guy in the photograph, but deep down, he wasn't. Especially not to Thea—who would never look at him that way again.

Thea had dropped off Irina with Jonathan on Monday, and then she arrived early to wait for Garret. She'd gone down the Cliff Walk, where three and a half miles of Newport's most scenic ocean views had been forever reserved for a public walkway. The air smelled of wet rocks and brine, and the clouds were knotty, low, and dark. Thea pulled her jacket tighter around her shoulders against the wind. Where she stood, the Walk was relatively isolated, but farther up or down the trail, the great mansions loomed over the ocean on their wide swaths of fading green grass.

She and Garret had met at these steps a hundred times before in what seemed like a different lifetime, and the steps had not changed. They marked the midway point of the Cliff Walk, and they led no farther than a platform halfway down the rock face, where she stood waiting. Below her, the waves were lapping the shore, and she was struck by the contrast of the hard rock and the soft, sloshing water. But she knew not to be fooled by appearances: in the game of the ages, the soft ocean waves would prove more unyielding and merciless than the rocks that sat so solidly on the shore.

She heard Garret's footsteps on the stairs behind her as he walked down to the landing where tourists regularly snapped pictures of the cliffs and water views.

"Hi," she said, suspicious of herself for the little buzz that shot through her when she saw him. He was dressed in work clothes, the rumpled and slouchy folds of a suit that had been worn over the course of a long day. No man had a right to look as handsome as he did when he was so obviously tired.

"Thea."

"Are you okay? Do you want to meet some other time?"

"No, I'm fine. It's just been a long day."

The wind caught her, chilly and slicing, and she reached into her pocket for a band to pull back her hair. Strands jumped out of her fingers, uncatchable as they swept across her face. She felt Garret watching her as she forced her ponytail under control. "Do you want to walk?"

He nodded, somber.

They scaled the stairs, then moved down the walkway that was so well known to them. There must have been a point, Thea thought, when they'd discovered parts of this path, when it had been new. But now she was familiar with every slab of concrete, every set of stairs, every rock, and she could not remember a time when the path felt unfamiliar. Garret, she thought, was much the same. It seemed the missing years had done nothing to dull their intimacy; what time had created was only a facade of separation— a painting of the horizon, the illusion of distance held as close as her own hands.

"I was thinking about what you said," she began.

"I say a lot of things. What thing in particular are we talking about?"

Thea knew he wanted her to say it. But she didn't trust herself to. "About how you think you feel about me . . ."

"Right. How I think I feel."

"We haven't properly talked about what happened. I think that if we got it out in the open, it might get easier for us, going forward."

When he sighed, it was such a big gesture that she could see it, almost feel it. "I shouldn't have said that to you."

"Do you want to take it back?"

"I didn't say I regret it. I just said I shouldn't have done it. Two different things."

They strolled slowly along the walk, and when the path narrowed they trailed one behind the other, until hard-packed red earth gave way to a wider concrete walkway. The waves crashed along the shoreline, spraying their faces with cold and salt.

"So it's attraction that we're dealing with," she said.

"We? As in both of us?"

She didn't look at him. "It's perfectly logical that there's still something physical between us. We'd thought we would be so good together, and then . . ."

"We weren't," he said. "I know. I was there too."

"What I mean is, it's like there's something unresolved. An open door that needs closing. I get that. That's all I mean."

They walked a few more steps. Ahead of them, the path dipped into a small, brown stone tunnel—perhaps built as some millionaire's concession to keep the Cliff Walk open to the public but to keep the public from making an appearance in his yard. Thea walked slowly, dragging her feet, hardly noticing she was walking at all.

"I'm sorry it wasn't good, your first time," Garret said. "You deserved better than that."

Thea shrugged. "I'm sorry I didn't know as much as you did. Maybe if I had it would have been better."

Garret stopped, and Thea too paused to look up at him. When he spoke again, there was something bemused and vulnerable in his eyes. "Thea . . . that time with you . . . it was my first."

"What? But you told me . . ."

"I lied."

Thea briefly closed her eyes. "You were a virgin too."

"Yes," he said.

When she looked at him again, his face had colored slightly; even now, it seemed hard for him to admit that he hadn't known what he was doing. For all these years, she'd believed that Garret had lots of experience with sex before he'd started dating her. She'd believed he had known the right way to make love to a virgin—if there was such a thing—but that he hadn't given her that courtesy. That he'd been as inexperienced as she was turned that whole pivotal moment of her life on its head.

"But . . . why didn't you tell me?"

"Because I was an insecure eighteen-year-old. I didn't want you to know. It was just . . ." He ran a hand through his hair. "You had all these huge expectations. It was like you'd built me up into this kind of hero, and I just . . . I didn't know how to live up to that. I wanted to, though. You have no idea how much I wanted to . . ."

"I'm sorry you felt like you had to lie."

"Thea." He touched her arm, fingers cupped gently around her elbow, and when he looked at her again, his face was focused and intense. "I can do better."

All at once, she was overwhelmed by the bigness of the afternoon, the glowering sky, the salt spray whipping in the breeze, and Garret—standing next to her, promising her once again that he was the hero he so badly wanted to be. "You're talking about sex."

He pulled her gently just inside the edge of the pedestrian tunnel, where the earth was soft under their feet. The rough-cut stones of a long barrel arch smelled of damp and moss, and the temperature dropped as if they'd stepped into an icebox.

"Haven't you ever wondered?" he asked. He touched her cheek. "What might have happened if we'd tried again?"

Heat snaked through her, years of compressed desire loosening, a fire unspooling within. She tried to fight it—to smother the fire that grew hotter and bigger—but his eyes wouldn't let her go, his fingertip burned her skin when he brushed her cheekbone, and she ached to her core for him, the memory of his weight, his hands, his mouth arresting her as if it was only yesterday that he'd touched her and she'd cried his name. "Yes," she said, swallowing hard, willing her voice to sound even. "I wondered. In the past."

"You still wonder," he said, his thumb skimming her bottom lip, pulling it slightly open. "And so do I."

And then he was kissing her. Not the kiss of a young man but the type of kiss he was made for—a kiss that was a dark question, a cord of heat cinching tight, a flagrant intent. And she remembered, everything at once coming back, the nights on the floor of her bedroom, the pinch of her hip bones against the floor, his seeking fingers in her mouth, her hair. Her heart caught in her throat as she wrapped her arms around his neck, dragging him closer. He tipped her head to the side, and the kiss slid deeper, into a hotter, more fearsome place—familiar and entirely new.

"Wait." She pulled away. Her breath faltered. "Are you kissing me because you think you have to prove something? Or is this more?"

"How can you even ask me that?" And when he kissed her again, her whole body went flush with heat. His hands were everywhere, traveling her back, tugging her hips tight against his, brushing her breast. He backed her against the wall, lifted her knee until their hips ground together, until agony and pleasure were indistinguishable, and Thea had never in her whole life felt such powerful hatred for her clothes. His kiss dragged her deeper, pulled her down, but it was a pathway leading nowhere. They were long past the days of making out—when a rushed and ill-planned collision could satisfy without leading to more. Eventually he must have felt it. He pulled away.

"This wasn't supposed to be about sex," she said, though her body screamed *liar*.

"What is it about?"

"It's about closure. About moving on."

He let her go. She felt the loss instantly, as if she'd been abruptly set back on the earth though her feet had never left the ground. "Some part of me will always wonder what might have happened if you hadn't married my brother . . ."

"And some part of me will always wonder what might have happened if you hadn't stopped talking to me when I needed to know that everything was okay . . ."

"I've said I'm sorry for it."

She crossed her arms. "This . . . whatever this is . . . it's just leftover energy that's been building out of proportion. That's all."

"How do you know it's leftover? How do we know it's not new?"

"I guess I don't know," she said. "If things had ended differently, more completely, we might not be feeling like this."

"Maybe," Garret said, and there was something pained yet resolute in his voice. "But either way, we can fix it."

"How?"

He walked away from her, out of the tunnel. She followed him, and he stood looking out over the bay, the whitecaps slicing the rough blue denim of the waves. He ran a hand through his hair, took a deep breath. When he turned to face her again, his expression was distraught.

"I hadn't planned to say this. I *shouldn't* say it."

"What?"

"How is it that I can argue before some of the most intimidating and powerful politicians on the East Coast without breaking a sweat, but *you* drive me half out of my mind?" She saw the moment he resolved to touch her again. He took her hand. "Thea. Sleep with me."

She stepped away. "You don't mean that."

"I know it's insane. But I don't know how else to get you out of my system."

She leaned her hands against the wet stones of the tunnel's outer wall. What if . . . what if he was right? What if sleeping with him once might be what she needed to end this terrible feeling that she'd faced since the day Garret had shown up back in her life?

"I think of you all the time," he said. "You keep me up at night. You make everything I eat taste like cardboard. I've imagined it—a hundred different times—what it would be like to touch you again. I don't know if sleeping with you is the best solution, but at the moment it's the only one I've got."

She said nothing, stunned and frightened to hear his confession—to encounter a desire that she'd once held so sacred here before her again.

"Look." He shifted his stance; frustration gathered around him like the first crackling electricity of a summer storm. "I'm not saying we should . . . see each other. I'm just saying . . ."

"I know what you're saying," she said. She pulled her hand away.

She'd meant only to talk with him today, to find closure. She'd meant for them to have a long stroll, deep conversation, and she'd pictured them laughing and shaking their heads afterward, arms linked, two old friends who'd found stasis at last.

But what she'd collided with instead was this: the force of her own desire and his, stronger now than it once had been. His suggestion appalled her—the idea of a quick screw. It was cheap, demeaning. Morally, she wanted to recoil. But physically, her body railed against her, heat fanned by the promise of a long-awaited—final—release.

"No," she said. What was she thinking—considering his offer even for a second? It was all wrong. "There's a thousand reasons we shouldn't even be talking to each other, let alone talking about sleeping together."

"I'm asking you for this," he said, stepping closer to her. "Once. Just once, and then we'll never talk about it again."

She looked him in the eye. "And what about Jonathan?"

"I don't want to do anything to jeopardize my relationship with him," he said, pulling up straight. "If we get this out of our systems, once and for all, the whole family will be better for it. Maybe you and I can start seeing each other without it feeling weird for everyone. It doesn't have to be a big deal."

She shook off his hand. "We're going to have to find another way. I'm not sleeping with you. Not now or ever again."

He nodded, and she noticed he wasn't breathing. For a moment, they stood quietly. Out on the water, seagulls sat on the surface of the waves, bobbing like buoys. The clouds tumbled over one another, shades of dark and light.

"You're probably right," Garret said. "We shouldn't see each other again in private. It hurts more than it helps."

"And we definitely shouldn't sleep together," she said, her mind racing with images so vivid she already knew the friction of his palms gliding over bare skin.

"Yes," he said. He leaned down, kissed her. His mouth was warm, sweet, and not enough. "But let me know if you change your mind."

Then he put his hands in his pockets and walked farther down the path, leaving Thea to stand alone, her brain reeling and the ocean battering the shoreline, wearing the rocks down.

From "The Coffee Diaries"
by Thea Celik

The Newport Examiner

Coffee had always been an important part of my parents' lives. In their home country of Turkey, the per capita consumption of tea far outweighs that of coffee. Yet it's the mystique of Turkish coffee that captures the imagination.

If you were a regular customer, wandering into my mother and father's tidy and crude little shop twenty years ago, they would have served you a fresh, hot cup of American-style coffee.

If you came in often enough and liked a bit of friendly small talk, my mother might have offered you the occasional piece of Turkish Delight, made in her kitchen and sold at ten cents a square.

But if you became one of my parents' true regulars—and you were invited to their home—they wouldn't dream of serving you American coffee. They would get out their Turkish mill with all the pride of a professional *kahveghi*, and they would make you a cup of thick, rich coffee flavored only with a bit of sugar.

My mother's grin would reach ear to ear, and guests didn't dare refuse a second cup. When a good friend offers you a gift, you don't say no.

FIFTEEN

As September blended into October, traffic into the coffee shop slowed down to a crawl. Only a very few tourists fresh off of bus trips or East Coast yachting excursions wandered in, their wool scarves falling loose around their jackets. The days grew shorter and colder, and Thea did her best to keep herself busy. She made plans to attend a coffee conference to kill time for at least one weekend. She worked hard with Irina on multiplication and the Revolutionary War—harder than she had to at times—and she called Jonathan often to make sure they were all on the same page. She reorganized all of her bookkeeping for the shop. She spent long hours at bedsides in the local nursing home, reading books to seniors who had lost their sight.

"What's wrong with you?" Claudine wanted to know one day while they sat trying out new pumpkin-flavored coffee at the shop. "You've been so depressing lately."

"She's depressed. Not *depressing*," Tenke said. "It's finally sinking in that she's divorced."

"I don't think so," Claudine said. "I think she needs to get laid."

Lettie too had a theory. "It's a matter of momentum. Meter, we'd say in music. When you were married you knew where you were going. You knew what came next. Now, the next bars aren't so predictable. But you should try to enjoy it—not knowing what's ahead."

"Maybe we should let *her* tell us what's wrong," Dani said.

But Thea had no idea what to say. Her relationship with the Sorensens—all of them—hadn't been so strong since she was a child. She and Jonathan were friends. Sue and Ken had not changed in their affection for her. Garret no longer wanted her exiled away from the people he loved. She had everything she wanted.

And yet, day by day, she felt her moods growing darker. Food was bland and unappealing; not even the smell of fresh coffee beans tumbling into a hopper could make her senses light.

She was petrified of being alone with her thoughts—for fear of the direction they would lead. For comfort she turned to the same tried-and-true standbys, and not without the guilt of knowing that she was supposed to be trying new things instead of relying on the old. When she had to be by herself—nights when she could not sleep—she read books with fast-moving plots that would keep her from lingering too long on any one passage. She watched movies about bank heists and road trips, or in the very worst situations, she took a sleeping pill. Her thoughts—when left to their own devices—ran amok. And no matter what trail her musings started down, they always found their way into the past, back to the girl who stood on the brink of a decision—and did the wrong thing.

As a young man, there was no one in the world Jonathan had looked up to more than his father. Ken owned a boat dealership, and he had a way about him that made other men feel comfortable enough in his office to put their feet up on the table, talk about their wives, and light a cigar. Ken had expected that Jonathan would go into the family business, and for a long time Jonathan tried—he practiced his handshake, he studied the art of small talk, he read books on negotiating. But in the end, he simply didn't have the personality for sales.

Eventually, Ken's focus on Jonathan shifted away, his plans for the family business slowly being transferred to his other son, the son who laughed louder than Jonathan, talked louder than Jonathan—the son who was good at talking people into doing things that they didn't want to do.

Despite the disappointment (it was never spoken aloud that Jonathan was no longer the favorite to take over the family trade), Jonathan had never stopped emulating his father. If there was one thing Ken could do that Jonathan could also do, it was to be kind to women. Jonathan had learned early on to treat women with dignity and respect—a lesson that Garret hadn't entirely mastered, since he was apt to treat the women in his life no different than his soccer or drinking pals.

Jonathan thought to hold Thea's coat for her when she was putting it on. He opened the car door. He asked what she wanted to order for dinner or what movie she wanted to see. He would have walked through fire for anyone who asked—but especially for Thea.

And so afterward—after Garret had stopped talking to her, after her heart had been broken and Jonathan's prediction had come true—he'd spent as much time with her as she'd needed, holding her hand, handing her tissues when she cried, reassuring her in every way he could think of that she was worthy, beautiful, adored. And when it became clear that she would need more to heal than words, he didn't shy away. He wasn't good at many things—not like his brother, champion of last-minute drives down the field, of coercing customers into the larger boat motor and leather steering wheels, of sweet-talking teachers into passing grades—but he was good at being there for Thea. He could protect her and be kind to her and help her in every way. It's what he'd always been good at.

Still, he could not—no matter how gentle, how patient, how good he was to her—get her to say *yes*.

Garret stood in the quiet of his apartment in Providence, drinking the last of the coffee that Jonathan had left when he'd moved out. At the glass windows, he gazed down on the city, the inky river snaking beneath fiery torches, the gondolas gliding silently along the water, the cars moving quickly over the bridges, the well-oiled machinery of it all.

For weeks, his condo had been empty. Irina had left a few of her toys behind by accident—a stuffed dog wedged behind the couch, a miniature Corvette parked beneath the coffee table—but all of her things had since been returned, and now there were no traces that Garret had ever had guests at all. He missed it—the noise and clutter of constant company. And it made him realize: he was getting older. If he was going to have a family, he needed to get started sooner rather than later.

But first, he had to get the roadblocks out of the way.

He drained the last sip of coffee from his mug, knowing he would not go to the Dancing Goat to get more. If he was going to see Thea again, she was going to have to make the choice to come to him. He fantasized about the moment a hundred different ways—that she was sitting on the park bench outside his work, that she stood when she saw him and said *I've been thinking*. He thought of coming home to find her in the lobby chatting with the doorman—the look she would give him that said *Thank God you're here.* In his real life, he'd even gone so far as leaving his door unlocked and making sure he was freshly shaved and showered at all times.

The minutes were murder. The seconds, each one a prick against his skin. The circle that he'd once thought was closed had actually always been open, and it was opening farther. But still, in his empty apartment, the phone did not ring.

When Thea arrived at Sue's house one day in early October, she was only half surprised when the lights came on and her family was there to yell *Surprise!* Irina blew a paper trumpet, and Ken showered her with a handful of confetti. She laughed and held open her arms for hugs all around.

"It was Irina's idea," Sue said. "We planned it together."

"Actually, it was all me," Irina said.

Thea messed up her daughter's hair and glanced around—Ken, Sue, Irina, Jonathan, Dani . . . no Garret. She hated that she felt so disappointed. She kept thinking that any day now things would go back to normal. And yet she suspected they were starting to slide back into the old ways—when he and she showed up for social functions only if each knew the other would not go. She couldn't bear the thought of going through this with him again—for her own sake, but her family's as well.

At one point, Sue pulled her aside. "Are you doing okay?"

"Of course," Thea said. "Why wouldn't I be?"

Sue's lips pressed into a fine line. "It's not my place, but you're not really yourself these days."

Thea gave Sue a quick hug. "Thanks for worrying about me. But I'm fine."

They lit candles and sang "Happy Birthday" while Thea covered her ears in mock horror. Afterward, when the wax had been picked off the icing and slices of yellow cake had been passed around, Sue sat Thea in a chair in the living room to open her gifts.

From Irina: a handmade clay vase that she'd been working on in school, lumpy and painted in smears of green and red.

From Ken and Sue: plane tickets to the coffee conference that she'd wanted to go to.

From Dani: a pretty new clip for her hair, beads and pearls covered in a clear, hard resin.

From Jonathan: a book about the history of coffee, which she already owned.

"Thank you all so much," Thea said. "This is so fantastic. What a great surprise."

"I almost forgot. One more thing!" Sue jumped to her feet and hurried into another room. When she came back, she held a small, hastily wrapped box in her hands. "Garret sent this."

Thea took it from her. "Did he get held up at work?"

"I have no idea," Sue said.

Irina jumped up and down beside her. "Open it!"

Anxious, Thea pulled at the paper. Inside was a cardboard package with a picture of a wooden jewelry box on the side of it. Thea opened the top and peered in: it looked just like the picture on the front. She had to admit that it was an odd gift—not really to Garret's taste, but she didn't want to let herself dwell on it too long. The jewelry box meant Garret had thought of her. She felt his absence like a clamp on her heart.

"How nice," she said, and then she closed the box, set it aside, and smiled at her spectators. "So what's a woman got to do around here to get another piece of cake?" she said.

At some point, Thea had begun to see the shape of her bones under her skin. Jonathan had noticed too. He'd refused to leave her side

after Garret had dumped her—guarding her not with any nervousness or obsessive crowding, but instead with a kind of steady,
simple companionship. When he wasn't with her, he called. He
cheered her up, brought her small things like a handful of wild
lilies or a chocolate bar. Thea leaned hard on him, not with the
sense that she was taking advantage, but instead, with the feeling
of coming back down to earth, to the place she'd always belonged.

Jonathan had been sitting beside her on the breakwater, his
skinny legs dangling down to the churning ocean, when she realized she hadn't had her period. She told him what worried her, the
way she always told him things, with complete trust. He assured
her. All they needed to do was wait a while. He made her feel as
if her period was a thing that she had temporarily misplaced, and
that it would turn up when she stopped looking for it.

She waited. The sun rose hot and crimson in the morning, set
in a blaze of sweaty orange at night, and still—no period. When
another week passed, he put his arms around her in the front seat
of the car and let her cry on his T-shirt.

"Don't worry," he'd said. "I won't tell anyone."

And she knew he wouldn't. He would support her. He'd always
been supporting her, even when she hadn't known it. Even when
she'd been too obsessed with Garret to see. And she felt some echo
of his tenderness in herself: the urge to protect him, to help him,
to comfort him in the way that he gave so much care and kindness
to her. He bought her a pregnancy test; it was pink and white like
candy, and he waited outside the bathroom at a local fast-food restaurant while she stared at her watch in a tiny stall. Afterward, she
slid into the plastic booth beside him, feeling as if she was floating
above the tile floor.

"Negative," she said.

And he gave her a long hug.

But still her period did not come.

*   *   *

After her birthday party, Thea accidentally let Irina stay up an hour later than usual watching television. She'd been on the phone with Dani, talking things over. She had the sense that her life was out of control—not that it suddenly was, but that it always had been. She'd fallen into her work at the coffee shop. She hadn't married Jonathan so much as she hadn't told him no. When Jonathan had suggested they have a child, she'd had no reason to hesitate. And her divorce—that probably wouldn't have happened if it wasn't for Jonathan as well.

She'd always been good at letting her life make her happy. She loved the shop and motherhood and even her relationship with Jonathan. But the idea that she had not chosen those things plagued her.

It's like coffee, she told Dani. *We're rarely born loving it—but drink it enough and you learn to love it.* She wondered: Were *all* the things that made her happy the result of slowly acquired tastes for those things—as opposed to instinctive, built-in tendencies? And if a taste had to be acquired to be appreciated, didn't that make it artificial in some way? How could she tell the things she'd learned to love from the things she was born loving?

When she hung up the phone with Dani, she still had no answers. Irina came into the kitchen, hopping up onto a chair, her slippers brushing the ground. It was only then that Thea realized how late it was.

"Did you brush your teeth?" Thea asked.

"Yes."

"Top and bottom?"

"Yes."

"Let me see."

Irina rolled her eyes but dutifully opened her mouth. Dark flecks of Oreos were still mashed into her molars.

"What did I tell you about lying to me?" Thea asked, her voice unusually tight.

"Mom, I'm not. I brushed them."

"You didn't really brush them. Irina—get back upstairs and finish brushing your teeth."

"Maaaaaah. No!"

"I said, *now*."

"No, you didn't say 'now.' You said, 'Get back upstairs and—' "

Thea grabbed her daughter's arms, harder than she meant to. She stood and brought Irina to the foot of the stairs.

"Ow! You're hurting me!"

She ordered her daughter to brush again, and when Irina's lip began to quiver, it only made her madder. "I said, GO!"

It wasn't until Irina had stomped as hard as she could one foot over the other that Thea realized how close she was to losing it, as if she'd been taken over by some entirely different person. Sue was right: she'd been snapping at everyone—her daughter, her friends, her employees . . .

She sat down at the kitchen table, where the gifts from her birthday party were scattered, each a treasure in its own way: Irina's lumpy, paint-streaked vase, Jonathan's thick book, Dani's glinting hair clip, and Garret's odd jewelry box. She wondered how long this could go on—the feeling that she was coiled like a spring, the shades of frustration and even anger that discolored everything she did.

Garret's offer—the fantasy of going to him at last—was constantly in the back of her mind. She wanted him; she wouldn't deny that. But she knew that she would not be able to simply shove desire under the carpet and expect it to disappear. Garret was the great, open-ended question of her life, and if she wanted that to change, she would need to do something about it—one way or the other.

She picked up the strange box he'd sent, pulled it out of its foam wrapping, and set it on the kitchen table. It was nice enough—thick wood, rounded corners, a little brass clasp—but given his taste for expensive things, the crude little box simply didn't seem like something he would be attracted to. She wondered: Why would he bother sending her a present if he wasn't going to show up at her party? What kind of mixed message was that?

It wasn't until she opened the box and pulled the velvet ring holders out that she understood. All her indecision had been condensed down into the finite point of the moment: a taunt, a lure, a choice. Inside was a single silver key.

The fact that Garret had been sitting with his arm around his date at the drive-in theater in North Smithfield when he'd found out that Thea had started dating his brother had not eased his shock. The rain had just begun to fall, dotting the windshield and making the inside of the car humid. The sky was not yet dark.

"At least that's what I heard," the girl had said. And she scooted next to him, her bare shoulder pressed against his chest. "Does it bother you?"

He'd said *hell, no* even before he'd realized he'd spoken the words. That Thea was with another man—a man who might do better than him—was enough to make his blood seethe. Thea with his brother was unthinkable. Rage tightened his whole body like a crossbow.

He didn't see a frame of the movie; he barely noticed when his date moved her hand to rest so suggestively on his lap. For the fullness of the season—so bloated with heat and humidity—he'd been living in a kind of time freeze, so that some part of him expected that everything would somehow settle back into its right place come the fall. As if the nightmare of his summer had been nothing more than a dream.

But if Thea was with Jonathan, he could lose her forever. He saw that now; the trance had ended. In the distance, thunder rumbled. Lightning flashed against the sky.

"Thea."

When he opened the door late on Saturday night, she was there. She was pushing him aside and moving past him, not waiting for an invitation. She was taking off her coat and dropping it over the back of his couch. She was pulling her hair from the constraints of a thick elastic and looking at him with all the hard intention of a woman who wanted something and meant to get it. He braced himself against his own hope—a futile effort—like trying to stop a mountain from crumbling with nothing but his two hands.

"This can't turn into anything serious," she said.

He didn't trust his voice. "I know."

"We do this, and it's the last time."

He nodded. All his senses were tuned in to her, the bend of her arm, the slight lift of her chin, the rate of her breath. She wore a dress he'd never seen before—an olive drab oxford, belted and hanging to her knees. He watched as she covered her face with both hands. The cry that came from her throat was caught between a laugh and a sob.

"I don't know how to stop thinking about you," she said, looking up. Her dark eyes were lustrous and wild. "I want it to stop."

He walked toward her, took her two hands in his, and kissed her palms.

In his bedroom, he closed the slats of the venetian blinds and lit the single candle on his dresser, his hand trembling so much he nearly lost the match's flame. He stood for a moment, looking at himself, seeing her come up behind him. The same nervousness that had stymied him as a young man racked him even now. And he realized: all of his training, his years of thinking of sex as science, of love as technique, had been preparation not for a string of nameless and faceless women but for this. A second chance.

He moved her to stand before him, so he could watch her in the mirror. He slipped open the buttons of her cotton dress one by one, from her clavicle to her knees, then eased it open. She was beautiful; he didn't know how he would be able to go slowly. Candlelight flickered, warm tones on her warmer skin. Her hair fell softly around her shoulders. Her bra was black as ink. He slid it down.

"Thea . . ."

She turned around and kissed him, hard, and left no question about what she wanted or how she wanted it. He bent to hook an arm around her knees, lifting her and carrying her to his bed. His own clothes felt heavy as lead on his body as he fought to get them off. A decade had passed since the last time they'd done this, but he couldn't wait a moment more.

And yet, if he let momentum take over, Thea would be gone before he knew it. But if he could hold out, could keep her with him as long as possible, he could stave off the end.

He was careful when he lowered on top of her, careful not to hurt her and careful to remember everything he'd learned. He kissed her mouth every way he knew how, drew back and teased her or demanded everything she had. He refused to give in to her pleas to hurry and rush. His hands traced her body: the plush pad of her lower lip, the sweep of her jaw, the curved undersides of her breasts. This was how he'd imagined it ages ago—and her moans and whimpers told him she too had known it could be just this way. He wanted more, to wring every last drop of pleasure from her, to show her that no one would ever make her feel this way but him. She was writhing like fire beneath him, all woman and liquid heat, and he kissed every inch of her to see if she still tasted the same.

He didn't stop her when she pushed at his shoulders, the need in her eyes bordering on anger. She balanced above him, nearly glaring, and he knew enough to hold himself still. His teeth clenched, the muscles in his neck tightened. She kissed him as her body welcomed him. She cried out against his mouth. And the last coherent thought he had was that she was his, finally, if only for a time.

Jonathan made an appointment at the local clinic, and while it was obviously scheduled for Thea, he'd found himself referring to it as "our appointment." They went together. They knew by now that she was pregnant with Garret's child; there was no other possibility. Weeks had passed, and Thea still hadn't bled. In the waiting room, Jonathan put his arm around her, and she leaned against him, her forehead pressing the skin of his neck, her body all angles and hard planes. Jonathan knew people might think that he was the father, but he didn't mind. Some part of him almost wished he was. Thea sighed against him. The air smelled of fear and chemicals.

"Listen," he told her. "I don't want to give you one more thing to worry about. But I want you to know that I'll marry you. I'll spend my life protecting your child. And you. You've got my promise."

Thea hadn't lifted her head, but she said, "You mean that?"

"Of course," he said, and a feeling of deep tenderness and protectiveness swelled up within him. "I would do anything for you. I love you."

"Let's not go in." She nestled closer to him. "Let's just sit here together. Forever. Just like this."

"Okay," he'd said. He knew what she meant. He too was

content—a moment of peace he wanted to live inside of, if only they could just pause their lives right here, before anything bad happened. He wondered if he was falling in love. He couldn't think of a better woman to fall for than Thea. He saw them: him, her, their kids. A house. Maybe a dog or cat when the children got older. He could take care of Thea—it was the one thing he knew how to do well.

When the nurse called her name, he held her hand and stayed with her as long as the doctor would allow. Later, after the exam, the doctor explained: She'd lost so much weight. Too much. And her body was conserving calories by making her miss her periods. He told her to start drinking meal supplements and taking vitamins. He told her to take it easy. Talk to a therapist. She left with her head hanging low.

"So you're off the hook," she told Jonathan with a pinched smile. And he was surprised to realize that he felt disappointed. "You don't have to marry me."

They were standing next to his car. It occurred to him that they hadn't so much as kissed, and yet he was thinking they should spend their lives together. He pushed her hair back off of her face, the face that had always given him such comfort, that always roused these feelings of protection and the knowledge of doing something *right*. He liked standing beside her when she was in trouble, holding her up. And he knew she would do the same for him.

He kissed her then, slow and shy. Her eyes were wet.

"Thea," he said, "the offer stands."

Later, Thea wondered that she hadn't lingered in Garret's bed longer. His arm was across her bare shoulders, his naked leg thrown over her hip. She'd thought of a thousand excuses to stay.

I'll stay because it's raining.

I'll stay because Jules is opening the shop in the morning anyway.

I'll stay because Jonathan has Irina for the night.

I'll stay because I don't want to be rude.

I'll stay because what's it really going to hurt if I do?

I'll stay because I think Garret wants me to.

But in the end, she stayed in his bed only long enough for the trembling of her muscles to subside, so she could trust her knees to hold her up. They were good together; the promise of their nights on her bedroom floor had played out, and it was better than she could have dreamed. It nearly made her want to weep, that two people could be so perfectly in tune together, and that she hadn't known it until now.

When she stood, he didn't say anything. He only watched her slip back into her dress, her bra and panties shoved in a pocket and buttoned securely in.

At the door, he didn't kiss her, and she wondered if he was mad. But she couldn't explain herself. Sue and Ken could not take one more jolt—the family could not survive it. And so she ignored his blue eyes, already icing over. She ignored the heat coming off of his chest. She steeled herself for the sake of her heart, for the sake of her family, and did the only thing she could do.

"See you around," she said.

From "The Coffee Diaries"
by Thea Celik

The Newport Examiner

Instant coffee is considered by many to be a modern miracle. And technically, instant coffee isn't all that different from traditional coffee.

To make instant coffee, beans are roasted as usual, then crushed into a powder (instead of being cut with fast-rotating blades), then steeped in hot water. Once the coffee flavor has been released from the beans, the brew is quickly dehydrated either by freeze-drying or spray-drying, so that the water is removed and the flavor is left behind. Coffee connoisseurs complain that the taste of instant coffee can't stand up to the taste of a cup of fresh roasted and brewed java, partly because instant coffee is, in a sense, twice brewed.

Yet the market for freeze-dried coffee remains strong—and some people will swear that they love instant coffee more than fresh. Some will tell you they started drinking instant because it was easier. Some will say their parents drank instant, and so that's why they do. I think you can get used to anything, even subpar coffee, with time.

Sixteen

Thea could no longer remember how it was that she ended up talking to Garret in the street that night—if he had knocked on the front door or called up to her window. Only a few of the details remained: the glare of red and blue lights licking like flames along the wood-sided homes, the feel of the asphalt under her bare toes, the windows up and down the street lighting up one by one.

"What the fuck?" he'd said. He grabbed her shoulders hard. Minutes passed that felt like hours, and she had no idea how long he'd been yelling at her. "Him?" he demanded, his voice a blade. "Thea? Really? Jonathan?"

Thea folded her arms over her chest, mortified that he'd tugged her into the street in her nightdress. It seemed he was trying to seize every last thread of dignity from her, here before the eyes of their prying neighbors and weeks ago on a crumbling concrete floor. She was past crying now—past feeling sorry for herself. She was ready to move on.

When she'd needed help, Garret hadn't been there. He'd

proven inconstant and incompetent too. Garret had shown that he couldn't handle the difficulties of being in a relationship—that he would not talk things out. But *Jonathan* had been there for her, to comfort her and help her find the pride she'd thought she'd lost. She wouldn't let Garret take her dignity away from her again.

"Just tell me one thing," he said, and he pushed her against the wall behind her. Even now, her body felt the nearness of his and grew hot, and she hated herself for it. The back of her skull pressed hard on the wood of her parents' home. "Are you in love with him?"

She ground her teeth together, furious and wanting. His fingers pressed her arms. "What's it to you?"

"I have to know."

She stuck out her chin. "Why shouldn't I love him? He's kind and gentle and good. And he wants to marry me."

"Bullshit!" He let her go with a shove, and a moment later the police were on him, holding him by the arms. Thea hadn't even seen them coming until they were there, dragging him back. He was yelling at her, struggling, but Thea couldn't make out what he was saying—or perhaps she didn't want to. She felt surrounded by him, confronted on all sides. His rage was the same nightmarish color as the squad car lights that bathed the whole street in red. And her own anger—that he'd ruined what was supposed to have been the greatest happiness of her life—rose up with a ferocity that matched his.

"Is this guy bothering you, miss?" one of the policemen asked.

Slowly, her focus on Garret eased, and she began to see the moment for its entirety—the neighbors coming to stand on their stoops to watch, her mother and father with their arms around each other, the policemen waiting for her answer. All her nights of loneliness, self-doubt, and anger had come down to this. It occurred to her that Garret's whole future, everything he'd ever wanted, was in her hands.

"Ma'am?"

She pulled herself up straight. Passion had not been what she thought it was. When she loved again, it would be without passion—a love that she could slip into comfortably. *Love*, she thought, *should be easy*. Love that wasn't easy was probably not love at all. And she wanted happiness for herself—not drama. Not *this*.

She couldn't put her finger on the moment in their lives that had led to *this* moment—the kiss on the beach, or the night in the barn, or the day she'd seen him underneath Price's Pier—but she knew for certain that this was where she would end it.

Jonathan parked beside the Newport library, welcomed by its rusticated stonework and matronly hipped roof. Inside, he asked the librarian where the science fiction book group was meeting, and then he made his way past the white marble busts of old Newport alums to find a group of chattering people in one of the side rooms. Men in jackets and tattered jeans sat cross-legged and talking in a circle.

"Jonathan!"

Irina's teacher—Lori, he made a mental note to think of her by her name—rose from a thin-legged wooden chair. Her hair was down, and he saw now that it was not very long, barely to her chin. Her greeting was so warm and friendly that, when she came to stand in front of him, he half expected a hug, as if they were old friends. By the glint in her eye, he thought she might have been thinking about it too—but she merely reached out to touch his upper arm, then stepped away.

"This is the writer I told you about," she told the group.

Jonathan laughed and explained that he hadn't been published yet. But secretly, his pride grew. He took a seat between an older man with a full white beard and a heavyset, bespectacled young kid. He knew well enough that he shouldn't read too much into Lori's friendliness; she taught ten-year-olds. Infectious enthusiasm was part of her job description.

"Are we ready to get started?" Lori asked.

Jonathan settled in. He pulled his book out of his briefcase and put it on his lap. He relaxed into his chair, feeling deeply comfortable among the wooden bookshelves, small statues on marble pedestals, and all these people—who loved books as much as he did. He wondered why he hadn't thought to join a book group before. Lori took her seat beside him, sending a brief smile his way.

Thea's booth at the Taste of Newport festival was not overly lavish or impressive. She hadn't hired models to hand out flyers, as some of the bars had done. She wasn't raffling off a new car or blaring loud music to get people to turn their heads. But she had staked a little corner of the pier as her own, and now Lettie, Jules, and Tenke were setting up their wares.

Along with a free coffee cupping so that guests could sample the differences between brews of various origins, Thea had also devised a new game for this year. Players could toss a brown "coffee beanbag" into a series of oversized cups and saucers for twenty-five cents a throw. Three well-placed throws could win them Dancing Goat mugs and shirts. The proceeds would go to the Fair Trade Federation, which advocated that coffee farmers should be paid a fair wage for their work. Irina was fantastic at running the game, calling out to passersby like any seasoned host at a boardwalk. In Thea's mind, her daughter could outshine nightclub PR people or flashy sports cars any day.

"Thea!" Sue and Ken came toward her, smiling. The day was chilly, and the sky was low and threatening rain, so they both wore thick jackets and carried umbrellas rolled up tight as cigars at their sides. Sue kissed her. Ken gave her a warm hug. Looking over his shoulder, Thea saw that Jonathan and Garret were not far behind.

She focused her attention on Sue and Ken. "How are you guys enjoying the festival?"

"It's fabulous!" Sue said. "What's this game you're playing?"

Irina jumped in. "It's a coffee beanbag toss. Want to play? You can be the first one! It's for charity."

"Of course I do!" Sue said.

Irina held out her hand. "Seventy-five cents."

"I thought it was twenty-five per throw," Ken said.

"It is. But trust me. You're going to need at least three if you want a shot at winning. You'll probably need more."

Sue and Ken glanced at each other and laughed. They headed over to the game, where Irina and Thea had made oversized coffee cups out of flour-and-water papier mâché. Thea was alone only for a moment before Jonathan and Garret stood before her—Garret looking as expensive and groomed as always. No one thing about him was showy or flashy, but when all the components were put together—his expensive clothes, his hundred-watt smile, his styled blond hair—the effect was dazzling. Thea's breath caught in her throat.

"Heya, Thea," Jonathan said brightly. He kissed her quickly on the cheek. There was something different about him, a brightness in his eyes that she hadn't seen in quite some time.

"You look great," she said, and she squeezed his arm. She glanced at Garret. "And you're all right too," she said, hoping to make a joke to break the tension.

Garret bowed, a slight nodding of his head. "Good to see you."

She put her hands in her pockets, warming them for a moment. Thea was sure that to anyone watching, the scene would have looked completely normal. But inside, her guts were rollicking.

Her awareness of Garret beside her was like a knife held to her back, a silent, secret threat. She thought of the span of his chest under his shirt. The smell of his skin when she'd pressed her nose to his neck. She felt her cheeks flush, and she realized that Garret knew why.

"Raking in the big bucks?" he asked.

"Hardly. But the festival is good for the community." Because she didn't trust her voice to hide her anxiousness, she turned to Jonathan. "How are you doing? How's the new place?"

"It's great," he said. "Nice view. Close to everything. Irina likes it too."

"I know. She tells me all the time," Thea said.

An awkward quiet settled among them. Thea looked out over the increasingly busy pier, watching an extended family of seagulls fight for a hot dog bun on the ground. "So," she asked Jonathan, "what are you reading these days?"

Jonathan looked away sheepishly. "Actually, I'm writing."

"Really?"

"Yep. A science fiction novel."

"He won't talk about it," Garret said. "It's a big secret. I can only assume it's about big-breasted alien women who come to earth to enslave the male population."

"That sounds just like something Jonathan would write," she joked.

The moment of awkwardness had passed. They stood for a few minutes, making small talk and watching Ken and Sue repeatedly miscalculate their beanbag throws—intentionally, from what Thea could tell. Eventually, Jonathan laughed and went to join them, leaving Thea and Garret alone.

She cleared her throat, searching for something to ask him about, some jumping-off point for a conversation. But all she could think of was the steely heat of his skin under her hands and how much she already missed it. That she was thirty-three years old and hadn't known that sex could be so powerful, so intimate, added a spark of anger to her already overheated thoughts.

"How's it going?" he asked.

"Okay," she said.

"Irina's having fun."

"Yes. She is."

"It's great."

"She does a great job."

The wind blew gently over the pier, sending a paper cup skipping along the weather-worn boards. The festival went on around them— the noise of blaring radios, the smells of popcorn and greasy meats, the shouts of cheerful vendors. She and Garret stood side by side, not speaking, and yet Thea felt the firm tug of the things they could not say passing between them. She tapped her hand against the side of her leg; he adjusted his sleeves. Together, they watched Irina instruct Ken on the best way to make a toss with the beanbag. When Garret chuckled, she felt the sound rumble through her whole body.

She started to speak at nearly the same time he did. "So—"

"Your—"

She laughed and turned toward him. "I'm sorry. You go."

"Your lips are chapped."

"Oh." She reached up and touched them instinctively, wetting her lower lip. His eyes narrowed, darkened. The look on his face was pained.

"Don't," she said. But she was there with him, remembering. Heat coursed through her, her skin burning with a memory all its own. His gaze held hers, and she could not bring herself to look away.

She was glad when Jonathan interrupted. "Quite a saleswoman we've got," he said. He'd jogged back across the planks of the old boardwalk to join them. His smile was easy and wide. "She just talked me out of five bucks because she said she couldn't make change."

"Sounds like Irina."

Jonathan glanced at Garret, then Thea. "Everything okay? You two aren't fighting again, are you?"

"No," Thea said lightly. "Not at all."

The newspaper had made it look so easy.

> *Newport—Multiple residents in the yachting club neighbor-hood phoned to report a disturbance between two recent Newport grads. Garret Sorensen was arrested on charges of disorderly conduct.*

Around the concession stand at the high school, the parents of good Newport children traded their theories over hot dogs and cans of Coke. *You know it was a temper tantrum*, some said. Veteran fathers joked: *It's always about a girl.*

At shiny, bright salons, where the women of Newport got their hair done and leafed through magazines, all their sympathy was with Garret. *So he made a mistake*, they said. *She didn't have to get him arrested. That was just cruel.*

And in the teachers' lounge of the high school, where coaches and tutors sat with the paper open on the old coffee table, the mood was much more somber. *Idiot*, they said, more with sorrow than unkindness. Garret's scholarship to Notre Dame for soccer had been provisional—and now it would be taken away from him. *What*, they asked each other, *had he been thinking?* One moment of overreacting because of a high school crush—and now his dream was gone. Those closest to him who saw how hard he'd worked felt the loss personally, deeply, as if all their own efforts had failed.

But Garret heard none of Newport's chatter. He stopped working at his father's boat shop and locked himself in his room. He ate little, slept less. He'd gone to Thea's that night to win her back; he'd hoped they might start over, that she might ask him up to her bedroom, that with his hands and his mouth and his attention he might heal the wounds he'd inflicted, using pleasure as a balm. But when he got to her house, he saw not only anger in her eyes but repulsion. She looked at him like he was small enough to squish under her foot. And he'd lost control. That he had blown it all—everything he'd worked for and wanted—in a few seconds, seemed unreal. And that *she* had been the instigator of that loss . . . he no longer thought that people were as good as they pretended to be.

In the darkness of his bedroom, his stubble began to soften; the air began to smell stale. Occasionally Sue or Ken came in, tried to talk to him. *Everyone has to get their heart broken*, his father said. *You've always done everything so much bigger than the rest of us. Seems like this is no different.*

His mother sat down on his bed and took a more practical approach. *Why don't you come out, let me make you some lunch to take on the patio. You'll feel better once you've had something to eat and some sunshine.*

Of everyone who'd come to talk sense to him, there was only one person Garret refused to speak to. Jonathan had knocked on the door, asked if they could talk. But Garret said nothing, staring at the panels of white and the doorknob.

I know you're mad at me, Jonathan said. *I wish you weren't. But she's not as tough as you think she is. She needs to be treated more gently. I just . . . I just don't think the two of you suit each other, and you should probably—I don't know—try to see that.*

Garret was too lethargic to bother saying *go away*. Eventually, Jonathan's monologue wound to a close and Garret heard footsteps disappearing down the hall. It would be a year before he considered speaking to his brother, and even then, the conversation was strained.

But Thea . . . he knew he would never see her again. He'd always counted on her warmth, her kindness, her generosity. And what she'd shown him was a cruelty that he hadn't thought she was capable of—not only because of how quickly she cast him aside and gave herself to Jonathan, but because when she'd found herself with the power to ruin him, she didn't hesitate. If she'd only said *No. No, he's not bothering me.* The police would have let him go that night. Rick Lazear, one of the cops who had showed up, knew Garret personally—knew his family. Rick would have vouched for him. He would have told them to break it up and go home. But the moment Thea said *yes*, she'd compelled the officers to take action.

Garret paced the floor in his room, stepping over hummocks of dirty laundry, aching for vengeance. Though he didn't think it consciously, something changed in him during those dark weeks. He would show Thea. He would show everyone. But first he had to get through his summer and the endless, aching sadness of hours spent alone.

The sound at the door came long after Thea had sent Irina off to her father's house for the weekend, long after she had slipped into her pajamas, and long after they'd packed up the beanbag toss and free samples of coffee at the Taste of Newport fair. Her heartbeat picked up speed as she made her way to the door. She knew Garret was there even before she let him in.

He walked past her into the kitchen. Beneath his jacket, he was still wearing the same dark jeans and green V-neck sweater that he'd been wearing at the pier. His face was pulled tight, his features strained. "What are you doing here?" she asked.

"Don't you know?"

She shut the door and stood across the room from him in

jogging shorts that had been relegated to her pajama drawer. She crossed her arms over her thin white tee. "We said once."

"I know what we said. It's not enough."

"It has to be."

"You know it's not just sex," he said, stepping toward her.

"But that's what you're here for, isn't it?"

"Yes," he said. "That. And more."

She moved around the table instinctively, putting it between them. Her hands grasped the top rail of a chair. "You can't just show up like this after all these years and expect to pick up where we left off."

"That's not what we're doing. I want to know you all over again. I want this to be *new*."

She laughed—an ugly sound. "We can't. Don't you see that? We blew our chance."

"You don't have to remind me," he said, his voice low. "I lost more than you did. You took my entire future from me."

"That's an excuse. If you'd really wanted to stay in soccer, you would have found a way. Played at a smaller school or something. Instead, you turned yourself into this . . . this *actor*."

"Excuse me?"

Thea pulled herself up straight, feeling as if a deluge of words was on the brink of spilling out, and she realized that in some strange way, she had been talking in her mind to Garret all day long—having this conversation again and again with him, so that if she ever got the chance to vent her feelings aloud, she would be ready. She cautioned herself to be moderate, to go easy. But when she thought of what they might have had, what they never would have, anger knocked out sense.

"I see glimpses of the real you from time to time—the guy I used to know," she said. "But it's like you hollowed yourself out over the years. What did it prove, Garret? That you're smart and good-looking? That you're powerful? Rich? That you're *happy*? Because I don't think you are."

He came toward her, moving around to the other side of the table. "Of all people, you've got no right to lecture me about being authentic."

"Maybe not," she said. "But at least I tried. You gave up years ago."

"You don't know anything about it."

"No?" she pulled herself up straighter. "I know that while you got to be angry and bitter and furious at me for what happened, I had to listen to your parents talk about you as if you'd hung the moon, knowing that you hated me—*hated* me—even though I never had the satisfaction of hating you back."

"Hold on here. *You're* pissed off at *me*?"

"Yes!" She dragged a hand through her hair. "Yes, I'm pissed off at you. You took something from me too, you know. I loved you, dammit. And that feeling—it never went away. I thought it did; I wanted it to. But it never went away."

She caught her breath. He was listening. When her anger settled, she saw that he was looking at her differently. His head was tipped slightly to the side where he stood before her. She could smell the saltwater on his jacket, and beneath it, the warm, alluring scent of his skin.

"You're still in love with me," he said softly.

She looked down, trying to think of how to recant. She didn't want to think of herself as having been in love with Garret for all this time, since she'd put him out of her mind on the day she got married. And yet, just because she'd closed her eyes to her feelings didn't mean they weren't there. "Maybe I was in love with the person I used to know."

"And what if he was standing right here, right now, with you?"

Her body felt very, very heavy. "Then I'd be in love with him too."

"Thea . . ." His arms came around her.

She reached up with both hands and touched his face. His eyes were as deep and sparkling as the bay on a spring morning. "I know," she said. She knew what he wanted—the desire in his eyes warmed her like sunlight on her skin. He made no apology for his kiss. Instead, it came fast and strong.

And then he was tugging her shirt over her head, her skin tingling as the cotton left her body, and her breasts ached in his hands. She tugged his undershirt from his jeans, all anger and worry turned to vapor by the force of need. He turned her so her palms were on the table, the wooden edge biting into the bones of her hips. Her shorts puddled around her ankles. His hands brushed the base of her spine as he loosed his zipper.

Once, she'd told him. But he was right: it hadn't been enough. *Once* was before. Once upon a time. But the sting and hot pleasure of his hands gripping her hips and tugging her flush against his body, the sound of table legs scraping the floor as they moved— this wasn't once. In fact, it had never been like this, so good that heat raced like particles of light along her every nerve. His hand clutched her hip, went seeking between her thighs, and moments later she was doused in pleasure, waves and waves of it racking her body like the surf washing the shore. This was now. A second time, a second chance, almost too much to stand.

He collapsed on top of her, his forehead pressed against her spine, and moments after her knees gave out beneath her, she was filled to bursting with love, with gratitude, and only the dimmest regrets about what might come.

That night, Garret dreamed of Thea—the same dream he'd had a thousand times. He dreamed he was holding her, that they were curled together comfortably skin to skin, safe, warm, happy. He always hated the dream; when he woke from it and discovered that he'd been dreaming, the emptiness ate holes in him. The momentary comfort and rightness of the dream had never outweighed the pain of waking up from it. He did his best to stay asleep as long as possible, to forestall the inevitable loss.

But sometime near daybreak, before the sun appeared, his sleepy brain began to realize that he was not only dreaming of Thea's soft breathing and the feel of her body against his, he was with her. She still loved him. And he knew: the bliss of reality far outweighed the joy of his dreams.

From "The Coffee Diaries"
by Thea Celik

The Newport Examiner

Coffee seeds are nestled within the cherry in pairs the shape of a heart or two cupped hands. But when only one seed is fertilized, only one seed matures. Single seeds are called peaberries.

When a farmer finds a peaberry in with the other, normal, dual-seed cherries, he or she must pull it out of the bunch. Peaberries have a different shape than their counterparts; the roasting process is different.

Some say coffee made only from peaberries tastes better than coffee made from normal seeds, because peaberries are round on all sides. And that may or may not be true.

But there's something so precious about two sweet little coffee seeds nestled together within a single cherry. It's ridiculous, but it almost makes you feel sorry for the seeds that come of age alone.

SEVENTEEN

On Harrison Avenue, the cramped streets of old colonial Newport gave way to rolling hills, bucolic estates, and a world famous
golf course. With the sense that he was running out of time—that
his life might explode into happiness or collapse into grief at any
moment—Garret parked his car beside the chateauesque old country club. Inside, he waved to the girl at the front desk whose name
he could never remember, then he searched for his mother.

She was reading a magazine in a large, sun-filled room when he
found her. She sat alone on a toile chaise before an unlit fireplace.
A dense bouquet of lilies glowed bleach white at her side.

"There you are," he said.

She jumped, startled. "Oh! Garret!" He rushed toward her on
long strides, and she turned her face for a kiss on the cheek.

"Dad still golfing?"

"He'll be a while," she said, folding her magazine closed and
setting it aside. "I had no idea you were in Newport today. I wish

you would have told me you were coming. Your father and I already have plans . . ."

"It was a spur-of-the-moment thing," he said. He sat down beside her on a settee that seemed so delicate he was nearly afraid he would break it.

"So what brings you here?" she asked, leaning on the armrest. If he hadn't known her so well, he might have missed the slight twitch of concern at the corner of her mouth.

"I need to tell you something," he said.

She stiffened visibly. "Go ahead."

He leaned his elbows on his knees, looked at the dark flooring between his shoes. For most of his adult life, he'd dedicated himself to hating Thea. And yet, what he was about to say felt like the most right and true thing he'd said in a very long time. "Mom . . . I'm in love."

"Oh Garret! That's wond—"

"I'm in love with Thea."

Sue lifted her forearm from the armrest and clasped her fingers together in her lap. "All right," she said. "Have you told Thea this?"

"I think she knows. And I think she feels the same way."

Sue stood, went to the empty black fire grate and stared glassy-eyed as if flames were burning there. "Did she have an affair with you? Is that why her marriage failed?"

"Good Lord, Mom. No. I wasn't even speaking to her until a few months ago. This would have never happened if she was still married."

"I'm glad to hear that, anyway." Sue's shoulders relaxed slightly. "All those years of posturing as if Thea was the devil herself . . . I suppose I knew better."

Garret stood, took his mother's hands. He was only slightly taken aback that she'd seen through all his years of holding a grudge even when he himself had not. "So you understand. Thea and I are made for each other. We always were."

Sue drew back. "Does Jonathan know?"

"No. Not yet."

"Are you going to tell him?"

"I want to know what you think I should do."

She moved away from him, walking aimlessly, her shoes clicking on the floor and echoing up to the skylights. "You want my blessing I suppose? My permission?"

"Yes."

She was quiet for a long moment. Too long. Her skin looked dull in the bright light, and the bags around her eyes told him that she was tired. He held his breath, waiting for her pronunciation. If Sue was behind him, his father would follow suit. And together they could help Jonathan to see that this was not a betrayal but the righting of a wrong.

"No," she said.

The air rushed out of his lungs.

"I can't give you my blessing unless you get Jonathan's first."

He crossed his arms. "I guess that's fair."

"Do me this one favor," she said.

"Anything."

"Don't tell your father. Not yet."

"Why?"

"I just don't want to cause any more waves than necessary. But *do* tell Jonathan. If you love her enough that you'd risk breaking up this family for her a second time—if you're sure about this, then you need to tell your brother the truth. And you need to do it now. The longer you wait, the worse it will get."

From down the hall, Garret heard his father's booming laughter carrying through the corridors. He walked toward her, kissed her. Her skin was cool. "I'll go see him today."

"Today?"

He smiled sadly. "I can't wait another minute. It's been fifteen years too long."

*　*　*

Thea was tired, physically exhausted, all through the morning shift. And yet, beneath the fatigue from a long night of lovemaking, she'd never felt more energized in her life. Some flame was burning deep within her, keeping her going, despite the outward tiredness. She thought, if she had to give a name to the energy driving her, it would be *hope*.

Now, she sat in Irina's room on the blue carpet, listening to church bells clang from far corners of the city. Around her, Irina's toys, clothes, and books were piled haphazardly, wreckage that reminded Thea of a debris-strewn beach after a hurricane. Jonathan had dropped Irina off at the house, but Irina had only been home for a few minutes before she pleaded to go watch a movie at the neighbors' house. Thea might have tried to persuade her to stay if she wasn't so tired, and if she hadn't been in need of some time alone.

For a week Thea had been threatening: *If you don't clean this room, I'm going to clean it for you.* And yet now that the day had come, Thea didn't hate the task at all. She moved through the room methodically, dolls going in one crate, books sliding into their places on a shelf, tiny metal cars collected in the pouch she'd made with the bottom of her shirt, then poured into a plastic basket and tucked away. Her daughter's messiness was a new phenomenon; Thea couldn't be sure if the disorganization was a kind of rebellion against her parents' separation or simply a result of being nearly eleven years old. She guessed it was both.

Her body was sore as she worked—her breasts abraded by the movement of her T-shirt, the muscles tender when she sat down. She tried to focus on the task at hand, but each new sensation reminded her of Garret: after their rushed coupling in the kitchen, they had spent the whole night making love, sleep alternating with tired but insurmountable desire. Garret had said he loved her. He was going to talk to his mother to see what they should do. Thea agreed.

Now, arranging her daughter's collection of stuffed animals on the net that Thea had strung on the wall, she wondered what Irina would think if her mother started dating again. How much should Thea go into detail with her daughter? How much would Irina understand? And if she did understand, would she approve?

Irina and Garret got along perfectly—almost better than Irina and Jonathan. They were cut of the same cloth, the two of them—both lovers of soccer and Saturday morning cartoons, of the occasional argument and adrenaline. But how would Irina feel once she learned that Thea and Garret were . . . *dating* wasn't the right word . . . were in love?

She reached under Irina's bed to refold the extra blankets that had been stored there, and when she pulled out the afghans that Thea's mother had made, she found a little stash of Irina's treasures too. They were in a small shoebox that lacked a lid. At first the collection seemed sweet: a picture of her father from when he was in high school, a ticket stub to a New England Revolution game, a bracelet made of fake pearls, a bell. But there were other items too that Thea hadn't seen before, more telling items: a small Swiss army knife (where had she gotten it?). A panty liner that had been opened, then closed again. An empty pack of cigarettes. A book of matches, just two inside. Was her daughter smoking? At ten years old?

Thea sat back on her knees, horrified but willing herself not to jump to conclusions. It wasn't out of the ordinary for a girl Irina's age to want to have secret things—adult things—for her own. Thea herself had kept a romance novel under her bed when she was twelve, and she'd been petrified that Garret or Jonathan or her parents might find out. But what Irina was keeping here was not so innocent as a novel.

She put the items back and got to her feet, her knees aching with the effort. Since Jonathan had moved out at the beginning of summer, Irina had been getting increasingly ill-behaved. The progression was so subtle, it might have been invisible to an outsider, but Thea was tuned in to even the slightest changes in her daughter's demeanor. At first, there had been nothing more than innocent back talk. Then there was the occasional blowup—a pushed-over cup, a broken toy. A few weeks ago they'd learned Irina had destroyed her textbook. And now—a knife. Matches. And if her daughter was smoking, Thea needed to know.

On the way down the stairs, Thea's muscles reminded her once again of the pleasure of last night. It struck her now how surreal, how dreamlike the whole thing had been, a pristine moment when she could think of nothing, feel nothing but the enormity and sweet trauma of so much bliss, all at once, after so much time. But as she made her way to find where she'd left the telephone, she had the sense that her night of ecstasy was boxed in by reality on all sides. In the kitchen, she did the only thing she could do. She called Jonathan.

Garret rarely second-guessed himself. But standing at the door of Jonathan's apartment on Sunday evening, his heart pounded with nerves and his palms were sweaty. It was the same brand of nervousness he'd felt the day he'd tried his first case alone. But there was much more at stake now.

"Hey, Gare!" Jonathan was bright-eyed when the door swung open. "C'mon in."

"Thanks." Garret walked into the big apartment. Over the last few weeks, Jonathan had done a great job of making his new home feel comfortable and personalized. A bookshelf ran along the far edge of the wall, the kitchen counter held a bowl of apples and pears, and the couch cushions were a frumpy, comfortable-looking mess. Garret could easily picture Irina here, lounging, laughing, falling asleep on her father's chest. A wave of longing swept over him when he thought of his condo—the expensive and top-grade showpiece he'd worked so hard on—as empty and pristine as a department store display. The hope that it wouldn't be so empty forever, that he was on the brink of rediscovering the life he'd always been meant to have, gave him courage to go on. "Looks like you're getting comfortable here," Garret said.

"Yeah. It's starting to feel like it's mine, you know?" He moved through the room quickly, sitting down on a chair to pull on his shoes. "And it turns out, I like living alone. I mean, I like having Irina here too. But there's something . . . I don't know . . . liberating about it. I don't have to care about leaving dishes in the sink. And if I want to spend all night reading until three a.m., I don't have to worry about turning off the light so someone else can sleep."

"That's great," Garret said. He watched his brother stand and grab a broken-in overcoat from the back of his chair. "You heading out?"

"Yeah," Jonathan said. "Going to the library to hear a lecture about the history of satellite making. Want to come?"

"It sounds great. But it's not really my scene."

"No worries." Jonathan shrugged with a smile. "Care to walk me over? It's just a couple blocks."

"Sure," Garret said.

The early evening was bright and crisp, the streets nearly empty. The colonial blue and clay red of Newport's oldest buildings were severe against the sky. Talking to Jonathan while they were walking was not the best timing; Garret would have preferred to talk somewhere quiet—and private too. But if life in politics had taught him one thing, it was that people who waited for the perfect opportunity would wait for it forever. Once Garret had decided to take action, action had to be taken—come what may.

At a stoplight, he shoved his hands in his jeans pockets. A cold wind swept down the street. "So, are you seeing anyone?" Garret asked.

Jonathan grinned. If Garret didn't know better, he'd say his brother's eyes were twinkling. "Not yet. But I've got prospects."

"Oh yeah? What kind of prospects?"

"The kind with pretty eyes and a warm smile," he said.

The light changed, and Garret realized he forgot to acknowledge his brother's good humor before they started down the crosswalk. He was too wrapped up in his own thoughts. He was glad that Jonathan was dating—or at least thinking of dating—because it meant his brother was healing. He was learning to make his life into the kind of life he wanted. But it also meant he was ready to move on, and perhaps let Thea do the same.

"I'm thinking of seeing someone too," Garret said, his voice strained.

"Anyone I know?"

He nodded. He started to say *yes* but the word got stuck in his throat.

"Really?" Jonathan's eyes flashed interest. "The blond from the cheese shop? That waitress you were telling me about from the airport?"

"No." Garret's stomach soured. "Someone you know better than that."

Jonathan stopped walking. He didn't seem to notice that they were blocking the entrance to the library, where people needed to go around them to get inside. His smile wavered. "You don't mean . . . no. You're not talking about . . ."

Garret said nothing.

Jonathan's confusion exploded into rage. "You've got to be *kidding* me."

"We didn't plan it. It just . . ." He was going to say, *It just happened*, but he realized how terribly cliché an admission it would be—a line from a movie, almost, and one that explained nothing.

"Bullshit." Jonathan lifted his arms and dropped them, the gesture rife with futility. "This is bullshit."

"You're mad . . ."

"Of course I'm mad. Of course I'm fucking mad!"

Garret glanced nervously at a woman hurrying her children away from them. He needed to get them out of the doorway area, out of the public eye. But even though Jonathan looked around frantically, as if searching for help, Garret knew he wasn't seeing. He was blinded by emotion—insensible to anything that was going on around him. Garret tried to calm him down. "Look, Jon. We don't have to talk about this here. Let's go somewhere. We'll figure it out."

"I'm not going anywhere. Not with you." Jonathan laughed, his eyes wild with disbelief. "What is this? Some kind of payback because I married her? You're gonna move in on her now to get back at me?"

"Jonathan." Garret tried to gentle his voice, but it didn't come out in the soothing tone he'd hoped. Instead, it sounded more like a warning. He'd never been good at backing down—not with anyone. And yet, he *had* to get good at it, fast. He couldn't let this blow out of control. "Are you mad that she still loves me? Or are you mad that she's making decisions without you for the first time?"

"She makes plenty of decisions without me."

"*Now*, she does. You cheated on her. And then you divorced her. You don't get a say in what she does anymore."

"Fine. I get that. But it's not about Thea. It's about you and me—being brothers again. Being friends."

"That's why we're talking about this . . ."

"Right. As if you haven't already slept with her."

A pang of guilt swept through him. "Look, Jonathan—"

"You *did* sleep with her. I can't believe this. All those years you wouldn't speak to her, all the years you and I had to tiptoe around each other because you *hated* her guts and thought she wasn't good enough for me, and now you're sleeping with her?"

"You can't honestly tell me you're shocked," Garret said, forcing his jaw to relax. "I *had* to hate her. Hate was easier. Hate meant I could pretend I didn't still love her. Jonathan—I know you can see this for what it really is."

"Oh. Right. What it really is." Jonathan laughed—cackled. "What you're telling me is that she never loved me. That it was always about you."

Garret heard Jonathan's phone ringing; they both ignored it. "No—I'm not—"

Jonathan grabbed Garret by the collar and pushed him against the wall. "Look. You're a selfish prick. You always have been. You want to know why Thea and I got married? Because she hated your guts. And because I had to clean up the mess you made."

Something hardened in Garret's brain—some primitive command that readied him for combat. If Jonathan wanted a fight, Garret wouldn't throw the first punch. But he would throw the last. "I'm warning you. You better step down."

Jonathan scowled for a long moment. Their eyes locked. And then, with a slight push, he let his brother go. "I've been stepping down my whole life. But now I'm done." He walked away from Garret a few steps. "You want Thea? Fine. Have her. But if you do, don't expect to have anything to do with me again."

At the coffee shop on Monday, Thea was too distracted to focus on her work. She'd stopped by with Irina during the evening shift to check on the shop, and as so often happened, she found herself drawn into the crises of the moment—a broken grinder, a clogged sink, the phone ringing off the hook. She sent Irina into the office to play and got to work, barely noticing what she did. She was waiting for her cell phone to ring. She was hoping for good news.

Garret had gone to talk with Sue yesterday, and she wished he would have called already and given her a much-needed update. She wanted the assurance that Sue would support them—that she and Garret would be allowed to see how far their love for each other could go. And she wanted to hear from Jonathan too—she *needed* to hear from him. Thea had no idea how to handle Irina's collection of contraband. Would it be best to ask Irina to tell the truth—and possibly set her up to get into even bigger trouble by lying? Or was it better to confront her outright?

She was surprised when she saw Sue walk into the coffee shop, her jacket zipped tight to her chin and a soft cream hat pulled down over her forehead. Her gaze homed in immediately on Thea, and the way she crossed the room—swiftly, directly, unsmiling—made the fine hairs on Thea's arms stand on end.

"Sue. What's happened?"

Sue glanced up at Thea. Her frown was stern—an expression Thea had seen in only the rarest moments over the course of their lives. "Can we talk alone?"

"Of course. Let's—we'll head in back."

Thea led Sue down the hall to her office, where her desk was strewn with last week's invoices and her daughter's toys littered the floor. Irina, who was sitting at her chalkboard, jumped to her feet when she saw her grandmother. Sometime during the last hour, she'd done her own hair: two ashy brown and lopsided pigtails.

"Grandma!"

"Hello, my darling." Sue kissed the top of her head.

"I didn't know you were coming!" Irina beamed up at her.

"I just stopped by to talk to your mommy."

Thea smoothed back Irina's bangs. "Go out into the store and stay with Claudine for a few minutes."

Irina looked from Thea to Sue and back. "But I want to stay here with you. Grandma, it's okay if I stay here, right?"

"Not this time," Sue said. Irina went instantly quiet. Thea too felt the ominous shift in the air around them, the caution in Sue's tone.

"But you'll come see me later? Right?" Irina asked.

"Yes," Sue said. "But for now you've got to run along." When Irina had gone, she closed the door to the office and did not sit. She pulled herself upright, and when she spoke she sounded as if she'd been rehearsing. "I've tolerated a lot in my life," she said, her voice low and tight. "When you were dating Garret, I welcomed you as a daughter. When you changed your mind and married Jonathan, I kept my opinions to myself. When you divorced him, I fought for you to stay a part of this family. But now, I don't think I can do it anymore."

Thea's head felt light. "What happened?"

"My boys are fighting again," she said. "Over you."

"So Garret told him . . ."

"I thought Jonathan might have been understanding. But he wasn't. And I'm not sure he isn't justified."

Thea leaned against the desk behind her, unable to process everything at once. In the hours before dawn, she and Garret had talked about telling Jonathan as soon as possible. Neither one of them liked the idea of keeping secrets. And yet she hadn't realized he'd meant to act quite so fast. He must have been following Sue's advice.

Thea hooked her hands on her apron. The possibility that she could lose everything was no longer some specter distant as a boat on the horizon. It was here and now. Sue was frustrated with her, and whatever Sue decided about the situation, it would be law.

"*Thea* . . ." When Sue spoke again her voice was pained, as if she was on the brink of tears. "I need you to make this stop."

"I don't know what you're asking . . ."

"Ken's retiring this year. He's worked so hard for this family—and he feels like he's finally going to get some peace and relaxation in his life. The doctor told him he needed to cut back on his work and his stress, or he's in danger of having a stroke."

"Do Jonathan and Garret know this? Why didn't you tell us sooner?"

"Because he didn't want you to know. He didn't want to worry you. Isn't that funny . . . *him* worrying about worrying *you* kids . . ." Sue shook her head, lost for a moment in her own thoughts. When her eyes cleared, she took Thea's hand. "You know I love you. But some relationships can only bear so much."

"What do you think we should do?"

"What do I think *you* should do?" Sue corrected her. "Please. Have some mercy on my family. We need peace. My whole family needs peace. And I would think you do too. The three of you have been trying to find a balance since you were kids, and it's never worked. Not once. It never will."

Thea began to tremble. She held on to Sue's hand. "So what are you asking me?"

"I'm saying that it's time to end all this."

"Are you asking me to stay away from Garret? From Jonathan? Even from you?"

"I'm sorry," Sue said. "But yes, I am."

The year after Thea had graduated high school—after Jonathan had proposed with a *real* ring this time and Thea had said she would think about it, and after Garret had paid his fine and started over at a two-year school—Thea became an orphan. Her mother and father had packed up what things they needed to start over in Turkey, and the deeds to the house and the Dancing Goat had been signed over to her.

She'd stood in the departure hall of the airport, escalators and sunglass kiosks and the echo of mile-high ceilings surrounding her on all sides, and when her parents had rounded the last corner of the gate and she could no longer see them, she knew for the first time what it was to be without them. In some ways, she was no longer their child—no longer a child at all. The responsibility of their business and their home had fallen on her, and she'd taken up the burdens gladly—her last connection to her family. Watching the planes nose higher into the atmosphere behind tall windows, she felt as if a part of her was going missing—as if her father had accidentally packed a piece of her heart in his suitcase with his socks, and now it was being loaded into some dark and anonymous cargo hold.

But then—from that place of such sorrow and loss—Thea felt someone take her hand. Sue. She held it firmly, solidly—less to give comfort than to give strength. And when Thea glanced up at the woman beside her whom she was only just beginning to understand was a friend, she saw that Sue had been crying too. For Thea's sake.

They stood for a long time in the airport, long after Thea's parents had disappeared, not speaking. Outside the windows, the sky grew subtly pink. The frenzy of the departure hall faded. And at last, Sue put her arm around Thea and spoke.

"Come on," she said. "Let's go home."

Thea dropped two bags of groceries on the kitchen table; the day's hours had passed like a dream she still wasn't quite sure she'd had. While Irina prattled on, making an argument for staying up later,

Thea began to put away the bags and boxes of food she'd picked up at the grocery store. She pressed play on the answering machine.

"Hi, Thea? It's Lettie. I got a very odd phone call today, and my phone box is telling me that it was from your house. I can't imagine that's right. Please give me a call."

Irina grew suspiciously quiet, leaving the kitchen quickly, and the answering machine beeped again.

"Hello, this is Len Dempsey. I'm just calling to let you know that my daughter says she got a prank phone call from this number today from another little girl. Totally harmless—the old is-your-refrigerator-running thing. But I thought you'd like to know."

Thea stopped putting away a box of pasta.

"Um, hi. I got a call that said I was supposed to call this number back about a free television—"

She pushed stop. She looked at the sleek black answering machine. *Eight new messages*, it read. She pulled out a chair at the table, brown paper bags standing before her like parapets, and sat down. She knew she should be angry, should call Irina out. But how much more could a person tackle in one day? She stared absently at the groceries she'd yet to put away, watching condensation slip down the side of a Popsicle box. She felt too empty to cry.

When she heard Irina come into the room, she didn't turn her head.

"It's eight thirty. Aren't you going to make me go to sleep?" Irina asked.

Thea glanced at her—the daughter who was as worried about the future as Thea was, but who had no way to express it. "No."

Irina's eyes narrowed. She had already gotten herself into her princess pajamas and brushed her hair so it hung straight and brown before her shoulders. The look on her face said she thought she was being led into a trap. "Really?"

"It's fine. Watch your TV show."

To Thea's surprise, the furrow between Irina's eyebrows spoke less of elation than dismay. "You're not going to yell at me?"

"No."

"Really?"

"No, I'm not going to yell at you."

Irina stood looking at her for a moment, uncertain, then gave a yawn that would have earned her the starring role in her school play. "I guess I am kinda tired. I can tuck myself in tonight. You don't have to. Okay?"

Thea closed her eyes. The tears that had been mysteriously absent a moment ago now gathered in full force. Her ten-year-old daughter—how could kids sense the things they did? When she opened her eyes, Irina was standing in the doorway with a mix of hope and confusion on her face that touched Thea's heart. "Come here."

In a moment Irina was in her arms, clinging tight with her head turned to the side. Thea kissed her hair. It smelled of strawberry shampoo and that indescribably sweet scent that Thea had come to love when she'd first caught it on her daughter's infant skin. Irina had been through so much—and with each day her acting out grew bigger and more dangerous. If Sue was the moral compass that guided her family, Irina was the measure of the family's emotional health. And she was wilting as any seedling in the pressure of drought and sun.

Thea rocked her gently, the resolve to protect her daughter as deep and enduring as on the day Irina was born. The feeling was more than duty—it was need. The promise to give safe passage through childhood. To guard against unhappiness while the opportunity was there.

Thea stood from the chair, carrying Irina with her gently, and walked her upstairs to her bedroom. She turned on the night-light and shut the blinds. She helped Irina into the covers, brushed back the hair from her forehead, and kissed her there.

It had been a hard year, filled with sweeping changes, the foundation of their family life shifted not by degrees but by miles. Thea had believed her and Jonathan's civility toward each other would be enough to reassure their daughter that life would not substantially change. The plan might have worked too, if Thea hadn't gone and selfishly altered the balance—believing in a weak and naive moment that she could have Garret without complications, that she could have everything.

Irina turned over onto her stomach, and Thea tucked the covers in around her. What had she been thinking? Last night, Garret had held her and promised her that they were doing the right thing, that their family would want them to be happy. But now, what fragile accord the family had found was gone. Jonathan was angry at Thea, angry at Garret. Sue was frustrated with all of them. And Irina—whether she knew it or not—was picking up on all the negativity and feeding it back to them in the form of torn-up textbooks and prank calls.

In the doorway of Irina's room, Thea paused, pain opening her up and deepening like a dark pit. This morning, she'd felt as if she'd finally—*finally*—had Garret back, but now, for the sake of her daughter, it looked like she would need to give him up again. The thought of life without him, of how close they'd almost come . . .

She shook herself out of her self-pity. The future was clear, without alternatives. It shone before her—forgiveness, redemption, acceptance—bought at the price of love.

*   *   *

That night, she wrote to Jonathan in an e-mail:

I left a message that I needed to talk with you. I found some things under Irina's bed—a knife and matches. I worry that she's smoking. And apparently she's been making prank calls.

We need to be together, all three of us. As a family. Let's do something together. Let's go to a zoo. Let's carve pumpkins. Anything. She needs to know her family is solid, that we're all behind her. Call me tomorrow—we'll set something up.

I know I'm the last person you want to talk to right now. But I'm not writing about us. I'm writing about Irina. I trust you, completely, to help me give Irina the best life I can. Will you trust me to do the same?

She started to write her name in closing, but when she looked over the letter one last time, she realized she hadn't said all she needed to say.

Just so you know, I've decided that it's best Garret and I not see each other.

The cursor blinked before her, asking her to write more. One sentence could not undo everything that had happened. No number of sentences could. So she erased it quickly, then without time for second-guessing, hit *Send*.

From "The Coffee Diaries"
by Thea Celik

The Newport Examiner

To kick the coffee habit, many people give up outright.

There are a number of theories about where the phrase *quit cold turkey* came from. Some say it's related to *talk turkey*, which at one point was slang for *speaking bluntly without thinking first*. Others believe it's from the idea of serving turkey cold—without preparation.

Regardless, quitting cold turkey is asking for trouble. Symptoms of caffeine withdrawal can be brutal—headaches, irritability, drowsiness, insomnia, stomach cramps, and more. To mitigate the discomforts, many experts recommend that caffeine be reduced gradually over time—as opposed to all at once.

And yet for some people, the only way to quit is to quit fully and completely. Weaning oneself off caffeine little by little may be more difficult to bear.

EIGHTEEN

The alleyway of the Dancing Goat was dark and cold, but Garret hardly felt the chill. The days were growing shorter, the brittle skeletons of leaves chattering along the brick walkways and skittering into corners. Above, the stars were obscured between the high walls of the buildings, but the clouds were white gray and moonlit, passing quickly as if they were sliding down the sky.

At last, Thea and an older woman emerged from the coffee shop, and when the woman looked up and saw Garret there, she gasped and jumped back. He recognized her a moment later: she was Lettie, who'd been at the Dancing Goat since he was just a boy. She used to give him a hard time for wearing his pants too baggy when he was a teen. He was glad to see her, glad she was still around.

"It's okay," he said, holding out his hands. "It's okay. I didn't mean to startle you. I'm here to talk to Thea."

"Garret." Lettie put a hand to her chest while Thea locked the door. "You nearly gave an old woman a heart attack!"

"Sorry."

Thea looked at him a long moment; he didn't like the distance in her eyes. "You waited for me out here?"

He shrugged. Standing in the cold had seemed like the best idea; he didn't want to end up milling around awkwardly in the coffee shop, waiting for Thea to close up, making pointless small talk while bigger issues loomed. "I just got here a second ago," he said.

Thea tipped her chin down; she obviously didn't believe him. But she said, "It's okay, Lettie. You can go."

Lettie gave her a quick look—even Garret could see it meant *Are you sure?* But the older woman took Thea's cue, cinched up her heavy coat, and started down the alley. "Good to see you," she said as she walked past him. "I hope we run into each other again. Though perhaps without the heart failure."

Garret laughed politely, and then, a moment later, he and Thea stood in the narrow alleyway alone. She wore faded jeans, a heavy black peacoat, and sturdy sneakers. She pulled a knit wool hat over her ears—it was thick and embellished with red and white Norwegian stars, and she tucked her hair inside.

"So what are you doing here?" she asked.

"I needed to see you." She stood a few feet away—too far. He wished she would come toward him, put her arms around him. But she only stood still. "Walk with me?" he asked.

"Okay."

Together, they made their way slowly out of the alleyway and onto the main thoroughfare of Price's Pier. Most of the stores had already closed for the evening, and the pier was nearly empty, lit only by streetlights and the glow of seasonal window displays. The scrimshaw shop, where old Charlie Rourke etched schooners onto recycled piano keys, had been decorated with oversized pumpkins, stalks of brown and white corn, and bales of hay. Soft shadows nestled beneath empty benches and clung beneath eaves.

"Let's go to the edge," Garret said.

"All right," she said, her voice blank.

The cold air blowing in from the harbor stung Garret's cheeks and made his eyes tear. At his side, Thea wrapped her scarf tighter around her neck, shivering slightly, and Garret knew they wouldn't be able to stay outside very long. They walked out to the old lobster market, a warehouse that sat at the far end of the pier. In the dark, its weather-beaten boards and doors the size of truck beds seemed vaguely ominous. Beneath a single lamp, Garret leaned his shoulder against the planks, facing Thea. The building blocked some of the wind.

"I need to talk to you," he said.

"I heard you had a fight with Jonathan."

"Did my mother tell you?"

Thea nodded. Her gaze slid away for a moment—a flicker of something he couldn't read.

"He wants me to choose. You or my family."

"I know," she said. She looked out into the distance. The water was dark as pitch tonight, all that opaque black speckled by boat lights as if by stars. "I love your family," she said.

"I know you do."

"I won't make you choose between me and them."

He moved closer, took her hand, even though all he could feel was her gloves. "What if it's a choice I want to make?"

She looked down at their fingers locked together. "You can't leave them again. Not after having been away for so long."

He sighed, and he knew she was right. He was only just beginning to see how much he'd missed—and how much he regretted—all the years of tension between himself, his brother, and his parents. And yet, some part of him was prepared to do anything to keep her at his side.

"What if we just take a break?" he asked. "We can wait a year.

Two. Five—I don't care how long. Things might look different then."

"They might," she said, offering a watery smile. "But right now, I know this can't work. I've got my daughter to think of—she's already been through a lot this year. You've got to think of your family. It's bad timing."

"I know." He leaned his forehead against hers for a moment. "I think if this had happened to us when we were kids, we would have just said screw it. Eloped. Gone and bought a house out West or something and never come to Newport again."

"But we're not kids," Thea said, drawing back. "So it's not that easy. And I love you too much to see you cut off from your family because of me."

For long moments, he looked at her—her brown eyes, the thick knit stitches of her hat running along her forehead, her pretty skin the color of tea. He felt the distance between them, the distance she'd wedged there, meant to lessen the pain. But he couldn't stand it—all this intentional numbness. If they were going to do this, he wanted to feel it—all of it. Everything good about what they were together and everything that made him feel like his heart was being ripped from his chest. He couldn't stand by and let her disengage—pretend this wasn't happening and that everything was going to go back to normal. He didn't want to be the only one acknowledging the pain.

"Thea . . ."

She looked into his eyes, some of the flatness already giving way.

"Dance with me?"

She hesitated: he could see the war within her, one part of her wanting to linger and savor these last private moments together, and the other part urging her to shut down her emotions and flee. He helped her make the decision. He took off his glove, lifted his hand to brush the backs of his fingers along her cheek. Her eyes fluttered closed, her breath drawing in, and he pulled her against him. His cheek pressed hers as he swayed with her, his arms holding her as tight as all their clothes would allow. He loved the cocoon of warmth they'd made together, tucked away in the shoulder of the lobster market. The wind's moan, the creaking boards of the pier, the clang of a hard rope knocking a flagpole—if he listened right it almost sounded like music. When he pulled back to look at her, tears had gathered in her eyes.

"Garret," she said, his name a plea.

He kissed her. Wanted to memorize her mouth, her taste. Memories stored up for days and years down the line. She leaned into him, her lips parting beneath his, and fire rippled beneath his skin. Everything he'd ever wanted, the life he dreamed of, was locked inside her heart. He kissed her forehead, her eyelids. He held her tight and buried his face in the crook of her neck, swaying with her body. He felt the wetness of her tears against his face.

"I'll always love you," he said, the words so important and yet so futile. "No matter what happens. No matter where I go or what I do. That won't change."

"I know," she said.

He kissed her again, long and slow. He felt her shivering, less from emotion than the bitter cold. He wished the evening were more gentle—a warm breeze, a pink sunset. But the hard Atlantic winter was already creeping in, and the time for bittersweet good-byes had lapsed long ago.

He eased his grip on her, though it cost him so much. "Can I walk you to your car?"

"Please—*don't*," she said, her voice breaking as she inched away. "Just stay here for a minute. Wait until I'm out of sight. Then—then, you can go."

He nodded. She squeezed his hand once, her eyes full of words, brimming over, words she couldn't say. And then she turned and ran, the wind blowing her scarf behind her in the streetlight. He waited in the shadow of the building, watching, until she had disappeared.

Dear Thea,

I have no interest in seeing you. What you did is awful. You are awful.

I don't think Irina is smoking. You didn't find any ciga-rettes, did you? And she doesn't smell like smoke. I think it's pretty clear what you should do: take the matches and knife away, explain that they're dangerous. Irina's a smart cookie. She'll get it.

And as for prank phone calls, don't forget you made your share when we were kids.

Jonathan

The windows of the old Newport library shuddered and clanged, and falling leaves danced in the streetlights outside. Though the library was warm, damp drafts drifted in among the shelves of books from hidden places. Jonathan had left his coat on during the discussion—Lori Caisse had too. The little group had been talking for an hour, and the librarians were beginning to mill about the doorway, a sign that they were getting anxious to close.

"Jonathan."

Jonathan had stood to gather his things to leave, and Lori stopped him with a hand on his arm. He smiled at her nervously. He'd never considered himself an especially handsome man: he had a long face and eyes that were a bit too close-set for his liking. But until he'd started seeing Lori every few weeks, he hadn't much cared about whether he was handsome or not. Now he found himself feeling shy under her bright and direct gaze.

"Please don't tell me that Irina failed her social studies exam," he said, half joking. "We've been studying so much, I think that girl could probably pass a citizenship test at this point."

"I haven't graded it yet." Lori tipped her head to the side; Jonathan couldn't have looked away if he'd tried. "Why? Do you need to bring a report back to Thea when you go home tonight?"

"Do I need to . . . Oh, no. No, we're not back together," Jonathan said. "If that's what you—I mean, if you were thinking we were—"

"Oh." The color in Lori's cheeks rose, and she blushed the most lovely shade of strawberry Jonathan had ever seen. "I thought maybe you were back together. Maybe that's why you haven't asked me out."

Jonathan could only stare a moment, tongue-tied. The rest of the book group had wandered out of the library, leaving them alone among the shelves and empty chairs. They stood face-to-face under the high dome, and Jonathan suddenly had the odd feeling that he was standing with her not in a library but in a place as important and quiet as church.

"Or maybe it's too soon," Lori said. She picked up her jacket and tugged it on. "You know what? I'm sorry. It's too soon, isn't it? Wow, this is embarrassing. Just forget it—"

"Lori." He touched her, his hand landing directly on her waist instead of her elbow. The electricity was instant, shocking. He saw her eyes go wide. "Hey. It's not too soon."

She reached into her purse, opened her calendar—an old, brown leather planner as thick as an encyclopedia—and scribbled something down. "Here." She handed him the piece of paper. "This is my address and number. Let's just . . . I don't know . . . grab a cup of coffee this weekend. Something low-key."

"I can't," he said. "I have Irina."

"All right. Another day then. A weeknight."

He wanted to say something romantic and intriguing. But all he could come up with was, "Sounds like a plan."

Later, as he walked to his car, the brown, wet leaves dropping like weights around him, he couldn't ignore the charge that raced through his blood. He had never asked anyone on a date before. He'd married so young, he simply had never needed to go on a formal date. The idea that he was going on one now felt as exciting as the first time he'd stood in line for a roller coaster at an amusement park. But in some distant and shadowy part of his mind, he thought of Thea. He wondered what she was doing tonight. If she was alone.

The way Garret told the story to Jonathan was this: *I made a decision—just like you asked me to. But don't ask me to be happy about it.*

The way Garret told the story to his colleagues was this: *No, I wasn't interested in the HUD project in the past. But you know me—once I lock onto something, I get it. Most of the time. Anyway, I wouldn't lie to you. I want this assignment. I love D.C.*

The way Garret told the story to his mother was this: *I have to get away for a while. You know why. I don't know how long.*

The way Garret told the story to himself was this: *It's not running. It's giving everyone space to breathe. It's giving me space to breathe. If I go through the motions of getting over her, then it just might happen. It just might . . .*

But somewhere over Virginia, after the captain had turned on the fasten seat belts sign, Garret began to wonder if he was making a mistake. The flight had been a short one; with the flight attendant bringing an endless supply of oaky añejo tequila to his seat in first class, he'd hardly boarded the plane before the captain was telling him it was nearly time to get off. He pulled his seat upright, upended his last shot, and stowed his tray. He tortured himself with his options: *I could fly back.*

But when the plane touched down and he felt the rumble of the wheels beneath him and the pressure of gravity as they lost speed, he knew that even if he returned directly to Newport, it would not feel like going home.

Thea sat in the car, waiting in a line of traffic to pick her daughter up from school on Friday afternoon in late October. All along Van Zandt Avenue, children with bright-colored backpacks were searching out their parents' cars and running energetically toward them. Thea sat listening to the news on the radio, keeping her eyes peeled for Irina. When she noticed her daughter, talking to a group of laughing girls near the stairs, she thought about beeping the horn. But Irina wasn't looking around for her ride; she was hanging out. Taking her time.

Thea opened the car door and stood. She called Irina's name and waved. Normally, she might have been more patient, but she needed to get to the shop to train a new hire. Irina glanced over and saw her mother. She turned to her friends, said something that made them laugh, then walked—in no hurry—to meet Thea. She slid her backpack on the passenger-side floor as she climbed into the car.

"Sorry," she said.

"It's okay." Thea checked the traffic and pulled out slowly onto the street. "How was your day?"

They went through the usual conversation—Thea prying details and answers out of Irina about her homework, her tests, her lessons for the day. The thought of Irina's stash under her bed still bothered her, and because she didn't want to hold off until Irina got into serious trouble (was she bringing the knife to school?), she'd decided that she could no longer wait to speak with Jonathan. Apparently, he'd felt that an e-mail was all that the situation called for. She would tackle this problem on her own.

"Irina," she said sternly. "I found the box under your bed."

Irina's eyes grew big—over-the-top innocence. "What box?"

"If you lie, you'll make this a hundred times worse."

She changed gears fast. "So what? Who cares?"

"Where did you get the knife?" Thea asked.

Irina looked out the window. "Are you going to take it away from me?"

"I don't know. Where did you get it?"

She slumped down in her seat. "I traded with a kid at school for it."

"What did you trade him?"

"Espresso beans."

"What did he want with them?" Thea asked.

"Energy," Irina said. "They make you run fast."

Thea shook her head. "It's dangerous to give children caffeine like that. How many did you give him?"

"I don't know," she said, annoyed. "A handful?"

Thea stopped at a red light. "Don't do that again. Understand? If I catch you giving espresso to kids, you're grounded."

"You're probably going to ground me anyway."

Thea drummed her fingers on the steering wheel. "What about the cigarettes and matches?"

"I don't have any cigarettes."

"You have an empty pack."

Irina turned to her mother, her bottom lip protruding in a

frown. "I don't smoke, Mom. I just like the way the box smells. Like apples. Smoking is gross. It's tar."

Thea breathed a sigh of relief.

"And anyway I tried smoking once."

Thea stopped drumming. Her heart may have stopped as well. "And?"

"It tasted disgusting. Like . . . like ash!"

Thea held back a smile, pleased that if there was one thing that would keep her daughter from smoking, it was smoking itself. The light turned green, and she pressed the gas. "All right, here's the deal," she said. "You agree to these terms, or I really do ground you. Ready?"

Irina nodded.

"First, no more giving espresso beans out. They *don't* make you run faster. But they can make your heart race if you don't know how you'll react to them, and that could be very dangerous. Especially for kids. Okay?"

"Yes."

"Two, when we get home, we're throwing away the matches. They're dangerous, Irina. Not for playing with. Understand?"

"Fine."

"Last, I keep the knife until you're old enough to have it back."

"When's that?"

"I don't know exactly. We'll have to see how well you behave. If you're mature enough to have it."

"Really?"

Thea nodded.

"Fine. As long as you won't ground me," she said.

They rode in silence, heading south toward the Dancing Goat, and Thea thought to herself that there was something almost too easy about the conversation. Irina, who so often dug her heels in, had agreed to Thea's terms without any terms of her own. Thea would have to keep an eye on her daughter for a while, just to make sure she wasn't getting into any trouble. She hoped Irina's rebellion phase didn't last too long. There was only so much Thea could take.

The week dragged into the weekend, and Thea knew Garret had left—she felt his absence like a thinning of the air or the change in temperature that happens when the sun dips behind a cloud. She forced herself to know it, to reconcile with it, to embrace his disappearance. He hadn't told her he was leaving Newport, and yet somehow she knew the moment he was gone.

The baristas at the coffee shop did their best to cheer her up, and she did her best to let them. Only Dani and Lettie seemed to have guessed what was wrong, but neither of them spoke about it. They asked Thea if she was eating and insisted on going out to lunch. They offered to watch Irina if Thea needed a break, and when business was slow and Thea lingered longer than necessary, Lettie put her foot down and sent her home.

On Saturday evening, Thea had flipped the sign on the door from Open to Closed, and the baristas put on eighties music and danced as they cleaned up, Claudine making advances on a broom and Jules twirling à la Ginger Rogers as he mopped. Apparently someone had told Dani there was a party, because she'd brought her civilian clothes to change into in the bathroom after her shift. Lettie showed up with her knitting bag full of all the fixings for mojitos.

Sure, Thea thought. *Why the hell not?*

They closed the shades and dimmed the lights and tucked in for a long evening. And, sometime around one a.m., Thea realized she was drunk.

Jules refilled her glass, and she shook her head and pushed it away. "Oh come on," he said. "Lettie's opening in the morning. You don't have to be up."

"No." She stood on wobbly legs and went behind the counter for a glass of water. It tasted fantastic—crisp and clear going down. When it was gone, she poured another. Jules turned around in his seat to look at her as she rejoined them.

"Why don't we get out of here?" he asked. "There's this little bar I know about around the corner; it's so adorable. The kitchen is open all night, and they make the best lobster rolls this side of the Penobscot Bay."

"Lobster rolls?" Thea said. "I haven't had one in twenty years."

"Then maybe it's time to try again!"

"No. No lobster rolls." Thea put down her water, suddenly feeling an intense need to explain. To make him—all of them— understand. "Look. I don't like them. And that's all there is to it. It doesn't matter why I don't like them, I just don't."

"Okay, okay!" Jules said, sitting back in his chair and laughing. "No lobster rolls!"

But Thea wasn't done. "Do you know why Irina likes soccer?"

Claudine grinned. "Because it's the *real* football?"

Thea rolled her eyes.

"Because she's a show-off," Dani said. "And I think she gets a kick out of outplaying the boys."

"It's because it suits her," Lettie said. "That's all."

"Right." Thea jabbed her pointer finger in the air. "Soccer suits her. I never taught her to like it. I figured I would have been carting her to and from ballet or piano lessons by now. But nope—she likes soccer. And I have no idea why."

"Where are you going with this?" Claudine asked.

"I have no idea," Thea said. "I guess . . . I guess the point is that—okay—I did what you guys asked." She looked around at her friends, Claudine with her purple fedora, Lettie with her necklace of pearls, Dani with her boy-cut hair, and Jules with all the best intentions in the world. "I tried to reinvent myself—you know, the whole new post-divorce me. But as it turns out, I *like* the coffee shop. I *like* being a mom, even though I had Irina young. And I like my house, even though I inherited it from my parents."

She noticed that her friends had grown quiet, listening.

"I mean, maybe I could learn to like Indian food. Or lobster rolls. Or kissing strangers at two a.m.—"

"Whoa, I need to hear this story," Jules said.

"But," Thea continued, "my life, the life I've been living so far, suits me for the most part. I don't want to talk myself into being a person that I'm not. I like what I like. And I love who I love. And it doesn't matter *why* I love. I just do. And that's all there is."

Lettie stood up and walked around the table to Thea. "Come on, darling." Thea glanced up at her. "Come on and let Lettie take you home."

Thea looked up, confused. The look on Lettie's face was filled with gentle concern, and it wasn't until that moment that Thea realized she'd been crying. When she touched her cheeks, they were wet. "Lettie . . ." She started to say she was sorry, but the words wouldn't come out.

"Shhh." Lettie took her hand and helped her out of her chair. "Come on, love. You've had a long week. A very long week."

The room spun. Time had slipped at some point, and apparently Jules had gone for her things. He helped her into her coat and handed Dani her bag.

"I'm sorry, guys," she said. She took a deep breath and pulled herself together. "Thank you for this. For the party. And the therapy."

"I'll expect an extra eighty-five bucks in my paycheck this week," Jules said. Claudine smacked him on the back of the head.

In the doorway, Dani hugged her and said good night while the others began to clean up. "Call me if you need anything."

Thea nodded. "I can't help what I like," she said. "I'm not a bad person."

"You're the best person I know," Dani said.

Lettie put her arm around her. "Time to get you home."

From "The Coffee Diaries"
by Thea Celik

The Newport Examiner

After you've made your morning pot of coffee, what do you do with your coffee grounds? Toss them in the trash?

Americans drink millions of cups of coffee every day—and that's a lot of coffee grounds. We can all make more conscious, responsible choices by drinking organic fair trade coffee and by being aware of the waste that is so often invisible when we grab a cup of joe from our favorite vendor. Even when you take that last sip of coffee from your mug, the journey of the beans has not necessarily reached its end.

You can use your coffee grounds to fertilize your garden. You can flush some down the sink with boiling water to scrape the pipes clean. You can dry them out and use them as a deodorizer—the same way you put baking soda in the fridge.

Whatever you do, the important thing is to pay attention, to not take the earth's resources for granted, and to make the most of everything you have.

NINETEEN

Weeks passed. Irina had dressed up as Hulk Hogan for Halloween, with cotton-stuffed muscles, a bandanna, and a blond wig. She'd won a best costume award in the town parade. The leaves dropped from the branches until there were no more to fall, and the street sweepers roared down the streets and brushed the stragglers away. The grocery stores began advertising free turkeys, the food pantries took out ads in the paper calling for donations, and in some stores, the first Christmas decorations were popping up among lawn rakes and fertilizer like vanguards hinting at the winter freeze. The first snow flurry of the year came while Thea was taking Irina to school one morning, flakes sweeping up and over the hood of the car. She nearly had to squint to see them, and yet they foretold so much.

At some point, Thea had made the decision to stop wishing for what wasn't: for Jonathan to help make important decisions about her child, for Sue and Ken, for Garret. She felt the loss of them at odd moments—she missed Sue when Irina was hawking cheap chocolate for a school fund-raiser, and her grandmother always bought so much and with such joy. She missed Ken when it was time to clean out the gutters of her house, since he'd always insisted on giving her a hand and she always insisted on making a pie for him afterward. She missed Jonathan when she came home at night, because she'd spent so much of her life exchanging stories with him, and she liked his easy companionship. And she missed Garret—so much—all the time; her longing was a low hum that followed her everywhere, a sound that she could get used to and live with and maybe even one day learn to ignore, but she would never stop hearing it completely.

She studied with Irina to help keep her focused and on track. She kept the house clean, and she tried to settle into a new kind of rhythm. She wasn't alone—she had friends—but aside from her daughter, she no longer was close with any of her family. Still, she knew she was strong—that she could stand it. Maybe, she thought, she would even come to like her new life—maybe being alone, too, could become an acquired taste.

Jonathan loved to watch Lori Caisse eat—the way she gave such perfect attention to her food, cutting meat and vegetables into neat little bites, and chewing each with a thoughtful, pleased expression on her face. At the Greek restaurant where he'd taken her for their second date, his own food sat nearly untouched on his plate. It was delicious enough—a rich moussaka of eggplant, meat, tomato, and Parmesan—but part of the reason he couldn't bring himself to enjoy it was because of how much he wanted to.

His parents were upset with him—they had been for a while. His mother hadn't questioned his ultimatum for Garret and neither had his father, and yet he knew deep down that they held him responsible for their son's sudden departure. And of course, they were right. It had been weeks since he'd seen his brother, weeks since he could bring himself to even think of his ex-wife. And yet, here he was, happier than he'd ever expected he might be, enjoying the twists and turns of taking a beautiful, interesting woman on a real date.

Some part of him felt that he didn't deserve to be happy because his family was not. And yet he *was* happy. Not just content, but really, truly happy for the first time in years—except for knowing that it was Garret and Thea who bore the cost of his own new-found delight.

"What are you thinking about?" Lori asked, smiling in her playful way.

He picked up his fork. "My brother. He's gone down to D.C. for a while."

"Are you close with him?" Lori asked.

"Yes." He wasn't sure how much he should share with her. They didn't know each other very well yet, and he didn't want to rush things. He liked the idea of keeping the conversation light. And yet it weighed on him—what he'd done. It sat heavy on his chest and heart. "My brother's in love with Thea," he said.

Her pale eyebrows lifted. "For how long?"

Jonathan thought it over. "Since forever, just about. Since we were kids—before Thea and I got married, anyway."

She stopped eating to give him her full attention. "Is that why he went to D.C.? Because he couldn't stand to be around her?"

"That and he couldn't stand to be around me. I told him . . ." Jonathan swallowed. Saying aloud what he'd done made him sound like a terrible person. And yet what he'd done seemed so very justified in his mind. "I told him if he wanted to be with her, I wouldn't count him as my brother anymore."

"Oh," she said, a little breathless. "Well, I understand you must've been angry. She *is* your ex-wife."

"Yes."

She pushed a chickpea around her plate. "Do you still love her?"

"Of course," Jonathan said. "When we were separating, I'd always imagined us staying friends. It's what we both wanted."

"But you don't still . . . you know . . ."

"Oh, no," Jonathan said. "It isn't like that."

Lori reached for his hand. "It's not really my place to have an opinion, but maybe it's time you let her go. You can't hold on to love and *not* hold on to it at the same time. It doesn't work that way."

"It's less about me and Thea than it is about me and Garret," he said. "He betrayed me. He went behind my back."

"But you said he's loved her forever." She frowned, an expression he so seldom saw. "Did you know he loved Thea when you married her?"

"Deep down? Maybe. I don't know. I guess I did."

"Then you know what he feels like," she said, and she pulled her hand away. "Be careful with your family. Don't take them for granted. You have to show them that you love them. Every day. Because you just don't know what tomorrow will bring."

"I know," he said, and he shifted in his seat. He really hadn't wanted to talk about this. And yet he felt a little bit better. Since the day Garret had essentially asked permission to see Thea, his pride had been smarting with the injury. He worried he would look foolish—to his friends, his family, to everyone in town—if Garret started dating Thea again. He was still angry, but he would have to think about it. What he was feeling toward Lori was thrilling and fantastic, and it was nothing like what he'd ever felt with Thea. It hurt to think this was how Garret and Thea might have felt, at some point, before Jonathan got in their way.

"Enough about my family," he said, smiling. "Tell me about yours. Brothers and sisters? Or at least a dog?"

She laughed, and he knew she was as willing to drop the subject as easily as she had been willing to pick it up. "I have seven brothers and sisters, and I'm the youngest."

He swallowed a bit of eggplant. "Why do I have the feeling this is going to take a while?" he said.

Like Garret's condo in Providence, the hotel room had a nice love seat. A flat-screen TV. Like his condo, it had a stove, a microwave, a kitchen table. It had a bathroom fan that hummed when he turned on the light. Like his condo, the hotel room had a dresser where he folded his sweaters, a closet where he lined up his shoes, and a pillow where he rested his head and dreamed. But that's where the similarities ended. His hotel room was not his home.

Fall crept slowly toward winter, and he filled his hours with long, long workdays. Mornings when he could not sleep, he got up early and dragged himself to the gym for the relief of breathlessness and sweat. In the evenings he went with coworkers to happy hour, and when happy hour was over, he often walked home, even though he was sober enough to drive. The hotel room waited for him—its perfect lamps, its little bottles of shampoo and lotion that were replaced by a housekeeper he never saw, its soundproof silence.

Once before, he'd known what it was to lose Thea—and yet he hadn't known at all. When he was a young man and he'd lost her, what he'd lost was the potential of their future together, their hypothetical, projected lives as lovers, partners, parents, and friends. His notions of an adult relationship had been hazy and vague at best.

But now, this second time, he knew what he'd lost. He'd seen what a good mother Thea was—the way she might have cared for and loved the children they would never have. He'd known what it was like to talk through problems with her, to fight with her—and he wanted her even then. Worst of all, he now knew what it was like to be loved by her, fully, completely, as an adult. He'd thought he would be able to withstand this second loss more easily than the first one. But he'd been wrong.

At night, he turned on the television and flipped mindlessly through the channels, waiting to get tired and wondering what he was missing back in Newport. He wanted to be there for the most important moments of Thea's life—moments as big as weddings and funerals, moments as small as holding her hand during a commercial that made her cry. He rented a movie and realized ten minutes later that he'd already seen it before.

In the morning, the phone rang and startled him out of bed—his heart racing with hope. But an unfamiliar voice greeted him. A wake-up call. He sat on the side of his bed, stymied by the prospect of the day, exactly the same as the one before.

The moment Thea heard Irina's cry, she knew something had gone wrong. There was something in her child's voice that was different than a cry for attention, for a refill of juice, for the answer to a question. What Thea heard was panic. Terror. Maybe pain.

Later, she would rationalize how strange it was when the unexpected occurred—how quickly—and not—a person could react in the middle of a boring weekday, when nothing much ever happened, and nothing was expected to go wrong.

She shut off the espresso machine mid-drink, and she hurried back to her office, where she'd left Irina to do her homework, and where Irina had cried for Thea to come quick. Her mind constructed possible scenarios: perhaps Irina had pinched her finger in a drawer. Perhaps she'd hit her head. But when Thea made the sharp turn midway down the hall that put her in her office, what she saw made her freeze.

"I'm sor-reeeeeey!" Irina said, tears streaming down her face. "Mom—"

Thea sprang into action. The garbage was on fire, a thick column of smoke rising out of it like a geyser. Without thinking, she grabbed the entire metal garbage bin so she could get it out of the coffee shop as quickly as possible. But she hadn't calculated the heat—she smelled her skin burning before she felt it, and then came the pain. Instinctively, she dropped the garbage, and when the contents of it spilled across the floor, the fire did too—catching the paper in her recycling bin through the silver wire mesh.

She grabbed Irina's hand with her good one. "Come on!" She pulled her daughter down the hall, shouting as she went. "Claudine, Tenke—get out! Everyone, get out! Call the fire department! Now!"

Two customers left their drinks on the table. One left her dollars crumpled on the counter. Thea picked up Irina and handed her to Claudine. "Take her. Get away from the building and call the fire department!"

"But—"

Thea reached for the fire extinguisher that was on the wall, and she prayed it would work. She'd never had to use it before. "Go!"

Claudine hurried out; Thea barely heard Irina's hysterical cries over Claudine's shoulder. She took a deep breath as she made her way back down the hall. Already it was filling with smoke—it smelled sweet, woodsy. It burned her throat and made her cough, but she squinted through it and read the directions on the fire extinguisher. She pulled the pin, tested it. A plume of feathery white rushed out.

Steeling herself, she fast rounded the corner to look into her office, thinking of all the people in the wharf area, of how close and old the buildings were, how the wooden beams and rafters were dry as kindling, and thinking *aim at the base of the fire.*

But there was no base—at least no single base that she might weaken as if pulling up a weed by its roots. She coughed, her eyes teared. The fire had spread. Going on instinct, she blanketed the room in white, the wheeze of the fire extinguisher barely a whisper against the crackling roar of the fire itself. Her desk was burning. Irina's chalkboard was burning. Her filing cabinets were burning. Dolls, crayons, printers, fax machines, and her computer were melting. And the blizzard of snowy spray that rushed from the fire extinguisher did little more than if she were attempting to fight off an intruder by tickling him.

She didn't realize how badly she was coughing. How she couldn't quite breathe. She forced her way into the room, thinking that if she could get closer to the fire, she could put it out. But the fire extinguisher had died—some part of the back of her mind realized that it had only lasted a few moments, though it had felt like an eternity. She dropped it but never heard it hit the ground. She groped for the door behind her. It was gone, swallowed by smoke. Instinct led her toward it, her hands reaching out zombielike, and she thought she was in the hallway. She turned left, heading toward the public part of the coffee shop—her espresso machine and cash register, the closet where Irina had first learned to play hide-and-seek, the tables and chairs that her parents had bought decades ago . . .

She prayed the fire wouldn't spread, that the other shops on the pier would be spared, that no one would be hurt, that the fire department would arrive fast—

For a moment, she thought the smoke was clearing. She could see the end of the hallway. Clear air. But then, without warning, darkness closed in, darkness that was not smoke but something else, and though she fought against it, fought hard, willing her weakening legs to move one after the other, her own strength seemed to have been split and sapped by the same fire that had turned her father's accounting desk into char, and at the very end of the hallway, her last glimpse of her life was the door leading out of the coffee shop and the thought that she should have told Irina that she loved her before Claudine had carried her away.

Garret had nearly hit *ignore* on his cell phone. He was about to walk into a meeting. But something within urged him to answer his brother's call. He stopped in the hallway, watching his colleagues file past him into the boardroom.

"Garret?"

"What's up, Jon?"

"I'm sorry. Please. There's been an accident. Garret—you need to come home."

"Is it Dad?"

"No, Gare. It's Thea. The shop is burning down. We think she's inside."

Disbelief was instant and fleeting. Thea was in trouble—and here he was, hundreds of miles away. He didn't think for another moment about the meeting, didn't think to tell anyone why he was walking down the hallway in the other direction. Everything that had seemed so important a moment ago suddenly meant nothing.

"Tell me what's happening," he said.

In the days after Thea had told Garret about her parents' plans to move back to Turkey—the plans that would keep her from spending her senior year in Newport—the three of them walked out to the edge of the pier, past the old lobster market and as far away from land as they could get. On a park bench, Thea sat between the boys—the boy she loved in secret and the boy she called her best friend. It was a mild autumn day, and the press of their shoulders on either side kept her warm.

They meant to reassure her: *Don't worry. We'll think of something. You don't have to move away.* Jonathan had suggested they talk to her parents, to reason with them, to ask them to stay and depend on them to know it was the right thing to do. Garret had suggested that they get an apartment together: Jonathan could sign the lease since he was eighteen, and they could pool their money to pay the rent. Thea had wondered if any friendship could be as meaningful and companionable and loving as theirs. And she'd put her arms around the two of them, because there were no words to say thanks.

"Promise me," she told them. "Even if I have to move away, promise that nothing will ever come between us."

Jonathan's eyes were warm. "Nothing and no one."

"Not even an ocean," Garret said.

Thea woke in the ambulance, jostled by potholes and speed. She looked around at strangers—a young Asian man with a mustache and a woman with her light-colored hair pulled back so tight she might not have had hair at all. "Irin—" She coughed, tears streaming from her gritty eyes. She smelled smoke in her clothes. "Irina? Where is she?"

"She's fine," the man—nearly a boy—said. "Just relax. We're taking you to the hospital to get checked out."

"I'm okay," she said. She realized that the girl was holding the hand that she'd burned, wrapping it in gauze, and she wondered how odd it was that she couldn't really feel it hurting. Maybe she hadn't been hurt that badly. Or maybe it was the adrenaline. Either way, she had bigger things on her mind. "Where's Irina? What happened to the shop?"

She saw the medics glance at one another, a secret pity in their eyes. She felt the ambulance make a slow but sharp turn.

"Your daughter's fine," the girl said. "I don't know about the shop."

"I'm okay now," Thea said, pleading. "Take me back. I need to go back."

"Just relax," the boy said.

She closed her eyes, breathing out and coughing a little more. She didn't want to go to the hospital. She wanted a shower. She wanted to get back to the coffee shop. She thought of her parents, of Sue and Ken, of Jonathan, Irina, and Garret. The ambulance motored slowly forward. She knew it only by the light that flickered on the walls.

Jonathan was waiting for his brother at the arrivals gate, so late at night that it was nearly morning. The shops and kiosks had been closed up with metal grates and padlocks. The airport was so quiet he could hear individual footsteps on the tile floors.

Garret had no bags when he arrived and was dressed in a suit and fashionable but uncomfortable-looking leather shoes. The bags under his eyes were a cloudy purple blue. "I couldn't get an earlier flight," he said. "Is she okay? What about the shop? Where are you parked?"

Jonathan walked with Garret away from the arrivals area, hurrying to keep up with Garret's pace. "They let her out of the hospital last night. She checked out okay. She's home now."

"Okay. Take me there."

"Garret . . ." Jonathan stopped walking, his heart rate high. "The fire's out. And it's four thirty in the morning. She's sleeping. She *needs* to sleep."

Garret turned to face him. And for a moment, Jonathan was transfixed. His brother had never looked so bad—his disheveled hair, the pallor of his usually perfect skin, the defeat and exhaustion in his eyes. It was the look of a man who had been pushed to the edge of what he could bear, then asked to go further. And yet Jonathan knew that he saw only a sliver of his brother's suffering, and the rest was obscured.

"Are you . . . are you really in love with her?" he asked, if only because he needed to hear the answer.

Garret didn't speak. His dull eyes hid none of his exhaustion, his fear. He barely nodded.

"All right," he said.

In the dream, Thea can smell the sweet tang of wood blackened to charcoal, hints of pine and cedar sap tingeing the air. The old boards pop, hiss, and steam. The rain comes, and it's so fine and cold, she feels it on her face and lashes less like raindrops and more like she's walking through a cloud. Again and again, she revisits the coffee shop in her mind. The ceiling is blackened with sprays of soot. The doorways have crumbled to wrinkly, fragile char. There is a smell of wetness—of ocean, of saturated wood, of the way the air changes after it's been bathed in flame.

Then she realizes she's dreaming of the empty catacomb of the coffee shop, and she knows she's in bed. The fire from the shop jumps to the walls of her bedroom, her house, and it licks up the doorways and alights on the curtains like a thousand fire orange butterflies. She can smell the smoke, but she can't pry her eyes open. They've been seared closed. Irina is in the next room, crying,

Please, help! She needs to get up, to save her daughter, to save their lives—the fire is growing, if she could only wake up, she has to save them—but she can't.

"Thea. Thea—wake up. Thea."

When Thea opened her eyes, she thought she was still dreaming. She could still smell the smoke in her hair, even though she'd shampooed it. She could still feel the heat of the flames on her face. And yet—there was Garret, looking down at her, his eyes flooded with concern. She felt his fingers brush back her hair, and she knew she was awake.

"Garret." Tears that she hadn't cried all night came to her eyes. His arms went around her, and she cried against him, sobs she hadn't known she'd been holding back. She pressed her face against his hot neck, clutched his shirt tight. "I dreamed the house was burning too . . ."

He rocked her close and whispered against her hair. "Shh. It's okay. You're safe. Everyone's safe."

She pulled away from him, kissed him. It was the rightest thing that had happened to her in hours, if not weeks.

He gathered her tighter. "I was so worried," he said. "No—worried isn't the word."

"I need you, Garret. I need you for when things like this happen. And I need you for when eveything's fine. These last few weeks without you—"

"I know," he said. He kissed her forehead. "I've felt the same way."

In the near-perfect darkness, she looked into his eyes. "Don't go away again."

"I won't."

"I just can't believe that your family wouldn't let us have this. I love them. I trust them. If they really understood what it was like, they wouldn't make us be apart. But—Garret—we can't give up. We have to make them understand."

"Let's not think about them right now," he said. "Sleep. We'll talk about it in the morning."

She wrapped his shirt in her fist. "You're not going?"

"No," he said. "I'm right here. Sleep now."

She felt his arms around her: She was safe. He loved her. All was not lost. She settled into the crook of his arms and sighed against him, the deafening clamor in her head dwindling, the threat of another nightmare retreating like driftwood floating gently out to sea. She was nearly asleep when one last pang of panic caught her in its grip. And she had to work hard to fumble the words out.

"Garret. How did you get into the house?"

"Jonathan unlocked the door for me."

The words barely registered. "*My* Jonathan?"

He smoothed back her hair, and she felt the deep pull of sleep already drawing her back into unconsciousness. "We'll talk about it in the morning." His breath was warm on her cheek. "I love you," he said.

But she never heard the words. She was falling deeper into his arms, deeper into his love, and deeper into sleep and gentler, safer dreams.

From "The Coffee Diaries"
by Thea Celik

The Newport Examiner

Dear Newport,

In lieu of my regular column, I wanted to write you this: consider it a love note.

Until the fire at the Dancing Goat last November, I hadn't realized just how many lives something as simple as a coffee shop could touch. But when tragedy struck, it became clear that the Dancing Goat was more than simply *my* coffee shop; it belongs to all of us, to the lobstermen who load up their boats in the early morning, to the tourists who stop in with their families and make fond memories of their vacations, and to those of us who work here.

Your support has been overwhelming—to me and to the baristas here who are as close to me as family. I've been blessed by your offers of assistance, your consolation, and your prayers. I've learned something tremendous in these last six months— that sometimes the life you build collapses and forces you to start over from scratch. You find reserves of strength within yourself that you wouldn't otherwise have known existed.

I'll say it this way: the Dancing Goat is going to be back and better than ever—but don't think that means it will ever change.

EPILOGUE

Thea stood near the Dumpsters behind the Dancing Goat. Behind her, the sounds of happy conversation and laughter were clipped off by the slamming of the door at her back. She was breathless and tired, her feet sore from hard work—and yet she felt good. An hour ago, she'd propped open the door of the shop for the grand reopening. All her baristas were working at high speed to get drinks out to the crowd. Lettie had been chatting with a young mother who had a dark-haired little baby on her hip. Tenke was singing along to the music, mostly for the benefit of a few teenage girls who had wandered in. Even Dani had been roped into lending a hand.

Thea knew there was still much work to do, but she needed a break—a moment of quiet. It struck her how ironic happiness could be, that a person sometimes had to step back from it to take it all in. All of her regulars had turned out in support of the shop's relaunch. Hollis and Dean had come with their chessboard, and they'd only grumbled a little when there wasn't enough room or quiet for them to set it up. Sue and Ken had staked out a table in the corner, and they watched in happy admiration as Irina worked the room. Only Jonathan had been a no-show—but Thea wasn't mad. He'd been at the shop last night helping her put in a new faucet at the last minute. Today, he had a long-standing appointment to meet his new girlfriend's parents. Thea wished him luck.

She heard the *whoosh* of the door opening behind her, and she turned.

"Doing okay?" Garret asked. He came to stand in front of her, and he held her loosely by both hips. She still couldn't quite comprehend how easy it was to touch him now that the stormiest part of the year seemed to have blown over. To be able to reach out her arms to him, to hold his hand . . . such gestures became so much more beautiful as they grew more and more insignificant.

"I'm great," she said. "It's a madhouse in there."

"And you wouldn't have it any other way."

She smiled. She knew they still had a hard road ahead of them. But they would go slow. Though the future was promising, everyone was still sore and raw from the past year. More than once, Thea had heard her daughter shout *Fire!* in her sleep. But sometime after Christmas, the nightmares had all but vanished. Thea and Jonathan began spending more time with her—the three of them meeting for dinner at least once a week—and Irina's reckless misbehaving had tapered off. She was a handful, but she wasn't malicious. She was getting used to a new idea of her family.

"Did you see the photographer from the paper?" Garret asked.

"Yes. It's really cool."

"People love this place," he said. "It's gets in your blood."

"I guess it does." She took a deep breath. The spring air was tinged with salt. Somewhere, the water was sloshing at the tall posts that held up the pier, and Thea thought about how long it had been here, weathering the years. The seaside was not an easy place to live—or make a living. Salt corroded anything that could rust. Wind peeled paint down to chips. The sun bleached the boardwalk and burned skin. And in the winter, ice storms inflicted their glassy chill on stairs and railings and stones.

And yet, when Thea had thought about taking the insurance money after the fire and starting over, starting somewhere easier and new, she realized there was nowhere else she wanted to be.

"Sometimes, I'd give my left foot to know what's going on in that head of yours," Garret said.

"You do," she said.

He kissed her, then opened the door. The sounds of the party streamed like sunlight into the late afternoon. "I have to get back to work. Are you coming inside?"

"I'm right behind you," she said.

NOTES AND ACKNOWLEDGMENTS

Great big heaping armfuls of thanks: To my editor, Cindy Hwang, for her keen eye and great taste in sushi, and to everyone at Berkley, including Erin Galloway, Leis Pederson, and Rita Frangie. To my agent, Kim Lionetti, for her encouragement, expertise, and lovely, musical laugh. To Rhonda and Jon Mallek (and also Jessica Maarek) of the Fine Grind in Little Falls, New Jersey. (Note: if you're in northern New Jersey, stop in!) To Lee Hyat, who knows I'd like to carry her around like an angel on my shoulder. To Mike P. Meeker, for policing sections of this book for errors. To Albry Montalbano, plotter, schemer, and friend. To my family—there just aren't enough words. To fellow book nerds who hang around my blog (you know who you are!): thank you—so much—for inspiring me with your funny, insightful, and supportive comments. Love love love!

A couple quick things: Price's Pier was inspired in part by Bowen's Wharf in Newport, Rhode Island. I've taken some liberties with geography (and with certain minor elements of scenes), but I've done my best to evoke the larger feel of that part of the city. FYI, I've also used the terms coffee shop and café interchangeably, though technically, they're two different things.

Finally, thanks to *all* readers: you give life to the books you love. I wanted to work the traditional closing lines of a Turkish story somewhere into this book. So, in closing:

Three apples fell from the sky:
the first for me, the second for you,
and the third for the one
who passes this story on to another.

READERS GUIDE FOR

Slow Dancing on Price's Pier

BY LISA DALE

DISCUSSION QUESTIONS

1. Discuss some of the most pertinent themes of "The Coffee Diaries" and how they relate to Thea's life. How does the "story of coffee" intersect with Thea's story?

2. Thea has a long and somewhat complicated relationship with the Sorensens. While they are like family to her, do you think the way she has treated them—and the way they have treated her—has been completely acceptable? Discuss some of the difficulties that they've encountered in their relationship.

3. Garret's playboy ways have kept him from settling down. Do you think that he is hopeful for a second chance with Thea, perhaps even before he realizes it? Is the perfect veneer he's created for himself a shield to make up for the failure he believes he is, especially in love?

4. Do you think Thea was right to marry Jonathan for "comfort and refuge"? (p.143) Is compatibility without chemistry enough to make a happy marriage?

5. After the divorce, Thea has "an unsought opportunity—a second chance she didn't quite know she'd needed until now." (p. 151) Discuss how this foreshadows her future encounter with Garret. Do you believe she was subconsciously seeking a second chance with him?

6. Thea's consistent advice to Irina in a bleak situation is that "it's going to be okay" (p.175), yet she seems to have difficulty believing that herself. Why do you think she has trouble following her own advice?

7. At one point, Thea describes her first romance as "One great, juvenile, operatic, and misplaced passion." (p. 171) She regards her relationship with Jonathan as a more mature and responsible kind of love. Do you think there's a gap between young love and adult love? Does it show when Thea falls for Garret a second time, or is there no difference at all?

8. Thea's column preceding chapter 13 talks about how coffee is an acquired taste. (p. 219) How is this a parallel to her life, and what she is seeking now that she is divorced?

9. Do you think Garret was right to blame Thea for the fact that he lost his soccer scholarship and that his journey into adulthood didn't go as planned?

10. Do you think Thea and Garret's relationship, from the beginning when they dated secretively, was destined to fail? Did everything that happened from the time they broke up to the time her marriage dissolved need to take place in order for them to find what was there all along?

11. Thea's family has obviously always come first in her mind. Do you think she is a good mother despite the emotional turbulence her family suffers because of her love for Garret?

12. Thea has a desire to think things through before she acts. Do you think she is missing out on life because of her need to not act impulsively?

13. As a teen, Thea put a lot of importance on losing her virginity; only later do we learn that Garret does too. What caused their first attempt at lovemaking to fail?

14. Through all their difficulties, the Sorensens try to remain close to one another. Was Sue right to demand "enough is enough" and evict Thea from the family? Should she have put her foot down sooner? Or not at all?

15. Do you think Thea and Garret were being selfish in rekindling their love, or was it a chance they had to take? Why do you think it takes a tragedy for the family—particularly Jonathan— to accept that Garret and Thea's love is the real deal?